"Compelling and wholly convincing—at once a vividly readable novel and a long-overdue presentation of Europe's unsung heroine to the broad audience she deserves. This telling of Margaret's story is captivating on a personal level, and classily comprehensive on 16th-century diplomacy."
— Sarah Gristwood, author of *Game of Queens, The Tudors in Love*

"Rich in history and filled with enticing drama, a diplomatic tale that celebrates the life of a brilliant European power broker of the early 16th century. Margaret emerges as a charming, savvy, and wily hero, capable of manipulating Europe's political chessboard."
— *Kirkus Reviews*

"Gaston's is a deftly-drawn rendering of this historically significant woman who embraced leadership at a time when women were discouraged from leading."
— Archduke Géza von Habsburg of Austria, author of *Princely Treasures*

"With sparkling dialogue and rigorous historical accuracy, Gaston brings Margaret of Austria to life, taking us along on her travels, sitting beside her at the negotiation table, and unearthing how she evolved into one of the most important rulers of the Renaissance."
— Susan Abernethy, *European Women in History*

"A must-read for anyone interested in the history of early modern Europe, women's history, or political biography."

— Lee Leho

"This is an excellent book about a fascinating woman during a period in which women played an important, and to-date largely unrecognized, role. I recommend it highly."

— Keira Morgan, author of *The Importance of Pawns*

"A captivating novel with rich layers of historical detail, Gaston's *Margaret of Austria* highlights the tenacity, resilience, and grace of a woman who crafted a unique role for herself in a time of patriarchal dominance, allowing her the freedom, power, and respect that few women in history have known. The drama weaves together Margaret's part as a political pawn; her years of love forsaken, love found, and love lost; and the turmoil created by her extended royal family. All while capturing the nuanced details and motives that spurred Margaret's decisions."

— Jules Larimore, author of *The Muse of Freedom*

"Margaret of Austria, an overlooked historical figure, who lived in the dynamic first half of the 16th century, comes to life in Rozsa Gaston's new historical novel. Margaret's life, especially her role as governor of the Netherlands, offers an insider's perspective on historic events with consequences that reverberate to this day."

— Ann McClellan, author of *Bonsai and Penjing: Ambassadors of Peace & Beauty*

MARGARET

OF

AUSTRIA

GOVERNOR OF THE NETHERLANDS
AND EARLY 16TH-CENTURY EUROPE'S
GREATEST DIPLOMAT

ROZSA GASTON

Renaissance Editions

New York

Cover image of Margaret of Austria from a stained glass window of the Royal Monastery of Brou, Bourg-en-Bresse, France

Chapter heading image from Margaret of Austria's statue by Joseph Tuerlinckx in the Grote Markt Main Square of Mechelen (Malines), Belgium

Cover design by Cathy Helms/Avalon Graphics

Published by

Renaissance Editions, New York

www.renaissanceeditions.com

ISBN-13: 978-1-7325899-8-8 (ebook)
ISBN-13: 978-1-7325899-9-5 (pbk)

Contents

FOREWORD

The few English-language books on Margaret, daughter of the great Emperor Maximilian I, common ancestor of all Habsburgs, all focus on her checkered life as Governor of the Netherlands and on her supporting role to her father, Maximilian, and to her nephew, Emperor Charles V.

Instead, as an art historian and specialist on early collectors, I have always been primarily impressed by Margaret as collector and patron of the arts. There is no doubt: of all early Habsburg women she possessed the keenest eye. Fortunately, through extensive inventories, we are very familiar with the furnishings of her residence in Malines (Belgium) where she held court for 24 years. surrounded by sculptors, painters, philosophers, authors, poets and musicians. We know of the precious tapestries and lavish codices with miniatures she commissioned, illustrating the family's history.

The extensive, detailed, inventories of her possessions even pinpoint the location of individual works of art in her *Cour de Savoie*, her palace in Malines. As one example among many others, we know that Jan van Eyck's *Arnolfini Wedding* (National Gallery, London), arguably her most prized possession, as well as other works by van Eyck and Hans Memling, hung in her bedchamber.

As one of the greatest patrons of the arts of the Renaissance, Margaret received artists such as Albrecht Dürer and Jacopo de' Barbari and was responsible for introducing Italian works to Northern Europe.

Rozsa Gaston, a Hungarian compatriot, brings a fascinating new perspective on Margaret of Austria to the biographical fiction canon. In this work, unlike others, she emerges as a woman increasingly confident of her abilities as ruler and statesman, and unapologetic about exercising her authority. Not just seen through the prism of sacrifice and duty expected of her as a female member of the House of Habsburg, Margaret springs alive as a woman who discovers she has a gift for governance and diplomacy, and delights in doing both well.

Gaston portrays Margaret in her well-crafted biography as a woman who enjoyed her work. She also enjoyed being recognized for her accomplishments, as evidenced by the exquisite flamboyant Gothic church at Brou, near Bourg-en-Bresse, France, leaving behind a lasting imprint of her time on earth. Gaston's is a deftly-drawn rendering of this historically significant woman who embraced leadership at a time when women were discouraged from leading.

— Dr. Géza von Habsburg, Archduke of Austria
Guest lecturer on "Celebrated Habsburg Women" for the Metropolitan Museum of Art, New York
Author of *Princely Treasures,* Vendome Press, 1997

Coat of Arms of Margaret of Austria and Burgundy
used by her from 1501-1530
Courtesy of Geraldiker

Of all the historians who have written about the history of the Burgundian Empire in English, Richard Vaughan is the most cognizant of the integral role played by women in its governance. In Vaughan's series on the Valois Dukes of Burgundy, he mentions these women in passing—peripheral to the male players.

But with this work Rozsa Gaston has given Margaret of Austria, the most powerful of Burgundian royal women, her long-overdue moment on center stage.

Gaston has chosen a worthy subject in Margaret, granddaughter of the last Valois-Burgundian duke, Charles the Rash. Her humanist education and sojourns to some of the most influential courts of Europe in the 16th century rendered Margaret uniquely qualified to govern the Netherlands as regent for her nephew, Holy Roman Emperor Charles V. Gaston shines a spotlight on Margaret's pivotal role in early 16th-century European affairs, but most of all what it was about her that made her so good at governance.

With sparkling dialogue and rigorous historical accuracy, Gaston brings Margaret of Austria to life, taking us along on her travels, sitting beside her at the negotiation table, and unearthing how she evolved into one of the most important rulers of the Renaissance.

— Susan Abernethy, historian and writer
The Freelance History Writer
European Women in History

What Comprised Burgundy?

In the days of Margaret of Austria Burgundy was comprised of two regions, roughly corresponding to the present day Benelux countries of Belgium, the Netherlands, and Luxembourg, as well as areas farther south, one of which was the duchy of Burgundy, and the other the county of Burgundy known as the Free County of Burgundy or Franche-Comté.

The term Burgundian-Habsburg Netherlands is interchangeable with Burgundian-Habsburg Low Countries, and refers to the Burgundian Netherlands under Habsburg rule from 1478-1556.

Four dukes of Burgundy successively built the Burgundian state, begun in 1369 and ended in 1477 with the death of Charles the Rash. They are all descended from Philip the Bold, younger brother of Charles V of France, of the French royal House of Valois.

Philip the Bold (1342-1404) b. Pointoise, France; reigned 1363-1404

John the Fearless (1371-1419) b. Dijon, France; reigned 1404-1419

Philip the Good (1496-1467) b. Dijon, France; reigned 1419-1467

Charles the Rash (1433-1477) b. Dijon, France; reigned 1467-1477

Charles the Rash and Charles the Bold are both terms used to denote the last of the four Valois-Burgundian dukes. I have chosen to refer to him as Charles the Rash, as the French denote him as *Charles le Téméraire*, the term *téméraire* meaning reckless, rash, or foolhardy. In contrast, the first Valois-Burgundian duke is known to history as Philip the Bold, or *Philippe le Hardi*. In French, the term *hardi* means bold or daring.

The House of Valois-Burgundy 1465-1477

From Karte_Haus_Burgund_4_EN

Statue of Margaret of Austria
by Joseph Tuerlinckx, 1849
Grote Markt Main Square of Mechelen (Malines), Belgium
Photo by Ad Meskens

CAST OF
CHARACTERS

IN ORDER OF APPEARANCE

FAMILY

Margaret of Austria (1480-1530) Archduchess of Austria, Duchess of Savoy, Governor of the Netherlands, Dowager Princess of Spain

Maximilian I of Austria (1459-1519) Archduke of Austria and Holy Roman Emperor, and Margaret's father

Philip I of Castile (1478-1506) Known as Philip the Handsome, Lord of the Netherlands, Duke of Burgundy, Archduke of Austria, King of Castile (1506), and Margaret's brother

Juana of Castile (1479-1555) Known as Juana the Mad, Queen of Castile from 1504 and Queen of Aragon from 1516 to 1555, wife of Philip the Handsome, mother of Charles V, and Margaret's sister-in-law

Ferdinand of Aragon (1452-1516) King of Spain and father-in-law of Margaret through his son, Juan, Prince of Asturias

Charles of Habsburg, the future Charles V, Holy Roman Emperor (1500-1558) Also known as Charles of Luxembourg, Prince of Castile, Archduke of Austria, Lord of the Netherlands and Duke of Burgundy (from 1506), King of Spain (from 1516), the future Charles V, Holy Roman Emperor (from 1530), and Margaret's nephew

ROYALS

Anne de Beaujeu (1461-1522) Regent of France from 1483-91 during the minority of her younger brother Charles VIII of France, daughter of Louis XI, known as the Spider King

Louise of Savoy (1476-1531) Countess of Angoulême, mother of Marguerite and Francis d'Angoulême, Duke of Valois, the future Francis I, King of France

Louis XII of France (1462-1515) King of France, formerly Louis, Duke of Orléans

Anne of Brittany (1477-1514) Duchess of Brittany and Queen of France

Catherine of Aragon (1485-1536) Queen of England and daughter of Isabella and Ferdinand of Spain

Henry VII of England (1457-1509) Known as Henry Tudor,

first Tudor king of England who sought Margaret's hand in marriage

Henry VIII of England (1491-1547) Second Tudor king of England, son of Henry VII, husband to Catherine of Aragon, Margaret's former sister-in-law

MEMBERS OF MARGARET OF AUSTRIA'S COURT

Mercurino di Gattinara (1465-1530) Piedmontese statesman and jurist in Margaret of Austria's service in Savoy then the Netherlands. Eventually became Chancellor of Charles V, Holy Roman Emperor

Jean Lemaire (c. 1473-c.1525) Poet and historian from Hainault (now Belgium) who served at Margaret of Austria's court from 1504-c.1512 then at the court of Anne of Brittany. One of the last of the school of poetic rhetoricians he was a forerunner of the Renaissance humanists

Jean de Marnix (dates unknown) Secretary and treasurer to Margaret of Austria

Laurent de Gorrevod (1470-1529) Savoyard nobleman who accompanied Margaret of Austria from Savoy to the Netherlands where he became a member of her privy council

Margaret de Croy, Countess of Horne (1480s-c.1513) Close friend and lady-in-waiting to Margaret of Austria

Elisabeth of Culemborg (1475-1555) Known as Lady Elisabeth, she was first lady-in-waiting or *dame d'honneur* to Margaret of Austria from 1506–1530. In 1509 she married Antoine de Lalaing, Count of Hoogstraten, member of Margaret's privy council and knight of honor of Margaret's household

OTHERS

William de Croy, Lord of Chièvres (1458-1521) Tutor and chief advisor to Charles of Habsburg

Charles of Egmond, Duke of Guelders (1467-1538) Ruler of Gelderland, he refused to recognize the legal transfer of his duchy sold by his father to Margaret's grandfather, Charles the Rash, in 1473. Egmond resisted submission to Habsburg rule for most of his life

Charles Brandon (c. 1484-1525) 1st Duke of Suffolk and right-hand man to Henry VIII of England

Jakob Fugger (1459-1525) German banker from Augsburg whose banking dynasty controlled most of northern Europe's economy during the 16th century and who financed the House of Habsburg's rise to power

Desiderius Erasmus (1466-1536) Catholic theologian from Rotterdam considered to be one of the greatest scholars and thinkers of the northern Renaissance

Albrecht Durer of (1471-1528) German painter and printmaker from Nuremberg considered to be one of the greatest painters of the northern Renaissance, whose major patron from 1512 on was Maximilian I

Fortune, infortune, fort une

The changes of fortune make one stronger
or
Fortune, misfortune, fortifies one

— Motto of Margaret of Austria

For Ann McClellan

PROLOGUE

In 1480, in a palace in Brussels, a daughter was born to fulfill a great destiny. Her name was Margaret, and she grew up to become Governor of the Netherlands and the most influential diplomat of her times.

Her mother was Mary of Burgundy, known as Mary the Rich, head of the House of Burgundy. Her father was Maximilian of Austria, head of the House of Habsburg. They were happily married, in a union that brought Habsburg domains to France's borders, too close for comfort for the French king, Louis XI.

Margaret had one older brother, Philip, who grew up to be called Philip the Handsome.

When Margaret was two, the winds of fate knocked Margaret's mother off her horse while hunting. Her back broken, twenty-five-year-old Mary of Burgundy succumbed to her injuries three weeks later. The heir to Burgundy was dead, leaving behind two motherless children, heirs to two of Europe's most noble dynasties.

Twenty-three-year-old Maximilian gave over care of his children to his wife's stepmother and Margaret's godmother, Margaret of York, widow of Mary's father, Charles the Rash. This politically astute and capable lady was sister to two kings of England: Edward IV and Richard III.

With Mary's death, Maximilian of Austria's claim on Burgundian lands weakened. The French king, a shrewd but unpleasant character, saw his chance to seize more territories on the French-Burgundian border. To thwart his aggressions, Maximilian countered with a solution superior to war: a marriage alliance.

With the Treaty of Arras of December 1482 Maximilian promised his daughter to the French king's son, along with a rich dowry of disputed Burgundian territories, the largest of which were Franche-Comté and Artois. The intent was to satisfy Louis XI's territorial acquisitiveness and commence an era of peace between France and the Holy Roman Empire. What better way to cement an alliance than to inject a Habsburg bloodline into the French royal House of Valois?

Three-year-old Margaret was sent to the French royal court to prepare her to one day become Queen of France.

Alas, it was not to be. Neither peace between the two realms ensued nor marriage between the Princess Margaret and Charles, Dauphin of France. But because Margaret spent the entirety of her childhood in France, from ages three to thirteen, she grew up speaking French as her mother tongue, and was adept in the ways and customs of France. Such a formation would serve her well when she went on to mediate treaties between Europe's most powerful princes.

Only Margaret of Austria knew all the players and how to handle them.

Marriage of Mary of Burgundy and Maximilian I

Ghent, August 1477

Artist unknown

Photo by Elena Borz of www.Nasvete.com

Diptych: Philip the Handsome and Margaret of Austria

By Pieter van Coninxloo, c. 1493-95

The National Gallery, London

Photo by The Print Collector/Getty Images

Depiction of Margaret of Austria
Stained glass window, Royal Monastery of Brou
Bourg-en-Bresse, France
Photo by Yann Kergourlay
www.theanneboleynfiles.com

1

AMBOISE

1491

"Blonde like the wheat from neighboring Beauce,
and with cheeks the color of roses of Provence."
—Louise of Savoy's description of her childhood
friend Margaret of Austria[1]

TROUBLE WAS BREWING. HER lapdog wouldn't settle down. Pacing and gnawing at the corners of the door, she seemed to sense something was afoot on its other side.

---

1. Paule Henry-Bordeaux, *Louise de Savoie: Régente et "Roi" de France* (Paris: Plon, 1954), p. 11.

Margaret's dream of the night before had unsettled her. Still shaking the cobwebs from her head, she reached for Fortuna to comfort her. But the dog kept jumping off the bed to scratch at the door.

She had been in a beautiful field, reaching to pick a daisy, a *marguerite,* after which she was named. But before she could pluck it a donkey appeared, an *âne*, spirited and kicking up its heels. She reached out to pet it but the donkey rushed past, trampling over the daisy she had spotted.

Saddened, Margaret looked around for another but there was none. The donkey ran off and only a vast empty field remained.[2]

"Fortuna, stop that! Come back here," she scolded.

The small white dog reluctantly backed away from the door and came to her bedside. But at the sound of the door opening she flew to it again, yapping excitedly.

"Good morning, Your Grace," Margaret's attendant greeted her, curtseying. The scent of the steaming mug of hot barley drink she held out filled Margaret's nose, instantly erasing any traces of her dream.

"I cannot get Fortuna to settle down. Is something going on outside?"

"Nothing much, my lady. Some of the men have arrived back from Brittany, that is all."

"Why are they back?'

---

2. Eleanor E. Tremayne, *The First Governess of the Netherlands* (New York: G.P. Putnam's Sons, 1908), p. 11. With reference to Pasquier, who originally recorded Margaret's reference to this dream.

Margaret's lady-in-waiting shrugged. "I don't know. Perhaps Madame de Segré will know when you see her."

"When is she coming?" Margaret asked. Her tutor knew everything. Even when she was nowhere near, she knew when Margaret had behaved less like the queen she would one day become. It annoyed Margaret at times, but she was being prepared for a large role and the day she would step into it was coming soon.

"She told me to help you dress for crossbow practice. She will see you after, at lessons."

"Crossbow practice!" Margaret sang out. What fun it was to practice at crossbow with her playmates, especially Philibert. The boy from Savoy was her age, eleven, and always helped her at practice. Philibert was good fun to be around and, though Margaret was training to be queen, she wasn't done with fun yet.

Jumping from bed, she held out her arms for her attendant to dress her. Once Madame de Segré appeared she must behave with decorum. But that morning she would run and play with the others. Who knew? Perhaps this would be the day she would finally hit the bullseye.

Promised to the young French king, Charles VIII, Margaret was the highest ranked princess at court. When she became queen she intended to run a joyful court, more lively than the court of her guardian, Anne de Beaujeu, the king's older sister, whom all referred to as Madame la Grande.

Charles did exactly what his sister told him to do, so Margaret imagined he wanted to get out from under her thumb. Once they wed, she would help him to become his own man. At the court they would create she would surround herself with music and laughter, games, dances, and tourneys. At least Madame la Grande allowed archery and riding, as well as hunting.

France's regent was an accomplished hunter herself. Anne de Beaujeu practiced in the forest what she did so skillfully as a ruler—bagging smaller territories adjacent to France to add to its kingdom. She was now hunting down Brittany to the west to snatch from its ruler, Anne of Brittany, a plum realm France's former king had cast his eye on before he died. Margaret didn't doubt she would get it, just as Anne de Beaujeu's father had acquired parts of Burgundy on France's eastern borders with Margaret's dowry.

Letting out a gay laugh, Margaret brushed off her attendant and ran her fingers through the wavy strands of her deep golden hair. She couldn't wait to get outside to the practice grounds on the great lawn at Amboise.

"Mademoiselle, let me dress your hair!" her attendant scolded.

"Then do so quickly that I may be off," Margaret cried, eager to feel the strength of her bow arm and the rush of excitement the moment she released her arrow. Crossbow practice was not just for sport. She thrilled to see her arrow fly to its aim, knowing it was her steady hand and careful eye that had sent it there. One day she would use a similar hand and eye to rule over all that she managed as Queen of France. For that role, she must practice with diligence.

Dancing out from under her attendant's hand Margaret escaped from the room, Fortuna running after her. What fun it was to enjoy her lessons. And Philibert had already told her she had a steady arm. She hoped he would be there that day.

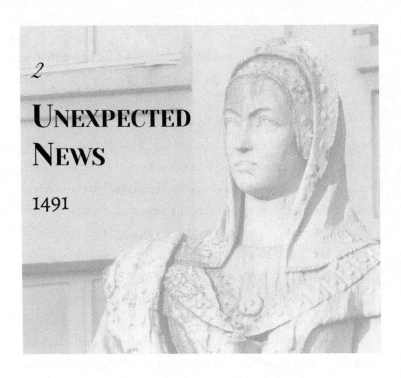

2

UNEXPECTED NEWS

1491

"This year's vintage (sarments) is as worthless as the
king of France's vows (serments)."
—Margaret of Austria's quip upon being offered bad
wine after being jilted by Charles VIII of France[1]

"WAIT HERE. I WILL speak to the princess alone," the King of
France addressed her attendant as he gestured to Margaret to follow
him.

1. Jean Lemaire, *Oeuvres, Jean Stecher, Vol. 4* (Geneva: Slatkine
   Reprints, 1969), pp.105-106.

She shivered, eying her betrothed. Had the moment arrived for her to become Queen of France? She wasn't ready, but she would do her duty.

"What is it, my lord?" She followed Charles to the small salon off the great hall of Amboise. Like the inside of a jewel box, it was richly draped with fine Flemish tapestries to keep out the December chill. She couldn't remember anything about the land of her birth, but all said that the finest tapestries in Europe were made there.

Proud of her heritage, she stood straight and lifted her chin to Charles. He looked even less attractive than usual, his bulbous eyes not meeting hers.

"There has been a change, little sister." The King of France's tone was strained.

"What change, my lord?" Why was her future husband addressing her as "little sister"? She was eleven years old. Not so little anymore, although she didn't feel ready to marry as her friend Louise had been forced to do at the same age. Four years earlier Louise of Savoy had wed the much older Count d'Angoulême, whom everyone knew kept two mistresses in the home he had brought his child bride to.

"Sit down, little one." Charles VIII of France pointed to a chair. She was not supposed to sit while the king stood, but he had ordered her to.

Margaret suppressed a giggle. Usually it was his older sister giving the orders. She must accustom herself to her future lord giving orders so that others would follow her example. But it was still strange to hear the young unsure-of-himself king tell her what to do.

"Am I so little, my lord?" Nearly as tall as Charles was she sat with a flounce, wondering at his strangely serious manner. Usually they ignored each other. Their ten years' age difference put them in different circles, although they saw each other when the court gathered for important events. Was he about to tell her another one was coming up soon?

Charles sat and wiped his face with a handkerchief. "You are still a child, are you not?" he asked, looking uncomfortable as he attempted a smile. But his eyes flitted past, alarming Margaret.

"That depends, my lord, on what follows your question. Do you ask if I am ready for marriage?"

Charles sighed. With elbows on knees, he rubbed his temples with both hands, looking older than his twenty-one years. Then he lifted his head and gave her a sad look. "I do not ask, Margaret. Because I know you are not. Yet I am."

Margaret's heart beat faster. She was not at all ready for what Louise had told her about married life. "You are ready to marry, my lord?"

Charles gulped but kept his gaze steady. As usual, his mouth hung open. He closed it, then opened it again. "I *am* married, little sister."

"We are betrothed, my lord. Not yet married," Margaret amended, wondering what he was getting at.

Charles' Adam's apple bobbed in the silence that followed. "We are no longer betrothed, because I have married the Duchess of Brittany," the short, ungainly king announced.

"What say you?" Margaret felt her voice rise to a childish pitch that her tutor had counseled her was unbecoming.

Charles' face flushed. "I have married the Duchess of Brittany."

"But you are trothed to me!" Margaret cried, forgetting her manners.

"No longer, Margaret. I am bound to the duchess now, and you will like her very much." Charles gave her a guarded smile, as if holding secrets elsewhere.

Icy shock congealed her limbs. "I will not like her at all and I do not like you!" she burst out.

Charles looked pained. "That is just as well, as you will not be stuck with me for a husband. But I will always like you, and my queen will, too."

"*I* am to be your queen, my lord! You cannot just take another!"

"My little one, I can and I have. It is not what I expected to happen, but it is done to keep peace between Brittany and France."

"But I am to be queen. You cannot just cast me aside," Margaret railed, thinking of all the stories she had heard at court of broken engagements when better offers had come along. It was done all the time. But never had she thought it would be done to her.

"I don't doubt that you will be a queen someday. But not my queen. It is best for you, little one. You will see." Charles reached out and put a finger beneath her chin.

Margaret batted his hand away. "What do you mean it is best for me not to be your queen? It is what I have spent my life preparing for!" she exclaimed.

"And because you have prepared, you will most likely become queen of a king far more worthy than me."

"But it was supposed to be you!" Margaret protested.

Charles raised his arms out to either side. Shaking his head, he gave her a wry look. "Do you really want someone who looks like me for a husband?"

"That's not the point. The point is you promised, and you can't just break your promise." A strange desire to laugh welled up within her. Charles was right. No woman with eyes in her head would wish for a husband who looked like a gnome. She had tried for years to overlook his deficits. But he was short and ugly, with an enormous nose, an oversized head, and a mouth that hung open. She had never been able to dream of him as her future husband no matter how hard she tried. But she had dreamt of becoming queen. Counted on it, in fact.

"Ah, but I can and I have. Think about it, little sister. Now is your chance for a more handsome prince to come along."

For the first time since their conversation began, Margaret found Charles attractive. Among his limited attributes, he possessed humility. He knew how ugly he was, as well as uncultured and unlettered, due to his father's preference of his older sister over him. Did she really want such a man for a husband? As long as she became queen of someone, somewhere, perhaps he was doing her a favor with this unexpected twist. But she was still angry.

"I can do better than you and I will!" she shrieked.

"Ah, my lady, now you are talking like the future queen you will be. I must go, but rest assured I will do all within my power to keep you happy here while arrangements are made."

"What arrangements?" Margaret asked, feeling as if the world was tumbling down around her.

"New arrangements. Until the prince of your dreams is found for you."

"But you—you were—"

"Don't say what you don't mean, little one. You have always been honest and true, which is why I wanted to tell you myself what has happened. You will do better than me, I promise you."

Margaret opened her mouth, but nothing came out. Why argue with the truth?

As Charles left the room, she pondered his words. She had just discovered his promise meant nothing. But to rebuke a king for such was treason, although she was not a subject of his kingdom. She would keep her mouth shut and write to her father that day, so he could begin the search for a more worthy king for her to wed.

"I will go to my chambers," she ordered as her attendant entered the salon.

"Is all well, my lady?"

"Very well." Her humiliation was great, but perhaps all was not lost. Certainly, Charles had a point with his observation that she could do better.

"Fetch my writing kit; I must pen a letter."

"Yes, my lady. Was there news from the king?"

"There was, indeed." Steeling herself, she put into action years of practice in concealing her feelings. All kings and queens did it. She would not let her composure slip in front of a courtier.

"Oh, my lady, was it that you will be wed soon?"

"It was not, but you will find out soon enough what it was."

"Oh, my lady, I do so love surprises."

"Usually I do, too."

"Not this time, my lady?"

"I haven't decided yet."

"Do tell, my lady!"

Margaret ignored her. "Get my writing things, and have Madame de Segré meet me in my chambers," she ordered.

"Yes, my lady." The attendant hurried away as Margaret turned in the direction of her rooms. She had trained her entire life to be queen, and she would not allow anyone other than her tutor see the shock that swept her at that moment. As Charles had said, although his word was worthless, she would be a queen one day.

Straightening, she held her head high as she traversed the great hall. She would tell her father to make sure it was to a king who was more noble and better-looking than the one who had jilted her.

THROWING HERSELF INTO MADAME de Segré's arms, hot tears spilled from Margaret's eyes.

"Madame, did you know of this?" she sobbed.

A heavy sigh escaped Madame de Segré. "I had heard rumors, but no more."

"It is done already, and I was given no say in it!" Margaret wailed.

Her tutor hugged her closely. "There, there, *ma princesse*. Perhaps the king did not have much say in it, either, but did what he did for the sake of his kingdom."

"How could he have no say in such a matter?" Margaret demanded. "Is he not king?"

Madame de Segré pulled back to meet her gaze, still holding Margaret's arms firmly. "The king is young, and takes counsel from others."

Margaret stamped her foot. "One other, you mean."

Her tutor said nothing but looked at her sadly. If France's regent had changed her mind, it was not for her to question. No one questioned Madame. Anne de Beaujeu ruled France as well as its king. It would remain to be seen if she would rule the king's new bride, too.

MARGARET WANTED TO HATE her. Yet she couldn't. Anne of Brittany was three years older than she, already a woman. Short yet commanding, she carried herself like the sovereign she was; although Margaret knew, as did the entire French court, that Charles' intent in marrying her was to wrest her realm from her.

Worst of all, Brittany's ruler was kind to her. Most of the court had backed off as Margaret's new status set in. No longer was she addressed as "Your Grace," but only as "*mademoiselle*" or "my lady."

She who was to become queen was now a hostage. As a foreign princess who had brought a sizeable dowry with her, she would not be allowed to return to her birthplace until her dowry was returned, too. As a child raised at court, she had grown up quickly. At age eleven, she was sharply aware of her plight.

Charles VIII of France and Maximilian I of Austria both wanted Burgundian lands Maximilian had ceded to France as part of the intended marriage alliance. But now that the marriage was off, Margaret's father insisted those lands must be returned to Habsburg-controlled Burgundy.

Charles was loath to do that, but Brittany and his new wife were a bigger plum. Overnight, Margaret had become *persona non grata* at court, with only one royal stepping forward to show her kindness—the woman who had replaced her.

Anne of Brittany, the queen Margaret should have become, showered Margaret with gifts and affection.

"I lost my sister when she was ten, *ma belle*. You are like a younger sister to me," France's new queen told her.

"And you, like an older sister to me," Margaret responded, although the only older sister she had known had been her friend Louise, who was nothing like the dainty Duchess of Brittany.

Louise of Savoy had been sharply aware of her impoverishment, whereas Anne of Brittany was as regal and self-assured as a royal born to rule. Now Louise was married and living in Cognac, far from Amboise. Her brother Philibert was still at court, but was in training to become a squire and as such was occupied with manly pursuits most of the day, no longer part of Margaret's coterie.

Margaret had one friend of the same age who remained close to her. Charlotte of Naples, the Princess of Tarente, also lived at court and was waiting for a marriage match to be arranged. Anne de Beaujeu decided that Charlotte and Margaret should be moved to Melun, far from Amboise and closer to Paris, while details of what portion of Margaret's dowry were to be returned, and when, were hammered out with Maximilian in Vienna.

But soon Charlotte was called back to join Anne of Brittany's court.

Margaret was distraught. She wrote to Anne de Beaujeu, who had supervised her upbringing throughout her childhood. A less maternal woman in all of France would be hard to find, but thankfully, Madame de Segré had been allowed to accompany Margaret to her new home in Melun. Yet her beloved tutor was in service to Madame la Grande, so Margaret penned her complaints in secret.

> 'Madame, I am saddened to see the departure of my sole companion and comfort, the Princess of Tarente. I beg you to return her to me or to return me to court where I may enjoy the company again of all who I hold dear. Why have you exiled me here, when you so diligently cared for me all the years of my childhood? I ask you what I have done wrong, when it is I, myself, who has been wronged by the broken troth of your brother the king.'

Margaret paused then crossed out her final sentence. It would not do to criticize the woman who had most likely engineered the coup to attain Brittany. Until recently, it was said that Anne de Beaujeu was the most powerful woman in France. She was still widely feared, although the young king was coming into his own now that his new consort was showing signs of an assertive personality.

Signing and sealing the letter, Margaret gave it to the stable boy to deliver. She had written countless times to her father, complaining of her treatment, but to no avail.

Maximilian needed her to stay in France until the return of her dowry was settled. He, too, had been jilted. Married by proxy to Anne of Brittany in 1490, Maximilian had been infuriated to hear that Brittany's young ruler had secretly married the King of France in December of 1491.

With her father as humiliated as she, Margaret burned whenever she thought of it. At such moments, Madame de Segré would assure her that an even better match would be found.

"As you were raised to be queen, it is certain to come to pass," her tutor would say. "Just not to the king you had thought it would be."

It was small comfort. And such efforts took time. Her attendants remained, but Margaret was painfully aware that she was no longer one of the most important demoiselles at court.

Now she knew the bitterness her friend Louise had carried all those years as a poor relation in Anne de Beaujeu's household. Louise of Savoy's status had risen with marriage to Charles d'Angoulême, a member of France's ruling Valois dynasty, but at a cost. Installed at Cognac, she found her husband's household run by the senior of his two mistresses, who had been assigned to Louise as her lady-in-waiting.

Margaret shuddered. It was too louche to think of. She prayed that whatever her future held, her husband would be an upright and honorable prince.

EIGHT SEASONS CAME AND went as negotiations over the return of Margaret's dowry dragged on between Vienna and Amboise. Margaret's education in the new humanist teachings continued, as did her lessons in drawing, dancing, painting, and music. But she was no longer referred to as *la petite reine*, the little queen. She was Margaret of Burgundy and Austria now, a foreign princess in a land far from her own.

Finally it was settled. The territories of Franche Comté and Artois were returned to the House of Burgundy-Habsburg, and Margaret was to be returned to the Burgundian-Habsburg Netherlands to the custody of her older brother, Philip of Burgundy, and her step-grandmother and godmother, Margaret of York.

Before setting out on her farewell journey across France, Margaret received a generous gift of gold rings and a richly embroidered coif from Anne of Brittany. The small but commanding queen came personally to bid her Godspeed on her return to her native lands.

"Margaret, I will miss you, but I will write to you and we will see each other again," she told her.

"Oh, Your Grace, I don't know what will become of me, but I will think fondly of you." Margaret lowered her voice. "Although not so fondly of France," she ended.

"I know how you must feel, but you will grow into a great lady and take your seat at the table of Europe's princes." The queen smiled, reaching out to caress Margaret's cheek. "Mark my words."

Margaret felt herself flush with pleasure. "Thank you, Your Grace, but how can you know that?"

"It is written on your face and in your stars," the queen declared, putting a hand on Margaret's shoulder.

"How so, my lady?"

"I have known you for two years. Just as befell me, fate twisted your path. But you have managed these long months of waiting with good grace. You have good sense and a steady character, Margaret. With your lineage and your good head, you will make the Houses of Burgundy and Habsburg proud."

"What counsel do you give me to ensure it is so?"

Anne of Brittany smiled brightly into Margaret's eyes, steel behind her gaze. "Don't let anyone or anything unsettle you. I have seen your mettle in handling yourself well over these months of uncertainty. When circumstances change, don't change with them. Ride through whatever comes your way, so that all around may depend on you as a rock."

"I see the court depends on you in the same way, Your Grace."

"It is because I have been tested," the Breton ruler said with no hesitation. "I have been through fire, but now I am Queen of France."

"Fortune smiles on you, Your Grace."

"Not always, Margaret. But you and I are not who we are due to fortune alone. We are doughty princesses, and we will withstand, no matter what fortune serves," the queen assured her.

Margaret nodded. Anne of Brittany's words rang true. She might be small, but there was something solid and immutable about her. Taking her hand, Margaret placed it on her forehead.

"Bless me, Madame."

The queen's hand pressed firmly. "Wherever you go and whatever happens, you will manage it well. I have already seen this in you. With God's blessing and mine, go in peace. You have everything you need within you already," she proclaimed, her voice as authoritative as it was warm.

Margaret's heart swelled. Anne of Brittany's words were the greatest of her gifts to her. She would not forget them.

Regarding Charles VIII and his older sister, she would never forgive their inconstancy. Yet she was a princess-born and, as such, sooner or later she would be re-enlisted to play on Europe's chessboard. Once she was older, and no longer a pawn in someone else's hand, she vowed she would play to win.

Upon reaching the border from France to Flanders, tears were shed and gifts given to Madame de Segré, Princess Charlotte of Tarente, and Margaret's retinue of ladies-in-waiting and household attendants. Bidding adieu to them, she bid goodbye in her heart to Louise and Philibert of Savoy, as well.

As for Charles VIII and Anne de Beaujeu? Margaret did not cast a single backward glance.

3

RETURN TO BURGUNDY/ MARRIAGE TO JUAN OF SPAIN

1493-1500

"No matter how perilous her situation, Margaret of
Austria lost neither her calm nor her composure, nor
even her sense of fun." — Leonie Frieda[1]

GROWN TO WOMANHOOD, MARGARET settled in at the Burgundian-Netherlands court. French was the language of most of Burgundy and was spoken at court, so she was at ease communicating.

---

1. Leonie Frieda, *Margaret of Austria, Duchess of Savoy – true to her own self* (https://engelsbergideas.com/portraits/margaret -of-austria-duchess-of-savoy-true-to-her-own-self/), p.1.

But her heart had hardened against France. She would not forget the betrayal of the French king, however happy she was to have escaped sharing a marital bed with him. He was now marching across Italy, making trouble for her father with his hungry eye on Naples. She had heard that Philibert was with him, a youth bursting to prove himself a man. He would manage well if he did not die.

Margaret found a fond welcome in her stepgrandmother and godmother, after whom she was named. Margaret of York was sister to the former King of England, Edward IV, and the widow of Margaret's grandfather, Charles the Rash, who had died before she was born. The refined and perspicacious Englishwoman had embraced Burgundy as her permanent home, and had become active in its political and economic affairs.

Margaret of York placed Margaret under the direction of Johanna de Halewijn, who had once been her mother's governess. The capable woman arranged for Margaret to study Flemish in addition to classical literature, drawing, and music. Regaling Margaret with tales of her mother, Madame de Halewijn related that Mary the Rich of Burgundy had loved falconing and had kept her favorite hunting falcons in her bedchamber, even after marrying Maximilian.

"Ah, my dear, you have inherited those full Burgundian lips from your mother, God rest her soul," Madame de Halewijn sighed, smoothing back Margaret's wavy dark blonde hair as she smoothed away the pain of the past few years of humiliation she had suffered in France.

Margaret soon discovered that Burgundy was a realm rich in tradition. Festivals, archery competitions, games, and feasts dotted the year, and Margaret eagerly participated in them with her brother Philip, now ruler of the Burgundian-Habsburg Netherlands. Her heart warmed to the land of her birth as she saw the high esteem in which their countrymen held them as the sole descendants of Mary the Rich and Charles the Rash.

Philip of Burgundy, known as Philip the Handsome, had been given the reins of rulership at age fifteen by their father, who had retreated to his native land of Austria. There Maximilian plotted to curb France's power. His plan to stake a Habsburg claim to Brittany to provide a hedge around France had fallen through with the failure of his attempt to marry Anne of Brittany. But there were other countries with which to ally against France. Casting his eyes on other great powers on the Continent, they came to rest on Spain.

By January of 1495 a marriage alliance with two of the children of the Spanish monarchs was signed in Antwerp. Philip the Handsome was to marry Juana of Castile, second daughter of Isabella and Ferdinand. Margaret was to marry their only son Juan, Prince of Asturias and heir to the Spanish throne.

Informed of these arrangements, Margaret exulted. Madame de Segré's prediction would come true. She would indeed be a queen, not just of an important country, but of the lands across the sea discovered by Queen Isabella's protégé, the Genoese navigator Columbus.

Philip wed Juana in Brussels in December 1496, and Margaret departed for Spain to meet her future husband in the spring of 1497. Ever quick with her quips, upon saying goodbye to her brother she bade him not to make her cry as the sea water might cause her to swallow all the salt water she could withstand.

Margaret's words proved almost true. The voyage by sea was horrific. Beset by raging storms in the Bay of Biscay, Margaret's shipmates despaired for their lives while she penned her own epitaph.

'Here lies Margaret, the willing bride,
Twice married—but a virgin when she died.'[2]

By some miracle the ship made it to port in Santander, where Margaret was greeted by her soon-to-be in-laws. Isabella of Castile was immediately warm and affectionate. Her husband Ferdinand of Aragon was gruff and intimidating, every bit a warrior. But from the moment Margaret grasped his hand and kissed it, against Spanish protocol, he melted in the bright sunshine of his new daughter-in-law's forthright nature and good cheer.

Best of all, eighteen-year-old Juan, Prince of Asturias, was handsome and refined. Enchanted by the sparkling and resilient princess who had almost lost her life then joked about it, Spain's heir welcomed her into his life and arms like a breath of fresh, northern air.

Margaret was everything the Spanish demoiselles were not. Spontaneous and informal, forever ready to laugh and jest, she won over the crowds that came out to greet the Burgundian princess their rulers had chosen for their prince.

On April 3, 1497, Margaret and Juan wed at Burgos Cathedral in the capital of Castile.

Margaret was as delighted with her new husband as he was with her. In contrast to her own sturdy and outgoing self, Juan was somewhat delicate of constitution. Sensitive and reserved, he was overjoyed to have his new wife draw him out.

---

2. Jean Lemaire de Belges, Oeuvres, by Jean Stecher (Geneva: Slatkine Reprints, 1969), p. 106.

A buoyant honeymoon ensued with a joyous progress through Spain. Margaret enjoyed teasing her prince, shocking him at times with her exuberance but capturing his heart in the radiance of her gay disposition. No woman in all of Spain conducted herself in such a fun-loving fashion. She was more outspoken than any young woman he had ever met, but he loved her even more for it.

At night, Juan's ardor amazed Margaret. In contrast to her friend Louise, with her much older husband and his two mistresses, Margaret's own introduction to married life was a far sunnier story. Her prince was young and ardent, with a heart wholly for her and a passion that burned nightly, as well as in mornings and during afternoon siestas.

Margaret flung herself headlong into an awakening of her senses to pleasures she had never imagined existed. Juan of Asturias was not as delicate in the bedchamber as he appeared outside of it. Her new husband was as fiery a lover as any she had read about in the old romances. At moments she worried that he would wear himself out with the life forces he spilled in his voracious passion for her. But they were young and in love, so she paid her fears no mind. This was her first experience of a man, and she marveled at his indefatigable desire for her.

By the first of October they had reached the city of Salamanca. There, Juan fell ill.

Margaret did all within her powers to nurse him back to health. But the Spanish prince's constitution had always been frail, and the non-stop festivities of their honeymoon trip had worn him out. Some said his new bride had worn him out, too.

Yet Margaret knew it was the other way around. She had happily matched her husband's ardor with newly awakened passion of her own, but it was Juan who had burned like a fiery comet until he had plummeted back to Earth.

With his wife and father at his side, the young prince of Asturias gave up his soul to God at age nineteen on October 4, 1497.

Margaret was heartbroken; his mother, the great Queen of Spain, devastated. But their grief was assuaged by news that Margaret was pregnant.

Isabella and Ferdinand's hopes rested on their daughter-in-law's unborn child to carry on the bloodline of their only son. With Castile's laws of dynastic succession not subject to Salic Law, a boy would be preferable but a girl would do.

Wracked by grief, Margaret soldiered on as her pregnancy progressed. Queen Isabella was a steadfast comfort, as great a warm mother figure as she was a political leader. Margaret had much time to spare, as her in-laws did all they could to make her comfortable in anticipation of the future King of Spain she might produce. She spent hours at her mother-in-law's side, watching her manage her network of informants, some of them reporting back to her on her husband's activities to stay one step ahead of him.

At the end of March, after an eternity of waiting, Margaret felt her first contraction. For two long days and nights she labored, terrified and barely touching food or drink. Finally, on April 2, 1498, the babe was born.

It was a daughter, stillborn. The experience had been so painful Margaret thanked God that it was over. She could not imagine ever enduring childbirth again.

Small comfort came to her in the whispered conversations she overheard between the midwife and her attendants in the hours after the birth, when she was thought to be sleeping. The midwife had told her assistant that Margaret would likely not be able to bear more children. As she drifted off, all she could think was that she was happy she would be spared another such ordeal.

Some weeks after the birth of her dead child, word came that Charles VIII of France had died in a freak accident at Amboise, not yet twenty-eight years of age. When Margaret heard the news, she thanked God she herself had not died. She had survived being jilted by Charles, almost shipwrecked at sea, widowed at age seventeen, and losing her child at eighteen. But she was still a princess of the House of Burgundy-Habsburg. Had not Anne of Brittany said she would grow into a great lady and take her seat at the table of Europe's princes?

Margaret raised herself up on her bed and reached for the goblet of strong Spanish wine mixed with herbs that sat on her bedside table. Sipping at it, she felt its warmth suffuse her vitals. Life beckoned to her; she would carry on.

Isabella was grief-stricken, her hopes snuffed out of seeing her son's line continued. Ferdinand too, but less so. Always a schemer, he decided to play the same game with Margaret that Charles VIII had in France. Ferdinand was in no rush to send her back to the Burgundian Netherlands, as he had no intention of returning her dowry. Instead, he began to search for a Spanish prince for his valuable daughter-in-law so he could keep her dowry in Spain.

As adaptable as she had been in France and in her homeland, Margaret did not press to leave the love and devotion of her mother-in-law. Unlike her attendants who longed to return home to Flanders, Margaret found Spain enchanting. She was struck by Spanish values of honor, solemnity and protocol, with an underlying depth of passion that she had experienced firsthand with her prince. All were in sharp contrast to Burgundy's less formal and more jovial atmosphere.

Observing and listening, Margaret absorbed lessons in the art of leadership from her mother-in-law. She had grown up with powerful women: Anne de Beaujeu, then Margaret of York. But Isabella of Castile commanded respect beyond any woman Margaret had known. She admired the Spanish queen's adeptness in handling both her vast realm and her husband. Margaret was struck by how Queen Isabella attracted great men to serve her: among them the valiant general Gonzalo de Córdoba, and the brilliant navigator Columbus.

In particular, Margaret noted how expertly Isabella managed Ferdinand, brushing off his imperfections and burnishing his pride when he infrequently appeared. The King of Aragon's domains were smaller than hers, with Aragon one-third the size of Castile. But Isabella was careful to include Ferdinand's signature on all decrees that went out, as well as to cultivate a loving relationship with him despite his long absences and rumored dalliances. The queen's reward for her deft skills in deflecting the bad and cultivating the good was that the king appeared to worship her, as did all of Spain.

Margaret guessed it was due to the queen's unwavering constancy. Isabella of Spain made all who came into her presence feel they could count on her, in sharp contrast to her husband, who was brave and capable, but not to be trusted.

As Margaret waited for Ferdinand, her brother, and her father to agree on what next to do with her, she grew close to Isabella and Ferdinand's youngest daughter, six years younger than herself.

Catherine of Aragon was being prepared to become wife to Arthur of England, oldest son of Henry Tudor and heir to the

English throne. Arthur's mother, Elizabeth of York, had written to Isabella, asking that Catherine learn French so that she could converse in the language of the court when she arrived in England. Who better to teach her than Margaret? The two princesses spent many happy hours together in the lush gardens of Isabella and Ferdinand's Alhambra palace, conversing in French and laughing over Catherine's strong Spanish accent.

In May of 1499, Margaret attended Catherine's proxy marriage in Spain to Arthur of England. With Catherine's departure for England imminent, the time had come for Margaret to return to her own realm.

In September 1499, the nineteen-year-old Burgundian princess began the long journey home, crossing through France with a safe conduct from its new king. Louis XII remembered her fondly from her childhood days in Amboise. Anne of Brittany had married him after Charles VIII's death and they had just had their first child together, a daughter.

By February, Margaret rested in Paris. Upon hearing the news that her brother's wife had delivered a son, she resumed her journey and arrived in Flanders' great city of Ghent in March 1500. Unbeknownst to her, Philibert of Savoy was amongst the crowd that cheered her return to her homeland. Escorted to her brother's palace, Margaret was invited to be the newborn prince's godmother, participating in lavish festivities surrounding the birth of Juana and Philip's second child and first son.

Named after his Burgundian great-grandfather, Charles the Rash, the newborn infant was heir to both the Habsburg and Spanish thrones. Never before had two such powerful and distant domains been united.

All of Europe recognized the significance of the boy's future. Not only would Charles of Habsburg rule over one realm stretching from the east of Europe to the west, but he would receive the revenues expected to stream in from the new lands Queen Isabella's navigator had discovered across the seas. As Margaret held the tiny prince in her arms, she vowed to watch over him as if he were her own son.

After the christening Margaret took up residence near the French border in a home Philip chose for her. Their maternal grandfather, Charles the Rash, had used Quesnoy-le-Comte as an animal sanctuary deep in the forest.

Margaret wondered if Philip had decided on the isolated spot to keep her far from court. Philip's household was so decadent and irregular that her sensibilities, honed in Spain's strict atmosphere, were increasingly shaken by what she saw and heard when she visited him.

She loved her brother but she could not fail to see that he was as undisciplined and self-serving as he was handsome and pleasure-loving. His wife had given him two children already—a daughter and a son—but what Philip truly wanted was Juana's title as hereditary successor to Castile.

Burgundy's dashing young duke dominated his Spanish wife, taking advantage of her impassioned nature by withholding then offering his affection. In return, Juana appeared obsessed with him. Her slavish devotion had begun to wear on his nerves.

Visiting Quesnoy-le-Comte without his wife, Philip ridiculed Juana in a way that jarred Margaret.

"Good God, if she would just contain herself I could breathe easier. As it is, she can't bear to let me out of her sight, and the more she sighs after me the less I can stand her."

"Brother, is it not a virtue for a wife to honor her husband?" Margaret asked, wondering why Philip wasn't charmed by Juana's interest, as she had been by Juan's. It was rare in royal alliances for couples to be interested in each other at all.

"'Tis no honor to have some sort of cow in heat mooning after me day and night," Philip grumbled.

"How can you say such a thing of your own wife?" Margaret cried, shocked to hear her brother so harshly describe Isabella of Spain's daughter.

"Sister, you were married yourself not long ago. Would it not have driven you mad to have your prince mooning after you every second of the day?"

"We mooned after each other at night and were very good friends by day," Margaret shot back, thinking sadly of how compatible she had been with her prince. She had felt protective of Juan, while he had been besotted by her.

"Well we're not good friends, and the more she comes after me the more I feel like kicking her away," Philip complained.

"You are talking about an infanta of Spain!" Margaret exclaimed, thinking how horrified Isabella would be to know of her daughter's treatment. The Queen of Spain had endured enough pain already with the deaths of her two oldest children in the past few years, along with their offspring.

Philip grimaced. "She is a woman at the end of the day. And she is no more capable of ruling Spain than she is of ruling her own household."

"Her mother rules Spain as a woman, and I saw with my own eyes the respect she commands," Margaret hotly retorted. "Surely your wife could rule her own household if you would let her. I heard you had all her attendants sent back to Spain," she added.

Philip made a sour face. "I can't bear having those glum pious types around. They understand nothing of our ways, and are forever turning their mouths down when any fun is to be had."

"Fun is only fun when it's not at another's expense," Margaret admonished, thinking that her handsome brother had not been sufficiently tutored in the school of honorable behavior. Perhaps too much luck in good looks and royal parentage had spoiled him.

"Sister, I can't explain it to you, but she brings out the worst in me. May you never find yourself caught in a similar position. It's enough to make one retch." Philip kicked the leg of the table in front of the couch on which he lounged.

"I will be sure not to," Margaret said, thinking it was her brother himself who had brought on his own marital unhappiness by not respecting his wife's background and customs.

The next time Margaret visited court, she watched Juana closely. The beautiful Spanish princess had all that life might offer: title to one of Europe's most powerful realms, two healthy children, and the most handsome husband in Europe, if not the most attentive.

Yet Margaret could see that Juana lacked one thing that all princesses need in their quiver. Anne de Beaujeu had had it, as well as Anne of Brittany, Margaret of York, and Isabella of Spain. All the women Margaret modeled herself after had burnished themselves strictly in the school of self-possession.

To Margaret's eyes Juana of Castile appeared to lack control of her emotions. Her passionate obsession with her husband had first charmed the Burgundian court, then increasingly caused alarm when it was clear that their archduke was not responding in kind. As Juana had no power over her husband's heart, but only over her own, she appeared to be losing even that, too. Philip had not helped matters by dismissing her Spanish attendants and insisting on her staying in her own rooms.

Rumors floated to Margaret's ears that Juana was mentally fragile. It had seemed inconceivable to Margaret that any child of Isabella and Ferdinand could be mentally weak, but Juan had confided to her that his mother's mother, Isabella of Portugal, had been unsound of mind and had lived in seclusion since the early death of her husband.

Now Margaret saw with her own eyes the dismaying spectacle of a royal wife overly dependent on her husband's regard. It shocked her almost as much as Philip's vicious response. The more she observed of Philip and Juana's downward spiral, the more Margaret resolved never to allow her emotions to control her. No ruler worth her title could afford such behavior. And no woman who valued her pride would allow a faithless husband to steal it, as Isabella of Spain had modeled so well.

Receiving a parting kiss from her brother, Margaret watched from the upstairs window as he strode across the courtyard: confident, glorious, cruel.

A chill passed through her as she turned from the sight. Trying to imagine the years ahead for the mismatched couple, all she could see was darkness and turmoil.

4

MARRIAGE TO PHILIBERT OF SAVOY

1501

NEWS FROM VIENNA ARRIVED. Her father had found a match for her. Philibert, Duke of Savoy, known as Philibert the Handsome, was to be her next husband.

Margaret could guess why. His duchy lay between France, Italy, and the Swiss Confederation, strategically situated to control access to Italy by foreign princes hungry to acquire a piece of it. By tying Savoy to the Holy Roman Empire, Maximilian hoped to cut off the French from making further inroads on the Italian peninsula.

Her childhood companion's epithet made Margaret smile. She remembered him fondly. The same age as she, he had been fun-loving and gay, unlike his high-strung older sister Louise. Margaret had not thought of him as handsome, but he had not yet ripened into manhood.

Margaret twirled a lock of her long, golden hair as memories flowed. Philibert's easy athleticism. His patient coaching at crossbow practice. Generous words of encouragement that had built her confidence and relaxed her arm before she shot. He had been fraternal, not competitive, and never dismissive of her skills as a girl. Perhaps it could work.

In August 1501, she began preparations to travel to Savoy to meet her intended husband. Juana had just delivered her third child, a daughter she named Isabella. Margaret wondered at the strangeness of her marriage with Philip, so unhappy yet so fruitful. She was eager to leave the unhealthy atmosphere of her brother's court, however much she loved him.

Negotiations over her dowry were not the only monetary issues on the table. Her brother wanted both a piece of her inheritance from their mother and Margaret's signature on a document renouncing any rights to Spain's throne.

"Brother, why are you so eager to grab out from under me that which is mine?" Margaret asked. She had found him in his study, where he rarely was.

Philip looked up impatiently, pushing himself away from his desk piled high with papers.

Margaret guessed they were largely unread and untouched.

"Sister, have I not just gifted you with 300,000 gold coins for your marriage?"

"I see they were given at a price. My mother's estates are dear to me, and I do not wish to relinquish them."

"Sister, be practical. You will make your home in Savoy and will not be able to manage lands in Burgundy. I am here, and can manage them better than you."

"I should like to retain rights to lands our mother left to me."

Philip waved a hand dismissively. "You will be far off in Savoy making fat babies and won't want the burden of faraway holdings."

"And you will be in Spain, even farther away, trying to grab your wife's crown from her in a country whose language you do not speak and whose people you will never understand," Margaret retorted.

"I would never grab Juana's crown, but rule beside her," Philip objected, looking exceptionally handsome, as he always did when he was lying.

"Will you, brother?"

"If she is capable of ruling, I will help her."

Margaret snorted. "As you have helped her here?"

Philip scowled. "It is hard to help those who do not help themselves."

"And so you kick her to the ground instead."

"Harsh words, sister. Do not say such a thing."

"I would not if I had not seen it with my own eyes," Margaret challenged.

"Speak no more of what you do not understand and sign this paper so I can manage your estates."

Margaret crossed her arms and leaned back against the door, ignoring the quill Philip held out. "I do not care to sign away my inheritance," she told him.

"I am simply looking after your lands while you are in Savoy," Philip explained, false innocence blanketing his tone like freshly fallen snow.

"Then you must stipulate they are to be returned to me when I return to Burgundy."

"Do not vex me, sister. The document is prepared and requires only your signature."

"You shall have it as soon as the clause is inserted that these lands return to me upon my return to Burgundy."

Philip's voice rose. "What difference does it make when you are about to begin a new life in Savoy?"

"If it makes no difference to you then I shall have it inserted, as it is important to me," Margaret resisted.

Philip glowered then threw the quill on the table. "Have it your way. But you are not to leave Brussels until you sign it."

"So be it." Margaret returned her brother's gaze, thinking how lucky she was to be his sister and not his wife, subjected to his wrath when she did not submit to his will, and his scorn when she did.

The following day Margaret met with the notary and had the clause inserted. As she signed, she vowed she would one day manage her own lands and her own affairs. Life had already shown her so many twists that she could not count on spending the rest of her years in Savoy. And come what may, her maternal inheritance was precious to her. She was the granddaughter of Charles the Rash, last of the great Burgundian dukes. No one must be allowed to wrest her birthright from her.

Chuckling to herself, she thought of how miserable Philip would be in Spain. He would wilt like a foreign flower there, where his superficial charm would not endear him to the serious Spaniards. Let him find out for himself.

How strange it was to love someone and not trust them at the same time. She hoped that her new husband would not be one of those types. But remembering Philibert's steady hand on her shooting arm and his quiet words of encouragement, she already knew he was made of different stuff than her brother.

Her mind flew to her wedding night ahead. Soon she would know if Philibert had grown into a handsome prince, with her eyes and with hands that would wander over every angle of his body. Shivering, she imagined its unknown landscape. That night their childhood friendship would deepen into a mystical bond no man could put asunder.

At the end of September, the marriage contract was signed. One month later Margaret set out for Savoy, accompanied by her own entourage, as well as a contingent of guards sent by her husband-to-be.

Maximilian, never one to venture far from his court in Vienna or Innsbruck, had traveled north to Brussels to see her off. Rarely did she see her father in person. But the force of his charm, his warm outstretched arms, and his unfailing affection melted her the moment she laid eyes on him, their brief meeting bringing them closer.

On November 22 she arrived at Dole, southeast of Burgundy's capital of Dijon. There she was met by Philibert's half-brother, René, Bastard of Savoy and Count of Villars.

Alerted by her equerry that her future brother-in-law was approaching, she began to prepare, freshening up from the indignities of the long carriage ride.

But before she was done, the curtain of the litter ripped apart to each side. A coarse man loomed before her, shocking her with his rough dispatch of her privacy.

"Ah, so you are pretty as well as rich," he greeted her.

Furious, Margaret raised her chin. "Who do you think you are, to address me in such a way?" she snapped. Shaped by Spanish formality after three years on the Iberian peninsula, she did not take well to such an insolent greeting.

"I am René of Savoy, your husband's brother and your proxy for him at our marriage ceremony tomorrow." Looking her up and down, he seemed ready to jump into the litter.

Margaret turned a glacial stare to the leering man and prayed his brother was nothing like him. If memory served, Philibert was not. He had been a sturdy boy, but gently raised. No one with manners like those of the man before her would have lasted long at the court of Amboise.

"Then I will thank you to leave me in peace until the ceremony takes place. And may you conduct yourself in a more seemly manner when you see me again," she berated, swinging shut the curtain of her litter. She would not tolerate being assessed like goods at a market by some swaggart, even if he was her new husband's natural-born brother.

The following day the proxy marriage ceremony took place. The cocksure René stood in for Philibert, touching his leg to Margaret's exposed calf in the usual bedchamber ceremony.

Barely tolerating his touch, she softened somewhat when he presented her with a large diamond before exiting the chamber. In the previous twenty-four hours she had learned that René ran the affairs of Savoy. Wondering how it was that the natural-born son of Philibert's father occupied a position of such high rank, she vowed to find out, once installed as head of her future husband's household.

The first day of December Margaret arrived in Romainmoutier, a charming village nestled in the Jura Mountains just outside Geneva. As her bridegroom rode toward her at the head of a large party, Margaret trembled. Memories of playing with her old childhood friend at Amboise melded with heady excitement at meeting him as a man.

From a distance it was apparent that he sat his mount well. As his face came into focus, she saw that his light brown eyes were fixed on hers with a look of wonder. She straightened in her saddle, feeling esteemed already, and willed herself to meet his gaze with her own. Already her instincts told her that he was nothing like his boorish half-brother.

Philibert dismounted his horse, throwing a finely muscled leg over its back. Feeling her insides hum, she allowed him to lift her down from her palfrey.

The moment her feet touched the ground, Philip bent one knee and kissed her hand. "Lady Margaret, I am delighted to see you again," he greeted.

Margaret blushed. "In far different circumstances, are they not, my lord?"

Philibert did not take his eyes from hers as he rose. "My lady, to gain you as a wife is beyond happiness."

"I hope it will be, my lord. I have had my share of misfortune, so I am ready for happiness, too," she answered. Philibert had, indeed, grown into a handsome man. Taking in the deep cleft of his chin and strongly-drawn mouth, she felt a thrill run down her spine. His features were well-defined, his physique sturdy, unlike her previous prince who had been delicately drawn.

The Duke of Savoy grasped her other hand as he searched her face.

With a slight nod she gave him leave to kiss her. As his lips touched her cheek a scent of cloves, horses, and heather hit her nose and she found herself responding. He was not overly tall, but a hands-length taller than she, suiting her well.

As he pulled back, years of thwarted plans and tragedies fell from her like dust shaken from a cloak. A slow blush crept up her body, one she had not felt since her brief months with Juan.

"Did you think we would one day find ourselves wed?" she asked.

Again, Philibert bent a knee to the ground, grabbing hold of her hand and placing it on his forehead. "Never did I think I would be lucky enough to marry such a highborn princess."

"And is that what you most care about?" It was an unfair question, since she, too, cared about position. Her father had assured her that Philibert, as titular King of Jerusalem, Cyprus, and Armenia, as well as Duke of Savoy, was worthy to become her husband.

"I did until this moment, my lady."

"And now what concerns you most?" Margaret asked archly, remembering how she had enjoyed their easy banter back in carefree Amboise days. Was it possible those days might return, this time ignited by an ardent flame?

"It is that I serve you as a good husband and a good friend, and that you find no fault in me other than the many you already discovered in our younger days."

Laughter welled in her throat. "Do you say you haven't developed any new faults in the years since last we met?"

"Only ones I intend to hide from you, my lady."

"As your wife, I will soon discover them." How at ease she felt.

"Then may they be as light as the feather you once used to tickle my nose."

At that Margaret's giggle escaped, eliciting sighs of approval from those standing near. "You have not changed, my lord," she exclaimed.

Philibert lowered his head and spoke in an undertone. "I have in some ways, which I hope will please you, my lady."

"I will let you know soon enough," she whispered back, over-joyed they had both been married and would be unencumbered by virginal flounderings.

With a merry snort Philibert offered his arm to her, and they proceeded into the town hall.

A crackling fire roared in the hearth at one end of the great room. There her gallant consort plied her with spiced hippocras and meat pastries until she was thoroughly sated. How exhilarating it was to know what lay ahead, having been a wife already. Even more wonderful to have a friend and peer for a husband, one she knew already but now looked upon with womanly eyes.

A shiver pulsed through her at the thought.

"My lady, are you cold?" Philibert asked, gesturing for an atten-dant.

"Not at all."

"Was I wrong to think you shivered?"

"You were not wrong," she said.

"But not from cold..."

Margaret gazed up at him from under her lashes. "No, my lord. Not from cold."

Philibert sprang to attention like a hunting dog scenting its prey. "Is it that I please you?" he asked in lower tones.

"I will not say." Margaret fluttered her eyes, warmed from the pit of her stomach that he asked in such attentive tones.

"Ah, my lady, then I am free to think what I may. And may I tell you what I think?"

She gave him an impish look. "No, you may not."

Philibert brought his mouth close to her ear. "Then I will show you later."

"I will show you, too," she replied, her unabashed Burgundian spirit rising like sap within her.

"I cannot wait," he murmured, a flame leaping in his eyes.

"You must wait, as we are not yet married," she reminded him.

Philibert's eyes twinkled. "So my brother's leg wasn't good enough?"

"Now that you are here, I will take the real man," Margaret riposted.

"So be it, my lady. We are to marry tonight in the chapel and then we will—"

Putting a finger on his well-shaped lips, Margaret stopped him. "Yes. We will."

Philibert grasped her wrist and kissed her hand, lingering upon it.

Margaret shivered at the velvety touch of his mouth on her palm. Perhaps, with this marriage, happiness would not come and go like some blithe and tragic songbird.

That evening, after a festive dance, Philibert and a small group of friends met Margaret and her ladies in the chapel one hour before midnight. There the bishop of Maurienne, Father Louis von Gorrevod, said the wedding Mass.

Philibert II, Duke of Savoy, and Margaret, Archduchess of Austria, Princess of Burgundy, and Dowager Princess of Spain, became husband and wife. Philibert's kiss was fervent; no Spanish formality reigned in Savoy.

By midnight the newlywed couple had been tucked into bed with the usual ribaldry. After Philibert had shouted away the last man in the room, his attendants drew the bedcurtains and stoked the fire before slipping out.

Alone, finally.

The night passed rapturously. Margaret felt even more at ease with Philibert than she had with Juan, who had been younger, less experienced, and someone she had just met. She had loved her Spanish prince, but it had taken them some weeks to adjust to each other.

In contrast, the younger brother of Louise of Savoy was an old friend, easy of manner, quick to make good cheer, and experienced in the art of pleasing a woman.

By morning, both bride and groom wore the rosy flush of a night well spent. The next day they set off for Geneva. In Savoy's largest town they were welcomed with a lavish wedding reception. There Margaret met Philibert's stepmother and younger half-siblings and bastard sister. Claude de Brosse, widow of Philibert's father, embraced Margaret warmly and invited her to her home as soon as she was settled into her own. Margaret could see that the children, all between the ages of five and fourteen, were as dazzled by her as she was charmed by them.

Philibert's sister Louise was there, too, with her daughter and son, Marguerite and Francis. For the first time Margaret met her old friend's children, ages ten and six. Louise was now a widow, capable and watchful, as tightly wound as her younger brother was not.

Margaret could see that her children were well-spoken and polished beyond their years. Both had inherited the darkly handsome looks of their father, Charles d'Angoulême, the King of France's first cousin. With Louis XII still without a son and heir, Louise's boy was in line to be France's next king. In a few twists of fate, her old friend had come up in the world. Margaret was as happy for her as she was for herself.

Several days of festivities ensued, until it was time for Philibert to bring Margaret to his ancestral home. The chateau of Pont d'Ain was halfway up a mountainside, looking out over the verdant valley of Ain. It was there that both he and Louise were born to Philibert II of Savoy, who had died four years earlier, and Margaret of Bourbon, who had died when Philibert was three.

It took Margaret only a few days to fall in love with the graceful chateau that would be her new home. Her husband was in his element in his charming aerie, surrounded by forests teeming with game, and protected from strong winds by the mountains behind it. She passed the first season of her new marriage in a whirlwind of dances and festivities, making good cheer before roaring hearths and nestled in the foothills of the snowy Jura Mountains as well as in her husband's arms.

Her handsome prince and she hunted and held court, laughed, studied, played cards and chess, rode their properties, and made frequent visits to his welcoming stepmother at her nearby estate.

At spring's emergence, the young Duke and Duchess of Savoy set off on a progress throughout the realm, greeted everywhere by Philibert's subjects coming out to meet their new duchess.

As their journey continued, Margaret noted that her husband was not overly concerned with the affairs of his realm. Content to put the reins of governance into someone else's hands, he had largely given over duties to his seven-years-older half-brother, appointing René Lieutenant-General of Savoy.

But Margaret had a better idea. Upon their return to Pont d'Ain, she reflected on two points she had observed on their trip across Savoy: firstly, the people had been well-disposed toward them; secondly, it was the Bastard of Savoy running the country. Not Philibert.

She saw that the moment was ripe for the Duke and Duchess of Savoy to embrace ducal responsibilities. As Duchess of Savoy, she was unwilling to allow her husband's powers to slip from its rightful holder to an illegitimate sibling, especially one as coarse and ambitious as René.

"My lord, it is time to take back what is yours by ancestral right," she remarked one morning, soon after their return.

"What do you mean, *ma mie*?" Philibert asked, tugging at his riding boot in his eagerness to ride out for the day.

"I mean you should not allow René to usurp your powers. It is not right for him to administer your duchy."

Philibert shrugged. "He enjoys doing it and I don't, so what's wrong with it?"

"He is eager to take over what is yours by birthright. You must not let him."

"What's your solution, then?" Philibert asked, looking peeved.

"My lord, this is your realm and I am duchess of it as your wife. I can see what needs to be done, and we have good counselors to help us manage it ourselves. Let me administer your lands so that they stay within your control and are passed on to our children and not René's."

"You don't like him, do you?" Philibert asked, searching for his hunting vest.

"I don't like that he seeks to upend the natural order. Your half-brother was born into a position he is eager to move out of, at your expense. As your wife, I will not have you shouldered aside by an upstart."

Philibert looked startled. "Do you think that's what he intends?"

"It is as clear as the sky is blue," Margaret said, warming to her argument. "And his wife encourages him. You must not let him continue in the position you yourself should occupy. If you do, one day what God has given you will be taken from you."

Philibert waved a blithe hand. "Leave off and come riding with me."

Margaret held firm. "Only if you promise to remove him from his position."

"If he hasn't done anything wrong, why should I do that?"

Instantly, Margaret knew what tack she would take. She had learned from mistakes made by her father and brother that any who held power made a wrong move sooner or later. Soon she would dig up something on René. "He has overstepped his boundaries by pressuring you to grant him an act of legitimacy," she replied.

"I can't just take it away from him. Your father affirmed it."

"And once it is revoked, he is no longer eligible to serve as Lieutenant-General of Savoy."

"But how can I revoke it?"

"Do nothing, and I will see to it that my father has it declared null and void."

"It seems harsh."

"It is to protect your birthright, so that you may pass it on to your children."

"Then we must get to work on creating some," Philibert jested as he reached for her.

"Let us ride out, my lord, and return to a pleasant evening ahead." Margaret sidestepped him, removing his arm from around her waist. She would let the matter rest for the moment.

Philibert kissed her. As she kissed him back, she sensed she would win her point. It would be easier to transfer power to their children one day if they themselves administered their realm. But her husband did not like to be bothered, so she would be the one to oversee Savoy's affairs, with a council to guide her. Meanwhile, she would exercise patience until the right moment arrived.

In her relationship with her father, Margaret had gained some experience managing men in power who did not wish to be bothered. Maximilian loved her dearly and trusted her judgment. If she told her father that René, Bastard of Savoy, should not be running Savoy in place of her husband, and pointed out evidence of René's pro-French policies, Maximilian would be alarmed. He could more easily sway Savoy to imperial influence with his daughter married to the man ruling it. Or ruling it herself.

As the months passed, she dug around. Soon enough, she discovered that René had promised certain parcels of Savoy's territory to the French in exchange for large sums of money without Philibert's knowledge or permission.

"Husband, did you know of this?" she asked one morning, once she had lined up evidence of René's land transfer.

"It is impossible. René would never let Savoyard lands pass from our realm," Philibert opined, dismissing her.

"He has done so with urging from his French wife."

Philibert's gaze was tender. "You are jealous, *ma mie*, because there is room for only one top woman in Savoy."

Margaret bristled. "Of course I'm not." Although she was. Anne Lascaris was from an important French family near Nice. She held many titles herself, and Margaret had no doubt that she exercised strong influence over René to sway him to pro-French policies.

"*Ma mie*, you are Duchess of Savoy. No one can take that title from you," Philibert reassured her.

"And as duchess, it is my duty to uphold the interests of my lord and his realm. Not to see it sold piece by piece to the French."

"Of course not, *ma mie*. Such a deed would be monstrous."

Margaret held out a paper. "Yet it is agreed upon here, with your half-brother's signature on it." She had gone to some pains to obtain the document. Remembering Isabella of Spain's use of informants, she had cultivated her own network. Soon enough, one of them had delivered the damning document into her hands.

Philibert took the sheet from Margaret and went to the window to scan it. Turning his back to her, he took several moments while Margaret schooled herself to say nothing. It was time for her husband to assert himself. If she stepped into his silence, she would never know if it was he or she who made the decision that must come next.

Philibert turned to her with an expression she had never before seen on his face. "My brother has sold pieces of my birthright to France," he intoned. Brows knit together, his light brown eyes had darkened. They looked ready to pop out of his head.

"It is so, *mon cher*. And I beg you to dismiss him before he sells more."

With measured steps Philibert went to one corner of the room and rang for the steward. Within moments the man arrived, bowing to the duke.

"You will go to the Count of Villars and tell him he is to appear before me without delay." Philibert's voice was a monotone, his face averted from Margaret.

"Yes, my lord." The steward dipped his head and backed from the room.

Margaret held her breath to see what her husband would do next.

Finally he met her eyes, with thunderclouds in his. "Let us say nothing more of this matter for the moment."

Margaret nodded, a heady excitement rousing her blood. Wordlessly, she moved into his arms and circled her own about his neck. Within moments he melted, his anger abated for the moment.

Several days passed and René did not appear. Margaret said nothing, watching her husband's ire grow with every hour his half-brother failed to show up.

On the afternoon of the third day René appeared. Insouciant as ever, he ambled into Philibert's study and draped himself on the couch.

Margaret slipped silently into the room behind him, her back to the door.

"You will stand before your lord," Philibert intoned, his voice like ice.

"What ails you, brother?" René asked, crossing one leg over the other.

"Stand now, or wait for my men to help you obey my order," Philibert barked.

"Why not?" René agreed, taking his time to rise to his feet.

Philibert's face looked carved from stone. "Why not explain to me by what right you have sold lands of my domain without my knowledge or permission?"

René looked perplexed. "I would never do that, brother," he said.

"You would never do that to my knowledge. And as you have already done it, you will not be given the chance to ever do it again." Philibert held out the document that Margaret had obtained.

The Bastard of Savoy took the paper. As he read, his Adam's apple bobbed. Handing it back, he attempted an amiable smile. "Brother—"

Philibert cut him off, his words like arrows shot from his mouth. "You will address me as 'my lord,' as you have lost the right to call me 'brother.'"

René's Adam's apple bobbed again as Margaret looked on, unnoticed. She would not interfere. This was between Philibert and René. But it was a new Philibert she was seeing. What she had begun, her husband was now finishing.

"My lord, this bit of business means nothing; pieces of barren land that have no value," René began.

"That is for me to decide as ruler of Savoy, not for you to take into your own hands."

"Bro—my lord, I did not wish to bother you with such small matters."

Philibert rapped the table before him with his fist. "It is no small matter to sell pieces of your lord's birthright to a foreign power."

"I wouldn't see it like that," René protested.

"It does not matter how you see it. What matters is that you did it without my knowledge or permission."

"My lord, I make many decisions each day without your knowledge, but with your permission as lieutenant-general of your realm."

"No longer."

René's eyes widened. "What do you mean?"

"You are dismissed."

"Dismissed from your presence, my lord?"

"Dismissed from your post."

René's mouth fell open. "But who will run your affairs if you dismiss me?"

"That is my concern, not yours."

The Bastard of Savoy's face darkened. "My lord, I have striven to make your life easier, and this is how you repay me?"

"You have striven to divide up my realm into parcels and sell it off to France."

"It was barren land that no one lived on, and the French are not so bad," René protested.

"It is good that you like them so much, for you will find your new home there."

René's face blanched. "What say you, my lord?"

"You will take your family and your belongings and leave Savoy forever within two days," Philibert commanded.

"My lord, what about my holdings?"

"Your holdings will revert to the duchy, in payment for its land that you unlawfully sold."

"My lord, that is preposterous!"

Philibert rapped the table again. "It is the order of your lord, and you will obey it now."

As René stood rooted to the floor, his face frozen in shock, Philibert rang the bell for the captain of the guard. He arrived with two men on either side.

"Escort this man to his home and keep guard over him until he and his family have packed their belongings," Philibert ordered. "Within two days you are to accompany them over the border into France."

"Yes, my lord."

"Once you have accomplished this, return here to report to me that it is done."

"I will do so, my lord."

As René turned, he caught sight of Margaret and let out a hiss. Quickly, the two sentries took hold of his arms and marched him toward the door.

Margaret moved aside to let them to pass.

"This is your doing, you dirty *salope*," René spat as he went by.

Eyes averted, Margaret raised a handkerchief to her nose. The arrogant cur was now being banished from the country he had run. She could hardly wait to step in and take up the reins she had caused to slip from his hands.

Within the month Maximilian's letter arrived from Innsbruck, reversing the Bastard of Savoy's legitimacy. But the power shift had been accomplished by Philibert himself. Just as he had ordered, the Bastard of Savoy and his wife and children were gone from Savoy within two days, never to return.

Margaret exulted, not only for her victory over the man who had leered at her on her proxy wedding day but for the assertion of power her husband had manifested.

It was a coup, resulting in much work falling into her lap. But she was ready.

She enjoyed the details of administering the duchy, meeting with her council members and maintaining good relations with France across the border, with a firm eye to maintaining Savoy's independence. Soon she was immersed in the daily affairs of her husband's realm. One day she intended for it to pass to their eldest son or daughter.

But no son or daughter came. Margaret wondered if the midwife's prediction had been true. Had the agonizing stillbirth she had endured ended her chances to become a mother? Truth be told, the thought of undergoing childbirth again terrified her.

Enjoying her youth and freedom from back-to-back pregnancies that royal women were expected to endure in the quest for heirs, Margaret threw herself into her work, leaving her husband free to hunt to his heart's content. She joined him often, having learned to hunt under Anne de Beaujeu, who had been as sharp with bow and arrow as she was with wit and tongue.

But one day, while riding in the Piedmont region of Savoy just south of Turin, Margaret's horse reared, throwing her. On the ground she cowered in fear as its hooves came down on her gown, then her hat and hair that had come undone. Waiting to be crushed, she narrowly escaped when the horse bolted off, as frightened by the voluminous folds of her gown as it was by the creature that had spooked it.

It was as if her mother's spirit had warned her not to follow in her tracks, her life snuffed out at age twenty-five by a fall from her horse.

Shaken, Margaret cut down on hunting with Philibert. Her decision freed her up to attend to even more administrative duties, as well as to enlarge their court, extending patronage to scholars and poets schooled in the new humanist thinking now wafting northward from Italy.

In their serene and politically neutral realm—obscure, mountainous, and untouched by the bustle of commerce of the Burgundian Netherlands—Margaret felt cocooned in happiness. She thanked God for the blissful existence He had brought to her after so many years of uncertainty.

Map of Savoy

By Raymond Palmer of English Wikipedia

Note: borders are similar to Savoy's borders in 1500

EARLY IN THE SUMMER of 1502, sad news arrived. Margaret's cherished former sister-in-law Catherine of Aragon had become a widow just six months after her marriage to the heir to the English throne. She and Arthur had both come down with sweating sickness. Catherine had survived, but her fifteen-year-old husband had succumbed.

Years of planning and careful preparation had gone into their match, snuffed out in the turn of two seasons. Margaret grieved for her former kinswoman, reduced overnight to a sixteen-year-old widow instead of a future Queen of England. How quickly the fates of foreign princesses could be upended.

With the news that Catherine was not carrying Arthur's heir, thus reducing her status to *persona non grata* at the English court, Margaret renewed her efforts to start a family with Philibert. Already they spent their days and nights together: blissful, healthy, and genuinely in love. Why, then, did the time not come when she would have joyous news to give her beloved?

The seasons passed, but no child arrived. Neither Philibert nor Margaret were bothered. They were happy enough with each other, and Margaret enjoyed managing the affairs of their realm. Every week she learned something new about building and maintaining the infrastructure of Savoy's towns and villages. What she didn't know she assigned to one of her counselors, who would identify local experts whom she would appoint to oversee the project at hand.

Under her eye roads were built, sanitation improved, hospitals enlarged, and almshouses created. When pestilence came to France in summer months, she saw to it that hygiene measures were expanded and villages sealed off. In the Alpen fresh air of Savoy, with Margaret's firm and consistent measures, pestilence did not come to call.

The more she oversaw, the more Philibert loved and admired her. His congenial nature possessed neither envy nor hunger for power. What he wanted was what he already had. He was content with what life brought him, especially his capable wife. Margaret could ask for nothing more, except for children to bless them.

IN THE SPRING OF 1503, Philip of Burgundy visited on his way back to Brussels from Spain. Juana had stayed behind with their fourth child, Ferdinand, who had been born in March. Leaving behind his infant son to be raised at his grandfather Ferdinand's court, Philip had passed through France before reaching Savoy. He had met with Louis XII and Anne of Brittany in Lyon to reaffirm their agreement to marry his eldest son Charles to the King and Queen of France's only child, the Princess Claude.

Margaret was only too aware of the flimsiness of betrothal promises, especially as made by the French, but she was overjoyed to see her brother again.

He and Philibert amused themselves with hunts by day, followed by evenings of dancing, music, and merrymaking. Margaret could see Philip's intemperate love of the ladies had not diminished. Philip flirted and dallied, scandalizing their small court and incensing her with the bad example he set for her husband. Still, she enjoyed his visit.

But suddenly both men came down with fevers. Margaret was terrified. After losing her Spanish prince, many said due to exhaustion brought on by too much merrymaking, she did not wish to lose two of the three men she loved most.

Putting her husband and brother to bed, she called the doctors and set her most skillful attendants to work. For three long days and nights they tended to their sick master and his royal kinsman with herbal tisanes and cold lavender-scented compresses.

On the morning of the fourth day both men's fevers broke. Margaret thanked God that they had pulled through and sent a large donation to the church in nearby Bourg-en-Bresse.

Greeting Philip the day after his recovery, Margaret dismissed his attendants and shut the door to his bedchamber. The past three days had shaken her. Death had come to call and left unsated. Was it not a warning?

"Brother, I am happy you have recovered. I hope you will treasure even more all that you hold dear, now that you have brushed death."

Philip looked at her blankly, his golden-blond features a handsome mask. "What meaning, sister?"

"Your wife and children. Are you not eager to see them again?"

Philip rolled his eyes. "I am as eager to see my prince and princesses as I am to get away from the one who gave them to me."

"Do you not feel blessed to have such a fruitful wife?" she asked, pushing away the worry that dogged her whenever she thought about Philip and Juana's marriage.

Philip sipped his tisane and put it down. Sourly, he looked at her. "What do you want from me? The answer you seek or the real one?"

Margaret sighed. "Things have not improved between you, have they?"

"She is unhinged, and her possessiveness drives me away," the Duke of Burgundy stated bluntly.

"She has a right to be possessive. She is your wife," Margaret challenged. As Philip's sister, she would speak up. With no mother to steer him, and their father far off in Austria, the Burgundian Netherland's enfant terrible was as rudderless as he was pivotal to Europe's affairs—embodying the link between the House of Burgundy-Habsburg with Spain.

"I am tired of it. She is also possessive of her title, although she has no idea how to manage it," Philip complained.

"And you do?"

"If only her father would keep his hands off my affairs, I would do fine."

Margaret shook her head. "Philip, do you understand the Spanish at all?"

"No more than my wife understands us."

"It is a shame, brother, to try to wrest from your wife what is hers by dynastic right."

Philip rolled his eyes. "She cannot manage it herself, even as she cannot manage her own actions."

"There have been many rulers with such challenges, but with support they administer their realms."

Philip's laugh was cynical. "She will never administer anything unless it be a dose of poison to one of my favorites."

Margaret shivered. "Do not jest in such a way." Perhaps it would not be one of her brother's favorites that Juana might dose with poison. She was Spanish, as impassioned and deep as Philip was not. He played with fire, but did not realize it in his blithe, uncomprehending way.

"She is capable of such a thing, sister. She cut off the hair of a fair lady at court last time we were in Brussels. It was a gruesome thing."

Margaret's eyes widened. So Juana had fought back. "Does that not tell you that she is capable of punishing those who cause her pain?"

Philip threw his head back and laughed. "What pain do any of my favorites cause her? It is she herself who causes her own pain by taking everything too seriously."

"You are right, brother. It is not one of your favorites who cause her pain. It is you."

Philip snorted. "She is besotted with me; she would never hurt me," he flung out.

"You do not understand Spanish pride, brother. She will revenge herself on you if you continue to disrespect her," Margaret warned.

"Sister, she doesn't respect herself, so how am I to show respect? It's all I can do to stand in the same room with her."

"Yet you manage to lie in the same bed well enough," Margaret noted.

Philip's eyes narrowed. "My aim is to claim Spain for Burgundy and the House of Habsburg. With two sons, I am on my way."

"Watch yourself, brother. You are married to a Spanish princess, heir to the Castilian throne. You think you have the upper hand, but if your wife should strike you down you may not recover."

Philip laughed, waving her away. "What bosh you speak. I thought you had more sense."

"I have the sense to know that Spanish passion burns hotter than Burgundian. And you will be its unhappy recipient if you do not treat your wife better."

"I already am, which is why I'm glad to get away," Philip scoffed, throwing up his hands.

"Treat her well when you see her next," Margaret advised.

"A discussion for another day, sister. I hope to host you and your duke in Brussels soon, so we can all make good cheer together."

In place of an answer she smiled tightly. She would not bring Philibert to visit him anytime soon, especially not if Juana was there. She did not wish her good-hearted husband to absorb any louche lessons from Philip on how to disrespect a wife.

A week later the Duke of Burgundy and his party departed. At Philibert's side Margaret waved goodbye, relief washing over her like cleansing rain. Her brother needed reining in. From what she had seen of Juana, his wife did, too. Both were ruled by their passions, a quality no ruler should rely on to do his job well.

Thinking of their oldest prince who would one day rule over most of Europe, she prayed her godson had not inherited the temperament of either of his parents.

Philibert II, Duke of Savoy

Chromolithograph, by Jean-Etienne-Frédéric Giniez, 1854

after a stained glass window at the church of Brou

Château de Versailles, Paris

From www.universalcompendium.com

5

THE CHANGES OF FORTUNE MAKE ONE STRONGER

FALL 1504

"MY LADY, I CANNOT abide this heat. Let us hunt today to escape it," Philibert suggested. Snug in bed they had just opened their eyes, their arms flung over each other. It was the first of September 1504, the hottest summer in memory for either of them.

"Nay, my lord. It is hot already, and I am mindful of my mother's accident since my own. Too soon she passed, at the toss of a horse."

"The forest will be cooler, *ma mie*. Why don't you ride out with me for a few hours?"

"You go. I've got papers to sort through. When you return, we can walk in the gardens at dusk." Margaret had much to attend to. But uppermost in her mind was her desire to conceive. It was coming up on three years since they had wed, yet no heir had arrived. She would not risk another fall from a horse that might end a pregnancy or her own life.

"As you wish, *ma mie*. Until this evening, then." Philibert threw on his clothes and headed for the stables.

Margaret tried to take her time getting up. Her doctors had advised her to slow down to improve her chances to conceive. But it was not in her nature to laze about. Even when she remained abed of a morning, her mind filled with plans—receipts to sort through, tenants to visit, counselors to confer with, roads and sewage ditches to improve. Soon she had set her plans for the day. Hopping out of bed, she slipped on her lightest summer silk gown.

By the time she was seated in her study the noise of the hounds, horses, and men had abated and all that was left was a dull, heavy heat whose cloying oppressiveness hung over everything. She hoped her husband would not ride too hard. In such torrid weather it was difficult to think, never mind chase prey on the back of a lathered horse.

Sorting through requests and receipts that had come in, she laid them out in separate piles. She delighted in being orderly and methodical, untangling the affairs of the realm just as she saw to the management of her court and household.

In the past year they had expanded their court, and she now paid stipends to several scholars and artists in residence. The poet Jean Lemaire had joined them earlier that year—a welcome addition from her homeland—whose poems and sparkling conversation entertained them on long evenings. Then there was Mercurino di Gattinara, a jurist from Piedmont, who had joined her administrative staff as counselor. She relied on him to help her in her dealings with the Savoyards, sorting out their grievances and untangling legal disputes.

Deep in study of a proposal to widen the roads in Bresse, she was startled to hear shouting in the courtyard and the noise of horses' hooves.

Margaret's heart jumped to her mouth. God forbid that Philibert had fallen from his horse. Had she not warned him to take care in the last words they had exchanged that morning?

Racing downstairs, she burst into the courtyard. Two men were helping her husband to dismount, his head hanging and his body slumped strangely.

"What has happened?" she cried.

"His Grace is taken ill, my lady."

"A fall?"

"Not a fall. He felt a pain in his side just after lunch, so we brought him back."

Margaret rushed to Philibert's side, taking his head in her hands. "My lord, can you speak?"

He looked at her and opened his mouth. A wheezing gasp came out, and he clutched his side.

"Take him to his chambers. I'll summon the doctors," Margaret ordered, motioning to her head steward.

She squeezed her husband's hand, surprised to feel no response in return. Two men grasped the duke beneath each arm and half-dragged, half-carried him to his quarters.

"He didn't fall from his horse?" she questioned the men outside his room as the doctors examined him.

"No, Your Grace. We spotted a boar and he took off after it. But he stayed his horse, although we lost sight of him."

"Where was he when you caught up to him?"

"We found him at the St. Valbas fountain. He said it was the first time that day he felt cool after drinking his fill."

An icy chill caught Margaret despite the heat of the day. The waters of Valbas fountain were fed by mountain streams. Their cold freshness could shock the body of one who was overheated and lathered in sweat from a hunt. She hoped Philibert hadn't drunk too fast or too much.

But she knew her husband. Peering at him, she moved to his side. With his buoyant lust for life, he would have drunk his fill and more.

"My lord, is the pain still with you?"

"Only when I breathe," he gasped out. Trying to smile at her, his head dropped and she caught it with her hands. Smoothing back his damp curls, she felt his forehead.

Fever.

"You will rest, and the doctors will have you better in no time," she assured him, keeping her tone even.

Philibert nodded. It was apparent that speaking sapped him.

"Has he broken a rib?" she asked the senior doctor.

"No, Your Grace. His ribs are intact."

"Then why does it pain him when he breathes?"

"It appears his lungs are inflamed. He will be fine if the fever subsides."

Margaret felt her chest tighten. "But what if it doesn't?"

The doctor looked grave. "I cannot say, Your Grace. We will make every effort to bring it down."

Margaret hurried to her bedchamber, where she found her jewel chest. Pulling out her pearl pieces, she ran with them to the kitchen.

"Grind these to powder to make a potion for the duke to drink," she instructed her head cook.

"Very good, my lady. 'Tis an age-old remedy."

"You must do all you can to bring down his fever," Margaret urged the cook and her helper.

"The duke is young and healthy, Your Grace. I'm sure he will recover," the cook said, a sturdy Savoyard, born and raised in the mountains.

Margaret left with a cool elderflower drink for her husband, her back to the cook and her assistant who had turned to each other with worried looks.

"What do you think?" the assistant asked.

"I think if his fever doesn't come down his soul will float to God."

"God forbid," the assistant gasped, crossing herself.

"It would be a shame, without an heir to leave behind."

"And to think those two are so in love."

"Uncommon, isn't it?" the cook remarked, reaching for the mortar and pestle on the shelf.

"I've never seen anything like it."

"Let's get him better so they can make that heir." Cook put the pearls in the mortar and handed her helper the pestle.

"Why haven't they already?"

Cook shrugged. "Save it for another day. We've got work to do." She pointed to the mortar and her assistant began to grind the duchess' pearls into a fine powder.

For the next nine days, the entire household of Pont d'Ain labored to save the Duke of Savoy's life. But his fever continued. Day by day Philibert grew weaker from the malady affecting his lungs that made him gasp for breath.

Margaret prayed, lit candles, and donated funds to every shrine in Savoy where miracles were said to have occurred.

More doctors were called, but there was nothing they could do. Philibert fell into delirium, unable to speak. Margaret slept on a pallet next to his bed.

On the morning of September 10, he finally awoke. Margaret was overjoyed, thinking the fever had broken.

"My lord, you are with us again!" she cried, covering his face with kisses.

Philibert's voice was a whisper. "Nay, *ma mie*. I am back to say goodbye."

"Do not say that, my love!"

"I have one request of you before I go." Too weak to sit up, Philibert tried to smile.

"You are not going anywhere, my lord. You are staying here with me and I will nurse you back to health," Margaret insisted. But looking down at Philibert's pale, sweat-covered face she knew she could insist on nothing. God would give and God would take away. She prayed that moment hadn't come.

"Will you do something for me?" Philibert whispered.

"What is it, my lord?"

"My promise to my mother. See that it is done."

"What promise, my lord?"

"To build a church and monastery in Brou, where she and I will rest."

"I will rest there with you, too, my love!"

"I pray that you do, but not too soon. If you build it, I will wait for you there," Philibert gasped out, wincing with each breath.

"I promise to see it done, but don't say you'll wait for me there. Be with me here and one day we will lie there together," Margaret pleaded.

"We will lie there together but I must go now. Call the priest, *ma mie*. My time is near."

Margaret's blood ran cold. She wanted to argue with him, but he was too weak. Her husband needed the comfort of his soul at rest if he was to journey home.

Motioning to the attendants to find the priest she returned to her patient, bathing his brow in lavender water as a mother might bathe her child.

Within moments the priest appeared and began the ancient rhythmic steps of the last rites. As he did, Margaret rubbed Philibert's hands and stroked his face to keep him awake so he could respond.

The short ceremony was soon over, the crumb of bread administered and the wine drunk. With the priest's final words of comfort, the Duke of Savoy closed his eyes, slipping into sleep.

"Get out! All of you. I must be alone with my lord," Margaret ordered.

She climbed into bed with Philibert. Gently she cradled him in her arms, racking her brain for something she could try that she hadn't already. Her mind wandered and she thought of the babe they had never had, imagining it was their child in her arms instead of her husband.

Looking down, she was comforted to see how peacefully he slept, the hint of a smile curving his lips. She kissed his mouth then drew back, horrified.

Savoy's amiable duke was already on his journey home to God.

Philibert the Handsome, Duke of Savoy
Walnut wood bust by Conrad Meit
to design by Jan van Roome, c. 1520
Bode Museum, Berlin, Germany
Photo by Daderot

Margaret of Austria
Terracotta portrait medallion by Conrad Meit, 1528
Kunthistorisches Museum, Vienna
From Susan Abernethy, *The Freelance History Writer*, and Natalie
Grueniger

**The Medallion of Philibert the Fair of Savoy
and Margaret of Austria**

By Jean Marende, early 16th century

From *The Numismatic Chronicle and Journal of the Numismatic
Society*, Vol. 3, London: Royal Numismatic Society, 1883.

"I am cursed!" Margaret howled, hurling herself toward the open
window of the room in which her husband had left the earth.

"No, my lady!" a man's voice called out behind her.

"I will join my lord!" she cried, trying to fling herself over the
window ledge.

Strong arms grasped her from behind and pulled her from the
ledge. Tumbling to the floor, she wrestled with her rescuer until two
more attendants came to pin her down then help her to a chair.

"Madame, you must not harm yourself." Jean Lemaire's face loomed over Margaret, concerned and full of pity.

"I have no more reason to live!" she sobbed. Her beloved prince was gone, in final rest on the same bed in which he had been born.

"You are needed here by us who love and admire you," the Low Countries scholar said, putting a cup to her lips.

Margaret turned deaf ears to her court poet, her eyes moving to the still form on the bed. The man who had loved and admired her most was gone, his sturdy frame still handsome and robust, finally relieved of the struggle to breathe that had enveloped him in his final days. His arm hung down limply, but she would not grasp his hand. Never had Philibert been cold to her touch. She could not bear that the life had gone out of him.

"Do not speak to me of love, when he who held my heart is gone!" Never did she wish to love any man again, only to have death snatch him from her.

Shouldering aside Lemaire, she ran to her room and locked the door behind her. When she reappeared, she had cut off her hair like a nun. Philibert had enjoyed wrapping those long, wavy locks around his neck in secret moments. They were reserved for him alone and, as he was gone, they must be gone, too.

In the wake of the duke's death, much needed to be done. It was a blessing for Margaret. She threw herself into arrangements, seeing to it that her beloved's remains were embalmed then commissioning an artist skilled in the new Italian techniques to make the effigy by which her handsome lord would be forever remembered.

"I will build a tomb for my husband, the likes of which Savoy has never seen," she told her council.

"To be put in the Cathedral of Notre Dame, Your Grace?" her head councilman asked.

"Not Notre Dame. He will rest in Brou, in the church of a monastery I will have built to carry out his mother's wishes."

"Madame, Brou is small and insignificant. I am sure you will wish the duke to be buried in Savoy's finest cathedral," another council member suggested.

"My husband promised his mother to build a monastery and church at Brou in thanks for his father's recovery from a fall from his horse," Margaret stoutly responded.

"Madame, the duke's mother died years ago. It is not your responsibility to carry out her wishes," the council member objected.

"Of course, it is. It was something my husband intended to do, but did not have time to fulfill." Her voice broke. How cruel Heaven was to claim back a man at the start of his prime years, snatching him from his plans and dreams. But Philibert hadn't been one for planning and dreaming. He had lived life to the fullest each day. For that she had loved him, a perfect complement to herself.

"Then it will fall to his brother the new Duke to see that it's done," the council member argued.

"I will not have it fall to anyone who might do it or not. I will see it done and rest next to him one day, along with his good mother."

"But Madame, how will the costs be paid?" another of Savoy's councilmen spoke up.

"To begin, I will use my dowager's pension from Savoy to build it."

"But—But, Your Grace, the realm may be hard put to even come up with that. And you must live on something in the meantime."

"I will manage, just as I have ably managed our realm," Margaret addressed her council, thinking of how tardy Spain usually was with forwarding her annual dowager's pension. But there were revenues from her lands passed down to her by her mother. She would need to wrest them from Philip's hands; as soon as she visited him in Brussels she would see to it.

"Madame, we will leave it for another day, but we are cognizant of your desire to honor your lord in death as you did in life," her head councilman offered.

"It shall be done. However long it takes, however much it costs," Margaret declared. She snapped shut the accounts book before her and rose. With her, all members rose, too, respectful of their duchess who had just lost their beloved duke. Philibert II, Duke of Savoy, had not been much for management, but his duchess was. If she said something would get done, it would. Their job was to ensure it didn't bankrupt Savoy in the process.

In the days and weeks that followed, Margaret reflected as she mourned. She was twenty-four, once jilted, twice widowed, and childless. With dowager revenues from both Spain and Savoy, she might be grief-stricken but she was also rich.

Philip wouldn't be eager to see her return to Brussels. He had had free rein over managing lands left to her by her mother. But since she had taken over administration of Savoy, she had gotten a taste of being in charge and found she enjoyed it. She was ready to manage her own affairs as a Burgundian-Habsburg princess, now Dowager Duchess of Savoy.

6

VISIT TO JUANA AND PHILIP IN FLANDERS

1505

BY THE SPRING OF 1505, Margaret had concluded negotiations with her brother-in-law over her intent to build a church and monastery at Brou.

Eighteen-year-old Charles, the younger half-brother of Philibert, was now Charles III, Duke of Savoy. His mother was Claude of Brosse, their father's second wife. It was not his affair to carry out the wishes of his brother's mother, to whom he bore no relation. Unwilling to undertake such a project, the new duke balked at the enormous cost it would entail.

But Margaret was determined to carry out her promise to Philibert. Fueled by love for her fallen prince, she was eager to draw up plans and begin. But first she needed to ensure that revenues due her from various regions of Savoy would be forthcoming.

Savoy's new duke was loath to cooperate, so Margaret called on her father, as Savoy's feudal overlord, to arrange a meeting in Strasbourg to hammer out an agreement.

In a rare personal appearance, Maximilian attended, along with a team of notaries. At Margaret's side was her Piedmontese counselor, Mercurino di Gattinara, trained in law and a skilled negotiator.

Within days, terms were decided upon. As Dowager Duchess of Savoy, Margaret would be guaranteed revenues from Bresse, Faucigny, Vaud, and Gourdans and was newly granted Villars, the former lands of the Bastard of Savoy. Overjoyed, she conferred with the governor of Bresse, where Brou was located, on plans and costs for the project.

The only cloud in this happy picture was word from her court poet. Jean Lemaire wrote to say that in her absence her beloved green parrot, which had belonged to her mother, had been killed by one of Pont d'Ain's hunting dogs. The poet enclosed a poem he had written to memorialize its death.

> Within this tomb, which is a harsh, locked cell, Lies
> the green lover, the very worthy slave Whose noble
> heart, drunk with true, pure love, Losing its lady,
> cannot bear to live.[1]

---

1. Jean Lemaire de Belges, *L'Amant Vert: Épitres de l'amant Vert* or *Letters of a Green Lover* written in 1505 from Oeuvres (Geneva: Slatkine Reprints, 1969), p. 52.

Touched by Lemaire's verses, she was also alarmed. Her court poet had been her anchor in the months following Philibert's death. Was Lemaire signaling his own feelings in his impassioned words?

Thoughtfully, she put down the letter. She had leaned on her countryman as a trusted member of her court. Anything more was out of the question. Her heart lingered with Philibert, as one day her body would rest next to his. The idea of being in any other man's arms revolted her.

She decided not to rush back home. Dangers might lurk there in the form of suitors eager to nudge her from her mourning. Instead of returning to Savoy, she would travel north to Brussels to visit her brother and his family.

Arriving on a bright June day, Margaret found neither Philip nor Juana on the steps of their palace to greet her.

"Is the duke or his wife here?" she asked, scanning the vast empty courtyard.

"My lady, the duke has gone out and Madame is resting in her rooms," a household attendant answered with a curtsey. As she lifted her head Margaret caught a furtive cast to her eyes.

"Take me to her, then." Margaret handed her traveling cape to a page.

"Would Madame like to be seen to her rooms while I tell her you have arrived?"

"I can tell her myself. Where are her quarters?"

The attendant looked fearful. "She is indisposed at the moment, Madame."

"I am sorry. Is she ill?"

The woman smiled for the first time. "No, Madame, but in her final months of confinement."

At least there was that between husband and wife. "Then take me to the children," Margaret said.

"The children are in Malines, Madame."

"Why in Malines?"

"The Duke says the air is better for them there than here in Brussels."

"I see," Margaret remarked, although she did not see at all. Ascending to her rooms she freshened her face then went to find her sister-in-law.

A lady-in-waiting stood in the doorway to Juana's chambers.

"You will tell your mistress that her sister-in-law is here," Margaret announced, annoyed to find her way blocked.

"Who is it?" Juana's voice called from within the room.

"It is me, sister. Just arrived from Germany."

"I am glad it is you and not him."

"Who, dear sister?" Although she could guess who. Moving into the room she spotted Juana by the open window. She was big with child, her dark-haired beauty enhanced by the bloom of pregnancy.

"That skirt-chaser who wishes to steal my throne from me," Juana sang out, a wild tone to her voice.

Margaret embraced her sister-in-law, sensing energy like coiled steel wafting off her, then kissed her on both cheeks.

"I see you are blooming," she greeted, choosing to ignore Juana's remark.

"I am always ready to bloom, yet your brother waters other gardens."

Margaret felt her cheeks pinken. How right she was. "Forget my brother. You are doing your duty and now you are Queen of

Castile," she encouraged, thinking sadly of Isabella of Castile's death of the November before.

"As if he cared."

"Why should you care if he cares or not?" Margaret asked, wishing Juana was made of sterner stuff.

"Because he needs to notice me," Juana said.

"It would seem he already does." Margaret's eyes flicked to her sister-in-law's belly.

"On occasion, sister. But not as I deserve to be treated."

You will be treated the way you inspire others to treat you, Margaret thought. "Then allow me to treat you like the queen you are while I am here," she offered, noting how unlike her mother Juana was. Instead of commanding respect, she demanded it. No wonder Philip failed to respond.

"My husband will not allow you to," Juana said, running her hands over her bursting belly in a most unqueenly way.

"Forget what Philip allows and what he does not. As queen of your own realm, it is you who decides," Margaret remonstrated.

"And as lord of my wife, I suggest you allow her to rest so that she may bring me another prince in short order," Philip's voice cut in. Looming in the doorway the Duke of Burgundy stood like a blond god, luminous and vital.

Juana's eyes fastened on him even as she berated him. "Where have you been?"

"It is none of your concern." Philip strode across the room, then leaned down to kiss Margaret on both cheeks. As he did she caught the scent of jasmine on his collar, telling her he had not been attending to affairs of state.

"You did not receive your sister when she arrived," Juana scolded.

Philip shrugged. "Did you?"

"I was resting as you ordered me to do."

"Then you are a good wife."

"As you are not a good husband."

Philip looked bored. "And why am I not a good husband today?" he asked, flicking a speck of dust off his doublet.

"You have not kissed me yet."

Margaret sensed a moment's hesitation before her brother responded.

"Then I am remiss." Philip leaned toward Juana and gave her a quick peck.

"You stink of scent!" Juana screamed.

Turning his back to his wife Philip rolled his eyes at Margaret.

"Who is she this time?" Juana railed, throwing herself at her husband's back and pounding him with her fists.

"D'you see what I put up with?" Philip said, shaking his wife off as he beckoned to her ladies to take her.

"I have seen more than I wish to." Disgust welled in Margaret's stomach.

"And you have only just arrived," Philip retorted, moving toward the door.

But Margaret got there before him. She couldn't wait to get back to her rooms and away from them both. How unspeakable that they were members of her own family.

As her visit unfolded Margaret could see that Juana was unprepared for her responsibilities ahead as queen of her mother's realm.

She had not been raised to ascend Castile's throne with an older brother and sister in line before her. But her two older siblings had both died unexpectedly. Now Philip was eager to seize the reins of ruling Castile as Juana's consort.

Margaret found herself caught up as a go-between for the baffled fathers of the unhappy couple, neither of whom understood the perverse dynamic between the two. Both Maximilian of Austria and Ferdinand of Aragon leaned on Margaret to try to fix it, so they could get back to their shared passion for weakening France.

One week after her arrival the ladies' maid assigned to her filled her in on the latest debacle. "Madame, I am sorry to be so slow today but I have been up all night."

"For what reason?" Margaret asked.

"The duke locked his wife in her room above his and she pounded on the floor all night long, demanding to be let out."

"Why didn't someone attend to her?"

The maid looked fearful. "It is difficult to calm her when she is in certain moods. She is stronger than she looks, and has attacked a few of the duke's favorites over the years. We were frightened to go in to help her..."

Margaret clucked her tongue. "Such nonsense. Why was the steward not roused to help you?"

"Madame, the steward could not get in until morning, as she had barricaded the door from the inside."

"Someone should have found a way to open it once she fell asleep."

"She did not sleep at all, Madame. She was pacing at first and shouting. Then she began to pound on the floor."

Margaret shuddered, grateful that she was quartered in the opposite end of the palace and had heard nothing. "In what state was she found this morning?" she asked.

"She had chopped up the table in her room with the cleaver she had been about to take to the duke's favorite. No one could get it away from her before he locked her in."

Margaret's stomach roiled. Such behavior would be unseemly for a peasant's wife. It was beyond shocking for a queen. If only Juana's mental fortitude could match her physical stamina, as her mother Isabella's had.

Juana of Castile
Master of the Magdalen Legend, c. 1497
Kunsthistorisches Museum, Vienna
From www.dailyartmagazine.com

Juana of Castile, the Young Charles V and his sister
Attributed to Nicolaus A. Mair von Landshut, c. 1504
From www.magnoliabox.com

Later that day, Ferdinand of Aragon's ambassador to the Burgundian court paid a visit. Gutierre Gomez de Fuensalida knew Margaret well from her two years in Spain.

"Madame, the situation is delicate and it is unclear to my king what his daughter's or her husband's intentions are with regard to Castile. As you speak her tongue, could you go to her and discern what her plans are?"

"I am not able to speak to her alone, and I do not have the heart to continue trying," Margaret replied, her stomach dropping at thought of trying to draw out Juana after what she had heard and seen over the past weeks.

Ferdinand's ambassador lowered his voice. "Is it possible that your brother is attempting to make the queen look unfit, so that he may rule Castile alone?"

"There is little good to be said of the situation between the two, so I will say nothing," Margaret hedged, fed up with both her brother and his wife. She ached for their innocent children, created from the maelstrom of their parents' outsized passions.

"Madame, I understand, but you are one of the few in a position to help, with your understanding of our language and customs," the ambassador urged.

"I cannot stay any longer in their household, as the indignities that take place there do no honor to either the Houses of Burgundy and Habsburg or the House of Trastámara," she replied, thinking she had never witnessed two human beings treat each other worse than her brother and sister-in-law did.

Fuensalida bowed and departed, but Margaret knew he would be back to work on her further for as long as she remained in Brussels.

Calling for her coach she decided to visit her nieces and nephew in Malines, a day's journey north of Brussels, where they lived in the palace Margaret of York had left to their father.

As she traveled, she reflected on the turmoil over who would rule Spain. She knew all the players too well to support any of them. Her former father-in-law would try to wrest the throne of Castile from his daughter. Her brother would, too, putting him on a collision course with Ferdinand.

As for Juana? The more Margaret saw of her, the less confident she was that the new Queen of Castile could administer the vast realm her mother had left her.

Spain had been one under Ferdinand and Isabella. But with Isabella dead the kingdoms of Castile and Aragon were pitted against each other, with Juana at the head of one and her father at the head of the other. No good could come of the present impasse, other than the passage of time. Once Ferdinand died, both kingdoms would pass to Juana and Philip's young prince in Malines, far from the furious scenes played out between his unhappy parents in Brussels.

ARRIVING IN THE COURTYARD of Margaret of York's palace in Malines, Margaret was greeted by her niece and nephew. As six-year-old Eleanor curtsied and five-year-old Charles made a stiff bow, she crouched and opened her arms to them.

"My doves, come to your Aunt Margaret," she bid them.

Shyly they shuffled forward as she smiled warmly at each one in turn.

"Would you like to see the baby?" Eleanor asked.

"Of course. But first let me look at you." Margaret held Eleanor by the shoulders and gazed into her face. Juana and Philip's firstborn was an auburn-haired brunette with a rosebud mouth. Margaret recognized its shape as the one she and her brother Philip both possessed.

"You are very pretty, Aunt Margaret," Eleanor said.

"But not as pretty as you, Eleanor," Margaret replied.

"I am clever, not pretty," Eleanor corrected.

Margaret chuckled. "Who told you that?"

"Charles did."

Margaret turned to her nephew and godson. "And why would you say that, Charles?" Relief surged through her to see little resemblance to his father, with a more protuberant lower jaw and a serious expression Margaret had never seen her brother wear.

"I told her it is b-b-better to be clever than p-p-pretty, and so she is."

"I think so, too, but it is nice to be both," Margaret remarked, thinking how grateful she was not to be as striking as her brother. She was convinced his flawless looks and easy charm had resulted in him not developing a stronger character.

"Will you come see Bella now?" Eleanor asked.

"Yes, take me to her."

Entering the palace of Margaret of York, Margaret felt a rush of affection for her godmother, who had died two years earlier. As second wife to Charles the Rash, she had been a loving stepmother to Margaret's own mother, Mary of Burgundy, and a substitute mother to Margaret, too, in the years she had lived in the Low Countries before and between marriages. Tender memories of the tall, stately woman with a beautiful, long face filled her thoughts as the children led her to the nursery.

Margaret gestured to her attendant to hand her one of the boxes she had brought.

A tiny three-year-old stared up at her, more delicately drawn than her older sister. She wore the same severe expression as her siblings, making Margaret wonder what sorrowful behavior between their parents they might have witnessed.

Margaret crouched, meeting the tiny child at eye level. "My dear, I am your Aunt Margaret," she said softly.

Silent, the child stared back with wary eyes.

"It is soon to be your birthday, is it not?" Margaret continued.

Isabella's eyes flickered, but she didn't smile.

"I have something for you that I hope you will like," Margaret said, holding out the box to her.

Isabella put her arms behind her back as Eleanor stepped forward and took the box.

"It's a gift for you, Bella," the older girl coaxed.

Charles moved forward and carefully took off the cover of the box. In that one small action, done with deliberation, Margaret could see he had not inherited his father's carefree, careless personality.

"Ooh," Isabella exclaimed, her eyes lighting up.

"'Tis a princess doll for a princess," Margaret said, enjoying the moment.

Isabella reached in and pulled out the doll, her face breaking into an angel's smile.

"Now, I am famished and so is your doll, so take me to where we may have cool drinks and cakes."

Eleanor and Charles laughed at the thought of their sister's doll being hungry, but Isabella hugged it closer as she beamed at Margaret. "Eat cakes," she said.

"Yes. Let's." Margaret held out her hand to the tiny girl and allowed her to lead her to the children's dining room, her joy burgeoning with every step.

The afternoon passed in charming conversation and slowly softening hearts, most of all Margaret's. Politics and powerplays dropped away, and all she thought of was getting to know each of the three exquisite children before her. What matter that she had none of her own? There were three here who needed love and attention, a fourth one in Spain and a fifth one on the way. She was happy to give them what their hearts desired, because her own heart desired the same. Their innocence touched her, their serious demeanors concerning her just a bit.

By the end of the day laughter and scampering feet resounded through the halls of Margaret of York's palace, and Margaret discovered maternal instincts she never knew she possessed.

Charles V and his sisters[2]
Eleanor (1498-1558), Charles (1500-1558), Isabella (1501-1526)
Master of St. George's Guild
Kunsthistorisches Museum, Vienna

UPON HER RETURN TO Brussels, the sweetness of her visit to Malines vanished with her first step out of the carriage. Don Juan
Manuel, Lord of Belmonte, a long-time envoy and Philip's closest
advisor from Castile, hurried toward her.

"Lady Margaret, I trust your journey was not too taxing." Don
Manuel's tone was unctuous.

---

2. Eleanor and Isabella's coat of arms are left half blank, to be filled
in with the coat of arms of their future husbands.

"Not taxing at all, Monsieur." Margaret wondered why he was there to greet her. She had noticed already that he was foremost among those intent upon swaying her to Philip's side against Juana.

"Very good, my lady. Then you will wish to know how things have been here," the Castilian envoy prompted.

Not particularly, and not from you. Margaret eyed him suspiciously. "I am sure my brother and his wife will fill me in when I see them," she replied.

Don Manuel sighed. "I am afraid you will hear different reports from each of them."

"And you are here to bolster my brother's version?"

The Castilian's face reddened. "I am here to assure you that your brother desires your full happiness as well as your full support in his role ahead in Spain."

"What role do you speak of, then?"

"Of helping the Queen of Castile to rule her realm." Don Manuel's expression was as meek as a lamb, as disingenuous as her brother's disarming glance when he was up to something.

"Monsieur, I have no interest to take sides in this tug of war, so desist from your efforts to influence me," she dispatched him as they arrived at the entrance to her quarters.

"Ah, but Madame Margaret, do you not see that good will come to Castile with your brother's careful guidance over his wife the queen?"

Margaret snorted and shut the door of her chambers in the slippery diplomat's face. Philip had not been careful of his wife's feelings from the day she arrived in the Low Countries in 1496. He had taken two full weeks to conclude his hunting trip before meeting her, leaving Margaret and her godmother to welcome Juana to a strange new land, instead. From such a dismal starting point, the marriage had briefly flamed then begun its agonizing downhill trajectory.

Furthermore, Margaret doubted Philip had the capacity to rule Castile. To begin, he did not speak the language. And from what he had confided to her and Philibert on his visit to them, he couldn't stand the country. She could imagine how displeased the Castilian Cortes would be with a Burgundian foreigner as their new king with no understanding of their language or customs, and a noticeable lack of respect for their queen. The Spaniards were sticklers for respect and protocol; they would be offended by casual Flemish bonhomie.

Then there was Ferdinand to consider. Between her blithe, pleasure-loving brother and the deeply cunning Ferdinand of Aragon, there could be no contest. Margaret worried to think of Philip at odds with his father-in-law. Even should Juana take her husband's side against her father, her erratic behavior would soon be noted and the Spaniards themselves might choose Ferdinand over Philip as their ruler.

Next to work on Margaret was her own servant, Louis, a long-time trusted member of her household.

"Madame, I am sure that the King of Castile has your best interests at heart as he does those of the queen," Louis remarked, one day soon after her return.

"My brother is the Duke of Burgundy, not the King of Castile. Who has spoken of him as such?" she corrected, thinking if her brother had Juana's best interests at heart she dreaded to think what he might consider to be in the best interests of Castile.

"Why, it is Don Manuel who refers to him as such, and certainly he will be crowned so when he returns to Spain, my lady," Louis replied.

"Until that time, refer to him by his correct title and remember that you are in my service to perform your duties, not to offer your opinions to me," she admonished.

Her servant bowed and backed from the room, not knowing Margaret had spoken her last words to him. By the end of the next day, she had learned from others that Juan Manuel had offered Louis an income for life on behalf of Philip, to come from Castile's revenues in return for gaining her support for Philip to rule Castile in Juana's place.

Margaret had had enough. With a heavy heart she dismissed Louis from her service, then called her remaining attendants to pack her things.

It was time to return to Savoy, far from the sullied air of her brother's court.

7

Henry Tudor's Proposal

1505

"I do not wish to marry again," Margaret told Philip as she tried to brush past him. She was eager to get to the courtyard where her carriages waited for departure.

"But why not? Think what advantage it would be to have you link our house to the House of Tudor, with all Henry's money and insecurity over his right to his throne."

"Those are his concerns, not mine," Margaret declared. "Besides, he is old."

Ignoring her remark, Philip offered a bright smile. "Think how you would infuse Burgundian and Habsburg blood into the country that is our biggest trading partner."

She saw through his smile, knowing him as well as she did. "Spoken like a true Fleming," she scoffed. "Commerce first, sentiment later. If at all."

"Sister, you had your great love with Philibert. Now think of your family and your country."

"Let me see, do you mean Flanders? Or Spain, or France, or Savoy? All have been my country at one time or another, and I am not about to make yet another my home. Especially not one with bad weather and worse food."

"Sister, do you not wish to be the queen you were meant to be?" Philip asked.

"Not particularly. I am happy in Savoy." She couldn't wait to get back to Pont d'Ain, where the air was fresh and pure, and she would no longer be subjected to daily pressure to support her brother's self-serving agenda.

"There is no reason for you to stay in Savoy. You are needed elsewhere by your family. And do you not wish to create one of your own?"

"I may not be able to create one of my own, which will not please the King of England should I be foolish enough to accept his offer," Margaret retorted.

"What reasons have you? You have had one child that God saw fit to take home, but why should you not have more?"

"I was not fruitful with Philibert, and I would not wish to run the risk of marrying a man who wishes for a brood mare and finds I am not one."

"I will write to Father. He will talk some sense into you."

"Maxi and I write all the time. I have already let him know I am not interested in this match."

Philip scowled. "Sister, what is it that makes you hesitate to marry again?"

"I cannot say," she answered, although she could but wouldn't. The example of marriage Philip had set with Juana had been enough to frighten her for all time from the thought of marrying again, but it would not do to point out what a despicable husband her brother had become.

Besides, a deeper reason lay behind her decision. Her heart remained with Philibert. She had no desire to direct it elsewhere. Already, she was bursting to get back to break ground on the church in Brou she had promised him to build.

As Philip opened his mouth to make yet another plea, Margaret put her hand over it. "I am done, brother. The coaches are waiting." Lifting her face to his, she gave him two undeserved kisses, one on each cheek, then turned and sped to the courtyard. She was bursting to return to the mountain realm where she was master of her own fate.

THE FOLLOWING MONTH MAXIMILIAN arrived in Brussels and drew up marriage contract papers with Philip for Margaret's marriage to Henry Tudor.

Receiving them in Savoy to sign, Margaret exploded upon reading through the clauses.

"Do I understand correctly that my supposed future husband is to manage my dowager pensions instead of me?" she raged.

Her counselor Gattinara frowned as he re-read the clause. "Apparently so," he grunted.

Margaret thought of her brother's cruelty in holding back his wife's allowance from Spain year after year, rendering her unable to pay her household or manage them with any authority. Never would she allow herself to be caught in a similar position. "Why in God's name would I put what is rightfully mine and which I bring to the marriage table into the hands of someone who may or may not dispense of my own funds according to my wishes?" she asked.

"I do not know, Madame. It does not seem a fair arrangement, especially considering your experience administering our realm."

"My father and brother are mad to think I wouldn't mind having my own revenues taken from me by a future lord," she exclaimed. If they thought she was so naïve as to allow others to manage her own revenues, they would soon find out otherwise.

"Perhaps they think you will be in good hands with King Henry."

"Nonsense! They wish for England's support and money against France, and what better way to tie him to Burgundy and Austria than to toss him their rich daughter and sister?"

"Madame, you are harsh." As her closest advisor, Gattinara was on frank enough terms to speak forthrightly to her.

"I love my father, as I love my brother, but I know them both as well as I know myself. My father forever needs money, and my brother does not know how to treat a wife."

Her counselor laughed. "'Tis a good thing you are daughter and sister to them, rather than wife to either."

"I am of a mind to be wife to none. And with my mother's inheritance and my dowager revenues, I am perfectly content with no lord trying to unload me of my fortune."

"Madame, they say that Henry Tudor is not a bad man. And he is bereft after losing his wife."

"They say that Henry Tudor is as cheap as they come, but knows how to save money," Margaret summed up. "I will not put my own revenues into his hands to save on my behalf, for who knows what he might do with them? And what if I am unable to give him heirs, and he should become displeased with me?"

"Madame, you are in a position to please yourself."

"So I am." With a flourish, Margaret took her quill and dipped it then drew a line through the offending clause. At the bottom, where her signature was meant to go, she signed: 'Never.'

Chortling, she pushed back her chair. "There. Send that back and we shall have a laugh at the thought of their faces when they read it."

Gattinara shot her an admiring glance. "Lady Margaret, Savoy has been in good hands under your administration. But one day you will leave here, and I will be bereft."

"There is only one way to fix that, Monsieur."

"What is that, Madame?"

"You must come with me."

Gattinara's eyes lit up. "That I will do gladly, my lady."

"Then be happy it will not be to England."

Gattinara threw back his head and laughed. "Just make sure the wine is good wherever you take me."

"You can count on it." Margaret joined him in laughter. Pointing to the carafe of fine Burgundy on the table, she smiled as her counselor poured out two goblets. With merry hearts they toasted to the future they would share as duchess and advisor. What pleasure to be in a position to please herself. And what nonsense her brother and father proposed, to think she would willingly give up what she already had.

8

NEWS THAT CHANGED EVERYTHING

1506

IN OCTOBER OF 1506, news came that changed everything. Philip the Handsome had been struck by a sudden illness while on progress in Spain. His wife had nursed him for ten days, never leaving his side, but he had succumbed in Burgos on September 25, 1506, at age twenty-eight.

The implications were enormous. With Juana, Philip had ruled Castile for less than two months. But now, Juana was sole ruler of the realm her mother Isabella had left her. Pregnant with Philip's sixth child, there was no doubt her father wished to wrest control of Castile from her until her oldest son Charles came of age and claimed his inheritance.

"Who will look after my brother's children?" Margaret cried, heart-struck to think of the four young children Juana and Philip had left behind in Malines. Eleanor was now eight, Charles six, Isabella five, and Mary just turned one. Three-year-old Ferdinand was being raised at his maternal grandfather and namesake's court in Aragon.

"Madame, the children are in good hands with their attendants, but your father will most certainly write you as to his wishes for their future," Jean Lemaire assured her.

"I am Charles' godmother. God knows it is my duty to look after him now that his father is dead and his mother still in Spain." Thinking of the serious young prince she had bid goodbye to in Malines, she winced. Who would guide him? Did he still stutter? And if so, who would help him to master his challenges so that he could assume the enormous role fate had assigned him?

"Will she return to Brussels soon?" Lemaire asked.

"Not in her pregnant state," Margaret guessed. "And not with her duties as Queen of Castile."

"Do you think her father will try to wrest Castile from her?"

"Do you think a dog's nose is wet?" Margaret replied. "He has had his eye on that plum since Isabella died, so now's his moment. Go and find out all you can about what happened to my brother, and what arrangements have been made to bury him."

"Whatever role you are called upon to do, you will fulfill it admirably, Madame," Lemaire assured her. He bowed and backed from the room.

Margaret sighed. Her life was again about to change. She would step up to whatever was asked of her. But no matter what, she would see to it that the church and monastery she was building to honor her beloved would be completed.

Now there was the ducal seat of Burgundy to fill, and a prince and three princesses in Malines to be raised. She hoped her new duties would once and for all lay to rest the question of her marrying the English king.

Over the next few weeks news flew in from all over. Jean Lemaire was well connected; he had gotten the details of Philip's death from his own sources.

"Madame, it is being floated that your brother was poisoned."

"Poisoned? By whom?"

Lemaire arched a brow at her. "One who would rule Castile in his place."

"Ferdinand?"

"That is the report. It is also said that the Queen of Castile thinks the same. But no one, other than she, has the authority to prosecute the King of Aragon."

What daughter would prosecute her own father? Margaret thought. "So, Juana believes Philip was poisoned?" she asked.

"They say she did not leave his bedside from the moment he fell ill at a banquet after a day of pelota."

"So like my last days with my lord," Margaret said, then mentally corrected herself. There could be nothing remotely similar between her final days with Philibert and Juana's ones with Philip. One bond had been true love, the other obsession and revulsion.

"Except that your lord had no enemies, whereas your brother had a dangerous one in Spain," Lemaire pointed out.

"Dear God, where is my brother buried?" Margaret asked.

"Madame, my sources say he is not buried at all, but is being transported through Spain by his wife."

Margaret gasped. "Transported to where?" Philip would wish only to be transported back to Flanders to be laid to rest. She and Philibert had heard plenty from him about his distaste for Spain when he had visited in 1503. He had scoffed at the rigidity of Spanish customs, hated the food, found the wine unpalatable, and been bored by the unwillingness of the Spanish ladies to offer their favors.

"They say the queen is out of her mind with grief, and not yet ready to bury him."

Margaret's eyes widened. "Then what is she doing with him?"

"Madame, it is a strange tale, and I hope my sources are wrong." Lemaire pulled a note from his doublet and laid it on the table.

"Good God, what do you tell me?"

"My lady, they say the Queen of Castile transports his casket by day with her entourage, then at night..."

Dread iced Margaret's veins. "Then what?" she asked.

"Madame, I do not wish to upset you nor desecrate the memory of your brother."

"Tell me now or I will hear it from others," she commanded.

Lemaire looked at the floor then up again, his eyes flitting from hers. "It is said that the queen orders his casket opened in the evenings and kisses his feet."

"That is beyond belief!" Margaret cried, revulsion flooding her. But she knew it was not. Her sister-in-law had her husband all to herself for the first time in their marriage. She could imagine Juana's joy at finally being the only woman to handle Philip's body, even if it was only his corpse.

"Perhaps they are rumors put out by her father, who seeks to discredit her so that he may seize her throne," Lemaire suggested.

"Does she not have a country to run?"

"I am afraid, Madame, that rumors say she is unfit to rule, and that her father has already seized power."

"But my brother's body should be brought back to Flanders!"

"The queen may wish him to be buried near to her."

"Then why doesn't she get on with it?" Knowing Juana, she would wish to keep an eye on her husband by burying him within sight of wherever she made her home. Finally, she would be assured of his faithfulness to her.

"Madame, you know the answer to that better than I."

Margaret nodded. Indeed, she did. No grieving widow would treat her husband's remains so, unless she was insane. Whether the loss of the husband she was obsessed with had driven her to that point or she was already there was unclear. But Margaret remembered Juan's words that their maternal grandmother had gone mad after the death of her husband.

As Lemaire left the room, Margaret pondered the horrors of what he had told her. She hoped it was untrue, but from what she knew of her sister-in-law it was entirely possible.

A thought scurried like a rat across her mind. Lemaire had said that Juana had not left Philip's side since the moment he had fallen ill. Had it been Juana herself who had poisoned Philip? Such an act would have accomplished two aims at once. His death had ended his quest to wrest her authority to rule Castile from her. At the same time, it guaranteed that he would never again be unfaithful.

Margaret froze. Such reasoning would be the work of an unhinged mind. It was exactly what Juana possessed.

Deciding to keep her misgivings to herself, she shuddered to think of Philip and Juana's children. Any rumors of their mother poisoning their father could only weaken the children's marriage prospects. As dynastic heirs, they must marry rulers to seed all of Europe with Burgundian and Habsburg blood. It was best for all to lay the possibility of poisoning—especially by whom—to rest.

With a shake of her gown, Margaret dispatched any lingering thoughts on accepting Henry Tudor's suit to become his queen. She was free of sentimental attachments, had wealth at her disposal, and no children of her own. Four fatherless children awaited love and guidance back at Margaret of York's palace in Malines. She would return to her homeland and mother them herself.

Queen Juana the Mad
By Francisco Pradilla, 1877
Museo del Prado, Madrid

ON OCTOBER 29, 1506, Margaret left Savoy for the Low Countries. She would visit her father in Germany before returning to the land of her birth. Unsure of what lay ahead, but wishing to be prepared, she brought her most trusted advisors and household members with her.

Her court poet and historian, Jean Lemaire, accompanied her. Born in Hainault in the Low Countries, he had come to Savoy by Margaret's appointment and so he remained with her court. Mercurino di Gattinara and Jean de Marnix came, too, eager to seek their fortunes in the prosperous Low Countries rather than remain in provincial Savoy. Laurent de Gorrevod also joined them, brother of Father Louis de Gorrevod who had married Margaret and Philibert. Surrounded by men who served her loyally and would be indebted to her for the rise in fortunes they were likely to see, Margaret felt well-armed for whatever she would face upon her return to Burgundy.

The meeting with her father afforded Margaret and Maximilian time to grieve Philip together, as well as make decisions about who would take his place in ruling the Burgundian-Habsburg Netherlands. Maximilian had no desire to return to the Low Countries to govern them himself. He had been increasingly unwelcome there after Mary of Burgundy had died.

Both Maximilian and Margaret were aware that the people of the Low Countries did not wish for a foreign overlord, and would only accept a ruler with native Burgundian blood in their veins. In the wake of Philip of Burgundy's death, that left Philip's children and

Margaret as the only royals who combined both Burgundian and Habsburg bloodlines.

Margaret knew she was of prime political importance in whatever transfer of power was to come. When Maximilian suggested she manage the Low Countries on his behalf, she was elated.

She would do it, but not for nothing. With Gattinara negotiating on her behalf, she told her father she would require him to make a legal and public appointment to ensure she assumed her duties with the full weight of Habsburg authority on her shoulders.

Maximilian agreed.

Years of administering Savoy had prepared her for the task ahead. Armed with confidence in her own abilities, a trusted staff, and imperial backing, Margaret bade her father goodbye in March of 1507, and continued north, then west to the Low Countries. Ahead of her lay the greatest role of her lifetime.

9

Margaret– Governor of the Netherlands

1507

"She ruled as a true heiress of Burgundy, and she governed the Low Countries with a liberty and an authority that no regent after her would ever possess."
— Shirley Harrold Bonner[1]

The moment she reached the Low Countries, Margaret made a strong show of her new authority. There was only one chance to make a first impression; she would seize it. Traveling to Malines she installed herself at Margaret of York's palace where her nephew and

---

1. Shirley Harrold Bonner, *Fortune, Misfortune, Fortifies One* (Shirley Harrold Bonner: 1981), p. 74.

three nieces lived, and set to work crafting the announcement of her appointment.

Before the Estates-General in Louvain on March 18, 1507, Margaret was formally sworn in as Maximilian's representative as Governor of the Netherlands and guardian of her nephew, Charles of Habsburg, Lord of the Netherlands, during his minority.

She was awarded a sizeable palace in Malines in July 1507, as her official residence. Maximilian had bought the property from a wealthy merchant. The Estates-General agreed to pay to furnish the residence for their new governor.

Located across the street from her nieces' and nephew's home, Margaret named her new quarters the Court of Savoy. Quickly, she set about learning who the key players were in her realm.

To begin, she met with those assigned by Maximilian to oversee her nephew's education. William de Croy, Lord of Chièvres, the Netherlands' former governor, whose role Margaret had taken, was named Charles of Habsburg's chief tutor, residing with him in his household. De Croy was from an old French family, a distinguished and dignified nobleman twenty-two years her senior. Immediately, Margaret could see he held great influence over her nephew. To counter his pro-French influence she made a note to provide Charles with a firm sense of Habsburg imperial authority as a counterbalance.

Adrian of Utrecht, a priest and noted professor of theology was appointed as Charles' second tutor. He would work with him on his stutter. Margaret did too, helping the seven-year-old archduke progress in making short intelligible statements.

Anna de Beaumont, Charles' mother's former lady-in-waiting, would continue as governess and head of household to the Burgundian-Habsburg prince and princesses. Margaret tasked her with filling out the household, to which Lady Anna added additional tutors for the princesses, as well as a music master, art instructor, and court jester.

Margaret threw herself into her new role. Within months she was cognizant of why her father had handed over such a challenging portfolio to manage. Seventeen different political entities comprised the Burgundian-Habsburg Netherlands, each with differing allegiances. Some were sworn to the imperial authority of the Holy Roman Empire, others to France, and one in particular—Gelderland—in a state of insurrection, although with close ties to France. Preparing for an uncertain welcome, she met with leaders from each province.

It did not take long to discern one unifying feature amongst those she spoke with: all but the rebellious lord of Gelderland were devoted to trade and commerce. To that end a happy relationship with England was essential, with English sheep providing wool to fuel the Flemish cloth trade.

But her brother had botched trade relations with his last visit to England in the spring of 1506. In return for receiving Henry VII's recognition of him and Juana as King and Queen of Castile, Philip had signed a new trade agreement with the English king that did away with all duties on English textile exports. No equal favor was extended to the Netherlands. The former *Intercursus Magnus* of 1496 had been replaced by what the Netherlanders referred to as the *Malus Intercursus* of 1506.

Members of the Estates-General of every one of the provinces Margaret visited in her first months in office complained that the new treaty's consequences had disadvantaged them. Informants that Margaret had engaged reported that the members also grumbled amongst themselves that they were now to be led by a woman.

Margaret saw her chance to show them what kind of woman she was. She would gain their goodwill by renegotiating the much-hated new trade agreement.

Henry VII continued to make marriage overtures to her. She would have liked to shut him down once and for all, but her political agenda required a more nuanced approach. Encouraging him to think she might be swayed, she floated the proviso that she could not consider his marriage offer while the 1506 *Malus Intercursus* caused her constituents economic harm. Repudiating the one-sided treaty, she sent her regrets to the English king that her assembly wouldn't ratify it, but she would be greatly pleased to see the original treaty of 1496 reinstated.

Henry VII took the bait, thinking he was making progress toward achieving his goal of a dual Anglo-Habsburg alliance: his daughter Mary to wed the Habsburg prince, and he to wed Margaret.

With the arrival of the English king's ambassador to Margaret's palace in Malines came the original treaty of 1496 reinstated, along with a gift of six horses and two greyhounds.

Margaret exulted. Her successful negotiation of the reversion to the original trade treaty was the deft masterstroke she needed at the outset of her reign.

Henry Tudor's personal gift charmed her. But it was not enough to soften her heart toward him. She kept one of the greyhounds and had the other animals delivered to her nieces and nephew across the street.

Murmurs of approval drifted through the halls of the Estates-General as Margaret presented the new favorable treaty to her legislature. Without hesitation, the *Magnus Intercursus* was ratified.[2] Word of the new governor's coup spread through the marketplaces to every corner of the Low Countries. Soon, all knew that Lady Margaret had restored to them what her brother had carelessly tossed away to the English.

But much work remained to be done. That summer, Margaret spent long hours in discussion with her closest counselors. After a particularly frustrating visit to Ghent, traditionally the most rebellious of the Flemish cities, she vented her worries to her inner circle.

"What tack should I take with these burghers? They all clamor for different privileges and seek to sniff out my womanly weaknesses," she complained.

"Use your advantages as a woman, Madame, and play up your position as Princess of the Blood of the dukes of Burgundy," Jean Lemaire advised. As a native of the Low Countries, he knew much about the history of the Burgundian dukes.

"Pah! The older ones remember too well the taxes and wars rained on them by my mother's father," Margaret disagreed, thinking of the storm clouds that appeared on the older burghers' faces when Charles the Rash was mentioned. It was best not to remind them of the last of the Burgundian dukes, who beat them into

---

2. Marian Andrews (Christopher Hare), *The High and Puissant Princess Marguerite of Austria*, (London: Harper and Brothers, 1907), p. 126.

submission and ignored their privileges until the Swiss cut short his life.

"Weaknesses can be attributes of either sex," Lemaire pointed out. "Your mother's father exhibited many, from lack of self-control to an unyielding nature that turned deaf ears to his subjects. But you, Madame, are adept at self-possession. And you know how to listen closely and appear to agree with your audience, whatever your true thoughts might be."

Margaret's eyes narrowed at the thought of the countless times she had used such skills to gain the advantage while learning her opponent's hand. "I have practiced for years in three different courts, and now here," she said. God knew being raised at the court of Anne de Beaujeu had trained her well in the arts of dissembling and self-control.

Lemaire turned admiring eyes to her. "Such qualities are ones Philip the Bold possessed."

Margaret sipped her tisane, pleased to be compared with her ancestor, Burgundy's acclaimed first duke.

"But the people won't accept my rule if I am bold. It is not seemly for a woman," she objected. Boldness wouldn't suit. She liked to get her way, but she enjoyed getting it by making others think they were getting theirs.

"No, Madame," Lemaire agreed. "Use the real strengths that you share with your ancestor."

"Which are?"

"Philip the Bold used personal charm to warm his subjects to him, just as you do," the court poet noted.

Margaret sniffed. "That is something, but not the greater part of what is needed to rule."

"As well, he was a master of diplomacy," Lemaire continued.

Margaret contemplated such skills. Charm and diplomacy were eminently attainable by a woman. She had been practicing both all her life. "Ah, Monsieur, now you are on to something," she agreed.

"As you are yourself, my lady, with your success in bringing back the favorable trade agreement your brother threw away," Mercurino di Gattinara put in.

"It was a way to bind my subjects to me." Thank God Henry Tudor had granted her appeal to reinstate the *Intercursus Magnus*. All because she had framed her request to leave the door open to further personal overtures.

"A clever tactical move at the outset of your rule," Gattinara observed.

"So, you suggest I rely on charm and diplomacy?" Margaret asked. Using such skills made her feel both powerful and womanly. Flexing a leg under her gown, she savored the satisfaction of having the natural attributes to do her job.

Lemaire's smile was subtle. "Precisely, Madame. Charm them personally and make each think he is being heard above and beyond the others."

"Then weave your subjects closer with artful diplomacy that preserves peace in your realm so that commerce thrives," Gattinara added.

Margaret looked from one to the other. "I have noted already that it is their greatest concern, no matter where I go," she said.

"Commerce is the religion of the Low Countries, Madame." Jean Lemaire's tone was dry. Born in Hainault, he was one to know.

"At all costs avoid fruitless wars and endless taxation," Gattinara advised.

Lemaire nodded. "That is the way Philip the Bold won love and respect, just as you will do."

"I will try my best, Messieurs. Your counsel has succored me." Fueled by her advisors' confidence in her, she was ready to take on the challenges ahead. She had already won both Lemaire and Gattinara's loyalty. Jean de Marnix and Laurent de Gorrevod, too. If they had not believed in her they would not have followed her from Savoy to seek their fortunes in a new land.

"You have everything you need already, Madame. Just use the skills God has given you and harness them to your authority as native princess of Burgundy."

Margaret thought of Anne of Brittany's long-ago words: *You have everything you need inside you already.* "I will play down the Habsburg stamp and play up my Burgundian birth," she announced.

Lemaire offered an encouraging smile. "'Tis a glorious birthright as Princess of the Grand Dukes of the West."

"That age is over, Monsieur, with the death of my grandfather," she reminded him.

"All ages are over at a point," Lemaire noted. "But the age you are ushering in is perhaps an even greater one, with the House of Burgundy joined to the House of Habsburg."

Margaret's pride flamed. "Do not forget Spain when my nephew comes of age."

"Nor the New World that comes with Spain," Gattinara added.

"It is fathomless to think of just one man ruling such an empire," Margaret mused. "I wonder at the weight that will be on his shoulders."

"One man will not be able to rule it all," Gattinara said. "Your nephew will appoint counselors to help him oversee each of his realms."

Margaret's lips curled into a smile. "Trusted counselors like you, Monsieur?"

"Trusted counselors like you," Gattinara answered. "Who could be more trustworthy than a member of one's own family, who has proven herself a capable ruler?"

Margaret pondered the years ahead. If she did her job well her rule might extend beyond just the years of her nephew's minority. It was a heady thought.

Lifting her goblet to her lips, she thought of the satisfaction she would have in applying her natural talents to the pursuit of statecraft. No widowed king of a far-off land must interfere.

Yet Maximilian continued to pressure her to accept Henry Tudor's marriage offer. In September 1507, he wrote to say he could not come to Flanders to aid her in deepening the imperial alliance with England, but she should do whatever she could to see that Henry did not turn to France or Spain instead. He concluded that should she accept Henry VII's proposal she could continue as Governor of the Netherlands by passing three to four months yearly in her own realm.

"Does he think I am Persephone, to pass from the underworld back to her own lands every six months?" Margaret grumbled.

Gattinara raised a brow. "It is an interesting idea, but will it be embraced by the English king?"

Margaret snorted. "Never mind the English king. What about my own people? Do you think my council will listen to anything I say if I only drop in on them for a few months each year?"

"To govern well, one must live where one rules," her counselor agreed. "How else could one know what the troubles are in one's own realm?"

"Which is precisely why the emperor has given me the Low Countries to govern on his behalf. The burghers think of him as an outsider, and will only accept one of their own to rule over them. What is he thinking with this absurd idea?"

"Madame, your father sees a prime opportunity to clinch England with your marriage to its king."

Margaret sniffed. "He can bag his quarry with my nephew's marriage to Henry's daughter."

"In the event it should not come to pass, he looks to you to ensure a second connection," Gattinara remarked.

"The role I play now is far more important for the Houses of Habsburg and Burgundy. Should I leave, you can be sure the Low Countries will fall back into spheres of influence, each one ruled by a separate overlord."

"So it would seem, my lady."

Margaret flipped back the ends of her white widow's coif. It had proven effective at setting her subjects at ease—far more so than the imperial crown Maximilian had worn during his unpopular rule in over the Low Countries after her mother's death. "I know so, Monsieur. And I enjoy my role, so why should I change it to suit someone else's pleasure?"

YET MARGARET'S PATH TO effective rule was frequently hampered by Maximilian's changeable decisions. She was her father's spokesperson, but even she couldn't fathom his thought processes, and didn't always agree with them. Yet she knew him better than anyone else, so when Europe's princes found themselves confounded by his elusiveness they came to her for clarification or support.

More often than not the inscrutable man who held the title of Holy Roman Emperor wished to be left alone, happy at his court in Innsbruck. Margaret found herself making decisions for the Netherlands on her father's behalf that he acquiesced to afterwards, relieved to have her take affairs out of his hands.

As 1507 progressed, she grew aware of the pivotal role she played in increasing the House of Habsburg's influence across Europe. With Philip dead and Maximilian viewed as an outsider, Margaret was the sole native Burgundian royal who could stamp the Habsburg imprimatur on the Low Countries. And with every visit to the provinces she governed, she saw that the only way her subjects would accept Habsburg authority was by maintaining peace to promote commerce.

Chivalric values had gone out with the last century. Business was in, and the Low Countries were at the hub of where trade took place between England and the Continent. Flanders was the foremost exporter of textiles and tapestries in Europe. To its north, Holland and Zeeland were outpacing the German Hanseatic League in shipping and fishing. Spices from the Levant were sold in lively markets in Antwerp, which had also become a major banking center.

Margaret embraced the spirit of the Low Countries. And they embraced her back. Undesirous of being ruled by a dreamy feudal-era overlord who would tax them in order to fight wars in Italy or against the Turks, the Low Countries burghers and bankers found their flexible and practical Madame Margaret far more to their tastes.

Reveling in their regard, Margaret was quick to take well-placed opportunities to remind her subjects that she was their native princess through her mother, Mary the Rich. It was an epithet that made the ambitious hearts of the Low Countries' merchants sing.

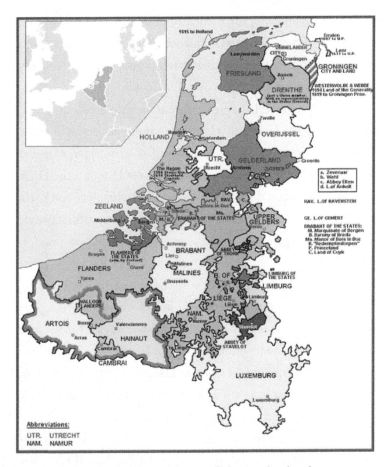

The United Provinces of the Netherlands
1609 (Author's note: borders similar to 1507 borders)
From ahnuniverse.weebly.com

The Court of Savoy, Palace of Margaret of Austria
Malines (Mechelen), Belgium
From www.emperorcharlesv.com

Charles of Habsburg, the future Charles V
After Barend van Orley, c. 1519
Municipal Museum of Bourg-en-Bresse, France
From the Netherlands Institute for Art History

Puppet Show at Margaret of Austria's Court
By Willem Geets, 1892
Museum Hof van Busleyden Malines, Belgium
Photos courtesy of Sue Ross (Margaret with Charles below)

10

THE LEAGUE
OF CAMBRAI

1508

"Margaret "the true great man of the Habsburg family and the founder of the house of Austria" obtained
her greatest diplomatic triumph by the 1508 League
of Cambrai."—Jean Lemaire[1]

By 1508, Margaret had settled into doing what she did best: running things.

Henry VII of England continued his suit. Early in the year
he sent a new ambassador to Margaret's court, an up-and-coming

---

1. Jean Stecher, *Jean Lemaire de Belges* (Louvain: Lefever Frères et
Soeur, 1891), p. 37 (with reference to Michelet within quotes).

commoner. Seven years older than she, Margaret soon recognized Thomas Wolsey's perspicacity as rivaling her own.

Wolsey probed as Margaret sidestepped him. She was aware that the real plum for Henry was for his daughter to marry her nephew. No matter what favors Henry VII offered, she had no intention of falling into his hands. She had enough on her own with managing the unruly lords and burghers of the Low Countries.

"My lady Margaret, my sovereign begs the favor of an answer before I return to English shores," Wolsey requested, looking eager to begin his journey back across the Channel.

Margaret guessed his sovereign hadn't given him sufficient funds for more than a few days' visit. All of Europe knew the English king was cheap. "Ah, Monsieur, if it were only for me to say, but it is my father who is to be succored."

"Lady Margaret, my sovereign tells me it is you yourself who can give the greatest nudge to your father to proceed with our proposed alliance," Wolsey persisted.

"My father is besieged by concerns on many sides," Margaret hedged.

"Could we put a finer point on it, Madame, so that I have something to report back to my king?"

"As you know, my father must pay his troops, so his most pressing concern is over how to accomplish this."

"In other words, how much the King of England intends to provide with his daughter's dowry," Wolsey spelled out.

Margaret pursed her lips. "That is a point that needs hammering out before further steps can be taken."

"I am here, Madame, to do just that, but your father's wishes are not easy to pin down."

Margaret's laughter floated across the room, as evanescent as Maximilian's wishes. Only two constants could be relied on: the Holy Roman Emperor would always be short of money, and he would always hate the French.

"Above all, my father and I both desire an Anglo-Imperial alliance to curb the French," she noted.

"As does my sovereign," Wolsey agreed.

"But my father worries that before the children are grown, your king may look elsewhere to place his daughter." *Or my father may look elsewhere to place his grandson.*

"Which is why a ceremony of *per verba de futuro* would deter this from happening," Wolsey swept in.

"There is the matter of your king's promise of 100,000 crowns to my father before such a ceremony can take place," Margaret checked him.

"My king has asked that a bond be put up for its guaranty by each of the Flemish towns, which has not yet been offered."

"And will not, as I cannot get my council to agree to such an arrangement," Margaret finished. "Do you think my burghers are made of money?"

"I think your burghers have a strong interest in holding on to their money," Wolsey replied. "But as this comes from my sovereign's coffers, we need a guaranty that it will be returned should the marriage fail to take place."

"I can give you a guaranty if each town is held to only a portion of the full amount, each according to their resources," Margaret answered. "Otherwise, it is out of the question."

"Ah, Madame, how sad it would be for your father and for my king should this result in the intended marriage being out of the question, too."

"Even worse for me, Monsieur. Your king has the sea between his realm and France; my father has the Alps. But I have nothing to stop the French from overstepping their bounds into my lands. So you may tell your sovereign that I count on him to consider my proposal in light of the friendship between my father and him."

Wolsey's eyes beseeched hers. "Madame, my sovereign seeks friendship with you, as well as friendship with your father."

Margaret gave Wolsey a radiant smile, the same one her brother Philip had used in his most disingenuous moments. "Ah, he shall have it then, as he already does. You may tell him as a special favor to me, that if the guaranty can be formulated according to my proposal, I will prevail upon my father to arrange the *per verba de futuro*."

"What manner of friendship do you offer, then?" Wolsey's large body relaxed into his armchair. He seemed sweetened by her smile.

"Friendship between rulers with mutual interests," Margaret proffered with diplomatic vagueness. What a gay dance it was to never quite allow anyone to pin her down.

"And are your interests mutual?" Wolsey asked.

"As regards the flourishing of our cloth industry, yes," Margaret effused.

"And as regards the flourishing of my king's interest in making you his wife?"

Margaret lifted her eyes to the window, thinking of how best to deflect without losing her quarry. "Ah, Monsieur, my heart's interests lie with those of my realm. If your king wishes to succor me, he can do so by offering that which leads to peace and prosperity for my people," she riposted.

"Anything more?"

Margaret offered yet another ravishing smile, enjoying her moment. "You have my answer," she said.

Wolsey grunted, looking as if he knew he had met his match in artful evasiveness. Rising, he bowed and departed.

Watching the envoy's burly form cross the courtyard, she chuckled. She must keep the English king on her and her father's side at all costs, save one. She would do anything except marry Henry Tudor. Once, twice, three times a pawn had been enough. Happily, the arms she had fallen into with Juan and Philibert had been loving ones.

But there was no guarantee any other man's would be, and she had heard enough about the English king to know he wasn't for her. With Henry Tudor as insecure as she was confident, the Lancastrian king might turn envious of her doubly royal lineage. Or threatened by her having been influenced by her godmother, Margaret of York, who had sheltered rival claimants to his throne.

Besides, Henry VII was old, soured, and to all reports ran a tight-fisted court. Never would she give up rule of the thriving Netherlands and the cultured coterie of scholars and artists she was building at her court for such a gloomy prospect.

In Brussels that October 7, 1508, a *per verba de futuro* ceremony by proxy wedded Charles of Habsburg to Mary Tudor, with Henry VII's 100,000 crowns flowing into Maximilian's war chest.

Margaret attended, having arranged the whole affair; Maximilian did not. Sending the signed intent of future marriage to Henry VII, Margaret had Charles include a short billet-doux to his intended bride along with a jewel engraved with his monogram, 'K' for Karolus.

It was done, although Margaret knew its legal weight was as light as the paper it was written on. Mary Tudor was twelve, but Charles of Habsburg was only eight. Much could change in the six years before Europe's most promising prince would be ready for marriage. Just as Margaret's alliance with the French king for the duration of her childhood had come to nothing, this too might crumble. Still, it served to keep ties strong in the interim.

THAT FALL, MARGARET CALLED for a summit meeting with the King of France. It was time to stop French meddling in Gelderland, and she had thought of a way to do it. She would divert the French to a more interesting target.

Equally, she needed to divert her father's demands for increased taxation in the Low Countries to fund his military campaigns. Not only had he asked for money for an army to fight Charles of Egmond, Duke of Guelders, but he also needed money for his campaigns in northern Italy against the Venetians, who had humiliated him earlier that year. He had made a pro forma request for his army to pass through Venetian territories to travel to Rome to be crowned Holy Roman Emperor by the pope.

To his shock, Venice had refused. Enraged, Maximilian had attacked Venetian-held towns in Austrian lands. The Venetians had pushed back, taking even more Habsburg territories. Maximilian had retreated, licking his wounds, unable to pay his army to continue fighting with them.

The Estates refused to raise funds for Maximilian's use, and Margaret agreed with them. But her father's dilemma had given her an idea. His anger burned hotly against the Venetians, cooling his usual animosity toward the French by comparison. If she could get Maximilian and Louis XII into treaty alliance with a mutual objective far from the Low Countries, the heat would be off her own realm. Her Netherlanders could return to what they liked doing best—making money, not war.

The proposed summit was to take place at the end of November in Cambrai, an independent prince-bishopric on Flanders and Hainault's borders with France.

When both Ferdinand of Spain and Maximilian asked Margaret to represent them in negotiations, she jumped at the opportunity. Ferdinand was too far away and Maximilian's excuse was that he had business of the Empire and the Netherlands to attend to in Malines.

Margaret chuckled, knowing his only business in Malines was to visit his grandchildren. At age twenty-eight, she now had a chance to prove herself on the European chessboard—no longer as a marriage pawn, but as a political negotiator.

Armed with the support of two of Europe's most senior princes, Margaret prepared for her international debut. Following her father's advice she rented half the lodgings in Cambrai for her entourage while Louis XII's minister of state, the Cardinal d'Amboise, rented the other half.

Mindful that she was representing Burgundy as well as the House of Habsburg, she spared no expense to exhibit the splendor that the Burgundian court was known for. She intended to dazzle all present, foremost, Georges d'Amboise, as sophisticated an aesthete as he was a statesman.

To soften d'Amboise further, she brought her nephew's tutor William de Croy, Lord of Chièvres, as a sign of rapprochement to the French. Chièvres and she were not best of friends, but his presence would conciliate the French party, many of whom knew him personally.

Margaret turned on her full charm with d'Amboise, twenty years her senior and a connoisseur of the art of fine living. As a Burgundian princess, having inherited the priceless art and book collections of her stepgrandmother Margaret of York, Margaret knew a thing or two about fine living herself.

She and d'Amboise talked the length of dinner and far into evenings of Italian painters and sculptors, and Flemish and Netherlandish masters. Margaret drew him out on the subject of the spectacular chateau he was building outside Rouen, France's great market town in Normandy.

While d'Amboise rhapsodized over construction plans for his chateau, Margaret plied him with the finest of Burgundian wines, served with sugared comfits from the rare spice markets in Antwerp. Evenings she had roaring fires set in the hearthplaces, scented with balsam and fir. Bathing the cardinal in sensory delights, she teased out his intellectual pursuits until she had established a firm rapport with the French minister.

Daytimes were a different story. The two spent hours wrestling over differences neither was willing to compromise on, d'Amboise as cunning as Margaret was determined.

But the problem of Gelderland was not easily resolved. Charles of Egmond's grievances dated back to the 1470s and the reign of Charles the Rash. Egmond had switched sides several times, and neither the French nor the Habsburg forces had control over his actions or could vanquish his brigands. But all knew the French king furnished Egmond with money for armed incursions that made the lives of Netherlanders miserable.

After one week of wrangling, Margaret and d'Amboise decided to accord Egmond his duchy of Gelderland in return for restoring to the Archduke Charles several castles he had taken elsewhere in the Netherlands and a promise to stop raiding bordering Habsburg-controlled territories. Details were to be hashed out in committees nominated by Maximilian and Henry VII and, on the other side, Louis XII and the King of Scotland to review the duke's grievances and render a solution.

Map of The Netherlands with Gelderland featured
From Ontheworldmap.com

Charles of Egmond, Duke of Guelders (1467-1538)
Artist unknown
Museum Arnhem, Arnhem, Netherlands
From familysearch.org

The moment arrived to turn to the second, far more enticing topic on the agenda. Margaret's intent was to divert France's interests away from financing the Duke of Guelders to the acquisition and dividing up of Venetian territories in Italy by all parties present.

Eager eyes fastened on Margaret and d'Amboise at mention of divesting Venice of its spoils. All four realms represented at Cambrai stood to gain by such an attractive prospect. In the name of aiding the Pope in regaining Papal lands seized by the Most Serene Republic, Margaret and her fellow negotiators got down to the real business of the summit.

On Maximilian's behalf, Margaret negotiated to regain Trieste and eastern Istria, as well as to take Padua, Vicenza, Verona, and the Friuli. For Ferdinand, she obtained the important ports of Brindisi and Otranto, gateways to the East.

D'Amboise negotiated for Louis XII, adding Brescia, Bergamo, Crema, and Cremoa to France's Milanese portfolio.

Pope Julius II, although not present, would receive Rimini, Ravenna, Faenza, and Cervia. D'Amboise assured her he would sign, as he was furious with the Venetians for poaching his territories.

A treaty was drawn up to push Venice back to its lagoon as punishment for its brash expansiveness over the past few decades. Framed as a holy war, nothing could be less so, with all the indignant defenders of the Church standing to divide the spoils of helping the pope to recover his lands.

On December 10, 1508, representatives of the Holy Roman Empire and Spain stood side by side with representatives of France and the papacy and signed the accord of the League of Cambrai against the Republic of Venice. It was the first moment of European unity of the 16th century, the seminal beginning of European coalition politics.

Margaret exulted. She had stood her ground with the more senior and experienced Georges d'Amboise, and negotiated more territory for her father than Maximilian could have done himself. Louis XII would be ecstatic to expand his Italian holdings and would divert France's military resources to Italy, thus drying up funding for the warlike Duke of Guelders. It was a crowning moment for her, one that raised her status to pivotal player amongst Europe's princes.

Upon her return to Malines, her governing body, the Estates General, awarded her 60,000 pounds for negotiating the peace settlement over Gelderland. Pleased to be rewarded by her frequently restive peers, Margaret felt transformed. She was now a known player on Europe's chessboard—not only Governor of the Netherlands, but a statesman of Europe.

When her father again raised the question of marriage to Henry Tudor, her refusal was firm. Never would she give up her newfound status to become queen-consort to a foreign lord, acquiescent and biddable to his whims. Having succeeded in spearheading the most unholy of holy alliances against Venice, Margaret was ready to embrace her new role as a political player on Europe's stage.

JUST BEFORE CHRISTMAS OF 1508, more good news arrived. Henry VII had officiated at the proxy marriage of his daughter Mary to Charles of Habsburg at Richmond Castle on December 17th, with Margaret's envoy standing in for her nephew.

The year had flowed with fortuitous treaties. Margaret gave thanks at Christmas Eve Mass for the successful negotiations she had taken part in over the past twelve months. With a twinge of conscience, she asked forgiveness for the pride she felt in spearheading many of them.

The Lord had declared that the meek shall inherit the Earth. But Margaret had not been raised to be meek, schooled as she was first by Anne de Beaujeu, then Margaret of York, and Isabella of Spain. Everything she needed to get done required resolve and firm action to accomplish. Now that she had presided over her first international negotiation, she reveled in the exhilaration she felt from the exercise of power.

"You have put the affairs of princes in my path, O Lord, so I ask You to give me whatever I need to carry out my duties well," she prayed, thinking meekness would not do at all. Certainly, it wouldn't help her to manage her Low Countries' burghers.

To maintain peace in her realm, she must be anything but meek. Charming, yes, seemingly flexible, then ultimately firm. Above all, she pursued the policy of planting the idea she wished to see done in the other party's head, then drawing him out until he suggested it himself.

It was a technique she had learned from Anne de Beaujeu, daughter of Louis XI, France's spider king and Charles the Rash's nemesis. How satisfying it was to avenge her maternal grandfather's defeats at the hands of Louis XI by taking a page from his daughter's playbook.

Thinking back to the hours she had spent bickering over Gelderland with d'Amboise while warming to a Venetian landgrab that instantly united French and Imperial interests, Margaret flushed with pleasure. It had been a breathlessly stimulating year that had unleashed a passion for politics within her. She looked forward to more to come.

IN THE SPRING OF 1509, France made the first move against Venice. Louis XII and his troops had marched across the Alps the moment the snows melted.

On April 16, 1509, the French army crushed the largely mercenary Venetian forces at Agnadello. One week later the papal army made their own move, with the pope excommunicating Venice on April 27.

When news arrived in early May that Henry VII of England had died Margaret felt the winds of change reshuffle Europe's prime players.

Within six weeks of Henry Tudor's death, his son Henry VIII married Catherine of Aragon, widow of Henry's brother Arthur. Margaret breathed a sigh of happiness to hear that her former sister-in-law had finally gained the queen's crown she had been sent to England in 1501 to attain.

By July Louis XII had taken possession of Venetian territories earmarked for Maximilian, holding them while awaiting imperial forces to arrive. The king of the country Maximilian most hated was delivering Venetian territories into his hands, without him having had to pay an army to fight for them. Margaret's work at the Treaty of Cambrai had resulted in the reconciliation of the two houses of Europe most at odds with each other—the House of Valois and the House of Habsburg.

Yet Maximilian delayed his arrival to claim the territories the French had won on his behalf. It was not until August 18 that he

arrived outside Padua to take over the siege of the city Louis XII had
begun for him.

Instead of setting to work to break down Padua's city walls,
Maximilian's army, much of which was mercenary, hung back in the
fields outside, becoming increasingly bored and disgruntled. By the
end of September it was not just the Paduans who were running out
of provisions, but their besiegers as well. Maximilian had exhausted
funds to pay his mercenary troops beyond the end of the month.

What he did next puzzled all of Europe.

Lifting the siege of Padua, the Holy Roman Emperor returned to
the Tyrol with most of his army.

"What was he thinking?" Margaret raged as she waved his letter.
Her father had written to say that his soldiers had wearied of the siege
and food had been in short supply. The vast number of his army,
with their horses and artillery, had turned their encampment into a
field of mud, dampening the spirits of all present. He had decided
to withdraw his troops.

"What news, Madame?" Gattinara asked.

"My father says his army wearied of the siege, but I know him too
well. It was he who was fed up with waiting around and tired of the
whole affair," Margaret fulminated.

"Madame, what reason would the emperor have for withdrawing
his troops when success was in sight?" Wrinkling his brow, Gattinara
looked perplexed. It was a reasonable question, likely being raised in
council chambers all over Europe at that moment.

"Do not ask, Monsieur. Because the answer I have from him will
confuse you further." Margaret tried to hide her dismay, a combination of disgust and anguish at her father's flawed decision-making.
What military leader, no matter how feckless, would let slip a prize

won for him by others, when all he had needed to do was wait for his target to run out of food and come to terms?

"Try me. I am not easily confused, as you have seen already, my lady."

"It is not easy to know the mind of my father," she groaned. How she wanted to throttle him. He had walked away from the rich reward she had negotiated for him, and the French king had all but delivered into his hands.

Her beloved, head-in-the-clouds Maxi, full of dreams of military grandeur, had not wished to persevere with the distasteful realities of war. To begin, the incessant need for money to pay for everything was beneath the dignity of the Holy Roman Emperor. Then the actual campaign in itself—a monotonous slog of tired or bored, increasingly filthy men, muddy camps, horses that needed exercise and feed, and nothing to do but wait until suddenly there would be too much to do and no soldier could know if they would live or die.

All of this was bad enough under an inspired leader. But when the leader chose to go home because it was all too ignoble for him, then who in their right mind would do their job with zeal—especially without knowing if they would get paid for their efforts?

Margaret slapped the desk she sat at then buried her head in her hands.

"No one in Europe knows the mind of your father, my lady, which is why they all come to you," Gattinara observed.

She shook her head. "Why did he not put together an all-out onslaught and get the job done?" she railed.

"Madame, you are not in agreement with your father's actions, but all will come to you for an explanation, so try to offer a good one."

"A good one? Or the real one?"

"Both. Then let me help you carve out what to say once word gets out of such a misstep."

"The one we will use is that he ran out of money to pay his troops," Margaret told him.

Gattinara looked less than impressed. "That is the usual reason—solid but tiresome."

"We will use it, as all who know my father have heard it before from him."

"What then lies beyond it?"

Margaret rose, moving to the window. Looking out, she expelled a long breath. "I would guess that my father would not wish to accept help from France," she surmised.

"So, he couldn't cope with the French king doing his work for him?"

"If you must put it like that. Certainly, he would have been amenable if it had been the English who had helped him."

Margaret thought of her former suitor, Henry VII, newly planted in his grave. Would his son and successor renew their Anglo-Imperial alliance? She had heard Henry VIII was young and vigorous, eager to prove himself.

"So, pride caused the Holy Roman Emperor to miss an opportunity so thoroughly that he is now being laughed at in all of Europe's courts?" Gattinara asked carefully.

Margaret gave her counselor a stern look. Her father would not wish to be laughed at. But any could see he was not in step with Europe's changing times.

"My father is a heroic man. But he requires heroic circumstances as his backdrop," she defended. Strangely, Maxi reminded her of

Charles of Egmond. Both were valiant knights who didn't quite fit the spirit of the new age. Born and shaped to manhood in the century before, they clung to feudal ways, exulting in glorious, un-profitable pursuits and disdaining filthy lucre or how to acquire it.

"Madame, that is all well and good, but I daresay we are no longer living in heroic times," Gattinara remarked.

Margaret arched a brow. "Were we ever?"

Her counselor laughed, and Margaret joined him. The past was the past. But she and the realm she governed were rooted in the present. If the House of Habsburg was to flourish she would need to carefully cultivate its next head, because the one who ruled it now was a figure who belonged between the pages of an ancient epic tale.

How she loved Maxi, and how she loved to read such tales. But when she was done, she put them back on the bookshelf and re-turned to the real world of men squabbling over who would pay for what. That was the world in which she governed. And she had only just begun to learn the craft of how it was done.

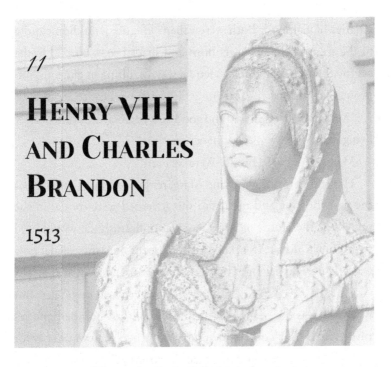

11

HENRY VIII
AND CHARLES
BRANDON

1513

> "'Praise the God of all, drink the wine,
> and let the world be the world.'"
> — French proverb quoted by Charles Brandon
> in *The Tudors* (2010 television series)

Henry VIII was arriving that day in Lille, fresh from the English and Imperial victory over the French at Thérouanne. The fortified town was in Artois, land that the French had held unlawfully for decades, although they had promised to return it to Burgundy as part of Margaret's dowry when she had been sent back to Flanders in 1493.

Margaret was cognizant that the English had done most of the work. Her father had supplied morale and some troops, but the

English had led the siege. Maximilian had joked to her that he had contracted with Henry to pay him one hundred crowns daily to serve in his army, a point that had made her cringe but hadn't surprised her. Maxi was endlessly short of funds. In his quest to expand his dominions, he dependably sought to pry funds from his allies to pay for his military engagements.

After the English rout of the French supply line at Guinegate, it had taken only another week until Thérouanne surrendered. Henry VIII was eager to prove his mettle on the Continent, and willing to pay Maximilian to provide a legitimate reason for why the English were there at all. Margaret was delighted to have the young and eager English king clear the French from territories bordering her realm, saving her from the trouble of doing it herself.

She was eager to assess Europe's newest player among princes. Her father wished to build a close alliance with Henry VIII as a hedge against France; she also wished for a hedge against France, but one that wouldn't require further taxation of her subjects. Henry VIII, with his burning desire to prove himself and ample coffers due to his father's strict fiscal governance, might be just the ambitious prince both she and Maximilian needed.

Positioning herself at the side of the window overlooking the courtyard of her town house in Lille, she watched as the English party rode in. As Henry VIII dismounted, she saw that he was tall and broad-shouldered, larger than any of the continental princes—most of whom she had met.

A man in officer's uniform dismounted behind him, equally tall and broad, to whom the king turned and spoke.

Margaret noted the way Henry VIII clapped a familiar hand on the man's shoulder. Was this the one her man at the English court had told her had the king's ear and should be cultivated? She had heard he had been the king's master of the horse and had been put in charge of the vanguard that had vanquished Thérouanne.

Watching the two stride across the courtyard, she saw that the officer did not walk behind his sovereign but at his side. Such familiarity would be unthinkable on the Continent, even at the relatively informal Burgundian court.

Descending the stairs, Margaret straightened her widow's coif and smoothed down her gown. She would take the measure of these two before the day was out.

The two men entered the hallway in a burst of male vitality, arousing Margaret's amour-propre. She would match them with equally potent feminine charm.

Henry VIII of England approached with strong sure steps, his small bird-like blue eyes set in a ruddy, broad face.

Looking beyond Henry, she glanced at his companion. As the officer met her eyes, a chill shot down her spine. This was no sapling king, but a full-grown man with every attribute a woman might dream of in the dark of night.

Margaret composed her face. She had seen male beauty at close quarters before. Her brother had possessed it. So had Philibert. But this man had something more, a cocksure confidence about him. It unsettled her.

"Lady Margaret, I am honored to meet you," Henry VIII said with a bow. "May I present Charles Brandon, Viscount Lisle, and captain of my forward guard?"

Margaret dipped her head slightly to acknowledge the king's companion, no more.

But the officer stepped closer and bent over her hand, not understanding he had not been invited to approach. Kissing it, Charles Brandon raised his eyes to hers and boldly stared into them.

His gaze sent a lightning bolt through her body. An ancient tune hummed within her, one she hadn't heard in years.

Margaret raised her chin, looking down her nose at the brash officer. Her duty was to stand firm and let the young King of England know she wished him to be an ally, but he must pay for the favor. As for the English king's master of the horse, she could see he might easily become master of more than the horses if given free rein.

That night a banquet was held to honor the English guests. Margaret left off her usual black widow's garb and picked out a gown of cloth of gold. Instead of her white coif, she put on a Burgundian headdress that glittered with rubies and pearls. Why not give the English king a taste of Burgundian opulence? Such a display might up the ante of what he was willing to pay her father for the privilege of joining forces with him on the Continent.

While the young King of England threw himself into the amusements, one moment playing the lute and singing, the next leaping about in a lively galliard with several of her maids of honor, Margaret surveyed the room using only her eyes. With head held high and neck arched, she savored her moment as a contender on the diplomatic tournament floor.

"May I have this dance, Lady Margaret?" a low voice rumbled.

Without turning to look, Margaret knew who addressed her. She had summoned him without a word.

Charles Brandon bowed before her, his officer's uniform exchanged for a resplendent silk brocade doublet in Tudor green and white.

"I am not much for dancing, Monsieur. But I am sure one of my maids of honor would be delighted, if you asked," she demurred.

"But I would not be delighted, Madame."

"Do you not appreciate female beauty, then, Monsieur?" She held his gaze, telling herself she would not be unnerved by the dark eyes that leapt out at her from under thick, well-shaped brows.

"I appreciate it more when it is coupled with intelligence and skill," Brandon replied.

Margaret felt herself flush. "Many men prefer female beauty to be served up alone."

"I am unlike many men."

"So I hear from my counselors."

The officer leaned toward her. "I would be honored if you would decide on your own."

Margaret narrowed her eyes, fluttering her lashes. "How shall I decide then?" She felt strangely thrown off balance, as if leading a negotiation and suddenly realizing it was she who was being led.

"You will have me figured out before our dance is ended," he riposted.

"I have no interest in figuring you out," she fibbed, as the sweet bygone tune thrummed within her, as insistent as the man before her.

"But you are interested in measuring up my sovereign, so you need to know what he sees in the likes of me," the English officer said evenly.

"Since you put it that way, you have a point." Without thinking she slid her hand into his outstretched one and glided onto the dance-floor as the music started up.

Expecting they would resume their conversation, she was glad when they did not. It was enough to be swept up in the music, the murmur of merry conversation and low laughter around them. Most of all, the grip of the confident Englishman's hand on her waist.

THE FOLLOWING DAY THE King of England visited again, accompanied by a small entourage including his right-hand man. The weather was heaven-sent—neither too hot, nor cool—with a playful breeze that ruffled the ladies' headdresses as they walked in the gardens of Margaret's townhouse.

Charles Brandon strolled next to her, the king up ahead, a boundless fireball of male energy at age twenty-two, cavorting at the side of one of the demoiselles.

As Margaret watched Henry VIII, she told herself to be on her guard against being duped. The English army had just taken care of a nice bit of work for Maximilian, at minimal expense to him. Margaret's job was to succor them, just as she guessed the English king might have advised his master of the horse to succor her, to strengthen England's reputation on the Continent.

But her heart fought her reason on a slippery slope, one she had not found herself on before. She had enjoyed the attentions of her court poet, Jean Lemaire. Yet she had not felt an answering chord within. When he had left her service to join Anne of Brittany's court the year before, she had been saddened, but not bereft, to see him go.

As for this new admirer? She had thought of little else since the night before when the English officer bade her good night.

"Does your sovereign ever stop moving?" Margaret asked Brandon.

"Not when there is a lady to impress."

"And when do you plan to tell him that is not the most effective method?"

"Madame, I will offer no such advice, as he would never take it, whatever I counseled."

"He is like a charming young pup," Margaret mused, observing Henry pluck a blossom from a shrub and present it to the demoiselle nearest him.

Brandon shuddered. "Madame, no man wishes to be taken for a pup by the lady whose favors he seeks."

"And what would you wish to be taken for by the lady of your choice?" Margaret asked, enjoying the moment.

"I would wish to be taken for a serious man, but with a sense of humor."

Margaret shot him a glance then flicked her eyes away. "Are you a serious man? Or a clever one who knows what pose to assume to achieve his aims?"

"Madame, you have uncovered me. But I will not say which I am, as that is for you to discover."

"Then I guess you are a man who is serious about achieving his aims," Margaret told him.

"Is it an unworthy quality?"

"It is one that stands a man in good stead if accompanied by honor and discretion," she volleyed back.

"But is there true honor among princes, my lady? You more than any other would know, as you have dealt with them all."

Margaret laughed, the breeze ruffling her headdress as she tossed her head. "There are alliances that shift with the wind, and those that remain firm," she answered.

"And which do you seek to make with my king?"

"If your king keeps his word to marry his sister to my nephew, their offspring will create a permanent alliance between our houses." There. She had delivered her most pressing objective for this visit. Although a second one was emerging.

"And if your father decides to marry his grandson to another princess, it will prove to be the usual shifting alliance," Henry's officer countered.

"Is there a lesson to be learned either way?"

Charles Brandon nodded. "I would value a marriage alliance over a treaty alliance every time."

"But if an alliance serves a purpose at one time, but is no longer convenient at another, a treaty does nicely."

With eyes like searchlights, he caught her own. "If the party one seeks to ally with is of the highest quality, there is no future time when one should end it."

Margaret felt a pang as she thought of Philibert, as solid and true as Savoy's pine-scented mountains. "You do not speak of politics, Monsieur, for in that arena there is an end to every engagement," she parried.

"No, fair lady. I do not speak of politics, but of something dearer."

Blood like a rushing stream coursed through her veins. "And what is that?"

"Of marriage, my lady. To one of the highest quality who has captured my heart."

Margaret sucked in her breath. "So your heart has been captured, Monsieur?"

"I will say no more of it if you tell me there is no hope."

"I am happily widowed, and much older than you."

Brandon put his lips close to Margaret's ear. "I am unhappily widowed, and close to you in age."

"I am perfectly content as I am, Monsieur." She had told her father so, repeatedly. But this time she was not so sure.

"I am the sad father of two beautiful daughters with no mother," Brandon pressed.

"Are they at court or at home?" Margaret asked, struggling to regain control of the conversation. The current between them was flowing fast. Much too fast for her usual banter.

"Madame, my eldest is just now flowering into womanhood. She would benefit from joining a court such as yours."

"Her name?"

"Anne, my lady."

"'Tis a good one. If you send her to me, I shall make a proper demoiselle of her," Margaret offered. Ordinarily, she withheld invitations until weighing them first. But nothing was ordinary about the moment at hand, tightening itself around them like a silk scarf.

"My lady, nothing would give me greater pleasure."

"I thought you just said there was something else that would." The teasing words flew from her lips, baiting him.

"My lady, do you give me a glimmer of hope?" Brandon's dark eyes swept hers like an oncoming wildfire.

"I give you an invitation to send your daughter to me." Margaret had not been captivated by such a gaze in almost a decade. Nine years of widowhood melted like spring snow in the crucible of his regard.

"My lady, I am indebted beyond words."

Margaret smiled, pleased with her outcome. It was outrageous to think a man such as Charles Brandon would sue for her affections. There was no way she could consider his suit. Yet as her mind rebuffed him, her senses rebelled.

Having his daughter join her court would ensure his regular visits. And should his rank rise with each visit, who knew what might ensue?

That evening Margaret once again left aside her widow's garb and donned an emerald green gown with a cream-brocade panel shot through with gold thread to honor the Tudor king. Making merry over dinner, she counted the minutes until the music began and she felt her suitor's hands take hers again.

The opening notes of a galliard sounded. Brandon caught Margaret to him and spun her around in a heady motion that left her breathless, her back pulled tight against his chest. He put his mouth to her ear; this time not to speak.

Margaret felt herself buckle. The dam had given way. Flinging the remains of her self-control into the churning river within her, she leapt into its current.

BY THE END OF September the English had accomplished a second victory, this one at Tournai, a French enclave due east of Thérouanne in Burgundian-Habsburg territory. After an eight-day siege, Brandon had taken a contingent of soldiers and stormed the gatehouse. To his surprise he had found it almost undefended and breached the town. Its leaders immediately surrendered.

In thanks for his victory, King Henry gave his top officer the keys to the town. And extended an invitation to Margaret and her nephew to join them in victory celebrations.

Margaret and thirteen-year-old Charles of Habsburg arrived outside Tournai on October 11, 1513. They were led inside its gates by the English king and his entourage.

As a bee to a flower, Charles Brandon attached himself to her side. Margaret did not discourage him. The ancient tune hummed once more as he stood next to her. All the qualities she derided in other men—among them unbridled ambition and swaggering confidence—she found irresistible in the charismatic Englishman.

Playing the game of courtly love, she served back Brandon's volleys with equal zest. The strong, athletically-built man reminded her of Philibert except that he was older, shrewder, and of questionable background. Concerning the last, alarm bells should have rung. But joyous chimes drowned them out, ringing so insistently they blotted out all other sounds.

Arrangements for their overnight stay were vague. Margaret was without her full entourage. She had brought her two most senior attendants, along with a handful of demoiselles. All were housed in the same palace that the king and Brandon stayed in, her nephew given his own suite of rooms in a separate wing.

"My lady, I have thought of nothing but you since last we met," Brandon murmured as they came together in the stately pavane that opened the evening's dancing.

"It seems you took a few moments to win the town for us," she parried, her spirits soaring.

"For you, my lady. So I would have cause to see you again with a prize to offer."

"You serve your king, but I serve my nephew who will rule over most of Europe one day," she checked him.

"Think what an alliance they will make!" Brandon exclaimed, his thumb stroking the back of her hand.

"One that will wax and wane as princes' alliances do, Lord Lisle." She kept her voice cool even as the feel of his touch shot flaming arrows down her spine.

"Unlike firmer ones of marriage," Brandon replied, squeezing her hand.

"Do you speak to me of such?" Margaret asked blithely.

"I would if you would have me," Brandon returned, his eyes boring into hers.

Averting her eyes, Margaret considered. In her three previous betrothals she had not been consulted. Now she was thirty-three years old with her own wealth. Never having enjoyed the opportunity to choose her own partner, she found her heart and her head at war. Charles Brandon was far beneath her in rank, of non-royal background. But his hand on hers was warm and certain. She had not felt such a degree of certainty since she had laid her gallant Philibert to rest.

But as for marriage? The man before her was on his way up. If not a peer now, quite possibly one in the future, as the king's favor raised him further. Should she, daughter of the Holy Roman Emperor, deign to take him as husband, his rank among Europe's nobility would soar.

"I have decided not to remarry," she told him.

"Madame, you are too young and too beautiful to renounce our sex," he protested.

"I am too busy with governing and raising my nephew and nieces to think of such pleasures."

Brandon bent to her ear and brushed it with his mouth. "Then don't think of such pleasures; just enjoy them."

"How like a man to say such a thing," she whispered back, thrilling to the velvet touch of his lips.

"How like a bright jewel you are, Margaret, hiding under your widow's garb. Allow me to polish your lustre," he murmured.

Margaret felt a blush spread over her. "You speak out of turn, Lord Lisle."

"Then let me know when my turn comes and I will serve you patiently until then."

Margaret fluttered her eyes at him, feeling as giddy as one of her maids of honor. She couldn't say yes, yet she wouldn't say no. All she could manage was to steer them both to a corner unoccupied by any in her entourage.

For the entirety of the evening Charles Brandon remained at her side. Through several more dances, then rounds of cards, his bracing scent filled her nostrils as he shifted next to her, brushing her arm at moments that flooded her senses and emptied her mind.

As the hour neared midnight, Margaret saw that the crowd was thinning.

"I am tired, Lord Lisle, and ready to retire. I will see you on the morrow," she said.

"You are not tired, and I will see you to your rooms," Brandon replied, taking her arm like a mighty Zeus.

"You will do no such thing," Margaret protested, a flame shooting heavenward at the thought of him at her chamber door.

"I must see that you have been quartered properly, as befits your dignity," her suitor insisted.

"I am perfectly capable of finding my quarters on my own," Margaret responded. Tingles ran down her arms as she considered what might befit her dignity that night. Perhaps a night off was in order.

"So, your ladies will not accompany you?"

"Of course they will." Looking around, she saw no sign of either Lady Elisabeth or the Countess of Horne.

"'I'm sorry we couldn't find room for them in the chamber I arranged for you." Brandon's tone was as guileless as his gaze was not.

"Do you mean there are no sleeping couches for my ladies?" Margaret asked, surprised.

"I have had quarters down the hall from yours prepared for your ladies."

"Next to my own?"

Brandon's voice was low. "No, my lady. They are several doors down, with an empty room next to yours."

"Then who will protect me during the night?" Margaret murmured back, the words spilling out before she could censor them.

Brandon's eyes leapt out at her. "I will see to your protection, my lady."

"It is the protection of my honor that I speak of," she warned, reminding him of her rank.

"I will see to it in every way." Brandon's eyes poured liquid gold into hers.

Desire seized her. "I trust you to do so," Margaret whispered as the Countess of Horne appeared at her shoulder.

Bidding Brandon goodnight she turned to go, her lady-in-waiting trailing in her wake. Perhaps her next steps would be folly, but she had thought only of duty for too long. She was a grown woman, with power and wealth. It was time to think of something else. Or not think at all.

"My lady, where is the couch where I am to sleep?" Lady Horne asked as she helped Margaret off with her gown.

"They have quartered you with Lady Elisabeth in the room two doors down," Margaret blandly answered, her heart thumping.

"But what will you do if you need something during the night?"

Margaret removed her headdress, busy brushing it off as she avoided her lady-in-waiting's eyes. "I will manage. As I have on other trips," she said.

"Shall I ask for a couch to be brought in so you will not be alone?"

"Don't bother. It will be amusing to look after myself. If men on the battlefield can do it, so can I." Margaret turned her back to hide her smile. It was one she had not felt in years.

"Very good, Madame. I will see you on the morrow." Lady Horne slipped out.

With the click of the door shutting behind her Margaret ran her fingers through her hair, luxuriating in the firelight that danced on the walls. Falling back on the bed she laughed for joy.

THE NEXT DAY MARGARET wrote to her father. Letting him know she was doing her part to pin down the English on the marriage between her nephew and Mary Tudor, she mentioned she had spent time playing cards with the English king and Lord Lisle.

'I am so very joyful that it is not possible to say more,' she ended, unable to contain her happiness. Signing and sealing it she sent it off, knowing her father would look into Lord Lisle's background and decide if it was of sufficient stature to arrange a match between him and his daughter.

Maxi would use the opportunity as an excuse for Henry to cough up more funds for use in future campaigns. Henry needed prestige and Maximilian needed money. If Margaret so desired, she could be the instrument by which both rulers achieved their aims. But did she wish to marry again at all?

Shifting her weight, she lingered on the thought of the most masculine of warm arms around her. She longed to feel those arms again. Beyond that, she was sure of nothing.

Ten days of merrymaking ensued until the eve of Margaret and her nephew's departure from Tournai. They would return to Lille the following day, feted and fully satisfied.

She was aware that others in their party had noted her high spirits in the presence of the English king's officer. But it was time to return to her duties. With Lord Lisle occupying her every moment, she found herself in a position she had frequently warned her maids of honor against: unable to think clearly and not giving a fig that she couldn't.

Following that evening's banquet, the guests broke up into small groups. Margaret found herself with Brandon, seated on a stool before her. The king stood nearby, his red-golden head bobbing in animated conversation with a cluster of demoiselles.

As the group made merry, Brandon bent over her hand and kissed it. Upon withdrawing, he slid off the diamond ring she wore on her ring finger and put it on his pinkie.

"A token, my lady?" he asked, his eyes twinkling.

Laughing, she grasped his wrist and tried to retrieve her ring. "Monsieur, do I take you for a thief?" she asked, using the French word *ladrón*.

"I do not know what I am, other than your devoted champion." Brandon closed his hand around hers, preventing her from wresting the ring off his finger.

"If you are my champion then return my ring to me," she protested.

Brandon's smile was devilish. "I will return your ring when you return my heart to me."

"If you choose to give me your heart it is your decision, but I do not choose to give you my ring, so you will put it back." Margaret held out her hand, wondering for the first time if her admirer understood the rules of engagement of the game they were playing. Was it possible he did not know the finer points of courtly love?

"It was no choice, my lady, but the command of your charm that has stolen my heart," Brandon parried, kissing her ring on his finger.

A frisson ran up Margaret's back as it hit her that she may have misjudged her suitor. "And the command of your lady is that you will return what is hers to her," she stated firmly. God forbid he would hold onto her ring and show it to others, as if to boast of his conquest. The token he had taken would prove a heady conversation point should others recognize it as hers.

"I shall wear this keepsake forever, so I may have you near me wherever I am." Brandon's voice was as velvety as a starless night.

"You will do no such thing, Charles. Give it back to me before I take you for a *dieff*," Margaret ordered, using the Flemish word for 'thief.' God's bones, if only she could remember what the word was in English.

As others glanced their way, she rued raising her voice. She must get the ring back before anyone noticed he had it and talk began.

"You may take me for whatever you like, but you hold my heart," Brandon hedged. With a roguish smile he stood and bowed to her, the finger of one hand stroking her ring on the other. As he raised his head, she caught the glitter of his eyes.

Dismay flooded her as she saw the pleasure he took in disobeying her. It was far from the way of a courtly knight with his lady.

But before she could rebuke him further the English king was upon them, a broad smile on his face. Turning to Margaret, Henry VIII raised his goblet.

"To Anglo-Imperial alliances!" he cried.

"More than one?" a pert demoiselle asked, looking at him then at Margaret and Brandon with a cheeky gaze.

"The more the better!" Henry VIII exclaimed, giving Brandon a wink.

Margaret raised her glass. In principal, she agreed. But she could not bear to look at Brandon. She had asked for her ring back and he had not returned it. He was not the man she had thought him to be.

THE MORNING OF DEPARTURE arrived. Margaret moved down the hall toward the courtyard where the carriages waited. At sight of the English king's officer, she sent Lady Horne off to fetch a fan and a pair of gloves from her trunk. As her lady-in-waiting disappeared, Brandon strode toward Margaret and pulled her into an alcove.

"I am desolate that you are leaving," he greeted.

"And I, too. But you have something of mine you must return before we part," she replied, relief easing her. Of course, he had come to make all right between them.

"Ah, my lady, it is a token I require to remind me of sweet moments with you."

Margaret gasped. There could be no sweet moments between them mentioned before anyone. Yet how blithely he had tossed out the words. It would take all of one conversation with his sovereign for him to spill the details of what had transpired between them. And if he was not believed, he had only to show her ring to drive home his boast.

"No token you have taken from me is to be shared with anyone. Now give back my ring so our parting will be as pleasant as our time here has been." She held out her hand.

Brandon leaned over and kissed it, infuriating her.

"The ring, Monsieur," Margaret said, her outrage building.

Brandon reached for her. As he did, Margaret grabbed his wrist. But he was larger and stronger. With his other hand he caught hers, preventing her from wresting the ring off his finger.

"My lady, I have found your gloves," Lady Horne called out as she approached.

Margaret released Brandon's wrist. She would seek to retrieve the ring later, through other means. Her feelings riled, she struggled to contain them as the English king's man melted from sight.

"Give them here," Margaret directed Lady Horne, looking at the gloves she held out instead of her lady-in-waiting. Taking a long moment to fit them on, she composed herself.

"Madame, you are pale," Lady Horne noted. "Shall I fetch a glass of water?"

"I am fine," Margaret answered. "But bring some water while I wait for the carriage."

Lady Horne backed from the alcove, her face telling Margaret that she was aware of the effect the Viscount Lisle had had upon her.

Avoiding her gaze Margaret fussed with her collar, straightening it out yet failing to straighten out the jumble of feelings beneath it.

It was no use. She could not tell if what had taken place had been felicity or folly. Would the man who had taken a token from her flaunt his treasure to all the world, or guard it close to his heart?

Back in Lille the following night, Margaret tossed in her bed. Had it been true love that had gleamed in her suitor's eyes? Or something else that had nothing to do with sentiment, and everything to do with an ambitious man's upward trajectory?

The next morning, she awoke and tried to laugh off events of the week before. She and her suitor had taken their game too far, each in their own way. But as she rang for breakfast, restless thoughts roamed. Neither Juan nor Philibert had ever made her feel so unsettled.

Moving to her desk, she pulled out parchment and dipped her quill. Hastily, she scribbled a note to her ambassador to England. If she were lucky, she would get this matter taken care of before the king and his party left the Continent and before anyone noticed the diamond ring on Charles Brandon's little finger.

But the matter was not resolved. One month later rumors reached her that the ring had been noted. When reports came that the king's master of horses had shown it off at the English court, proud to have others wonder what his status might be with the daughter of the Holy Roman Emperor, Margaret's cheeks flamed.

Further humiliations came with word from Germany that traveling merchants were taking wagers on whether the Lady Margaret would marry the King of England's trusted companion.

Meanwhile, Brandon had not communicated at all.

Her heart twisting like a broken weathervane in the wind, Margaret told herself she had had enough. Her suitor had overstepped the bounds of proper conduct; he was not a suitable husband for a woman of her rank.

If only such a reasonable conclusion could end thoughts of him that stalked her nightly.

Charles Brandon, 1st Duke of Suffolk
Master of the Brandon portrait, c. 1514
From Sotheby's, Public domain

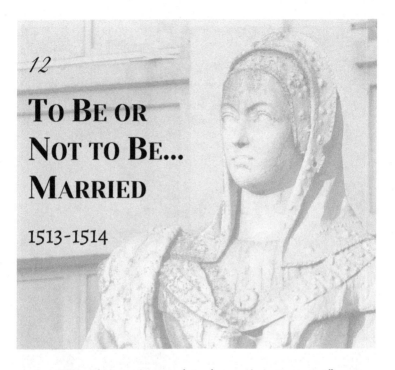

12

TO BE OR NOT TO BE... MARRIED

1513-1514

"Let others wage war: thou, happy Austria, marry."
Bella gerant alii, tu felix Austria nube.
— Habsburg motto ascribed to
Hungarian king Matthias Corvinus

"Have you heard she is to marry the Viscount Lisle?"

"Viscount Lisle?" a female voice sniggered. "Do you mean the English king's stable boy?"

Margaret braced herself against the arras she stood behind. She flushed, shaken to think her Englishman had spread such a rumor. How galling to hear him referred to as a stable boy.

"He's quite high up with the king. But if he weds the duchess, he will rise even farther."

"I can't believe our duchess would agree."

"It's hard to imagine, but 'twas said she was taken with him when she and the prince visited Tournai last fall."

"It's one thing to enjoy a flirtation. Another to wed such a man."

Margaret clenched her jaw.

"What manner of man is he, then? If the king likes him so much, he must have some qualities."

"Oh, he does," the merry voice replied, ripe with insinuation. "They say he's as cunning as he is brave."

"In battle you mean? Or in sport?"

"Both of those and more."

"And more?"

"He knows his way around the ladies."

"So he must if he caught the eye of our duchess. She is not one to give her favors lightly."

"He is as slippery as a lamprey with the ladies."

"Our duchess would never consort with a rogue," the second voice bristled.

With the arras blocking her view, Margaret could not determine who the speakers were. Her stomach roiled to think word of her dalliance had spread farther than she wished it to, as such topics do.

"She most likely did not know he was one when he waited on her hand and foot in Tournai."

"How do you mean, then?"

"Have you heard how he came by his title?"

Margaret sharpened her ears. She had wondered herself.

"How then?

"He betrothed himself to his ward, who is an orphaned heiress."

Glass shards of laughter rained down on Margaret's heart.

"How could he speak of marriage if he is already betrothed?"

"Ask him, not me. His ward is only an eight-year-old girl, but he engaged himself to her so the English king would award him her title and land revenues."

"Does the duchess know of this?"

"I think not. She would never have favored him so if she had."

"He'll need to break the engagement to marry her, but without his title he's nothing."

"She'll never have him."

The first woman cackled. "They say she already has." Whispering ensued, punctuated by giggles, each one a catapult launch of burning arrows to Margaret's dignity.

Her Englishman had mentioned nothing of this. He had not written to her nor had he returned her ring. Instead, Henry VIII had sent an even more valuable one with rubies surrounding a large diamond to replace it.

Yet that was not the point. Her reputation had been besmirched by Charles Brandon's bad behavior. And as senior member of the Houses of Burgundy and Habsburg, the honor of two of Europe's most preeminent houses was on her shoulders. They were the cornerstones upon which she based her life.

Margaret slipped away to find her private secretary. It was time to get to the bottom of this. If what the women said was true, Charles Brandon had much explaining to do. Henry VIII had sent the replacement ring to smooth the path to his sister's marriage to the Archduke. But the Viscount Lisle had yet to right himself with her.

Opportunists, both of them, she fumed. Yet she could ill afford the proposed marriage match between her nephew and Mary Tudor to fall through. If it did the thousands of pounds Maximilian was anticipating Henry to shower on him would not materialize, and he would be unable to continue with his Italian campaigns.

But she would not be taken in by a stable boy. It must not be said that the English king's master of the horse had been promoted to master of the emperor's daughter.

Tracking down her secretary, she tasked him with researching the complete background of Viscount Lisle as soon as possible.

WITHIN TWO DAYS SHE had her answers. Not only had Brandon affianced himself to his ward to gain the title the young girl brought with her, but he had behaved dishonorably toward the mother of his two daughters as well.

"Madame, it is a most mixed-up affair, but it seems that Viscount Lisle was betrothed to his first wife by whom he had a daughter, but married her aunt instead." Jean de Marnix raised a perplexed brow.

"Why would he do such a thing?"

"The usual, my lady. The aunt was a wealthy widow much older than he, and the match afforded him opportunity for advancement."

"Then what became of the mother of his daughter?"

"Her family was angered, and protested the marriage. It was annulled and he was forced to marry the child's mother, who died a few years back after giving him a second daughter."

Margaret felt her blood boil. So this was the wife he had referred to when he had described himself as a lonely widower with two young daughters.

"There is more, but it is not about him: rather, his father," Marnix continued.

"Pray tell." Margaret beckoned to an attendant for refreshment. She would need something strong to fortify her through such revelations.

Marnix hesitated. "I am sorry, Madame, but 'tis somewhat unseemly."

"Go on."

"The viscount's father—"

Margaret snorted to hide her hurt. "Leave off with 'viscount,' now that we know how he came by such a title."

"The person of interest's father was arrested for rape when he was a young man."

She fell back in her chair. "Pray tell me not of an innocent young girl?"

"Not only, Madame." Marnix's mouth curved downward. "Of a young woman and her mother, an older gentlewoman of means. While he was husband to another older woman, a widow with two children."

Margaret blanched. Reaching for her goblet she sipped to hide her face. It would seem Charles Brandon had inherited his way around women from his father.

"Was he prosecuted?" she asked.

"The records say he was held in ward in 1478, but nothing more. Apparently, he got off and fled to France, then Brittany, where he joined up with Henry Tudor."

"And ingratiated himself, I suppose."

"Apparently so, Madame. He was knighted by Tudor the moment they landed in England, then killed at Bosworth holding the king's standard."

"At least he died a hero."

"A great favorite of the old king, Madame."

"Much as his son is this king's favorite." How close the apple had fallen from the tree. Both father and son had won their king's favor while using wealthy older women to make their way in life. Sucking in her stomach, she struggled to quell her nausea.

"So they both were, Madame. They served their sovereigns well, but not so their wives."

"Refresh yourself. You have told me all I need to know."

Marnix poured out some spiced wine and sipped. "'Tis a curious history, is it not?" he remarked.

"It is one I would not wish to associate with," Margaret replied. *How appalling that I already have.* "Nor any member of my house," she added, hating the look of sympathy Marnix cast in her direction. She, senior member of the House of Habsburg, would not stand for anyone pitying her for making the mistake of allowing a man with such a sordid family background into her life.

"Madame, you have raised the Archduke so well that he would never consort with such types."

"Of course not, Monsieur. He would see through such a one in a day and throw him off."

"So he would, Madame. Thank God, he has had you all these years to guide him."

Margaret felt sick at the thought of how poorly she had guided herself. "You may go now, and tell my ladies to bring the musicians," she bade him. That evening she would shake off every vestige of Charles Brandon's memory. What a fool she had been to dally with a rogue.

Saying a prayer for those who might come after her, Margaret guessed there would be a few. Such ambition in a man knew no bounds. With the skills he had exercised on her, he would doubtless find others to ply them on.

Telling herself she was over him and any others of his ilk, her thoughts flew to her upright Philibert. No other man could take his place. None other ever would.

"Madame, you are deep in thought this evening," Lady Elisabeth noted as the trio of musicians tuned up.

Margaret turned to her, wondering if she had any inkling of her distress. The Countess of Horne would have known. But her close friend and lady-in-waiting had died earlier that year, carrying to the grave whatever she had seen in those heady days at Lille and Tournai.

From the sympathetic expression on Lady Elisabeth's face, Margaret guessed she knew what was on her mind. She burned to think her courtiers felt pity for her over her involvement with a man beneath her dignity. It was one thing if she had made a mistake in affairs of state, something that invariably happened to any ruler. But it rankled her to have others know she had stumbled in affairs of the heart.

Margaret turned to the music master and clapped her hands. "Let us dance a pavane," she called out.

"Shall I call the men to join us?" Lady Elisabeth asked.

"Not tonight. I am not in the mood for men's company this evening."

A discreet smile crept over her lady-in-waiting's face. "Very good, my lady. Sometimes it is more pleasurable to be without them."

Margaret rose, putting out her hand for her lady to lead her to the dance floor. *Perhaps not more pleasurable. But certainly more prudent.*

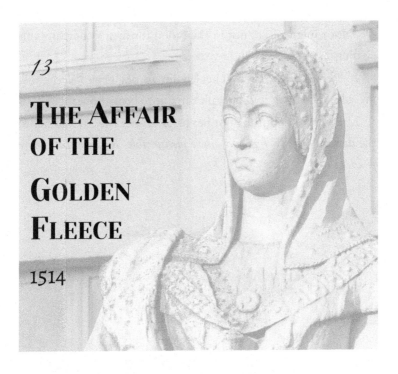

13

THE AFFAIR OF THE GOLDEN FLEECE

1514

AT THE END OF December 1514, a letter arrived for Margaret from Ferdinand of Aragon. Her former father-in-law praised her to the skies, lauding her as "the most important person in Christendom, since she acts as mediator in almost all the negotiations between the princes of Christendom."[1]

Her pride flaming high, Margaret schooled herself to be wary. The King of Aragon never offered compliments without a request far behind.

---

1. Shirley Harrold Bonner, *Fortune, Misfortune, Fortifies One* (Shirley Harrold Bonner, 1981), p. 137.

"I am delighted to receive such words of praise from my dear Spanish father. Pray tell, what does he want?" she asked the ambassador who had handed her the letter.

The Spanish ambassador cleared his throat. "Lady Margaret, it is about the lord of Belmonte."

Margaret stiffened. Juan Manuel, Lord of Belmonte, had caused her problems in the past. But she had not kept an eye on him in recent years. "What about him?"

"My sovereign wishes you to know that he has stirred up trouble for him, and speaks maliciously of you."

She felt her back prickle. She had distrusted Juan Manuel ever since he had bribed her servant to sway her to her brother's side when Philip had sought to have his wife declared unfit to rule Castile.

"What does the King of Aragon say he has done?" she asked.

"He is instigating support for Castile to revolt against Aragon."

Margaret was not surprised. She imagined Ferdinand would be as eager to put a stop to his activities as she was to quash her adversary Charles of Egmond's incessant aggressions on Gelderland's borders. "And what does your king wish me to do about it?" she asked.

"He wishes you to arrest him, Madame, and turn him over to him."

"That is a large request!" Margaret exclaimed. But she had ceased to trust Juan Manuel since the affair with her servant in 1505. There had been an older incident, too, one that dated back to 1495, when Juan Manuel had been sent to Maximilian by Isabella and Ferdinand to arrange for the double marriage of their son and daughter to Margaret and Philip. It was said that Juan Manuel had tried to bargain a higher dowry price in 1495 for Margaret to marry the Spanish infante. He had argued that she was of less value, since she had already been married by proxy to the French king. Margaret had been incensed when she heard of it years later.

"Madame, the King of Aragon thinks highly of you and knows you alone have the authority to do this. His relations with your father and your nephew will be greatly improved with the man rendered powerless."

Weighing the idea, she sharpened her quill. "I will think on it," she finally said. She had wanted to be free of Juan Manuel for some time. The man was always up to something. If he was inciting Castilians against Aragon, he might incite them against her nephew's rule over Spain once Ferdinand was gone. And, finally, she could pay him back for the double hurt he had inflicted upon her. As for whatever malicious words he had spoken against her, it was time to put an end to his wagging tongue, besmirching her reputation.

Margaret pushed back from her desk and stood. She would act on Ferdinand's request.

JUST AFTER THE CHRISTMAS holidays she made her move. Under her authority as Governor of the Netherlands she arrested Juan Manuel de la Cerda, Lord of Belmonte, along with two other Castilian nationalists on charges of inciting sedition, and had them sent to Vilvoorde prison, midway between Malines and Brussels. As soon as arrangements could be made, she planned to return them to Spain and into Ferdinand's custody.

Two days later a contingent of the highest-ranking members of the Burgundian nobility visited her at the Court of Savoy, her nephew included.

"Madame, you have overstepped your authority with the arrest of the Lord of Belmonte," Charles addressed her, drawing himself up to his full height. At not quite fourteen years old he was slight, still a boy. But the stern look on his face belonged to a man. William de Croy stood behind him, along with others, her military captain among them, all of the highest echelon of Burgundian nobles.

"As Governor of the Netherlands, Monsieur, I have full authority to arrest any in our domain who incite sedition," Margaret told Charles brusquely. What cheek for the boy she had raised to tell her she had overstepped her authority.

"Madame, in the case of the Lord of Belmonte, your jurisdiction does not hold," Charles retorted, his face a stone mask.

Margaret felt herself redden. Never had she heard her nephew use such a cold tone toward her. And since when had his voice deepened? It was as if he had turned into a stranger overnight.

"Of course it does," she shot back. "What do you say?"

"The Lord of Belmonte belongs to the Order of the Golden Fleece and may only be judged by knights of our order," her nephew intoned. "We ask you to deliver him to us so that we may weigh his actions and proceed accordingly."

Margaret's temper flared. "You do not mean to say that you intend me to abrogate the laws of this land to hand over a criminal just because he is a member of your order," she exclaimed.

"Madame, the order is a sacred trust founded by our ancestor, Philip the Good, and presided over by the Holy Roman Emperor. It is not in your hands to imprison one of our members," Charles continued.

"Of course it is in my hands. I have and I will continue to use my authority to try anyone who breaks the laws of this land in a court of law under my jurisdiction," she argued. Flustered, she felt her control crumbling. Never had she heard her nephew speak to her so harshly. It was especially galling, as he was questioning her authority in front of men she must maintain it before in council meetings.

"Madame, we cannot condone you breaking the statutes of our order," Henry of Nassau put in.

Margaret lost her temper. "If I were such a man as I am a woman, I would make you bring your statutes to me and have you sing out passages from them!"

"We will inveigh upon the emperor to release him into custody of the order," Charles responded coolly, as his fellow Golden Fleece members glared daggers at her.

Margaret rapped her knuckles on the table. "And I will inveigh upon the emperor to have my authority upheld."

"Madame, we ask you for the final time to release him into our custody," Charles' chief advisor, Chièvres, spoke up.

"He stays where he is until we get this sorted out," Margaret barked.

With baleful glares the men departed, leaving her astonished and unsettled. Never before had her nephew stood up to her in such a way. Clearly, he was under the influence of his Golden Fleece confrères. Not having been invited to join their male-only order, she had rarely given it a thought. What rot that she should hand over a legal prisoner for the sake of the pride of its members.

"What did I do, other than my job?" she exclaimed as her counselor entered the room.

Gattinara's smile was rueful. "You stepped on the toes of the most elite group of knights in Europe."

"They stepped on mine to ask me to hand over a prisoner arrested under my authority," she protested.

"Your father will need to sort it out."

"This is my domain, and I will sort it out myself."

"Madame, you do not know what you are up against. You will never hear the end of it if you do not cede them something."

Margaret pondered. If she conceded, she would look weak before her countrymen. "Until I hear from the emperor, I will keep Juan Manuel under lock and key in Vilgoorde instead of sending him to Spain," she concluded.

"Very good, Madame. I will let them know before they make further trouble for you."

"And the emperor will uphold my position," she asserted.

Gattinara looked doubtful. "Madame, the emperor is the Grand Master of their order," he reminded her.

"What bosh." Margaret threw her quill on her desk. And how is it you know that?"

"It is something that noblemen of this realm aspire to and women don't concern themselves with."

"That is true. I don't care about such orders in the least."

"But you need to know how highly the men on your council do."

Margaret slammed shut the book of legal statutes on her desk. "They must abide by the law of the land, and by my authority as governor of it."

"Madame, I urge you to show flexibility before you lose their support."

Margaret pointed to the door where the men had just exited. "It is their job to support me!"

"Then do not step on their toes overmuch."

"I should like to stamp on all of their precious toes," she railed.

"Madame, I am glad you are not a man, for if you were, you would be called Margaret the Rash at this moment, after your grandfather."

"I think not," Margaret huffed.

"Then school yourself and write to the emperor. Whatever you do, don't offer abroad your opinion on what you think of the Knights of the Golden Fleece," Gattinara advised, giving her a sympathetic look.

FURTHER TROUBLE ENSUED. IN January 1514, Maximilian's response to Margaret's letter was that if Juan Manuel committed a crime punishable by law she was within her rights to arrest him. Otherwise, it would be enough to banish him from court.

Therein lay the rub. While Margaret set her team of legal advisors to work preparing the case against Juan Manuel, Charles came again with two Golden Fleece members. This time they complained that it was Margaret herself who was trampling on the laws of the land by not abiding by their order's statutes.

Margaret stared at her nephew, suddenly grown up and defying her. She could not tell him what she really thought of him and his order in the presence of his fellow knights. Instead, she repeated what Gattinara had already informed them, that she would not transport the prisoner to Spain until his case was tried in the Netherlands and she had heard from the emperor.

Gattinara reported back to her on what happened next. In February a joint letter by the irate knights was sent to Maximilian, complaining that the governor had not handed over the prisoner, as requested.

Maximilian had not replied, hoping to dodge the issue. Another letter was sent in March with signatures from every one of the Burgundian Knights of the Golden Fleece, the Archduke Charles' at the top.

Maximilian sent his response to Margaret instead of the knights, directing her to release Juan Manuel from prison and send him to Vienna, so he could judge the case himself. It was an equitable solution, saving face for both Margaret and for the Knights of the Golden Fleece.

Margaret told her nephew and his cronies that she would obey the emperor in his capacity as the one who appointed her Regent of her nephew and Governor of the Netherlands. She would have the prisoner transported to Vienna under armed escort. As for Maximilian's role as Grand Master of their order, that was not her affair.

By the end of April Margaret had dispatched Juan Manuel from the Low Countries and sent him under guard to Maximilian.

But damage had been done. Trying to repair her relationship with her nephew, she saw that he was no longer willing to follow her counsel, as he had as a boy. He was now being advised by fellow Knights of the Golden Fleece, whom she had thoughtlessly insulted.

Telling herself it would blow over, she turned to the English alliance she had devoted so many years to cultivating. Charles would come of age in less than a year, and she needed him to follow through on plans to marry the English king's sister.

WITHIN TWO MONTHS ANNE Brandon arrived at Margaret's court. With her came two others. A note from Charles Brandon introduced the youngest of the trio as Magdalen Rochester. He wrote to say that he had saved Magdalen from drowning at the age of eight and had taken an interest in her future ever since. The daughter of an Englishman from Calais, he could think of no higher placement for her than serving at the court of Europe's most illustrious princess. Would she include Magdalen amongst her demoiselles?

Refolding the note Margaret tried to fold up the muddle of emotions she felt to read Brandon's words. She didn't trust him, but she would take the girls into her household. Perhaps she could train them in correct deportment in place of the untamable man who sent them.

The third English girl was also named Anne—the younger daughter of Thomas Boleyn, an Englishman who had served as ambassador to the Low Countries the year before.

Margaret set the girls to work on improving their French and learning the nuances of court life. She was happy to host them, for the bonds they made would strengthen Low Countries' ties with England. All three showed promise: Anne Brandon with a quiet grace so unlike her father's brash charm that Margaret could scarcely see a resemblance, and Magdalen Rochester with a steady character and loyal nature.

As for the third demoiselle, she soon stood out from the others. Anne Boleyn exhibited a lightning-quick wit and catlike charm that was far beyond her young years. Margaret guessed that she had inherited her father's ambition, for Thomas Boleyn was on his way up in Henry VIII's inner circle, just as Brandon was.

On Valentine's Day 1514, the English king's envoy, Richard Wingfield, arrived.

"What brings you to our court, Sir Richard?" Margaret asked.

"Madame, I have a letter from my sovereign for you as well as news of his esteemed courtier whom you met in Tournai."

Margaret hid her face by straightening a painting on the wall. "And what is that?"

"The Viscount Lisle has been awarded one of England's three dukedoms. He is now Duke of Suffolk."

"My, what favor he has found with the king," she remarked. Did Charles Brandon not know that a fast rise ensured fast enemies? How might Thomas Howard, Duke of Norfolk, and Edward Stafford, Duke of Buckingham and a descendant of Edward III of England, feel to find the son of a yeoman joining their ranks?

"Indeed, Madame. And here is the king's missive for you, a most pleasant duty to discharge on Valentine's Day." Sir Richard pulled a sealed envelope from his dossier.

Opening it, Margaret read the short note extolling her virtues and asking for a date to be set for the marriage of the Princess Mary to the Prince of Castile, Archduke of Austria, Duke of Burgundy and Lord of the Netherlands, now that he was about to turn fourteen.

"I see that your king is eager for the match to move forward between my nephew and his sister," Margaret observed. It would take months of haggling over funds to accompany the bride before her father would commit to a date.

"My sovereign is eager for consummation to take place within eighty days of the archduke's fourteenth birthday, as is stipulated in the proxy marriage agreement," Wingfield spelled out.

"As I am eager, too." Surprised, too, that Henry VIII was intent on keeping to the exact terms of the agreement. So much had happened since the proxy marriage at the end of 1508 that she had forgotten about the eighty-day clause.

"Could we set a date and place so preparations can begin for the Princess Mary to arrive?" Wingfield asked.

Margaret hesitated. "I would not wish to set a date before consulting with the emperor." A strange letter had arrived from Gattinara two days earlier. He had written that there had been three suns and three moons in the night sky of the evening before. She had consulted with her court physicians, schooled in astronomy, on what it might mean. Ever since, she had been troubled.

"Lady Margaret, my king has asked me to point out that eighty days after the archduke's birthday brings us to the middle of May. A fortuitous month for a wedding, is it not?" Wingfield asked.

Margaret shivered. The middle of May would mean three moons past the date the three moons had been seen in the night sky. It was just when an unexpected extraordinary event would be due. Could it be her nephew's marriage to the English princess? But there was nothing unexpected about it at all; they had been planning it for years. "Indeed it is, but much must be done. I fear it is too soon for the preparations needed," she hedged.

"Madame, the king is ready to move quickly. He is concerned that the emperor is not committing himself to an actual date and place."

Margaret was concerned, too. Whenever she sensed Maximilian was up to something, he usually was.

"I cannot speak for my father, but should the wedding take place in May I propose a location closer to us, as the princess will make her home with the archduke here in the Low Countries."

Wingfield nodded. "My king proposes Calais for the nuptials."

Margaret's heart leapt. Calais was English-held, due west from Malines. By hosting the wedding on English territory, Henry VIII would bear the brunt of the costs. Maximilian would be overjoyed.

"Calais is a possibility," she replied.

"We would need to know how many and of what rank would be in the archduke's party, the emperor's, and in yours."

Margaret motioned to her secretary to scribble down details of the envoy's requests. "That can be supplied."

"We would wish to know how many days' festivities to plan for, so that lodgings can be arranged."

"I will think on it and give you an answer by tomorrow," Margaret responded.

"The king will be pleased to hear this, and even more pleased to hear from the emperor that it will finally take place."

"I will write to him forthwith, as I'm sure your king has written to him."

"My king does not know his present whereabouts, my lady. We rely on you to reach him to get us a firm answer."

Margaret pursed her lips to prevent a laugh from escaping. A firm answer from the head of the House of Habsburg would be as extraordinary as three moons and three suns in the night sky. She would do her best to extract an answer, but it was not in Maximilian's nature to be pinned down to actual dates and places.

Her uneasy thoughts returned. Especially not if he was plotting another alliance behind her back. Why she thought he was, she couldn't say. But the portent Gattinara had seen in the night sky troubled her.

OVER THE NEXT FEW weeks, Maximilian's elusiveness was not the only resistance Margaret encountered on the impending nuptials.

"Good aunt, I am not ready to marry," Charles protested.

She eyed her nephew. "We are in contractual commitment to the English king for your wedding to take place within eighty days of your birthday," she explained.

"But I am to be fourteen, not twenty-four," he argued.

"You will be of an age to marry, and many a prince has married at age fourteen."

"Who?" Charles' stare was glum, his mouth hanging open as it frequently did.

"King Louis, my dear. He was fourteen, and his bride twelve, when he married the old king's daughter." It had been a disaster, ending in an annulment, but she wouldn't mention all that.

"And got rid of her years later to marry his queen who just died," Charles noted.

So he knew the story. "Ah! 'Tis a shame to have lost Queen Anne at such a young age," Margaret remarked. Anne of Brittany had passed from kidney stones the month before just short of her thirty-seventh birthday.

"The French king was no more ready to marry at fourteen than I am," Charles exclaimed, his usually sleepy eyes snapping at her.

Startled, she spotted dark blond down on her nephew's upper lip. The boy she had raised was becoming a man. One that resisted her. "That may be, but your grandfather and the English king have made an agreement. And you are the instrument to see it kept," she spelled out.

Charles raised his head and stuck out his long Habsburg jaw. "I am soon to be nobody's instrument. I will be fifteen next year and answerable to no one," he announced.

Stunned by his defiance, Margaret kept her tone light. "Ah, nephew, do you really think you will ever be answerable to no one?"

"Of course I will. I will rule in my own right, and will decide for myself when I am ready to marry."

"Charles, you will break your grandfather's heart if you do not go ahead with this wedding."

"Will I, *bonne tante*?" Charles met her gaze with a mature skepticism she had not witnessed before on his narrow face.

"Of course you will. I will have him write to you so that you know where your duty lies and see to it that it gets done."

"I will see to it that I am not to be bossed around when I come into my rule, good aunt. You have ever been my counselor, but now I am ready to take up my own counsel."

Alarm bells rang in Margaret's head. "Charles, no good ruler relies on just his own counsel. When Charles the Rash did, it ended badly for him. "

"He was a mighty ruler."

"He began as a mighty ruler and ended as a rash one," Margaret noted. "The burghers feared him, and he lost all sense of reason in the end."

"It is good to be feared so that one will be obeyed, *bonne tante*."

"It is good to be feared, but not to be hated. And that is what happened to your great-grandfather." She could gloss over the past. But it was imperative that her nephew learn from it rather than repeat it.

"How would you know?" Charles challenged. "You were not even born until after he died."

"Because when the burghers fight with me over taxes, they say they were taxed to death by Charles the Rash and will not allow themselves to be bled dry again."

"I will take over those fights from you in a year's time when I run the Council myself," Charles declared.

"My boy, you will see soon enough what I am up against."

"You said it yourself, aunt. I am still a boy, yet you push me into marriage with a princess old enough to be my mother."

Margaret glared at him. "Nonsense. She is only four years older than you."

A terrified look crossed Charles' face. "She could be a mother, then."

"That would be the idea, in time," Margaret agreed.

"Do I look as if I'm ready to be a father, Madame?"

Margaret offered an encouraging smile, but he was right. Her spindly nephew with his jutting jaw and serious eyes looked anything but ready to be either father or husband.

"You will be ready for the responsibilities fate has showered on you when the time comes," she reassured him.

Charles gave her a warning glance. "My first responsibility is to assume rulership of my realm."

Margaret started. It was her job he would take. "All in good time, nephew."

"All in one year's time, good aunt. And until I come into my own, I will not marry."

"But it is promised!"

"I am not a pawn to be moved about."

"You are a king about to make a princess your queen."

"I will wait until I truly am king. Until then, I am too young to marry."

"But Charles—"

"You can't have it both ways, aunt. You are regent until I'm fifteen, another year away. If I am too young to rule, then I am too young to marry."

"Who says?" Margaret struggled to keep the petulance from her voice.

Charles crossed his arms. "I say."

"You should listen to your aunt."

"I do, and I have made up my mind."

"You are too young to make up your own mind."

"Then I am too young to marry," Charles countered.

"We shall see what your grandfather says."

"I know what he will say," he replied mysteriously.

"What, then?"

"He will say nothing at all, and so I will not need to marry now."

"I—you—but..." Charles appeared to know Maximilian better than she had thought he did.

Seeing that she was stumped, Charles softened his tone. "Do not worry, good aunt. All shall be accomplished in time."

"But Princess Mary expects to marry now."

"If she is so eager to marry, let her marry someone else," the young Archduke retorted. With a curt bow, he turned and left the room.

Watching him go, Margaret shuddered. That was precisely what she feared might happen. And now that Anne of Brittany was dead, the King of France was on the market.

In early March, another letter from Henry VIII arrived. Quaking to read it, with as yet no word from Maximilian, she scanned its contents. Instead of any reference to his sister or her nephew, Henry VIII apologized for the rumors that had been spread about a possible marriage between her and the Duke of Suffolk.

"...we are trying in every way possible to know and understand from where this rumor comes and proceeds; and if we discover that it proceeds from this side, we will make such grievous punishment that all other inventors and sowers of lies will take example."[2]

Margaret was taken aback. Was the English king trying to assuage her hurt feelings in order to speed up Mary Tudor's wedding to her nephew? Or was Henry VIII making up with her so that she would be less offended when she learned he had made other plans for his sister?

Motioning to Lady Elisabeth, she asked her to find out what was being said around court about England's new Duke of Suffolk.

The following day her lady-in-waiting reported back.

"I overheard a few snippets, Madame. One in particular from Sire Erasmus."

"Pray tell." The word of Europe's most esteemed theologian counted for much by her.

"It is rather harsh, my lady."

---

2. Shirley Harrold Bonner, *Fortune, Misfortune, Fortifies One* (Shirley Harrold Bonner, 1981), p. 131.

"Out with it."

"I mentioned that the Duke of Suffolk has risen high in the English king's esteem."

"And what did he say to that?"

Lady Elisabeth's mouth twitched. "He said 'from a stableboy to a nobleman,' Madame."

"How was his tone?"

"Most disdainful, my lady."

Margaret's heart sank. "I see." So even Erasmus referred to the English king's newest duke as a stableboy.

"Did he say anything more?"

"Not about the Englishman. But he praised Princess Mary."

"Do tell."

"His words were 'Nature never formed anything more beautiful.'"

"Quite a compliment." And yet Europe's most beautiful princess was in danger of slipping from their grasp.

"Yes, my lady. Do you think the Archduke will marry her?"

Margaret stiffened. "Why do you think he would not?"

"No reason, my lady. Only that he is younger than her, and may not be ready to wed."

Margaret studied her lady-in-waiting. "Have you spoken to my nephew recently?"

"No, Madame. He is busy these days with Monsieur Chièvres and hides himself away."

"Then what makes you think he may not be ready to marry?"

Lady Elisabeth looked uncomfortable. "'Tis nothing, my lady."

"'Tis something. Speak frankly."

"It's something that some of the maids of honor say among themselves."

"And what is that?"

"That the young prince is shy, but longs for some experience before being married off."

"And who amongst my maids of honor has said such a thing?" Margaret probed.

"My lady, it is not just one. It is commonly spoken of amongst the demoiselles."

"Is there any one of them he favors?"

"Oh no, Madame. It is said that is precisely why he is not ready to marry."

"Because he does not like women?"

Lady Elisabeth giggled. "Oh no, Madame, it is not that he doesn't like them."

"Then what?"

Her lady-in-waiting paused. "It may be that he is afraid of them," she answered, the hint of a smile curling the ends of her mouth.

It was Margaret's turn to laugh. "Are they not all afraid of them at the moment they spring from boy to man?"

"Indeed they are, Madame. And our prince wishes to be ready when it is time to wed."

"Ready for what?"

"Ready to be lord of his wife and not the other way around." Her lady-in-waiting rolled her eyes.

Margaret sighed. "You have been frank. Thank you."

Lady Elisabeth curtseyed. "Is there anything else I can do, Madame?'

"Nothing more. You may go." There was nothing more anyone could do. Her biggest dream of an English alliance was slipping away; as were her feelings for a certain Englishman who was not a stableboy, but certainly not a gentleman.

14

ANNE BOLEYN

1514

IN LATE MARCH 1514, the Duke of Guelders attacked Arnhem in the north. Margaret was furious to hear he had broken the treaty she had made with him the summer before. Immediately, she sent him a stern reminder that their treaty stipulated four years of peace. Charles of Egmond withdrew, leaving behind only minor damages but lasting anxiety for the locals.

Writing to her father to let him know the attack had been quelled, she again turned to the more important topic.

> 'My lord, the eighty-day deadline bears down on us
> and still I have not heard from you on the intended
> wedding of your heir and the English king's sister.
> Any promises we have made to him should be kept.

If we do not abide by them, he may turn to other
alliances. I beseech you to act upon what we have
sought with the English before the moment slips a
way.'[1]

Maximilian's response dodged Margaret's request. Instead of answering, he rhapsodized over bagging a mountain goat on a recent
hunting trip, then closed by asking for his granddaughter Mary to be
sent to Vienna to prepare for her future marriage to the Hungarian
king's son, Louis. It was a reasonable request, but far from urgent,
as Mary of Habsburg was only eight.

Margaret crumpled the letter and tossed it to the floor. Surely, the
more pressing marriage was the one concerning the other Mary, of
England, regarding which the English envoy awaited an answer.

But in the past month Sir Richard Wingfield had ceased his visits.
Margaret feared the worst. Was Henry VIII making other plans for
his younger sister?

May came and went with no wedding taking place. Then in June
an unexpected event diverted Margaret's attention. Charles' next
youngest sister, Isabella, was promised to the King of Denmark,
as per negotiations of the year before. On Saturday, June 10, the
Danish ambassador arrived, requesting an immediate audience with
Margaret.

"What is it?" Margaret asked, alarmed that something had happened to thwart the proposed marriage. Her father counted on

---

1. Eleanor E. Tremayne, *The First Governess of the Netherlands*
(New York: G.P. Putnam's Sons, 1908), p. 133.

bringing the King of Denmark into the Habsburg fold. With three princesses to marry off, Maximilian was eager to get the first of them wed.

"Lady Margaret, my lord King Christian requests a marriage by proxy with the esteemed Princess Isabella to coincide with his upcoming coronation date," the Danish ambassador stated.

Relieved, Margaret smiled. At least some marriages amongst her charges were going ahead as planned. "'Tis a sound idea. When will his coronation take place?"

"'Twill be held in Copenhagen on Trinity Sunday, June 11."

Margaret's mouth fell open. "But that is tomorrow!"

The ambassador made a wry face. "My lady, I have just now received instructions from my sovereign to put in this request. He is eager to wed the princess on an auspicious day, so all of Denmark will celebrate the date in years ahead."

"I cannot possibly put together a wedding worthy of a princess of the House of Habsburg with just one day's notice," Margaret objected.

"Madame, I regret the lateness of this request, but the king has had much on his mind with preparations for the coronation. He intends to hold a splendid wedding ceremony in Copenhagen once the princess arrives."

Margaret eyed him disapprovingly. "I shall see what my niece says," she told him, although it didn't matter what Isabella would say, as she would decide. But she needed time to think.

"I shall be at your disposal tomorrow, Madame. It will be an honor to stand in for my lord king." The envoy bowed and left, his manner somewhat abashed at having made such an unreasonable request.

She had been through her own proxy marriage ceremony with the King of France long ago. It had no meaning unless followed up by a fully consummated marriage. But it was a step in the right direction, and it boded well that the Danish king wished his bride to have her own reason to celebrate on the anniversary of his coronation. With Maximilian pushing for the match it might be best to move full speed ahead.

Yet still, Margaret fumed. What cheek to offer only one day's notice. She hoped it wasn't a sign of Isabella's future husband's lack of consideration.

"*Bonne tante*, how will I ever get ready in just one day's time?" Isabella asked, surprise spread across her fine-boned features upon hearing the news.

"That is my concern, not yours. Madame de Beaumont will help you to dress, and my maids of honor will be your attendants."

"Oh, Madame, we cannot possibly get everything done in just one day!"

"Nonsense. Of course we can," Margaret insisted, although she thought the same. Scanning her niece's anxious face, she knew she must show no uncertainty so as to quell her worries.

"But my dress and my hair. So many decisions!" Isabella cried.

"You are marrying by proxy. There is no need to impress your future husband's ambassador. Save making a grand impression for when you meet your husband in person and have a proper wedding."

Isabella blushed. "He is very handsome in his portrait. I hope it is a good likeness."

"May he be as considerate as he is handsome," Margaret said, thinking of Philibert. He had been the same age as she, as ardent as he was devoted. But Christian of Denmark was twenty years older, and Margaret had heard rumors of his household being run by his mistress and mother. Isabella would be hard put to assume her rightful position as its head.

Troubled, Margaret surveyed the second-oldest of the three princesses she had raised. More delicate than either of her sisters, Isabella was sweet, biddable, and meek. It was likely she would be overrun by the more dominant personalities in her new husband's home.

"Will there be a reception tomorrow?" the princess asked.

"Of course, my dear." Setting aside her worries, Margaret trained her mind on one overriding goal—the match would extend the House of Habsburg's reach into yet another corner of Europe.

"With dancing?" Isabella pressed.

"With dancing and merrymaking. Now go tell your brother he is needed as your escort. Off with you!" With a hug and a reassuring smile, Margaret pushed her from the room. She had much to attend to.

The following day's ceremony went off well, with the bride and her proxy groom reciting their vows before the assembled court in the great hall of the Court of Savoy. A banquet followed with music and dancing.

"Thank you, *bonne tante*! I do not know how you arranged it all so fast, but I am enjoying my own wedding!" Isabella gasped, falling into a chair after a lively galliard with her brother.

"Brava, my dear. May you enjoy many more days ahead like this one," Margaret replied. *And may you enjoy your own marriage,* she thought, deciding that she would keep Isabella at home for another year before sending her off to Denmark.

At not quite thirteen, Isabella was too young to join her husband's household. Margaret worried if what she would find there might rival what had happened to her childhood friend Louise of Savoy, who had encountered two of her husband's favorites running his home when she arrived as a young bride. He had died when Louise was only nineteen and she had never remarried.

Margaret could guess why not. Louise must have been overjoyed to be her own mistress. How well she herself knew its satisfactions.

Her eyes roved over the dancers, thinking of her years of happiness in Pont d'Ain. There had been endless festivities, with Philibert leaping and spinning over the dance-floor, cavorting with the ladies, but with eyes that always returned to her.

With blissful memories melding with the scene before her she sipped the fine white Burgundy she had commandeered from the wine cellar. When her life's work was done—her nieces married off to Europe's princes to expand the House of Habsburg, and her nephew the ruler of Europe's largest realm—she would return to Savoy to take her rest beside her ever young and golden prince.

The following day Charles came down with a fever. Margaret was beside herself with worry. With phantoms lurking of her dead husbands, all of whom had left behind no children to carry on their line, she wrote to Maximilian describing the success of Isabella's hasty marriage ceremony, and only briefly alluding to Charles' fever. God knew her father would worry as much as she did the moment he read it.

At the children's palace across the street Madame de Beaumont tended to the young Archduke with sage and lemon verbena tisanes and cool lavender compresses, with Margaret visiting between council meetings. Within two days her relief knew no bounds to find that her nephew had recovered. All was well again in the two households facing each other on the Keizerstraat.

As summer deepened, she made her annual progress through her domains. Away in Zeeland, north of Flanders, she listened closely to the concerns of local council members. The refrain was familiar: Maintain peace to promote trade. Avoid war to avoid high taxes.

To achieve this goal she was determined to marry Charles to the English princess as soon as possible. It was the surest road to economic success in the Netherlands, with England's wool trade and her own realm's cloth industry interdependent upon each other.

"A messenger is here to see you, my lady," an attendant announced as dusk was settling.

"Where from?" she asked. Margaret and her counselor were enjoying a carafe of cool Rhenish wine as they watched the sunset on the North Sea coast facing England.

"From France, Madame."

Margaret bid him enter, recognizing him as the man she had placed at the French court to keep her abreast of what was brewing. She guessed he came with an update on the latest secret funding the French king was up to with her biggest domestic bedevilment, Charles of Egmond.

But Louis XII of France had been up to an even greater secret.

"What? It is not possible!" Margaret cried as the man gave his news.

"The English arrived on August 4th, my lady. A peace treaty was finalized on the 7th," he reported.

"What clauses?"

Her contact shifted. "Madame, there is one you will not like."

"I don't like any of it! How dare the English go behind our backs to make peace with France!" Margaret complained. Yet it was not just the English going behind her back. Her sources in Germany and Spain had reported that her father and Ferdinand had been going behind her back all summer to treat with France. Whatever happened, she could not afford the Anglo-Imperial alliance to fall through. Without favorable trade conditions with England, prosperity in the Netherlands would wither.

"My lady, it is said that the King of France is to marry the English king's sister," the man reported.

"Which sister?" Margaret asked.

"The Princess Mary, Madame."

She blanched. "That is impossible. She is to marry the Archduke!"

"Madame, the word is that they will wed by proxy next week. The princess will then travel to France, where they will meet in October."

"But the English are not in treaty alliance with France!" Margaret cried.

"They are now, Madame." Her agent bowed, waiting for further orders.

Margaret was speechless. Waving him out, she stared at Gattinara. "How could this be?" she exclaimed.

"Madame, you well know, as you have been the victim of such deceit yourself by the French."

"It is not the French who have deceived us. It is the English!"

Gattinara gave her a dry look. "Perhaps the English king tired of waiting for your father to make up his mind."

"We must get word to our envoy in London to find out what is happening."

A messenger was dispatched before the sun set. But before he could reach the English court another arrived from London confirming the news. The marriage had taken place on August 13 with the Duke of Longueville as proxy. Henry's tennis partner and prisoner, since the French nobleman's capture at the battle of Guinegate, had stood in for Louis XII at Mary Tudor's side.

"Marriage by proxy means nothing," Margaret sputtered.

Gattinara's mouth set in a grim line. "This one will probably go through."

"We must get word to my father!" Margaret cried.

"If he is treating with the French king himself, then he already knows."

Margaret stamped her foot. "Why was I left out of these plans?" she fumed, anger at the father she loved welling up alongside the sting of being hoodwinked by him.

"Madame, your father's concerns sometimes differ from yours for the Low Countries," Gattinara observed.

"But they are within his realm!"

"They are part of his realm, but without you to govern them the Estates would seek to throw him off, as they did before."

"It is the only way my burghers will submit to Habsburg rule." Well did she know the story of Maximilian's failures in the Low Countries in the years after her mother's death. The burghers of Ghent had not taken kindly to the foreign Habsburg prince's rule over their lands and had held him prisoner until they chased him out, declaring their loyalty only to the offspring of their native duchess.

"It could not be expected that the English king would sit idly by, waiting for the emperor to make up his mind," Gattinara noted.

Margaret threw up her hands. "And see what it has come to."

"You will steer through this, Madame. At least it's marriage and not war."

"You sound like my father," she huffed.

"No one could sound like your father. He is sui generis, is he not?"

She chuckled, the storm clouds scattering. "I do not know what to do with him."

Shaking his head, Gattinara gave her a merry look. "You are not alone."

Margaret locked eyes with her trusted friend. "And I don't know what I would do without you."

"Madame, I am here for you through thick and thin."

"Unlike my father," Margaret muttered.

"Let us drink to your health and to his," Gattinara suggested.

She narrowed her eyes. "Only to mine at the moment."

Gattinara raised his glass. "As you wish, my lady."

Margaret clinked her glass with his and took a moment to hurl silent invectives at her father. But as the sun sank into the North Sea, her anger sank with it. As usual Maxi had been up to tricks. But he and she stood for the same aim: increasing the glory of the House of Habsburg. She would work around his blunders because she loved him.

AT THE END OF August, Margaret returned to Malines to find a letter waiting for her from London. The English king's diplomat, Thomas Boleyn, was requesting an end to his daughter Anne's service at Margaret's court. He needed her to return home to prepare for a new position.

"What new appointment is this?" Margaret asked Anne, although she could guess.

"My lady, I am to serve Princess Mary at the French court." The English demoiselle's raisin eyes flamed. She had sprung from girl to striking young woman in the year she had served at the Court of Savoy.

Margaret's stomach churned. Of course. Unwittingly she had prepared her most promising maid of honor for a career at the French court, attending the woman who should have been her nephew's bride.

"And do you want to go?" Margaret asked.

"Everything I know, Madame, I have learned from you."

"That is not what I asked."

Anne cast down her eyes. "My lady, forgive me. But I wish to serve my king's sister as best I can."

"As you would have here, if she had wed my nephew."

"Oh, Madame, I am sorry it did not come about, but perhaps the Archduke is still too young for marriage."

"Why do you say so?" Margaret asked, remembering Lady Elisabeth's words.

The dark-haired girl raised eyes that danced with an allure beyond her years. "Because he is close to me in age and I am sure I do not wish to marry yet."

The message was clear. Her nephew was still too young in mind and body to wed, and no amount of pressure she put on him would change that fact. "Then go, and sparkle there as you have sparkled here," Margaret bade her.

"Thank you, Madame, for teaching me all that has polished me. I will never forget you, nor your lessons." The girl curtseyed, as demure a maid as Margaret knew her not to be, with her sharp wit and uncanny charm.

She nodded, waving her promising demoiselle out. Anne Boleyn had shone at her court. No doubt she would shine at courts beyond.

THAT AUTUMN, EVENTS TOOK place that Margaret had hoped would not come to fruition. Louis XII married Mary Tudor on October 9, 1514. The following month she was crowned Queen of France. All of Europe waited with bated breath to see if the nubile nineteen-year-old would gift the French king with the son he had longed for his entire life.

Margaret was angry with Wolsey, who she suspected had engineered the whole affair. But her displeasure was nothing compared to what she imagined her former sister-in-law must feel. Should the new Queen of France produce a son and heir, Louise of Savoy's son—Francis d'Angoulême—would be shouldered aside for the French throne, destroying her hopes for his future.

"Is the dauphin's mother worried that the queen will become pregnant?" Margaret asked her contact from the French court.

"My lady, it is worse than that for Madame Louise," the man replied.

"What do you mean?"

"It is not just that she worries the queen will beget a son with the king. It is said that the dauphin himself is in danger of losing his own position by his closeness to the queen."

Margaret gaped. "How close do you mean?"

"He can barely be kept from her side when she is not with the king."

"Good God, does he not realize the danger of what might happen if he seduced her?"

"He is young, Madame, and thinks of nothing but the moment at hand."

How unlike my nephew, Margaret mused. "His mother must be beside herself," she exclaimed.

"So she is, Madame. She thinks of everything that the dauphin does not. They say she has spies watching him to ensure he is never alone with the queen."

"Go back and keep your eyes and ears open. 'Tis a light assignment I give you this time."

The man chuckled. "Thank you, Lady Margaret. I will be back with the latest before Christmas."

Upon his return, the gay tone of goings-on at the French court had darkened. "The King of France is crippled by gout, Madame, and spends much of his time in bed," her contact reported.

"I hope that doesn't mean his dauphin spends time in bed, too, with his queen," Margaret jested, imagining her former sister-in-law's terror at a possible pregnancy ensuing.

"No, Madame. The queen's time is taken up comforting the king. She sings to him and plays the lute. Or does needlework at his side."

Margaret shook her head. "Not much fun for a newly-wed bride."

"She manages all with a smile on her face and a cheerful demeanor. The entire court is enchanted by her."

"The dauphin, too?"

"Especially the dauphin. But he is closely watched by those his mother has enlisted to keep him out of trouble."

Margaret laughed. "I hope he will run his country better than he feeds his passions," she quipped.

"They say, Madame, that if he ascends the throne 'twill be his mother running France while he runs after skirts." The agent's eyes twinkled.

Margaret stifled a snort. Despite her anger with Louis for stealing her nephew's intended bride, she felt sorry for him. Finally given a chance to beget a son, France's king was too ill to accomplish the deed.

She felt sorrier still in the second week of January when dark tidings came.

Louis XII of France had died the first day of January, at age fifty-two. Francis I was now King of France, and his mother, Louise of Savoy, the power behind the throne. The queen had been sequestered for forty days while all of Europe waited to learn if she was pregnant.

Margaret hid a grim smile. What agonies Louise de Savoy must be going through, on tenterhooks until Mary Tudor's flowers arrived.

But arrive they did, and two months later Mary Tudor returned to England. She was escorted home by the Duke of Suffolk.

"Was her dowry returned?" Margaret asked her man.

"It is said that it was, and her dowry revenues guaranteed by the new king."

"Is he still besotted with her?"

"He is, Madame, but she is already taken."

Margaret raised a brow. "What do you mean?"

"It is reported that she married the Duke of Suffolk in Paris before starting her journey home."

Feeling as if the floor had dropped out beneath her, Margaret stared at the man. "You must be joking," she choked out.

"I am not, Madame. It is said that King Francis was witness to the ceremony. He supported her choice, so as to take her off the marriage market before she got back to England and her brother forced a new dynastic marriage on her that might threaten France."

"Do you say it was her choice to marry that—that—"

Her contact looked amused. "That stable boy, you mean?"

"I mean the king's close friend," she replied, her stomach roiling. Thank God she hadn't married him herself. It was bad enough that rumors had wafted all over Europe of their dalliance.

"It is said that it was she who asked him to marry her."

"Whyever for?" Margaret examined a snagged fingernail.

"They say she was in love with him before leaving for France to marry the French king."

"And was he with her?" The moment she asked, she regretted she had.

"Madame, the Duke of Suffolk is in love with ambition. Any lady who leads him farther up the ladder of success would be of interest to him."

"And who says that?" Margaret shifted, squelching the white-hot twinge of envy for Brandon's new wife that shot through her. Well could she understand Mary Tudor's reasoning, for she had possessed it herself. It was reason born of the heart and not the head.

"All who know anything of the duke say so, Madame. And now the king is angered with them both, since he wished to marry her off to another prince."

"Instead of his best friend."

"Yes. But they say that Mary Tudor didn't want to wed the King of France and only agreed if the English king promised to let her marry a husband of her own choosing once the French king died."

"I hope she finds happiness with him," Margaret lied. It was all she could do not to throw her glass goblet at the imagined head of the man she had once allowed too close to her heart.

"Yes, although my wife says it's quite a comedown for a former queen to marry the king's master of the horse," the man remarked.

"Umm," Margaret murmured, waving him out. Not only a comedown, but a scandal. The Dowager Queen of France had married the most ambitious stableboy in all of Christendom. Tongues would be set afire across Europe's courts. In a swirl of emotion, she prayed her own name wouldn't come up, although she knew it would.

Over the next few days, Margaret wrestled with the unpleasant truth that the man who had fueled rumors that he might marry her had been consorting with Mary Tudor at the same time.

Cad. Rogue. Knave. No matter what term she assigned him, they all left a metallic taste in her mouth. Trying to take satisfaction in having eluded the snares of a scoundrel, she felt stung to the quick instead.

Mary Tudor had not only jilted her nephew but had won the prize that she had secretly hankered after herself.

Anne Boleyn, c. 1533-36
By Hans Holbein the Younger
Metropolitan Museum of Art, New York
Lent by Her Majesty Queen Elizabeth II
for the 2022 Met Tudor Exhibit, photo by R. Gaston

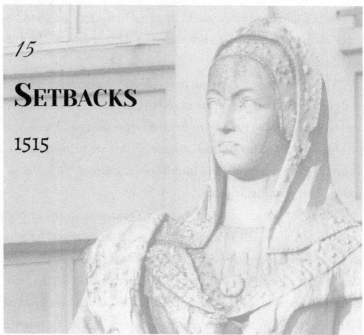

15

SETBACKS

1515

ON JANUARY 8, 1515, Margaret was summoned to attend an address by her nephew in Brussels. It was usually she who called the twice-weekly Council of State meetings, but the young archduke had convoked this assembly himself. Miffed that he had not told her privately what this was about, she steeled herself for changes ahead. Her nephew would reach his majority that year. What that meant for her role as governor remained to be seen. Three days earlier, Maximilian had proclaimed his grandson Charles ruler of the Low Countries in anticipation of his fifteenth birthday on February 24. The following day, the Estates-General in Brussels ratified Maximilian's proclamation recognizing Charles' emancipation, and the Netherlands celebrated their native prince's ascendancy to the ducal seat of Burgundy.

What adjustments this would bring to Margaret's position became clear as she listened to her nephew's short speech to the Burgundian nobles.

"Very dear and well beloved, it has pleased the emperor my lord and grandfather, to emancipate us and free us from his guardianship and regency, placing the government of our country and lordships on this side in our hands, and consenting that we be received and sworn to the principality and lordship of the same,"[1] Charles intoned in his new, manly voice.

The rest of the short speech blurred as she took in the import of her nephew's words. Without mentioning her by name, Charles in effect had done away with her position as regent of the Low Countries. Her nephew had grasped the reins of rulership himself. She could guess that his closest advisor, William de Croy, Lord of Chièvres, had counseled him that he was now entitled to rule the Netherlands, and no longer needed his aunt to do the job.

Stiff as a stone, she sat through the rest of the stinging speech that ended her position. To distract herself from her shock she mentally prepared a few words to say when Charles thanked her before the assembly for her years of service.

But that moment never came. Her nephew drew the meeting to a close without mentioning her at all.

With her features frozen into a dignified smile Margaret rose to greet her colleagues. She was numb with pain.

OVER THE NEXT FEW weeks Margaret was advised that Council of State meetings would be held in Brussels, no longer at the Court of Savoy in Malines. She was not informed of meeting dates, nor was she invited to attend. Her presence would no longer be needed, as Charles would head the council himself. Simply put, she had been dropped from the government of the Burgundian-Habsburg Netherlands.

Summoning her contacts, she pieced together what had happened that had motivated her father to hand over her position to his grandson without so much as a word to her.

The explanation turned out to be simple: money had been offered and Maximilian needed money.

The December before, under the influence of Chièvres, the Estates-General of the Netherlands had called for Maximilian to put Charles of Habsburg in charge of its government. Furthermore, they called for the rights of its present governor, the Lady Margaret, to be revoked, offering a sizeable payment of 140,000 florins to be paid to Maximilian for the emancipation of the archduke in light of his upcoming fifteenth birthday. A pension of 50,0000 florins was voted on for Margaret for services rendered as governor and regent during Charles' minority. All this had taken place at a meeting in Brussels to which she had not been invited.

Without a word to her, Maximilian had accepted a payoff to revoke her role as governor. She had been retired from her position without being informed. Apparently, the Knights of the Golden Fleece had not forgotten her insult to them of the year before.

Margaret was furious. Not to be consulted at all on the revocation of her role as Governor of the Netherlands was more than she could bear. She didn't know who to be most angry with: her nephew's chief counselor—the French-loving Chièvres—her father, or her nephew himself.

"It seems I have been put out to pasture," Margaret complained to the English ambassador. She had become close to Richard Wingfield despite the botched marriage arrangements between her nephew and Mary Tudor. England's economic interests were too aligned with the Netherlands to let slip an important relationship. And the more the Lord of Chièvres nudged her nephew toward the French, the more determined Margaret was to deepen ties with the English.

"Madame, the wheel turns and our fortunes go up, then down. I am sure yours will rise again," Wingfield assured her.

"I'm glad you are sure, but I am not. How dare my own family go behind my back to take my position from me?" she railed.

"Madame, it has always been understood that you served as governor in the minority of your nephew. Now that he has come of age, is it not reasonable that he would wish to take the reins himself?"

"Without consulting me first?" Margaret huffed.

"Lady Margaret, may I be frank?"

She glared at him. "Do. No one else has been frank with me at all, beginning with my own family."

"Madame, they did not consult you on this because they knew you would not wish to step down from your position."

Margaret threw up her hands. "Why should I? Have I not done a good job?" she exclaimed.

"You have done a magnificent job, but put yourself in the shoes of a fifteen-year-old prince who has just come of age."

"I am hard put to do so, as I have no sons of my own and I am not a man."

"Madame, every boy seeks to seize power once he comes into manhood. Think of England's Henry II and his son, the young king."

"The one who died early?" Margaret asked, remembering something had gone wrong with Henry II's heir by Eleanor of Aquitaine.

"Yes. The Plantagenet king crowned him, but gave him no authority. The young king hated his father as a result."

"Henry didn't do well with his sons, did he? They all seemed to hate him." She was angry with her nephew, but she could never hate him. Nor could she hate her father, that haphazard, foolish man who had not realized that by removing her from power he had weakened his own hold over the Netherlands. Chièvres would steer Charles toward the French, who would be only too happy to incite the Netherlanders to throw off Habsburg authority.

"My lady, Henry II did not understand the thinking of a young man, although he had once been one himself," Wingfield related.

Margaret raised a brow. "And you are an expert?"

"I am the eleventh of twelve brothers. They are all difficult at age fifteen. Believe me, Madame, the struggle between a boy and his father at that age is far worse than one between a boy and his mother."

"Or his aunt." She crossed her arms to hold in the hurt.

"I can tell you what is likely to happen, Madame, if you care to hear my thoughts."

"Prophesy away, Sir Wingfield." Margaret glanced at the hunting tapestry on the wall. Was she the wounded stag she saw there, just delivered a mortal blow?

"The archduke will take over governorship of the Netherlands and realize in a short time what a difficult job he has on his hands."

"Of course he will. Can you image how trying it is to find consensus with counselors of seventeen different provinces, then have to constantly deal with that bandit, Egmond?" she exclaimed.

"I cannot imagine, Madame. Which is why all of Europe admires you. None would envy you your job."

"Well, it's mine no more. Charles' problem, not mine." Why were all the men in her life who had made trouble for her named Charles? First there had been Charles VIII of France, who had jilted her, then Charles III of Savoy, who had opposed her plans to build the church at Brou, then Charles of Egmond, who year after year attacked her lands, then Charles Brandon, whose phantom stalked her on sleepless nights. Now the latest Charles to hurt her was the boy she had loved and raised to manhood. *Fie upon the lot of them,* she told herself, her heart aching at thought of the last two.

"The young archduke will tire of his troubles as Lord of the Netherlands soon enough," Wingfield speculated. "And once he becomes King of Spain, he will look for someone to govern the Low Countries in his place. Who do you think he will pick?"

"If he picks the Lord of Chièvres he may as well hand over the Netherlands to France," Margaret spat out.

Wingfield drew his chair closer. "Here is where what you do next is important."

Margaret bent her head towards his. "How so?" She had always thought most of what she did in the public eye was important. How galling to find herself demoted to a person of no importance, when she had prided herself on a job well done.

Wingfield looked her in the eye. "Act as if nothing has changed."

"But all has changed," Margaret protested, then felt Anne of Brittany's words waft to her from across the mists of time: '*When circumstances change, don't change with them.*'

"You still retain a seat on the council."

"But with no vote," she fumed.

"Makes no matter. Everyone seeking influence or wishing to sway a vote will come to you, just as they always have."

"Why would they? I have no power anymore."

"Wrong, Madame, if I may say so. Your power lies in knowing all the players. It is a position no one else occupies."

Margaret eyed him bitterly. "I am to be a go-between for others who retain power, when I have lost mine?"

"You have lost your position. Not your power. Think of the wheel. You are up today, down tomorrow. How many times have I faced you at cards when you bluffed having a stellar hand?"

A snort escaped her. "I have much practice in such matters." It was the first merry thought she had had in days.

"Carry on as if nothing has changed and the world will continue coming to you for advice and direction. And when your nephew is called to Spain he is likely to leave the Netherlands again in your charge."

"What if he hands it over to Chièvres?" The thought sickened her.

"You will see to it that Chièvres accompanies him to Spain," Wingfield spelled out. "Do you not think your nephew will need his chief counselor there?"

"Most likely." She had brought Gattinara with her from Savoy. It stood to reason Charles would bring his most trusted advisor with him to Spain.

Wingfield slapped the arm of his chair. "Then who do you think that leaves to rule the Netherlands in his absence?"

Margaret sniffed. "If only affairs play out as you foresee."

"There is one thing you can do now that will aid such a scenario in coming to pass," Wingfield said.

"What is that?"

"Conceal your anger. Hide your disappointment. Maintain your sangfroid and you will continue to be sought out."

"With no vote." Margaret's tone was acid.

"Forget the vote for now. In time, it will become clear to your nephew that all turn to you for advice. Soon enough he will turn to you, too, if you have not angered him or shown a bitter face."

"It is hard to dissemble so well and for so long."

Wingfield sat back, a smile breaking out on his face. "Ah, Lady Margaret, you do not fool me. I have played cards with you many an evening, and you are the master of us all. You are a person of expertise who knows the problems of each of the Netherlands' provinces as well as you know the minds of every one of Europe's princes. Soon your nephew will see that you were the one for the job all along."

"I hope you are right, Sir Wingfield."

"Only you decide if I am right. You either convince them that you are the one best-suited to govern the Netherlands, or not."

"Of course I am." What an outrage that any might question her competence. Then it struck her that this was not about her own record. This was about a fifteen-year-old prince proving his abilities to rule. She was in her nephew's way, for the moment. If she stepped aside without rancor, he would feel comfortable bringing her back. Or not. Either way, she would save face by maintaining her dignity.

"And soon enough, those who voted you out of office will realize they are worse off without you than with you and bring you back."

Margaret felt the first rays of sun warming her since her cold dismissal. "Sir Wingfield, you have done me a world of good. Come back this evening and we shall have a game of cards," she bade him.

"I will be honored, my lady. And if once again I lose, it will be no shame to lose against so great a player as you."

The Card Players
Lucas van Leyden, c. 1520
Museum of Fine Arts, Budapest, Hungary
From www.pixels.com

The Card Players
(identified as Charles V, Margaret of Austria, Thomas Wolsey)
Lucas van Leyden, c. 1520
Museo Thyssen-Bornemisza, Madrid, Spain
From Fine Art America

The following day, Margaret met with Gattinara at their usual time of nine in the morning.

"I have been tossed aside," she huffed, coming straight to the point.

"You have not been tossed aside, my lady, so much as your nephew is ready to step up to his duties," Gattinara replied, echoing Wingfield's words.

"Then what am I supposed to do now?" Her twice-weekly two o'clock council meetings had been taken over by Charles, throwing off the rhythm of her days.

"You will accompany him on his joyous entries, so he sees the good rapport his subjects have with you," her counselor advised.

"I have spent eight years building that rapport, striving for peace and keeping taxes low despite my father's endless requests to fund his wars." Margaret looked daggers at Gattinara, wishing he was Maxi instead.

"I know it, Madame. And as you and your nephew journey from town to town, you will inform him of each of their privileges and grievances."

"'Twill be an education for him to see what I go through to keep unity," Margaret griped.

"You will show him how to present himself to his people, so they bond with him in a way they never did with your father."

"They will never see my father as anything but an outsider. When my mother died, they put their trust in Philip, then me, as her descendants."

"And now a native prince rises to rule them again. Who better than you, a Princess of Burgundy, to present him to your people as your successor?"

"Their princess forever, but no longer their governor," Margaret grumbled.

"Ah, Lady Margaret, Charles takes your place now; but soon enough he will be called to Spain to assume his duties there. Once he sees how well-regarded you are by the people of your realm he will know there is only one person like himself, with native blood in her veins, whose authority the people of the Low Countries will accept in his absence."

Heartened, Margaret thought of Sir Wingfield's similar counsel. "Then I am ready to accompany my nephew," she acceded.

"You will make good cheer, and soon enough you will feel good cheer in your heart."

"I doubt that, Sire Gattinara."

"Count on it, Madame. Reap the reward of eight years of labor and rest a moment. Soon enough, more will be placed upon your shoulders."

Margaret reached out and adjusted the frame of her grandfather's portrait, askew on the wall. She frowned at the limp sheep hanging from Charles the Rash's necklace, insignia of the insufferable order whose members had taken her down. "I don't like having nothing to do," she complained.

"Madame, I remember our days in Savoy. You have not spent a single day of your life without putting your mind to a task at hand."

At mention of Savoy memories of carefree days with Philibert flooded her. "I did, Monsieur, when my lord was alive. But those days were numbered and few."

"You were blessed with a lord and prince, Madame, who delighted in your abilities, and gladly handed over responsibilities to you."

"Once blessed, but not now," Margaret burst out.

"You were once blessed, and you will be again. Show your nephew your prowess, and I assure you he will hand over responsibility to you again. Just be patient."

Margaret pursed her lips as she restlessly scanned her receiving room. Van Eyck's painting of the Arnolfini wedding that her courtier Don Diego de Guevara had given her hung too close to less important works. She had been meaning to have it rehung in her bedchamber for months. Finally, she had time to get it done.

The Wedding of John Arnolfini and Joan Cenani of Lucca
By Jan Van Eyck, 1434
National Gallery, London
Photo by Gennadii Saus i Segura

THAT FEBRUARY 1515, MARGARET set off on progress with Charles. Making joyous entries in Malines, Ghent, Bruges, and Antwerp, they would continue on to the northern cities of Bergen-op-Zoom, Delft, Den Haag, Haarlem, Leiden, and Amsterdam. In each town Margaret privately coached her nephew in the specific privileges agreed upon then watched as Charles, in a public ceremony, vowed to respect them, after which the townspeople swore loyalty to him.

"*Bonne tante*, it is a different situation in each town we visit. How did you ever keep track of it all?" Charles asked at the end of the day as they retreated to their quarters in Bruges.

"I kept a dossier on each province and engaged a contact in each town to tell me what the people desire and dislike," Margaret told him, pleased that Charles sought her counsel.

"Are all seventeen provinces different?" her nephew asked.

"They are all different in how you must present yourself," Margaret explained.

Charles rolled his eyes, tossing off his feathered hat and reaching for a handful of sugared almonds. "How will I remember all this?"

"Just remember to reflect back to the people what you see from them yourself."

Her nephew's eyes widened. "What do you mean?"

"Malines and Brussels are always loyal. Do nothing and they will love you. Ghent and Bruges are prosperous and proud. You must show them Burgundian splendor, but allow them some independence while making them puff with pride as you praise their history."

"What about Antwerp?" he asked.

"Less proud, but most up and coming of all. Promise them increased trade, and marvel at how far they have come so fast. The people will love you for your praise, especially if you compare them favorably with snobbish Ghent and Bruges."

Charles nodded as he sipped his ale. "What about farther north?" he asked.

"There you must rein in lavish displays," Margaret counseled, making note that she must also rein herself in by not dominating her nephew. But it was hard to hold back advice when she knew there was only one chance to make a first impression. Charles must make a good one.

"*Bonne tante*, I am not one for lavish displays."

Margaret smiled, resisting the urge to reach out and ruffle her nephew's hair. Those days were over. "No, you are not, my lord, but some in our entourage are, so we must ensure that our entry is more modest than our joyous entries farther south. Holland's towns of Amsterdam, Delft, and the others will think we are wasting their hard-earned taxes if we appear in the full splendor our ancestors are known for. We must present ourselves as sober rulers intent on increasing Holland's fishing and shipping interests over their North-German competitors."

Charles groaned. "I will never remember all this."

"I will be at your side, nephew. You have the right demeanor to win them over. Just nod wisely and keep your mouth shut, unless it is open to agree with whatever the city leaders ask for," she encouraged.

Charles lifted his narrow face, his jaw jutting out even farther than usual. "But what if I don't agree?"

"This is their first introduction to you. Make it go well, and when you are back in Brussels you can find a way to knock back their demands by getting their own local councils to vote them down. All of the provinces hate spending money. Once they see that what they ask for will cost them, they will vote against it themselves."

Her nephew sighed. "Good aunt, it all sounds such a game."

"It is somewhat a game. One that you will play well, as you think first and do not say too much when you speak."

"Sometimes I am not thinking at all, just listening," Charles confessed.

"To listen is a good thing, my lord. I have found that our people want to know we are listening to them, whether we can give them what they want or not. Our subjects are bound by love of commerce, and if we can offer them favorable trade agreements, low taxes and peace, they will be content with our rule."

"And what if they are not?"

"We must avoid war and civil conflict at all costs, for it destroys business. If there are differences, we must seek consensus," Margaret counseled.

Charles face looked glum. "It is not the way of a mighty ruler."

"It is the way of a ruler of the age we live in."

"I do not know what you mean," Charles said.

"A mighty ruler of this age knows his subjects submit to his authority because he shows them he cares to safeguard their interests."

"I do, *bonne tante*, but what if all seventeen of my provinces have different ones?"

"Seek consensus," Margaret repeated. "Your subjects know that the only way for trade to flourish is to cooperate with each other. If they forget for a moment, remind them that the alternative is war or rebellion that disrupts what they like to do best."

"Which is what?" Charles asked.

"To make money and to live in peace," she said firmly. How well she knew what her people wanted—far better than her father ever had.

On July 26, 1515, Margaret and Charles made their final joyous entry in Brussels, headquarters of the now fully-vested Lord of the Netherlands. The journey had bonded them once more after their fallout of the year before.

But upon her return to Malines, Margaret was startled to hear of rumors of her overspending and government mismanagement. Her trusted sources reported they were fueled by Charles' counselor Chièvres and a handful of council members, all Knights of the Golden Fleece.

Furious to hear her reputation was being savaged, she summoned her advisors to her privy chamber.

"I am not letting this pass," Margaret fumed. "Chièvres is behind all this, and I will not allow my reputation to be destroyed by his slander."

"Madame, was it not Chièvres who was governor before your father appointed you in 1507?" Gattinara asked.

"He was, which is why he laughs at my reversal of fortunes now."

"Demand a full rebuttal of these charges before your nephew's council," the Savoyard jurist advised.

"You can be sure I will," Margaret sang out.

Over the next three weeks she set her secretaries to work, combing her account books to prepare for a formal rebuttal of the criticisms being leveled against her. Not only had she been careful not to overtax her constituents, but she had dipped into her own dowager revenues to fund expenses incurred during her eight years of rule. The more she looked over her accounts, the more she burned at the thought of the lies her accusers had spread.

On August 20 she presented her case to the Council of State in Brussels. Detailing the ongoing war against the Duke of Guelders, she cast a baleful eye at Chièvres sitting next to Charles. Pointing out that Egmond, Duke of Guelders, had been continually aided by the French, she decried his revolt against the Lord of the Netherlands' authority. To continue, she included an accounting of all monies given her by the Estates-General, and all monies and gifts dispensed by her to fund costs or as gifts.

Both Charles and Chièvres looked increasingly surprised as the accounts were read and the account lists passed around. It soon became evident that Margaret had dipped into her own dowager funds from Spain and Savoy time and again to pay for expenses for the benefit of the Netherlands, rather than raise additional taxes.

At the end of her presentation, Charles addressed the council, clearly moved by her spirited defense. As always his remarks were brief, concluding with "Madame is held fully discharged from all things."

Then, much to Margaret's satisfaction, Chièvres spoke up. "Madame has proven beyond doubt that she performed her duties with exceptional fiscal responsibility," he concurred.

Signing off on the back of the accounts document she had prepared, Charles passed it to all twelve counselors, each of whom signed in the presence of the attending auditor.

Margaret's defense of her regime had been a success. Not only was she officially vindicated, but it was apparent to all present that she had worked hard to prosper the Netherlands. She had done her utmost to fob off enemies, as well as Maximilian's requests for money, so that the people of the Low Countries remained content with the peace and central authority that Habsburg rule brought.

Surveying the room before she left, she noted the glimmer of admiration in the eyes of some who had not previously been her supporters. They had witnessed that she was not going to disappear, felled by a whispering campaign. Perhaps at some future point they would look to her again to uphold the Netherlands' interests on Europe's stage. If such a time came they would remember how ably she had fought to defend her case that day.

Portrait of Charles the Bold (Charles the Rash)
By Rogier van der Weyden, c. 1454-1460
Gemäldegalerie, Berlin, Germany
Photo by Franz Meyer

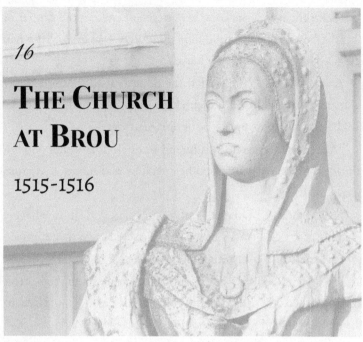

THE CHURCH AT BROU

1515-1516

MARGARET PULLED OUT THE will she had drawn up in 1509. Finally, she had time to go over it. When her mortal moment was up her heart was to be buried alongside her mother in Bruges, her entrails in Malines, and the rest of her transported to Brou.

Suddenly she remembered the sketches for the church her designer had sent in July. Where were they? She had not had a moment to get to them that summer.

Lifting them out of her desk drawer, she was about to dive in when a knock at the door interrupted her.

"Someone here to see you, Madame."

Annoyed, Margaret looked up. "I am not expecting anyone. Who is it?"

"A surprise for you, my lady. Sent by Madame de Beaumont from across the street."

"Send them in," she bade her attendant, setting the dossier of sketches to one side. Why did something always get in the way when she tried to do something for herself?

A small woman curtseyed at the door. "Good morning, Lady Margaret," she said. "I am Neuteken[1] from the children's household. Sent by Lady Anna to be of service to you."

"And what service do you intend to offer? I have staff enough already." Margaret recognized her nephew and nieces' fool from across the street.

"Not like me, Madame. Lady Anna says you do not have a Neuteken, so here I am." The woman curtseyed again then tumbled forward, making a complete somersault.

A laugh escaped Margaret as the little woman sprang to her feet and smoothed down her rose and gold-striped dress. "Come back in the evening when I need entertaining," she told her.

"If I please you, Madame, I hope you will add me to your court." The agile woman lounged against the back of the door, perusing the paintings on the wall. She showed no signs of leaving.

"What else do you do besides tumble?" Margaret asked, thinking Anna would not have sent her unless she thought highly of her skills. She had been an entertaining companion to the children. But now they were grown, with Charles and Eleanor moving to Brussels to live at Charles' new court, Isabella married off in Copenhagen, and Mary sent to Vienna.

---

1. Jane de Iongh, Margaret of Austria: Regent of the Netherlands (New York: W.W. Norton & Company, 1953), p. 246. Neuteken is mentioned as a member of Margaret's household.

"Ah, Madame, I have many tricks up my sleeve. You will discover them all in good time."

Margaret pursed her lips. "I shall be the judge of that, not you."

"I shall help you decide, Madame. You will take me on once you see how I cheer you."

"You are quite cheeky to say so, but we shall see how good you are at keeping things lively."

"I am a devil at tumbling," the small woman offered, her blue-green eyes flashing.

Margaret shot her a stern look, but her interest was piqued. "We shall see what you can do." Certainly it would add some excitement to nightly card games.

"Many things, Madame. Not just to entertain, but to lift your spirits when they are down."

"How would you know how?" Margaret asked, thinking she would very much like to have someone around who could cheer her instead of need cheering.

"I am a quick learner, Madame. Light on my feet and fast in my thoughts."

"You are confident of your skills," Margaret noted.

"Like you, Madame. That is how I know we would get along."

"My skills are not needed these days," Margaret groused, forgetting herself for a moment.

"Ah, Madame, your skills will be needed again. And in the meantime you must keep them sharp."

"Who are you to tell me to stay sharp?" Margaret asked.

"I am Neuteken, Madame. At your service." With that the woman made a dramatic bow and pitched headlong onto the floor, where she executed a neat roll and jumped up again.

Margaret waved her out. "You may serve me now by going away and coming back tonight."

"'Twill be my pleasure, Lady Margaret." With a final curtsey Neuteken backed out of the room, bumping into the doorway and bouncing to the other side, where she bumped again then fell onto the floor.

Stifling a chortle, Margaret returned to her work, thinking of the jester's graceful tumbles and cocky speech. Perhaps a little Neuteken was just what she needed.

Settling down to the drawings for the church she pulled them out, one by one. Construction had begun in 1506, then advanced in 1509. But she had been caught up with affairs of state in the ensuing six years and had only read occasional reports on its progress. She had engaged the Flemish artist, Jan van Roome, to design the church's most salient interior features: above all, the three tombs that would hold her beloved prince, his mother, and herself.

Turning over the first sheet, her breath caught in her throat. The sketch of Philibert's mother's effigy showed the same cleft chin that he had possessed. How she had admired it on him.

Picking up the sketch of Philibert's effigy, she went to the window. Golden late-summer sunlight spilled over her as Margaret again fell in love with the features of the man van Roome had captured.

In athletic repose Philibert rested with head tilted to one side, his face as strongly-chiseled as his stalwart character had been. The large straight nose, well-cut lips, and cleft chin formed a landscape her fingers had traversed countless times.

Leaning over the windowsill, she savored the breeze on her face, imagining it was Philibert's hand. The thought floated to her that he wished for her own effigy to be placed across the church nave at the exact same distance up the aisle as his so that he might be turned to her in eternal repose. She would make a note of it in her instructions.

Breathing in the fecund smell of ripening fruits and fields, her mind's eye saw him on that fateful hot day at the mountain spring, drinking deeply and pouring icy fresh water over his head. Rivers of cooling relief must have run down his face as he tipped it to the sky and laughed with the sheer joy of being alive.

One day she would laugh like that. Then it struck her that she had laughed in such a way only moments earlier with her entertaining visitor. Had her beloved prince sent the tiny woman to ease her days?

Effigy of Philibert, Duke of Savoy
By Conrad Meit and others
Royal Monastery of Brou
Bourg-en-Bresse, France

Effigy of Philibert, Duke of Savoy
By Conrad Meit and others
Royal Monastery of Brou, Bourg-en-Bresse, France
Photo by Frantz

17

LESSONS
LEARNED

1517

"THE KING OF SPAIN is dead, Madame."

"God rest his soul." Margaret crossed herself. She was saddened but not shocked. The past two Januarys had taken first Anne of Brittany, then Louis XII of France. This January it was Ferdinand of Aragon.

"Have we word of who he named as his successor?" She held her breath as she awaited the answer. Ferdinand's favorite grandson was his namesake, Charles' younger brother. The twelve-year-old prince had been raised at the court of Aragon. Margaret prayed he had not been named to Charles' rightful place as King of Spain.

"Here is the letter from the new King of Spain." The messenger bowed, handing her a folded note.

Margaret read it quickly. 'Good aunt—Praise be to God, my grandfather has designated me successor to the throne of Aragon. Yours, Charles I, King of Spain and Lord of the Netherlands.'

"Adrian did his job!" Margaret exulted. When Charles received word a few months earlier that his grandfather was ailing, he had sent his former tutor to Spain to convince the old king to name him as his successor instead of his younger brother. Adrian of Utrecht had succeeded in his mission.

"What say you, my lady?"

"Never mind." Scrawling her congratulations at the bottom of the note she handed it back to the messenger with two silver coins. "Take this back to His Most High Grace, the King of Spain."

"Thank you, my lady. May God bless you and bless Spain's new king."

It was good news indeed. Not only had Ferdinand done the right thing, but Charles had communicated directly with her to let her know. She rejoiced on both fronts.

Ringing for refreshment, she invited Lady Elisabeth to join her in toasting Ferdinand's memory. As she waited, she thought of her cunning former father-in-law. He had been her admirer ever since her years in Spain. Although buoyed by his regard, Margaret knew Ferdinand to be a trickster of the highest order. How she had laughed when she heard of his response to Louis XII when the French king had accused him of stealing Naples from him in 1504.

"The King of France complains that I have twice deceived him. He lies, the fool; I have deceived him ten times and more," Ferdinand had riposted.

"What will it mean for the archduke, Madame?" Lady Elisabeth asked the moment they set down their goblets.

"He is no longer just the archduke, but Charles I of Spain," Margaret corrected, thinking how apt her lady-in-waiting's question was.

"And what dominions come with Spain?"

"He will rule over Aragon, Castile and Leon, Naples, Sicily and the New World that is Spain's portion," Margaret listed.

Her lady-in-waiting's eyes widened. "But your nephew is only sixteen."

"He has many advisors," Margaret assured her.

"Of which you are one." Lady Elisabeth's eyes met Margaret's over the rim of her goblet.

"Not anymore," Margaret retorted. It was the same answer she had given any who asked over the past year.

"Forgive me to disagree, my lady. The chessboard has reconfigured, and you will be needed once the new king heads to Spain to take up his duties."

"How is he to manage there?" Margaret deflected, ignoring her companion's allusion to her possible new status. Her nephew did not speak Spanish, nor did he know the customs of that far-off land she had come to love.

"He will manage, just as you managed when you went there at the same age," Lady Elisabeth pointed out.

"I had help," Margaret said.

"He will have help, too," Lady Elisabeth rejoined firmly. "His brother is there, and the old king leaves behind a wife, does he not?"

"His brother is still a boy, and I have not met Ferdinand's widow," Margaret noted, trying to recollect what she knew of Germaine de Foix.

"How old is she?"

"Not old, as I recall." Margaret thought back to letters from Anne of Brittany, mentioning the choice she had made for Ferdinand when he had asked her to find him a wife from amongst her maids of honor after Queen Isabella had died.

"She is French, is she not?"

Memories of Anne of Brittany's description crystallized. "She came from the Queen of France's court and is the niece of Louis XII, God rest his soul."

"Ah, so your nephew will have someone to converse with in his own tongue," Lady Elisabeth exclaimed.

"To give him the lay of the land, I would hope," Margaret said.

"You enjoyed your time there, did you not?"

Margaret sipped as visions of Spain washed over her: the sound of the fountains in the gardens of the Alhambra where she had strolled with Catherine of Aragon, the outlines of majestic mountain ranges against brilliant blue skies, the smells of oranges and jasmine. She would not mention the deaths of her husband and child. "It is an enchanting land," she told her.

Lady Elisabeth's eyes sparkled. "Do you think your nephew will fall in love there?"

Margaret let out a tinkling laugh. The idea of her reserved nephew falling in love was difficult to imagine. "If he is to fall in love anywhere, it will be there."

"Then, here's to the new king's success." Elisabeth raised her goblet.

Margaret touched it with her own. "The king is dead. Long live the king!" she toasted, hoping that Spain would cast its spell over Charles the way it had for her.

As the year progressed, Margaret took part in ceremonies and festivals, tourneys and competitions.

In March she attended services for Ferdinand of Aragon. As she bowed her head during the funeral Mass, her father's face came to her. That great and valiant knight would ultimately return to God, too. It was unimaginable to think of life without him, but the years had shown her that life went on even when the unimaginable happened. One day her beloved Maxi would give up the ghost, and she would be senior member of the House of Habsburg, just as she was now senior member of the House of Burgundy.

She prayed she and her nephew would be closer by that time. But she would not seek him out. Her feminine instincts told her to draw him to her like a moth to a light. She would do so by representing her lineage well, attending Burgundian festivals and showing her people their native princess among them, fanning the flame of their richly cultured heritage. Word would trickle through to her nephew of the esteem in which the people of their realm held her. She would enjoy herself, too.

In June, Margaret brought Neuteken along when she took part in the national crossbow competition of the confraternity of Saint Sebastian. While her fool entertained the crowds by tumbling and making faces Margaret took steady aim, savoring the moment before she released her arrow. Each time she shot she thought of

Philibert behind her, his hand steadying her arm, offering words of encouragement as he had done in childhood days.

"For you, my love," she whispered as the final round took place. Sure enough she hit the moving parrot target, making her feel as if she were a young girl again and earning her the title of Queen of the Popinjay.

With a light heart, she offered the prize she won to the confraternity, then gave Neuteken a bag of silver coins to hand out as she pleased. The little woman slid silver into tiny hands and smacked larger ones away as the crowd roared with laughter.

Margaret delighted in being out and about with her countrymen now that they were no longer flooding her with grievances and grumblings. And Neuteken was good fun to have at her side. She could hardly wait for the next festival to come 'round, giving her another opportunity to mingle with her people and revel in carefree merriment.

With fewer daily burdens of governing, Margaret relaxed her stance toward Charles' chief counselor. Ever since Chièvres had spoken in her defense at her nephew's council meeting of the August before, Margaret had changed her tack. Instead of endlessly opposing him, she began to explore ways to work with him to support her nephew. There was no getting rid of William de Croy. The older man was like a father figure to Charles—too important to be shouldered aside.

Margaret bluffed her way through countless evenings with Charles and Chièvres across the card table, as insouciant and gay as she had never been in council meetings. Without the endless duties of twice-weekly meetings and all their attendant sub-meetings, she felt less beset by worries than she had in years.

By setting aside her hurt, she learned much. Most surprisingly she discovered that Chièvres' devotion to her nephew was as sincere as her own. For that, her heart softened.

She watched in silence as Charles spent the year familiarizing himself with governance of the Low Countries. For the moment, a voyage to Spain was out of the question. Instead, he named two Spanish clerics as regents to rule the Iberian peninsula until he arrived.

And now Charles' contemporary, Francis I, was on France's throne. At age twenty-one, the young French king was as urbane and debonair as Charles was not and never would be.

Margaret felt disgust when Chièvres steered Charles into a treaty relationship with the new French monarch with the signing of the Treaty of Paris in March 1515. Yet sticking to her policy of restraint, she held back and said nothing. With Ferdinand's death, she saw the sense in it.

Charles would need France's recognition of his ascendancy to the Spanish throne. It was more likely to be given if relations were already established between him and the French king, even though various points over Burgundian lands had yet to be settled.

With initial rapport established, a further treaty was signed in August 1516, with Charles recognizing France's claim to Milan. In return, Francis I promised Naples to Charles through the dowry he would offer with one of his daughters in marriage, or the youngest daughter of Louis XII and Anne of Brittany.

With this second treaty signed, Margaret's father found himself with no more allies in Italy. By December, having no alternative, Maximilian made peace with France over Italy in the Treaty of Brussels.

Margaret grieved for him to see his dreams crushed. But his Italian campaigns had cost the lands of her mother dearly. As a Burgundian princess, Margaret stood on the side of her people. Who could blame them for not wishing to see their hard-earned money wasted in faraway lands by an Austrian overlord too lofty to bother with fiscal oversight?

As for Charles marrying a French princess royal, she was sure that he had no intention of marrying any of Francis' family members. Nor did he give a fig about Naples. He had signed the treaty to maintain peace with France and to ensure the French king made no trouble for him in his new role as King of Spain.

By fall of 1516, Charles was asking Margaret to sit in on more council meetings. Better rested than she had been in years, she saw the benefits to being an observer. Sitting back, she listened and watched as her nephew and Chièvres, along with Charles' chancellor Jean Le Sauvage, managed the muddle of seventeen provinces with conflicting aims and allegiances.

As the leaves on the trees glittered gold then fell, discussions began of plans for Charles to travel to Spain.

WHEN MAXIMILIAN MADE A rare visit to Brussels in February 1517, he wasted no time in reuniting his grandson with his daughter.

Enveloped in her father's arms, Margaret felt his maddening, mystical warmth and love fill her heart like an early spring thaw. Then he turned to Charles and embraced him in a bear hug, pinkening the cheeks of the reserved sixteen-year-old.

Before the day was out, the head of the House of Habsburg had sprinkled his visionary allure over all present. For once, he was not asking for money.

Instead, he asked his grandson to reach for the mantle of the Holy Roman Emperor. Bursting with eloquence Maximilian filled Charles' head with visions of wearing the crown of Charlemagne, ruler of more territories than any other prince in Europe.

Charles looked dazzled, but held back. Margaret knew her nephew well, better than her father did. She saw he was weighing the responsibilities that lay ahead, wondering how he could handle them all. Thus far, he had his hands full with managing the Low Countries and treating with his rival in France who outshone him in every way.

"My lord, how am I to rule all these dominions at once?" Charles asked as his grandfather quaffed his mug of ale.

"My boy, you will rely on those you trust. Above all, your family," Maximilian instructed.

Charles' eyes met Margaret's. Neither fully trusted Maximilian, who could be counted on to change plans or run out of money as frequently as the wind shifts.

"Yes, my lord." Charles' tone was neutral.

Maximilian placed a weighty hand on Margaret's shoulder. "Look to your aunt, who has loved you as a mother and ruled your lands capably all those years of your minority."

Margaret warmed to the glow of her father's words. As Charles glanced at her again, she saw trust brim in his eyes.

"She has done a good job, my lord. And now I know what a tough job it is," Charles replied.

Margaret's heart swelled. It was the first bit of credit her nephew had offered since he had supported her defense of her governance at the 1515 council meeting.

"So leave the Low Countries in her hands again when you go to Spain," Maximilian advised. "It will be one less worry for you, and since she already knows the job she will not make a mess of it."

Margaret locked eyes with Charles again. Both knew who the master was of making a mess of things. Yet she could not help but feel devotion to the shaggy-haired graying-blond prince who had spread the House of Habsburg from Vienna to the Netherlands and would now see his grandson bring it to Spain. Her father had finally come to her defense two full years after tossing her aside for 140,000 florins.

"I will consider it, my lord," Charles responded.

Margaret silently rejoiced. In that moment all bitterness over her demotion of the past two years melted away. Charles never responded to anything impetuously. He was neither glib nor dashing like his Habsburg grandfather. But if he said he would consider handing over the Low Countries to Margaret to govern once more, she knew he would weigh the idea seriously. With his grandfather's words about family, she could see her nephew's heart had been touched. The only family Charles had was Margaret and his three sisters, with occasional visits from Maximilian.

That night at a banquet at Charles' palace in Brussels, Margaret sat on one side of her father as Charles sat on the other. Warm words were exchanged and toasts made as three generations bonded over a shared dynastic vision.

By the end of Maximilian's visit, Margaret sensed her star was again on the rise. Her father was impossible, but impossible not to love.

Judging by the gleam in Charles' eye when his grandfather had spoken of the glorious future that lay ahead of him, she had no doubt the House of Habsburg would stand together. God willing, she would get her position back. And if her nephew decided to reach for the crown of Charlemagne, she would do all she could to see him elected Holy Roman Emperor one day.

THE YEAR 1517 UNFOLDED with Charles consolidating his plans to visit Spain. His sister Eleanor would accompany him. The eighteen-year-old princess had fallen in love with his close friend, Frederick, Count of Palatine. But Charles was planning a more important match for her. The King of Portugal's wife had just died. His country was on the rise with its navigators bringing back ships laden with wealth from the New World. Charles sent Frederick from court and told his sister he needed her in Spain.

Eleanor acquiesced. She had been raised for one role only—to expand the House of Habsburg by marrying well. All other considerations were secondary: love, passion, personal inclination. The role of a Habsburg prince or princess was clear—duty trumped all.

Margaret saw that her nephew's head ruled his heart in his decision-making. It boded well for one who would oversee more dominions in Europe and beyond than any other prince.

To be ratified as King of Spain, Charles would need to present himself to the Cortes—the Spanish legislative body—of both

Castile and Aragon. With no knowledge of the language or exposure to Spanish customs, Margaret feared he faced a large challenge ahead. But with his reserve and serious demeanor, she sensed the Spanish would take to him better than they had his father.

Philip the Handsome's lighthearted and pleasure-loving ways had offended Spanish sensibilities. Charles of Habsburg would do better.

By August, Charles finalized the regency council that would rule in his absence. This time Margaret was included in proceedings. As they sat on the loggia of the Court of Savoy one hot afternoon her nephew made his intent clear.

"I would like you to take a seat on the Council while I am in Spain, *bonne tante*," Charles announced.

"I am already sitting in on meetings, so what do you mean?" Margaret asked.

"I wish to formalize your seat."

"How so?" She would wait for him to say the words. After two years of suffering in silence, she had learned her lesson. She must give her nephew agency. The boy she had raised had grown into a man. Charles was slow to make decisions, but he was not biddable as his father had been, with the nickname his Council had given him of "Philip Follow-Advice."

"You will have a seat with a vote," Charles spelled out.

"I accept," Margaret replied, her heart leaping in her chest. She busied herself with pouring another glass of chilled mint water. The young man she had raised was at a self-conscious age. It would not do to embrace him or stand up and dance a jig.

Reining in her elation, she reminded herself that it was only a seat at the table she had previously presided over. Yet it was a step in the right direction.

This time she would listen more to the concerns of the other council members, especially those who wore the collar of the Golden Fleece. She would never be invited to join their precious group, but no matter. Her forefather, Philip the Good, Burgundy's most glorious duke, had founded their order. If it helped to maintain Burgundy's unity, she would support it.

"Ah, Madame, you are back to your old job," Lady Elisabeth exclaimed as she helped her dress for that day's council meeting.

"Yes, but this time I sit at the table, not at its head."

"Your time will come again, Madame."

"Do you think so?"

"Just play along with those stuffed doublets who think they are so important with their limp sheep insignias. Your moment will come."

"It irks me to think they exclude me from their order when I am Burgundy's Princess of the Blood," Margaret admitted. She had spent two full years pretending not to care, but still it stung.

"'Tis something men do, Madame. It is a defense for them against us taking over," Lady Elisabeth opined.

Margaret smiled at her lady-in-waiting's insight. Philibert had been delighted to have her take over. Other men might not. "I don't think there's much chance of women taking over, is there?" she asked.

"Ah, Madame, men with wives at home and mothers who raised them know only too well we have already taken them over with invisible golden threads," Lady Elisabeth noted.

"And so they resist us with visible golden chains that they hang about their necks to feel superior," Margaret groused.

"Let them have their trinkets, my lady. We already own their hearts and minds, so they must have something for themselves."

Margaret chuckled as she stepped into her gown. "Then I declare myself a member of the Order of the Golden Threads."

"Ah, Madame, now you have it. Just be sure to keep it a secret from them. If they think you've come up with a rival order, they'll be looking for something new to lord over you."

"Did not Anne of Brittany in France found an order for the ladies of her court?" Margaret asked.

"It was the Order of the Cord, Madame. All her ladies had one hung from the waist in finest spun gold."

"I shall wear one myself then."

"Be sure to have it spun from invisible threads," Lady Elisabeth counseled.

"Why so?"

"So the men won't see it, Madame. What is known but invisible is more powerful than what is known and visible."

"How is it that you are so wise, Lady Elisabeth?"

"Because I have served at your court for all these years."

Margaret smiled, her pride stirred. "A fine answer."

"Thank you, my lady. Now go to your council meeting and bind their minds to you with invisible threads."

"I will let you know how I fare."

"Madame, I already know you will fare well."

Margaret and her lady-in-waiting erupted into laughter as she glided from the room. She was back in the game. This time she would play a more subtle hand.

ON SEPTEMBER 8, 1517, Charles and Eleanor set sail for Spain. While waiting for news of their arrival, Margaret heard from Maximilian. He wrote from Innsbruck that a young monk had caused an uproar after nailing a list of complaints demanding Church reform to a church door in Wittenberg.

Focused on her nephew's and niece's safety, Margaret gave little thought to the news. All that mattered was that Charles succeeded in Spain.

Some weeks later, word came. Charles and Eleanor had arrived safely. After logistical troubles due to an unexpected landing, they had been located and greeted by Castilian dignitaries and had met their brother Ferdinand, their youngest sister Catherine, and their mother.

Staring at the letter, Margaret wished it said more. But her nephew was a man of few words. She shivered to imagine what their meeting with their mother had been like. Perhaps it was fortunate that they had seen so little of Juana of Castile before being separated from her. Margaret guessed that no strong bond had been formed in the first place, so perhaps the impact of whatever condition they found her in would not be too grievous.

She wrote back, advising Charles to learn the language quickly and encouraging him that he had just the right temperament to win over the serious Spaniards. She hoped he would move quickly beyond the shock of meeting his mother. With the likely recognition that she was forever lost to him, he would need support. Worried that Charles had no wife at his side to succor him in a strange new land, Margaret took comfort that Eleanor was there.

Once again, January proved a month of deaths. With an epidemic circulating, both the chancellor and chairman of the Regency Council died, leaving two leadership spots vacant.

Margaret moved closer to the head of the table. By June, 1518, Charles appointed her chief counselor Gattinara as chancellor, indicating a vote of confidence in Margaret's court. She bided her time and remained careful not to step on the shoes of her fellow council members. Learning to build coalitions, she put aside minor issues to come to agreement on more important ones.

Yet, no longer would she assume certain issues were minor just because they were minor to her. What a misstep she had made in not recognizing how important the Order of the Golden Fleece was to the knights who belonged to it.

By August 1518, her improved skills were rewarded. A diplomatic pouch arrived from Spain. As she opened it, a large object fell out.

Picking it up, she flushed with pleasure. In her hands lay the seal stamper of the government of the Netherlands, without which no financial outlays could be made. Unfolding the letter, she saw Charles' seal at the bottom.

Margaret of Austria and Burgundy, Duchess of Savoy, was again granted the right to sign state papers and distribute state funds in the name of Charles I, King of Spain and Lord of the Netherlands. The official seal stamper of the government was to be held in her keeping alone. For her services, she was to receive an annuity of 20,000 florins.

"God be thanked, I am governor again!" Margaret exulted.

Her counselor smiled broadly. "Did I not tell you your fortunes would return?"

"The changes of fortune make one stronger," Margaret intoned as she handled the heavy copper stamp. How well she remembered its weight from the eight years she had used it in her first run as governor.

"Let us hope, Madame, that this time fortune will smile on you for even longer," Gattinara remarked.

"I have learned a few things. I will not be so easy to show my hand."

"Good Lord, Madame. You were not easy before, but now I am terrified to play you at cards."

"You should be, Monsieur. Now if I can just curb that brigand Egmond, we shall be in fine shape for whenever my nephew returns from Spain."

"He will be caught up with affairs there for some time to come," her counselor observed.

"Good. I look forward to having a long run. If I am to set policy I need time to institute it." Margaret weighed the heavy stamper in her hand, savoring her joy over governing her realm again.

"A wise word, Madame. And now that I am chancellor, you have someone who will work well with you."

"I do indeed, do I not, Monsieur?" Not only did she feel vindicated, she felt brought back to life.

Gattinara dipped his head. "I am at your service, my lady, at council and at cards."

Portrait of Mercurino Arborio Gattinara
by Jan Cornelisz Vermeyen, c. 1530
Royal Museums of Fine Arts of Belgium
Brussels, Belgium
From the Yorck Project

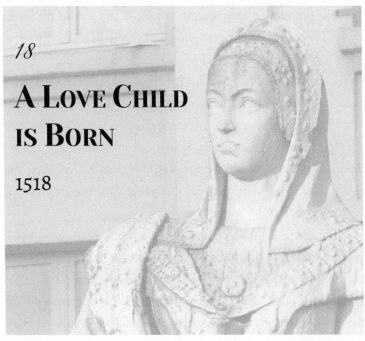

18

A Love Child is Born

1518

THAT FALL, MARGARET'S CORRESPONDENCE with her father increased. Now that she was reinstated as the Low Countries' governor, she felt warmer toward him. Their mutual ambition to see Charles elected Holy Roman Emperor in Maximilian's wake had lit a common fire between them.

Seven prince-electors of Germany must be reached and convinced to vote for her nephew. Such an undertaking was comparable to the lobbying that went on each time a pope died. Spiritual concerns were tossed out the window, and all involved in getting their candidate elected had only one goal in mind: raising enough money to buy votes.

No wonder the monk in Wittenberg had posted a protest against similar practices such as selling indulgences to fund the pope's building project in Rome, Margaret thought. But playing the hands dealt to her, she would play to win.

Whatever funds she raised to see Charles elected she would get to the electors directly, bypassing her father. Otherwise, Maxi had a tendency to skim funds for his own projects and campaigns. To that end, she organized her secretaries to arrange meetings with each of the electors from Brandenberg, Bavaria, Saxony, Bohemia, Cologne, Trier, and Mainz. Much money would be needed to secure the election for Charles, especially as the French king had also thrown his hat into the ring.

Amused by the thought of Louise of Savoy's sybaritic son holding any title possessing the term 'holy,' Margaret began a whispering campaign that quickly spread across Germany. Francis I, King of France, was painted as a foreign outsider likely to interfere with the special privileges of the German princes. The position of Holy Roman Emperor had been held by princes of German blood since the 10th century. It was unthinkable to have a French king as head of an empire east of the Rhine.

Although not to be trusted with money, Margaret knew her father to be a master at marriage alliances. He wrote that the Elector of Brandenburg was in the bag. He had offered his granddaughter, Catherine, to the son of the Margrave of Brandenberg in exchange for his vote.

The Infanta Catherine of Castile was already eleven and would bring a substantial dowry when the marriage took place—all from Spain's coffers, not the Netherlands' or Austria's.

As Maximilian worked with Charles in Spain to arrange Catherine's betrothal to the Brandenberg prince, Margaret sought to arrange loans from the Fuggers banking houses in Antwerp and

Augsburg. Visiting the offices of the Antwerp Fuggers, she laid out her case.

"Do you wish to back the horse that wins or the horse that loses?" Margaret asked, directing her question to the clean-shaven man most likely to be Jakob Fugger. Of all the men around the table only he wore a gold beret. It could only be Europe's richest banker, she thought, who would wear a hat that looked like a halo and shone like a gold coin.

"Madame, we have no need to back either horse, as we are not in the business of betting," another of the bankers replied, his tone flat.

"Ah, but you are in the business of moneylending, so you must see the wisdom of lending to the winning candidate instead of one sure to lose," she countered, hoping her mention of wisdom conjoined with the Fugger banking house would soften her targets.

The men at the table turned to each other with amused glances.

"Madame, it is likely to be the one who receives our support who wins." Jakob Fugger's eyes glinted steely blue. Not a hint of warmth lay there.

"Then back one of your own and not a foreign prince," Margaret responded.

"Madame, we do not dabble in politics. We look for opportunity and put money behind those who offer it." Fugger's thin lips curled into themselves.

"Surely you can see the opportunity behind my nephew's election as head of the Holy Roman Empire," she answered briskly. Charm was not going to sway Fugger. Talk of profits might work.

"What do you have in mind?"

"As King of Spain, Lord of the Netherlands, and head of the Holy Roman Empire, he will be in a position to repay every florin you offer toward his election," she spelled out, as if upending a bag of diamonds on the table.

"From where do you propose repayment to come?" another banker asked.

"To begin, there is his grandfather as present emperor."

As eyes rolled around the table, Margaret sensed she had misstepped. What had she been thinking to bring up Maximilian in a discussion on money?

"Your father has tapped out his credit with us," Fugger told her. "We have supported him for years, with the result that we now own all mining rights to the lands of his realm."

Margaret had not realized the full extent of her father's agreements with the Fuggers, but she could well imagine he had gotten himself in over his head.

"Then do you say you will not support the House of Habsburg continuing on the Holy Roman Empire's throne?" she asked. Never mind that there was nothing holy about the position nor was there a throne. The title held prestige, and Charles must have it.

Jakob Fugger's smile unfurled like a grimace. "I have long supported your father, but he has tapped the well dry."

"Then what do you propose?" Margaret asked. She had learned from years of presiding over council meetings that it was best to ask another's opinion before presenting one's own.

"That any funding to come from us is to be repaid from revenues to the Spanish crown," Fugger replied.

Margaret drew in her breath. "That is a whole other matter."

A muscle twitched at the side of Fugger's mouth. "A more interesting one," he remarked.

"I shall have to see what my nephew says to such an arrangement."

Fugger barely moved. "As King of Spain, who wishes to see himself head of the Holy Roman Empire, I'm sure he'll agree," he countered, his eyes unblinking as they bored into hers.

"He has many other resources, of course," she hedged.

Fugger raised a brow. "Such as?"

Margaret froze, caught in the searchlight of Fugger's hard gaze.

"Such as assets from new sources." She would not go so far as to say from the New World, since she had not yet discussed it with Charles and had no idea what those assets might prove to be. Neither would he, she guessed.

"Which new sources?"

"I will confer with him and let you know," Margaret feinted, raising her chin. She would not to be cowed by Jakob Fugger, no matter how rich he was. There must be something he wanted that only her side had. She would dig deeper until she discovered what it was.

"Repayments must be guaranteed by the crown of Spain, no matter what source they come from," he stipulated.

"It is possible they will come from the Low Countries as well," she said, not meaning it at all.

"Now you sound like your father." Fugger's tone was wry.

"I will let you know." Margaret felt her blood rise. How dare he compare her with her father, who hadn't the slightest idea how to hang on to money. Yet Fugger had bankrolled him through the years, so she held her temper.

"We will consider repayments guaranteed by Spain alone," the banker specified. "You know as well as we do that your own realm will not stand for being parted from their profits."

Margaret cleared her throat. How well she knew. "Then we are agreed that if terms can be reached, you will help us with my nephew's campaign."

"Your father is still emperor," Fugger pointed out.

"My father wishes to prepare for a fortuitous succession," she replied.

"Then we wait for your fortuitous response to our conditions."

"I will get back to you with possible terms," Margaret repeated, keeping her tone even.

"The terms will be made by us. Repayment guaranteed by Spain or we cannot help you." Fugger's voice was like ice water.

"You must help us!" Margaret burst out. "Charles of Habsburg is your countryman, and the Holy Roman Emperor must have German blood," she cried.

Fugger's face remained unmoved. "You decide," he answered, rapping his knuckles on the table.

All rose in unison with Europe's most powerful banker. The meeting was over.

Portrait of Jakob Fugger
By Albrecht Dűrer, 1518
Staatsgalerie Altdeutsche Meister
Augsburg, Germany
From the Yorck Project

BACK IN MALINES, MARGARET returned home to startling news.

"Are you sure this is true?" she questioned the man before her. Fresh off a merchant ship from Spain, he brought a short note from one of her contacts there. Unfolding it, she saw four words followed by her agent's seal: 'Trust what he says.'

"I am sure a child has been born to the dowager queen," the man related. "And she has been seen coming and going from private meetings with the king."

"That means nothing," Margaret remarked.

"That is not what is being said at the king's court."

"And what does the king himself say?"

"He has said nothing of the matter."

"Then there is nothing to say." How careless of Ferdinand's widow to toss away a queen's dignity by producing an illegitimate child. But what concern was it of hers?

"Quite a deal is being said, Madame, but behind closed doors."

"Then tell me what it is so I may get to the bottom of it." Margaret crossed her arms and waited.

The messenger cleared his throat. "It is said that the child's father is the king."

Margaret blanched. How could such a thing be possible? Ferdinand's widow, Germaine de Foix, was thirty, stepgrandmother to Charles, who was eighteen. Her nephew was young for his age in the area of sentimental attachments. If the news was true, he had grown up since leaving for Spain the year before.

"When did this happen?" Margaret asked, mindful to maintain a calm tone.

"The child was born last August."

Margaret moved to the window as she calculated dates. A child born in August would have been conceived in December, only three months after Charles landed in Spain. It was unthinkable that so much could have transpired between him and Ferdinand's widow in three short months. Yet it took only one night to conceive a child.

"Have you spoken to anyone else about this?" she asked.

The man shifted uneasily. "Not here, my lady."

"But back in Spain?"

"Back in Spain, many are speaking of this at the present time."

"What sex is the child?"

"A girl, Madame."

Margaret thanked the stars for such good news. The birth of a boy would raise questions of succession, with both parents of royal lineage. A natural-born daughter would be easier to manage. Or to hide.

"You may return now to your country, and do not share with anyone the news you have given me."

"Very good, Madame."

"I will have my men escort you to your ship," Margaret added.

The man's eyes widened. "I do not need an escort, Madame, if you don't mind."

"I do mind and you shall have one. But you have done nothing wrong, other than deliver news that I should not like to see spread." Margaret pulled a small pouch of coins from her desk. "Take this for your trouble and be on your way," she directed, motioning to the two guards at the door to accompany him. She would not like such news getting out until she heard from Charles himself.

As the men receded down the hallway, Margaret paced in her study. Months had passed since August, yet she had heard nothing from Charles of this.

Should she write to Eleanor to confirm it? Yet she had been in Portugal when the child was born. Her eldest niece had married Manuel I of Portugal in July 1518. He had previously been married to two of her aunts, Isabella and Maria, both sisters of Juana of Castile. Charles had arranged the match in order to gain the King of Portugal's support for his ascension to the throne of Castile.

Her nephew was beginning to show good sense in his political decisions. How shocking that he had not shown similar sense in his personal affairs.

Wishing to confide in someone, Margaret decided not to. If the news was false, she did not want it spread. And if it was true, it was a scandal. She was appalled to think he would have gotten involved with his stepgrandmother. Ferdinand had asked Charles to look after his widow upon his death. If the rumors were true, he certainly had.

As for Germaine de Foix? To bear a child out of wedlock was an extraordinary act for a dowager queen—foolhardy, scandalous and audacious, all rolled into one.

Margaret weighed the situations of both. Germaine de Foix had been widowed since January 1516. Bereft of her husband, but with a substantial widow's pension, she was still young, with both money and independence. Margaret did not know what she looked like, but if Anne of Brittany had chosen her for Ferdinand she must be fair.

Then there was Charles. To her knowledge, he was not well-experienced with women. Had Ferdinand of Aragon's widow offered guidance in the first months of his arrival in Spain? She and Charles shared French as their native tongue. He must have welcomed her help with Spanish language and customs. What else had she helped him with?

There had been the meeting with his mother. Word had reached Margaret that one of Charles' entourage had tried to enter the room behind him, but he had stopped him, barring the door. Spain's new king had not allowed any company to witness what had gone on between himself and the mother he had last seen at age six.

Whatever had passed between them, Margaret could guess Charles would have needed support in the weeks that followed. The mother whose arms should have encircled him had most likely shocked him instead.

Chièvres was there to help but he was almost sixty years old, cool and reserved by nature. Margaret could imagine her seventeen-year-old nephew turning to a woman for solace. Most likely, Germaine de Foix had been at his side: advising, consoling, and more.

Margaret said nothing of the affair to anyone, not even her father. Her nephew was making his first forays into manhood; missteps would happen along the way. She would wait to see if he recognized the child. If he did, it would make for a complicated situation. If he didn't, it would be better for all.

Trying to guess what he would do, she was flummoxed. The boy she had known so well had become a man with sides she did not know well at all.

19

DEATH OF AN EMPEROR

1519

THE FOLLOWING JANUARY SNATCHED yet another of Europe's
princes in its cruel maw. On January 12, 1519, Maximilian I of
Austria, Holy Roman Emperor-elect, died at his hunting lodge in
Wels, Austria. Two months shy of his sixtieth birthday, the report
came to Margaret that he had died peacefully in the deep hours
before dawn, bidding those at his bedside not to weep.

Yet Margaret did weep. "My father is gone, along with almost all
the princes I have loved," she choked out.

"Your father's love for you remains, my lady." For once,
Neuteken took a serious air, coming to her mistress' side and
stroking her hand.

"How can it remain if he himself is gone?" Margaret moaned.

"It is the armor you wear as senior member of the House of
Habsburg."

Margaret stared at her through her tears. "How serious you are."

"Do not fear, I will be back to pranks and jests once your tears have dried." Neuteken's woebegone smile told her she shared her sorrow.

"My tears will never dry for his loss," Margaret mourned. Thinking of his last letter in December, she thanked God they had been back on good terms after their rift in 1515. He had written a newsy report on tactics to use in winning Charles the coming election. But more dear to her, he had expressed how grateful he was that his grandson had restored her to her position, in recognition of her abilities. She had warmed to read his affectionate words, signing off as 'Maxi' in his familiar way.

More tears poured out at thought of her exasperating, indispensable Maxi. "How will I go on?" she lamented.

"Madame, you will go on less encumbered to serve the cause of the House of Habsburg, now that your father is no longer in a position to make a muddle of things."

Margaret glared at Neuteken. "If you were not my fool I would slap you for that."

"Madame, you engaged me to tell you the truth when I'm not telling you jokes. Allow me to do my job." The little woman took Margaret's hand and gave herself a smart slap on the face.

"Stop!" Margaret protested, giggling despite her sorrow. "You are making me laugh when I would cry."

"Cry your fill. And once you're done, you need to make your father's dearest wishes come true and get the King of Spain elected King of the Romans."

"Right you are, little one." They were her dearest wishes, too. She would ensure her father lived on by carrying them out.

"I am always right, Madame. All that I know I have learned from you." Neuteken raised Margaret's hand in hers again and slapped herself on the other cheek.

"Stop that and leave me to my sorrow," Margaret scolded, a welter of emotions swirling inside her.

"I will stop, but I will never leave you." Neuteken laid her head on Margaret's lap.

"If only that were true," Margaret murmured as she stroked her fool's soft hair. Her father, her brother, Philibert, and Juan had all left her. Only her nephew remained of those she had loved most.

Neuteken raised her head and looked gravely at her mistress. "It is true for as long as I have breath," she declared.

"Then that is the most comfort I can hope for," Margaret replied, thinking how final the moment was when breath left the body. Had her father suffered? His secretary had written that he had died with a smile on his face. Philibert had smiled, too, wrapped in her arms as he had given up his soul to God.

Unable to bear any more of such thoughts, Margaret rose from her couch, lifting Neuteken up with her. She would act on her fool's advice. With Maxi no longer able to pull strings on his end it fell on her shoulders to cajole, bribe, or intimidate the seven prince-electors of Germany into voting for her nephew.

Time was short, and the King of France must not be allowed to make further headway. Whatever devious methods Francis was up to in winning support, she must outmaneuver him.

All this while keeping her nephew in Spain far from the fray so that he would not object to the time-honored techniques used by every European prince or cardinal seeking to win an election.

How indeed had Charlemagne won his crown? She had heard it said that Charlemagne's father was major-domo in his sovereign's household, but had amassed so much power that when the king died it had been the major-domo who had his own son declared the king's successor.

She would rely on similar methods to achieve her aim. Money would buy power, and power would attract money. As much as she mourned the loss of her father, it was a good thing he was out of the way so she could see to it that the money she raised poured into the right coffers.

"Ready to face the world, my lady?"

"I am ready, Neuteken."

"And I am ready to comfort you whenever you need me."

"What would I do without you, little one?"

"You would rely on your dogs to soothe you, but they would not give you any advice."

"I do not need your advice, but what you offered was sound," Margaret said.

"I am your mirror, Madame. I hold up to you what you already know yourself capable of." Neuteken made the same stately expression that Margaret used to intimidate her councilmen.

Squelching the urge to laugh, Margaret straightened her white widow's coif. "Then let us get on with it," she announced. With a pat to her greyhound she sailed from the room, Neuteken following in her wake.

CHARLES WAS PROVING TO be difficult with the Fugger proposal. He did not want anything to do with the House of Fugger. In his view, it was an overly powerful institution that relied on usury to tie Europe's impoverished princes to its outstanding notes.

"He does not understand the way the world works," Margaret complained to Gattinara.

"He is young, Madame. Tell him Francis will go to the Fuggers if he doesn't agree to their terms."

"He will be furious if they deal with the French."

"The Augsburg Fuggers will not wish to deal with the French," Gattinara noted.

"But the Antwerp Fuggers will have no objection," Margaret continued thoughtfully. She knew her people. The merchants of Antwerp did not put too fine a point on who they did business with, so long as profits were to be made.

Under his bushy brows, Gattinara gave her a meaningful look. "Unless you stop them."

Margaret paused, tapping her finger on her desk. "Perhaps a decree prohibiting the bankers of Antwerp from dealing with foreigners."

Gattinara raised his eyes to the ceiling. "It must be passed by the Council."

"Of which you are chancellor," she noted.

"And signed into law with the stamp of the Lord of the Netherlands."

A slow smile spread across Margaret's face. "Of course."

"Madame, we see the way forward. Do not trouble your nephew with details. Just tell him you have taken action to prevent the French king from borrowing from bankers in the Netherlands."

"He will be pleased to hear it."

"Don't let him hear more," Gattinara advised. "His ears are too tender to absorb how elections are won."

"But what if he discovers I've gone against his wishes and borrowed most of what he needs from the Fuggers?"

"He has been angered with you before, Madame, but you are the senior member of his house. His wrath will vanish the instant he is elected King of the Romans and has you to thank for making it come about."

Margaret smiled. She would enjoy seeing her nephew beholden to her again.

ON JUNE 28, 1519, in Frankfurt, Charles I of Spain became Charles V, Emperor-elect of the Holy Roman Empire and King of the Romans as well as the German nation. He had won the unanimous vote of all seven prince-electors of Germany.

Margaret had spent a fortune campaigning for him. She owed almost 500,000 florins to the Fuggers banking house, and another 350,000 to the Welser and Gualterotti bankers. Borrowing such vast amounts had enabled her to secure the votes of five of the seven electors for her nephew.

The two that remained in favor of Francis I were persuaded to change their minds by the presence of Charles' mercenary troops stationed outside Frankfurt. They had arrived ten days earlier, ostensibly to prevent a French invasion. While Margaret had provided money, Charles had come up with a show of power. Together, they had got it done.

The combination of outspending the French king and debunking him as a foreign outsider had worked. Although Charles V did not speak a word of German and lived in Spain, he was perceived as the safer choice and more likely to uphold the privileges of the German princes in the hands-off tradition set by his great-grandfather, Frederick III, Holy Roman Emperor before Maximilian I.

In May of 1520, Charles left Spain to return to Germany to be crowned Emperor-elect. On his voyage back he visited his maternal aunt, Catherine of Aragon, and Henry VIII in England.

The timing was fortuitous. The King of England was about to attend a summit meeting with the French king outside Calais the following month.

Margaret's nephew had not been invited. She sent letters to both her nephew and Cardinal Wolsey at the time of Charles' visit to the English court, suggesting that Charles and Henry meet at Gravelines on the Low Countries border close to Calais after the summit. There she intended to unwind whatever goodwill had been struck up between the English and French at their summit and win back Henry VIII to an Anglo-Imperial alliance.

Charles V left England the same day Henry VIII and his queen set sail for Calais. The summit was to be a lavish affair, held in a valley to the south of Calais and named for the occasion as the Field of the Cloth of Gold. Margaret had already arranged for her contacts there to report back to her on whatever took place.

Traveling to Bruges to meet Charles, Margaret was overjoyed to discover the man he had grown into.

Her once-halting and timid nephew had matured greatly in the three years he had been gone. Reserved and serious, a new air of Spanish formality cloaked him. Amongst the courtiers accompanying him was Germaine de Foix, dowager-queen of Aragon and mother of the daughter he had sired two years earlier according to further sources Margaret had tapped to confirm the rumors.

Charles did not mention the child at all. Margaret took this in without comment as they traveled to Brussels to be received by the Estates-General.

There, he praised Margaret's and her council's governance of Low Countries affairs in his absence, and expressed his pleasure at being back in the land of his birth. Margaret was gratified, but cognizant that he wouldn't stay long. He was soon due in Germany to receive his crown, but first he must treat with the English after their summit with the French concluded.

Over the next few weeks, Margaret and her court enjoyed frequent missives reporting on events unfolding outside Calais at the Field of the Cloth of Gold. Her contacts informed her that Francis I was besting Henry VIII, making cordial relations on the surface while daily outshining the English king with superior displays of prowess and gallantry.

Margaret chuckled. Francis I would unwittingly undermine whatever goodwill Henry VIII had held for him in arranging their summit. The result would be to leave the English king in a more receptive mood to treat with her unostentatious nephew.

Travelling to Gravelines with Charles on July 10, 1520, Margaret counted on her nephew's natural reserve and unflamboyant demeanor to provide the antidote necessary to restore Henry VIII's good humor and win his favor. After spending two weeks being bested by Francis I in everything from a wrestling match to the attentions of the ladies, the English king was in sore need of having his vanity stroked. Who better but her sober nephew—good at listening, uninterested in occupying center stage, and sufficiently respectful of Henry's more senior age and experience?

Within days the old Anglo-Imperial alliance had been reaffirmed. A treaty was drawn up that promised the English king's daughter in marriage to Charles.

Privately, Margaret laughed. Such a promise was unlikely to be carried out, but it was better than none. Princess Mary was only four years old. Charles was twenty, already a father. But any treaty strengthening a relationship with England was welcomed. Invariably it would weaken whatever alliance England had made with France.

While Charles humored Henry VIII, Margaret met with her former sister-in-law. They had shared joyful moments in Spain, with Margaret teaching Catherine French to prepare her for her marriage to the ill-fated Arthur, heir-apparent to the English throne before his untimely death.

The Queen of England was now in her thirty-fifth year, with one daughter and no sons. She had borne a son and heir to Henry in 1511 and had named Margaret as godmother. But the babe had died a month after its birth.

Sipping on cool celery tonics, they sat in a corner of Margaret's gardens at the Court of Savoy. As the hum of summer's insects cloaked her low tones, Catherine confided her childbearing troubles. After losing her first child—a girl—in a stillbirth, then her newborn prince, she had borne two stillborn sons and another stillborn daughter. Her luck had not been good, and Henry VIII was not a patient man.

"My good sister, may God grant you a prince in the fullness of time," Margaret encouraged. But she worried for her sister-in-law. If she failed to produce sons, what would become of her?

"The fullness of time has already passed for me, sister, and I fear I am to bear no more," Catherine confessed.

"Then be happy with your princess and think of Queen Anne and King Louis in France, who were so happy with theirs," Margaret suggested.

Catherine's face fell. "King Louis was far older than his wife, and doted on her," she said.

"As I'm sure your husband dotes on you," Margaret said, although she wasn't sure at all. Already she had noted that the English king's energy far outstripped Catherine's, who was six years older.

She had also heard that the king had sired a son with his mistress just the year before.

"You know he has a son by one of his favorites," Catherine divulged, as if reading her thoughts.

"A son is not an heir," Margaret pointed out.

"Well do I know, but time is passing and mine may have run out."

The bleak look on Catherine's face made Margaret's heart ache. "Then may your princess be strong and healthy, and when the time comes she will marry my nephew and create children who will unite your kingdom with the land of your birth," she exclaimed, knowing such a union was unlikely to take place. Henry VIII would not wish to see his kingdom overshadowed by the might of Charles' empire.

"May it come to pass," the Queen of England responded, her eyes flicking away.

Margaret gazed at her former sister-in-law, thinking how much she resembled her older sister Juana in features. Yet how different Catherine of Aragon was in temperament and dignity of bearing. "May God hold you tight in His arms," she exclaimed, holding out her own.

"May my husband hold me tight in his arms, and may something come of it," Catherine responded as she fell into her embrace.

"I have missed you, sister," Margaret murmured, her heart full.

"I have missed you, too. And one other, so badly," Catherine whispered, as if she were twelve again, and Margaret seventeen.

"Who?" Margaret asked.

Catherine's voice caught in her throat. "I miss my dear mother."

"God rest her soul." Thinking of that great and loving queen who had taught her the rudiments of rulership, Margaret held back tears. Isabella of Spain would be grieved to know that her youngest was alone and worried in a far-off land, unable to produce the male heir her husband and his kingdom sought.

Drat kings who expect their queens to be brood mares, Margaret thought. And curse the fates who gave numerous children to mothers who were mad, and denied good mothers who wished to bear more but couldn't.

A steward appeared. The emperor had arrived with the English king. As Margaret accompanied Catherine to meet them, she thought that Isabella must look down from Heaven and grieve over the sorrows of her children. Her strong bloodline with Ferdinand had succeeded best through Juana, the most mentally weak of all five of their offspring. How capricious the fates could be. And how lucky Margaret felt to have escaped their vicissitudes by eluding further marriages.

Charles emerged from the shade of the loggia. Behind him loomed the tall, robust form of Henry VIII, his eyes glued to the back of the serving girl who was bringing in refreshments.

Margaret thought back to her brother's similar disrespectful behavior in front of Juana; she would have chastised him on the spot.

But Queen Catherine of England was not her hotheaded sister. Calm and collected, she tightened her grip on Margaret's arm, the only indication that she had noticed.

Squeezing Catherine's arm in return, Margaret greeted the men.

AT THE END OF October, Margaret traveled eastward to Aachen to see Charles crowned. In Maastricht, the last Low Countries town before crossing into Germany, she attended a public assembly Charles held. There, he formally installed her as Governor of the Netherlands and accorded her additional powers to rule in his absence.

Margaret basked in the warmth of his approval. Already, she held all the powers Charles had granted her, including the seal of the Lord of the Netherlands. But the investiture by Charles himself, on his way to be crowned Emperor-elect of the Holy Roman Empire, gave her additional validation before the nobles and burghers. Such official recognition would strengthen her authority once her nephew returned to Spain.

From Maastricht it was a half-day journey to Aachen, due east. There, Germaine de Foix joined her to watch Charles receive the crown of King of the Romans.

As the two ladies sat together in the Cathedral of Our Lady of Aachen, Margaret speculated on what the relationship was between Ferdinand's widow and her nephew.

At thirty-two, Germaine was closer in age to her than she was to Charles. It was apparent that Charles regarded her highly, as he had invited her to accompany him on his trip from Spain. Margaret had heard he had also arranged for Germaine to be married the year before to the younger cousin of Joachim I, the prince-elector of Brandenburg. Somehow Charles had fobbed off the mother of his daughter onto a less illustrious prince than himself while still retaining Germaine's loyalties.

Margaret glanced sideways at the Dowager Queen of Aragon. She guessed Germaine had long been schooled in the world of political maneuvering as wife to Europe's most cunning political operator. How had Germaine explained her one-year-old daughter to her new husband, Johann of Ansbach-Brandenburg? Or had Charles offered something to both Germaine and Johann so that all questions over the child had been quieted by the clink of gold or the promise of a sizeable reward ahead?

Gazing at her nephew's prostrate form on the floor, his arms outstretched to make a cross with his body, Margaret marveled that he had developed such deft political skills in managing his private affairs.

"Now that the emperor has been crowned, will you return to Spain with your husband?" Margaret asked, not too pointedly she hoped.

Germaine de Foix gave Margaret a cryptic smile. "We will remain in Germany for a time, and then one will see."

Margaret wanted to ask about the child, but Charles had not recognized her. Unless Germaine brought it up, she could not raise a subject that her nephew had chosen to keep to himself. "May you enjoy your visit to your husband's lands in Germany," she remarked.

"My husband has no lands in Germany. But we will visit his cousin before returning to my own lands in Spain," Germaine replied.

"They are in Aragon, are they not?" Margaret asked.

"Yes. In Valencia, where my lord Ferdinand and I made our court."

"How lovely it must be there." *And how agreeably far from where Charles holds court in Castile, on the other side of Spain*, Margaret thought.

Germaine de Foix nodded, her carefully arranged face a study in royal training.

Margaret saw a master of the art of dissembling before her. She prayed that her nephew would reward her well for keeping a distance from him. If Germaine remained in his life, Margaret feared the time would not come for Charles to find a wife.

Returning to Brussels with her nephew, all thoughts of Germaine de Foix vanished. War had broken out in both the north and the south, with Charles of Egmond revolting in Gelderland again and French troops threatening to invade the Low Countries' southern borders. With Charles' presence and support before the Estates-General Margaret was able to get funds approved to outfit the Burgundian army, which she oversaw.

But she struggled to contain both outbreaks as Charles returned to Germany to conduct the Diet of Worms. There, he was to meet the German monk stirring up so much trouble for him. Opening on January 23, 1521, the assembly met until the end of May, with Margaret receiving regular updates. At the close of the Diet reports came that the emperor had made two important decrees.

Issuing the Edict of Worms on May 25, Charles V decreed that Martin Luther was a heretic and forbade the people of the Holy Roman Empire to defend or support his teachings. Despite the severity of the edict, the emperor allowed Luther to leave safely. The increasingly influential monk had been given a writ of safe passage by the Prince of Saxony, one of the most important of the prince-electors who had supported Charles in his bid to become emperor-elect.

Secondly, the emperor delegated his younger brother Ferdinand as his representative in Germany, and named him Governor of Habsburg hereditary lands in Austria. Ferdinand had married Anne of Hungary just weeks before the Diet ended, bringing Hungary and Bohemia into the House of Habsburg's portfolio. It was a marriage which his grandfather Maximilian would have applauded.

Margaret paid scant attention to the matter of Martin Luther in her jubilation over her nephew's decision to appoint a family member to govern the German and Austrian dominions of his empire. With such an appointment, she guessed Charles was thinking about returning to Spain. Eager to see him again, she looked forward to his return to Brussels.

But sad news arrived before Charles did.

William de Croy, Lord of Chièvres, was dead. Charles' right-hand man had succumbed in Worms just days after the Diet had ended. The messenger reported that it was said he had been poisoned by reformers as reprisal for Charles' edict against Martin Luther.

Margaret grieved for her nephew. For many years she had disliked de Croy, but they had arrived at an entente in their mutual devotion to Charles. It was inconceivable to her that any would seek to poison such a venerable man.

When the messenger related that the Lord of Chièvres had argued against persecution of Luther at the assembly, Margaret speculated it was more likely that the elderly counselor, at age 63, had died of natural causes. Whatever the case it was a large loss for Charles, comparable to her losing Gattinara, or Henry VIII losing Wolsey. Margaret prayed that her nephew had sufficiently absorbed de Croy's lessons in rulership to be capable of taking the helm himself.

As she awaited the emperor's return, an unexpected visitor arrived. The German painter and printmaker, Albrecht Dürer, called on Margaret at the Court of Savoy. Accompanying the celebrated artist was his wife Agnes and her maid.

"Lady Margaret, I am honored to be received by you." Dürer bowed low, still handsome at age fifty—although the hand he held to his chest was gnarled and knotty.

"I trust you have met with success in Antwerp, Monsieur," Margaret greeted. She had heard he had widened his circle of patrons from amongst Antwerp's wealthy Portuguese merchants, endowed with sophisticated tastes and deep pockets from the past twenty years of seafaring successes.

"It has been a pleasurable visit that I hope will gain me new commissions. But I am here to thank you for prevailing upon the emperor to support me."

"My father patronized you, and so I thought it right for the emperor to continue your annuity," Margaret said.

"I am grateful for such support in the wake of your father's death."

"And you are now on your way back to Germany?" she asked, unsure of the reason for his visit.

"Yes, my lady, we are on our way back to Nuremberg, and I am here to present you with an expression of my thanks for your patronage." Dürer gestured to his wife's maid, who stepped forward with a wrapped canvas.

"I have not commissioned anything from you, to my recall," Margaret said, wondering what it was he was about to show her.

"No, my lady. It is a work I did of your father in his final month. I thought you might like it."

Margaret watched as the portrait was unwrapped and set on the arms of a chair.

The first thing her eye was drawn to was the prominent insignia medallion of Austria with the ram fleece of the Order of the Golden Fleece hanging from it. It seemed much too large to her. Her father's image appeared to be studying the medallion, his head dwarfed by its imposing size. She would so much rather see his image appear to be looking at her.

Cocking her head, she tried to appreciate the portrait. But the stab wound was too deep as she viewed her father contemplating his order, the one from which she had been excluded. To make matters worse, another limp sheep hung from his neck.

"It doesn't suit me," she blurted out, forgetting her usual tact.

Dürer's mouth dropped open. Behind him his wife and her maid exchanged worried glances.

"But my lady, I had wished to present this to honor you, as well as him." Wounded pride laced Dürer's tone.

Margaret felt a similar wounded pride with the oversized insignia staring her in the face, as if taunting her. How well she remembered those two painful years that members of the order had caused her.

Avoiding the insignia she again studied the canvas, this time focusing on Dürer's depiction of Maximilian. The painting portrayed him accurately; her beloved father looked tired and old. But it captured none of Maxi's charm, his ability to inspire, to rally men to his causes—not for love of gold, but for love of the nobility in their souls that he stirred.

"It doesn't look like him," she remarked.

Dürer's face colored. "But my lady, this is what he looked like when I visited him in Innsbruck in 1518."

Margaret cast a gimlet eye at the aging artist. "I know what my father looked like, and this is not how I wish to remember him."

Beads of sweat broke out on the painter's temples. "Lady Margaret, forgive me, but I thought you would be pleased to accept this token of my appreciation for your support and your father's."

Margaret's usual ability to dissemble had fled. The painting offended her. She could not stomach viewing a tired and ailing old man with a dead sheep slung around his neck on a daily basis.

"It does not suit, Monsieur Dürer. Wrap it up so I am not reminded of my dear father's final months." *Or of that precious order that almost cost me my position.*

Dürer looked shocked. "Ah, Madame, I fear I have offended you when I had wished to esteem you." Behind him, his wife's eyes darted between him and Margaret.

"Do not fear, Monsieur. I will see to it that your annuity continues. May God grant you a safe journey home and many years of prosperity ahead." With a wave of her hand Margaret signaled the end of the interview.

"Thank you, Lady Margaret. I will be on my way." As Dürer wrapped up the painting, his gnarled hands trembled slightly. Bowing, he backed out, along with his wife and her maid.

Margaret turned to her lady-in-waiting. "Was I too harsh?"

Lady Elisabeth arched a brow. "It was not your finest moment, Madame. But I know what it was that soured you."

She sniffed. "I could not have those dreadful sheep mocking me every time I passed by."

"No, Madame. And the emperor was not looking his best."

Margaret's heart caught. "I don't see why such a talent would not have tried to capture the soul rather than the jowls and fatigue."

"Monsieur Dürer is known for his verisimilitude. It is what has made his reputation," Lady Elisabeth demurred.

"And it was my father who first noted his genius. But he overdid the verisimilitude this time."

Lady Elisabeth chuckled. "Madame, when you have your next portrait done, find another artist."

"May it be an artist who captures who I am rather than what I look like."

"What you look like is not so bad, my lady."

Margaret glanced into the Venetian mirror on the wall and frowned. "If I am to be remembered to posterity, may it be in a likeness I can bear to look at."

"Do you think your father would not have been pleased with this one?"

"He would have said, 'Albrecht, liven up my face and make that medallion smaller than my head.'"

Lady Elisabeth burst out laughing. "Madame, that is what *you* would have said. But your father must have wanted it that way."

"I cannot imagine why," Margaret grumbled.

"Neither can I, but I can see why you wouldn't want it up on your wall, annoying you for all times."

"Quite right." Margaret marched from the room, her hound trotting behind her. She would go find Neuteken to cheer her up.

Portrait of Emperor Maximilian I
By Albrecht Dürer, 1519
Germanisches Nationalmuseum,
Nuremberg, Germany
From www.albrecht-durer.org

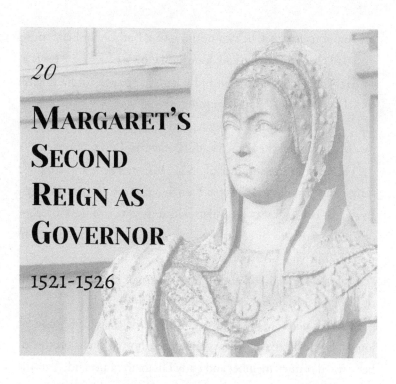

20

MARGARET'S SECOND REIGN AS GOVERNOR

1521-1526

"Without women nothing is possible—neither military courage, nor art nor poetry, nor music or philosophy, nor even religion; God is only truly seen through them." — Castiglione, *The Book of the Courtier*[1]

When Charles arrived back from Worms, Margaret could sense what a blow the loss of his closest advisor must have been. Keeping

---

1. Dorothy Moulton Mayer, *The Great Regent* (New York: Funk & Wagnalls, 1966), p. 5.

his emotions in check he said nothing of it but sought her counsel on a daily basis, just as he had done with Chièvres.

Margaret stepped up. She and Charles appealed to the English to help resolve what was beginning to look like war with France. Henry VIII's counselor Wolsey replied that he stood ready to act as mediator between the French and the imperial Low Countries.

Throughout the summer of 1521, Margaret sent and supplied forces that Charles led to repel French advances on their borders. By fall the emperor was headquartered at the estate of the Governor of Oudenaarde, to direct imperial troops besieging the French in nearby Tournai to the southwest.

Charles' army prevailed, and once Tournai was taken at the end of November Margaret expected him back in Brussels.

But her nephew lingered in Oudenaarde for several months longer. She surmised he was in good hands, hosted by the brother of her trusted council member and Lady Elisabeth's husband, Antoine de Lalaing.

By January, reports arrived that Charles was keeping company with a beautiful young Flemish woman serving in his host's household.

Margaret was not surprised. Her nephew was not yet twenty-two years old, barely a man but already an emperor, trying to manage Martin Luther's revolt against the Church in Germany, war with France in the Low Countries, and a Castilian uprising against his rule in Spain since he had left. If he sought comfort in the arms of a serving girl, it was a natural response.

But when Charles returned to Brussels in the spring then set sail for Spain in June 1522, Margaret had no inkling of what he had left behind.

In December 1522, reports came to Malines that Johanna van der Gheynst of Oudenaarde had given birth to a daughter sired by Charles V.

"Do you know anything of this?" Margaret asked Lady Elisabeth.

"No more than you do, Madame, but I can ask my husband," her lady-in-waiting said. She would speak with Antoine that evening. He was sure to know something of the goings-on of the winter before at his brother's home.

"Will he tell you the truth?"

Lady Elisabeth shot a sly grin. "If he is hiding something, I will sniff it out."

"What do you think?"

"I think that the emperor spent a good deal more time in Oude-naarde than we expected him to."

"Indeed. Find out more."

Within days, Lady Elizabeth reported back to Margaret. "My sources say the child is likely to be the emperor's," she said with a smile.

"And why do you seem so pleased?" Margaret asked.

"It is you who should be pleased, for you have been honored."

"How so?"

Lady Elizabeth looked coy. "The babe's name is Margaret."

Margaret hid her own smile. Her lady-in-waiting was right. She was gratified. "If it is his, I am honored."

"Your nephew must have spoken highly of you to the mother, my lady."

"I would doubt he spoke of me at all, as apparently he had better things to do," Margaret quipped.

Lady Elisabeth giggled.

"And what of the mother?" Margaret inquired.

"She is from a good family, Madame. Her father is a carpetmaker from near Oudenaarde, her mother an educated woman who manages the family business accounts."

"I am glad to hear it," Margaret breathed out, relieved that Charles had at least favored an honest Flemish girl in his indiscretion.

Writing to her nephew in Spain, she put it tactfully. "I have heard that a daughter named Margaret has been born to a member of the household of the Governor of Oudenaarde. Pray tell me if you have news to share. I will be delighted to hear it, if you do."

With his next letter to her, Charles confirmed paternity in his usual succinct manner. He made no mention of his intentions for the child's future.

"The emperor has let me know the child is his," Margaret related to her lady-in-waiting.

"The mother chose wisely when she named her," Lady Elisabeth remarked.

Margaret's pride flared. "I am not displeased. But I need your help to see that the child is properly cared for."

"Do you think he will acknowledge her?"

"I will see to it that he does," Margaret affirmed. And if the babe was worthy of the name she bore, she would ensure that she grew up to assume a role of importance. Royal blood ran in the child's veins. Margaret would harness her namesake to expand the House of Habsburg, one way or another.

As MARGARET'S TROUBLES GREW over France's incursions on the Low Countries' borders, her family responsibilities grew, too.

In 1523, her niece, Isabella, arrived in Malines with her three children and husband Christian II, newly deposed as King of Denmark. Margaret did not think highly of Christian, and was suspicious of both his and Isabella's reformist sympathies. But their children were innocent victims of their parents' mistakes, just as the children of Philip and Juana had been. Most importantly, they were Habsburgs.

Margaret settled them in Lier, to the north of Malines. Prince John was five, the princesses Dorothea and Christina three and two. Along with support of her young namesake, whom she had placed with a noble family in Brussels to raise, Margaret found herself reprising her role as surrogate mother to a second generation of Habsburg heirs.

Conferring with Charles in Spain on what to do about Christian II's pleas for money to regain his throne, Margaret advised not to offer any. Such aid would anger her Low Countries' burghers, who were loath to part from their guilders to support foreign causes. And more trouble lay ahead should Charles back a ruler who supported the reformists' cause, which might then spread to the Low Countries.

Charles listened. He declined the appeal of his brother-in-law, whom Margaret could see had made her niece miserable.

The rumors had been true of Christian II's household being ruled by his commoner mistress and her mother, a former tavern keeper. His mistress had been poisoned in 1517 and Christian had executed the nobleman thought to be responsible, angering the aristocracy, who had subsequently deposed him. But his mistress' mother had continued to exert undue influence over him, serving as his financial advisor and dominating his affairs until the Danish nobility had chased him from their realm.

Yet still, Isabella supported him. Margaret put them on a small stipend and appointed a Catholic Flemish woman of good repute as governess to their children. She would not condone Habsburg princes and princesses being raised in a Protestant household.

Christendom might be splintering to the East of the Rhine, but in her own realm she would support the Church. One day she hoped to see Charles V crowned by the pope as Holy Roman Emperor and not just emperor-elect. It was a supreme validation Maximilian had never attained.

But when the first Flemish pope in history, Adrian VI, the former Adrian of Utrecht, suddenly died in Rome in 1523, Charles V's plans to be crowned by his childhood tutor died, too. Cardinal Wolsey in England threw his red hat into the ring for the papacy and was defeated, beaten by Giulio de Medici, who took the name Clement VII. Devastated, Wolsey blamed Charles V for not supporting him and cooled off from Margaret, too.

Busy attending to the concerns of her seventeen provinces, Margaret bided her time until fortune's wheel turned up once more. That day came on Charles V's twenty-fifth birthday, solidifying Habsburg ascendancy in a way that none could have foretold.

On February 24, 1525, the Imperial Army captured Francis I of France at Pavia, south of Milan. It was a wholly unexpected event, made possible by the French king's insouciant belief in his invincibility and an unfortunate funneling of funds into his mother's pockets instead of to his mercenaries, who had gone unpaid.

Louise of Savoy, France's regent while her son was in Italy, had pulled a maneuver worthy of Maximilian. Margaret's sources related that funds had been released to the regent to get to Francis I to pay his army. But instead they had disappeared into Louise's private account, and Francis had found his unpaid forces less motivated to fight on his behalf.

Also disastrous, the French had lost one of their most important military commanders. Two years earlier Charles, Duke of Bourbon, had defected, offering his services to the emperor. Bourbon had been enraged when Francis I had seized certain of his land inheritances without due process of law. As a further blow, Bourbon had insulted Louise of Savoy with a public rejection of her marriage offer.

Margaret guessed that Louise had wanted the Duke of Bourbon's lands, not so much the duke himself. But Bourbon, fourteen years younger than Louise, had been infuriated to receive a proposal from the woman who had intrigued with her son to steal his inheritance. He had leapt into the arms of France's enemy, the Holy Roman Empire.

With the capture of Francis I, imperial domination of Italy was won. Charles V had the French king transported to Spain, where he was held prisoner in Madrid.

Margaret rejoiced. Finally, Burgundian territories that the French had seized in 1477 could be recovered. And with such unexpected good fortune, English support was no longer needed to vanquish the French.

Charles wrote to Henry VIII in August 1525, asking to be released from his promise to marry the English king's nine-year-old daughter. The young emperor reasoned that he was ready to marry and his legislative body wished for him to marry an Iberian princess who would be capable of acting as regent when he was occupied with other parts of his domains.

Henry VIII agreed. Now that France was at the mercy of the Empire, the English king was loath to further strengthen Charles V's hand by giving him his daughter.

After the Castilian revolt of a few years earlier, Charles V saw the wisdom in making an Iberian union to ease the discontent of his Spanish subjects over having their country run by Burgundian foreigners. His choice of bride was his cousin, the Infanta Isabella of Portugal, daughter of Manuel I of Portugal and Maria of Aragon, Charles' mother Juana's younger sister.

Upon hearing the news Margaret enquired from discreet sources about Germaine de Foix. She learned that Charles had appointed her and her husband as joint viceroys of Valencia, on Spain's east coast, far from his own court in Castile. Relieved, she thanked God that her nephew had seen to it that his bride would not suffer the indignity of entering marriage with her new husband's former favorite nearby.

In January of 1526 Charles V set the French king free under the Treaty of Madrid; accepting as hostages, in his place, his two oldest sons, ages seven and six. Five days later, Margaret's niece and Charles' younger sister, Isabella, died at age twenty-four, doubtless weakened by the unhappy marriage she had endured with her disgraced husband.

By March, Margaret's sorrow turned to joy when word arrived of Charles V's wedding to Isabella of Portugal in Seville on March 10, 1526. The marriage was both politically and economically astute, bringing Charles a large dowry which would help pay off some of his debts for his 1519 imperial election. But Margaret was impatient to learn more of what manner of match her nephew had made.

Sweet tidings arrived that summer. The emperor had fallen deeply in love with his bride, whose beauty was matched by her intelligence, education, and good head. They had taken up residence in the Alhambra in Granada.

Margaret rejoiced for Charles. Well she knew the wonders of the vast palace where she had lived with the Spanish monarchs and their princesses in the wake of her first husband's passing. With its tinkling fountains and lush gardens, she could imagine what raptures her nephew was discovering there with his well-matched bride.

In September, fortune's wheel spun again. Margaret's niece Mary's husband, King Louis of Hungary and Bohemia, had died at the hands of the Turks at the Battle of Mohács on August 29, 1526.

Mary of Hungary, youngest of the princesses Margaret had raised in Malines, had lost the husband she had loved, too soon and without issue, at the tender age of twenty-one.

Feeling her niece's pain as if it were her own, Margaret thought to bring Mary back to the Low Countries to teach her the ropes of governing. With Charles settling into married life in Spain, she would need someone to whom she could hand over governance of the Netherlands one day. Who better than capable and plucky Mary, the most resilient of all of her three nieces? But first, a new king of Hungary and Bohemia must be found.

Margaret and Mary conspired with Charles to see that it was a family member who ascended the throne. Ferdinand of Austria was chosen, whose wife Anne of Hungary was sister to the fallen Hungarian king.

Putting down Mary's letter announcing the good news, Margaret chortled. How proud Maximilian would be of their success in shooting the House of Habsburg's fortunes to the stars.

21

HENRY VIII, THE SACK OF ROME

1527-1528

IN THE SPRING OF 1527 Margaret's contact at the English court arrived from London. The King of England had sent an envoy to Rome to petition the pope for an annulment.

"What possible grounds can he have?' Margaret railed. Her former sister-in-law had been married to Henry VIII for eighteen years and borne him both a daughter and a son, although the boy had died.

"It would seem that the king makes the argument that his marriage to Queen Catherine was not legal in the first place," the man related.

"Why ever not?"

"He bases his argument on an Old Testament verse that forbids marriage to the wife of one's brother."

Margaret gaped. "And this is bothering the king's conscience eighteen years into his marriage?"

"It is the king's pretext for freeing himself to marry his favorite," her contact replied grimly.

"You must be joking," Margaret exclaimed. Kings and princes frequently had favorites. One did not throw over one's queen to marry one of them.

"No one is joking at the English court now. All whisper about the king's obsession behind closed doors, fearing the wrath of his favorite as much as they do the king."

"Who is this favorite, who has captured the king's reason?" Margaret demanded.

The man cleared his throat. "You know her, Madame. She served at your court years ago."

Margaret's eyes widened. Several English girls had served at her court. Only one had promised to be extraordinary. "You cannot mean the young Boleyn girl."

"The same, Madame. No longer so young, but still young enough to enchant the king."

"Good God, I heard he had favored the older one," Margaret recalled, thinking back to rumors about Mary Boleyn. Had he discarded her for her sister?

"Long over with. But the younger is not cut from the same cloth. She refuses to succumb unless the king weds her."

Margaret drew in her breath. "Do you tell me a courtier is demanding the King of England divorce his wife to marry her?"

Her agent lowered his voice "All say that Mistress Boleyn has turned his head, Madame. But they say it quietly. She is a force, and one does not wish to get on the wrong side of her."

Margaret was flabbergasted. "How can a young woman of twenty-something years be a force that directs the King of England to overthrow the laws of Church and State?"

"The king wishes for a son, Madame. He has one by a mistress, but he wishes for one by a wife and queen."

"And so he thinks to just replace the one he already has?"

"Apparently so, Madame. But none may refer to the queen as his wife now, as he argues that he does not have one, but has mistakenly lived in sin all these years."

"He sins at this present time to think he can toss off his wife just because she has only given him a daughter." Margaret paused, contemplating the full weight of her agent's words. "And what would this mean for the Princess Mary?"

"It would mean that she is no longer recognized as his heir," her agent replied.

"But that is absurd!" Margaret cried.

"Most women in England think the same, but those at court are careful not to say so."

"What position does Cardinal Wolsey take in all this?" Margaret inquired.

The man's face took on a fearful look. "He has been tasked by the king to make sure the annulment is granted, my lady. But…"

"But what?" How could Wolsey, who had sought the papacy himself, be in favor of such an upending of Church law?

"But it is said that he insulted Mistress Boleyn years ago, when she first caught the king's eye and no one thought of her as more than a trifle."

"And now what?"

"He fears she will seek revenge and turn the king against him," he related in a lower voice.

"So he carries out the king's mission, not because he supports it, but because he is afraid of a young woman?"

The man's eyes widened. "He is not the only one, Madame. She has a fierce temper, and is said to hold reformists' views."

Margaret shook her head in amazement. What manner of woman had she helped form at her court so long ago? "I worry for Wolsey," she remarked. As much as they had not been close in recent years she was pained to think of the untenable position he was now in.

"As do I. The king is beginning to perceive him as more loyal to the Church than he is to him. If the pope does not grant the annulment, Mistress Boleyn will seek the cardinal's downfall."

"And what does the king's close friend, the Duke of Suffolk, think?" Margaret queried, unable to resist asking.

"He supports the king in all ways, Madame. But his wife serves at Queen Catherine's court, and wants nothing to do with the king's favorite."

"So it is causing trouble in his marriage." Margaret indulged a delicious moment before checking her feelings.

"All I know, Madame, is that the situation is causing trouble and fear between husbands and wives all over England, as everyone has a different opinion on it."

"Ah, then I am happy to be widowed, for I do not need to hide my position for fear of anyone."

Her contact's face was bleak. "You have just described the state of the English court, Madame."

"Go now and report back to me on anything more you hear of this matter," she bade him, reaching for her writing implements. She would urge her nephew to sway the pope not to grant the King of England an annulment. It would destroy Catherine of Aragon's position. Far worse, it would set a precedent that would upend the Church. Charles V, protector of the Church as Holy Roman Emperor, could not allow such a thing to happen.

"Madame, Rome has been sacked and the pope is held hostage," the messenger panted out.

Margaret's hand flew to her throat. "Good God, no! By whom?"

"It is said by imperial troops, my lady." The messenger looked fearfully at Margaret, as if to implore her not to punish him for such news.

"That is impossible! The emperor would never allow such a thing."

"It is said that the troops were under command of the Duke of Bourbon and had not been paid for some time."

"That is no excuse for taking the pope hostage!" Margaret cried. What was Europe coming to?

"Much worse, too. It is said the soldiers have raped nuns and killed women and children."

"Dear God, my nephew will be aghast. How could the Duke of Bourbon have allowed such license?"

"He was shot outside the city walls as he approached with his troops. When his men saw he was dead they breached the walls and ran amok, pillaging and looting," the man reported.

"But who was second in command?"

"It was the commander Philibert of Châlon, my lady, but the soldiers neither knew nor obeyed him. The Duke of Bourbon had promised them bounty when they reached Rome, in place of the money they were owed, and they were determined to get it."

"'Tis a disgrace unworthy of the Imperial Army!" Margaret exclaimed. *Or of the Habsburg name*, she thought. Thank God her father was dead, not to have to hear of this.

"The army was mostly mercenary, Madame—landsknechts who follow the new Lutheran teachings. They wished to destroy the papal city as revenge for wrongs of the Church they say they have suffered."

"And where is the pope now?" Margaret demanded.

"Since that day of May 6th, he is held prisoner at Castel Sant'Angelo," the messenger reported.

A twinge ran down the back of her leg. "Has the emperor been informed?" she asked. The world was turning upside down. Habsburg rule meant law and order. What had happened in Rome was unthinkable. And it was still unfolding.

"Messengers are on their way to him."

Two weeks later she heard back from Charles. He was horrified to hear of the sack of Rome, and took full responsibility for the unconscionable behavior of imperial troops. On a brighter note, the Empress Isabella had given birth to their first child on May 21, 1527, a son they had named Philip. Margaret's heart leapt to hear such good news, despite the dreadful tidings from Rome.

News from Austria followed in July. Ferdinand's wife, Anne of Hungary, had borne a son named Maximilian. The next generation of Habsburgs was arriving. Margaret vowed to do whatever she could to see that members of her dynastic house upheld order within the guidelines of the Church. A splintering of Christendom would lead to social chaos and war, both within Europe and against the Turks.

The ongoing detention of the pope was transferred from marauding Imperial Army deserters to a law-abiding contingent that Charles sent in. Clement VII was safe, under the protection of the Holy Roman Emperor.

Margaret was heartened that Europe's balance of power had shifted even more dramatically into Habsburg hands, yet she could not ignore the growing underswell of support for Luther's reform movement. The Church itself was no longer the impregnable institution it had once been, with the pope threatened with bodily harm and his city sacked.

As the year 1527 progressed, Margaret's unease grew. Reports came that Rome had crumbled into anarchy. It was not until the early months of 1528 that the situation was contained. Pillaging had ended due to no food left to steal and no prominent Romans left to ransom.

Unburied corpses piled up in the streets had resulted in disease. With the arrival of plague in February 1528, the various armies—both legitimate and bandit-led—withdrew. Rome's population had been decimated from over 55,000 to 10,000—some murdered by marauders, but most fleeing from the complete economic and cultural collapse that had ensued.

Margaret told herself that such a scenario could never happen in her own realm. But the fuel that had fired the rage of the mutinous troops had been fed by growing calls for reform of the existing order. Social revolution was on her doorstep. She was determined to slam shut the door on it.

"What can I do to keep this unrest from spreading to my lands?" she fretted to Gattinara in their usual morning meeting.

"Madame, keep the Low Countries at peace so commerce thrives. In such a way you will put out any kindling flames," her counselor advised.

"Then I must stop the Duke of Guelders once and for all from waging war in my domains," she exclaimed, thinking of what a thorn in her side he had been all these years.

"There is only one way to stop a man like the Duke of Guelders, Madame."

Margaret shot him a sharp look. "I cannot have a man as noble as Charles of Egmond killed. Such an act would make his legend grow even larger. Plus incite every nobleman in Burgundy against Habsburg authority."

"No, of course not," Gattinara agreed. "What you must do is give him enough of what he wants combined with enough of what you need, and make peace with him."

"Have I not tried that countless times before?" Exasperation tinged her tone.

"Have your nephew try it this time, since Guelders won't listen to you. Now that the emperor's men have sacked Rome, Egmond may be fearful of having them visit Gelderland."

Margaret tutted. "He thinks he is as invincible as the hero of his own tale."

"He is older now and knows his time soon runs out, as all men face at a certain age," Gattinara said.

"How old is he?"

Gattinara made a wry grimace. "Ancient, Madame. Almost as old as me."

Margaret chuckled. "Come now, Monsieur. You are not so old that you will leave me anytime soon. I will not allow it, as I need your help to manage my burghers."

"And convince your warlords to put down their arms."

"Egmond will never put down his arms," Margaret grumbled. "Pride puffs his spirit too fiercely."

Gattinara looked thoughtful. "Egmond may be thinking about the legacy he will one day leave."

"He will leave only his reputation, as he has no heirs," Margaret noted. She too, would leave only her reputation. It was something of great value to her in the absence of children and grandchildren. For the first time, she wondered if Charles of Egmond might feel the same.

Gattinara's glance was shrewd. "With no heirs to leave it to, Gelderland passes to the empire."

"Only if Egmond concedes he owes fealty to the empire," Margaret qualified.

"Do you not think it wise for the emperor to offer him something to ensure he does?"

"Some sort of recognition you mean?"

Gattinara nodded. "Perhaps a treaty between princes so that Egmond feels he is finally recognized as lord of his own lands."

Margaret weighed her advisor's words. "… as lord of his own lands, but under fealty to the empire," she spelled out slowly. "Otherwise, the French king will come courting and he will shift like a weathervane." She did not wish to treat with bandits. But Egmond was more than a bandit, although he behaved as one. His father, Adolf, had imprisoned his own father when Philip the Good had supported him in his quest to become Duke of Guelders. There was something more to it, too. She searched her mind to remember.

"Did not my ancestor give Egmond's father some sort of investiture?" she asked.

"Philip the Good knighted him as a member of the Golden Fleece," her counselor noted.

Margaret smarted at mention of the Golden Fleece. Then it came to her. Here was her chance to use the mystique of the order that had caused her so much pain to curb the Netherlands' most insubordinate lord. "I shall suggest to my nephew to reach out to Egmond with a treaty that recognizes his control of Gelderland, but in feudal allegiance to the empire, just as his father swore allegiance to our forefather," she declared.

"And in return for such recognition, the Duke of Guelders is to name the emperor as his heir, should he leave behind none of his own," Gattinara added.

"As a continuation of the knightly brotherhood that bound his father to the emperor's forefather," she concluded, suddenly feeling as light as air.

Pushing back from her desk, Margaret laughed aloud. What did it matter that she would never be asked to be a member of their brotherhood? She was a woman. She would get things done her way. And if that meant harnessing the power of the Order of the Golden Fleece to get her worst enemy to behave, then she was all for it.

22

DEFT DIPLOMACY

1528-1529

"... ladies might well come forward in a measure for submitting the gratification of private hatred and revenge to the far nobler principle of the welfare of nations." — Margaret of Austria[1]

IN THE FALL OF 1528 a letter arrived from the French court, from Louise of Savoy. The mother of the French king had written that her son wished to make peace with Margaret's nephew. Suggesting that too much pride might be involved between the two princes for them to negotiate an agreement themselves, Louise asked what Margaret

---

1. Sarah Gristwood, Game of Queens (New York: Basic Books, 2016), p. 139.

would say to brokering a peace as representative for the emperor while she represented her son.

Margaret put down the letter and walked to the window. Flinching at the sharp pain that traveled down her leg, she rued her age. At forty-eight, she was no longer young. But she still yearned to accomplish more in her lifetime—something that would leave behind a lasting imprint when she was gone.

Leaning on the sill, Margaret gazed out onto the verdant plains surrounding Malines. A vision took shape in her head, larger and broader than any she had previously entertained.

Before her was an opportunity to broker a peace for all Europe, to restore order to Christendom, and to unite Europe's princes in a common aim to push back the Ottoman Empire on its borders. And with Francis I's loss of Naples to Charles V earlier that year, the French king was in a weakened position. It might prove the right moment for her to win concessions for the Empire the French had previously refused.

In April 1528 the French army had besieged Naples, under imperial rule since 1516. Initially the siege went well, but Francis I made the same mistake he had at Pavia in 1525—he failed to pay those who fought for him. This time it was his brilliant naval commander, Andrea Doria, whose nephew had led a French victory over the Spanish Navy in the battle of Capo d'Orso. It was a foolish oversight, bungled in the French king's usual blithe manner.

When Francis I further insulted the Genoese condottieri by not delivering Savona to Genoa as promised, Andrea Doria turned against him. In June 1528, his contract with the French expired and the fearsome warlord offered his services to the Holy Roman Emperor, just as Charles of Bourbon had done a few years earlier.

Doria's defection turned the tide in Italy for the Spanish-Imperial Army. Genoa withdrew its support of France, creating a chink in the wall of the 1526 League of Cognac that Francis I had formed against the emperor.

As summer progressed, the commander of the French forces destroyed the aqueduct that fed water to the city of Naples. But his attempt to cut off food and water to the imperial garrison inside backfired.

The waters of the dismantled aqueduct flooded the marshes around Naples. In the sweltering southern Italian summer, mosquitoes bred and pestilence arose. The French troops began to sicken and die. On August 15th the French commander succumbed, his successor following him a few days later. Dropping like flies, their soldiers were in no shape to continue.

Withdrawing from the siege at the end of August, the French Army soon found themselves pursued by the Imperial Army. Within days Charles V's forces regained control of Naples.

By summer's end, the French were routed from southern Italy. Their only remaining territories were in the north. Just as Louis XII's dreams of conquering Naples had ended in 1504, Francis I's foothold in Italy's boot was over.

Margaret's nephew now held the advantage. The moment was apt to favorably respond to Louise's invitation to broker a peace. But what was to stop Francis I from breaking any new treaty created? Had he not ignored the 1526 Treaty of Madrid he had made with her nephew and conspired with the pope, Venice, Milan, Florence, Genoa, and England to form the League of Cognac against him just months later?

The French were dependably deceptive, Margaret fumed. One could count on them to go behind one's back; therefore, there was no point in treating with them.

Like a phantom knight, her father's figure sprang into her head. He had gone behind her back more times than she cared to remember. The French were not the only ones.

She wrote back to Louise to say she was receptive.

Louise's response was swift. Addressing her as her dear sister-in-law, she pointed out that her son had signed the Treaty of Madrid under duress, as the emperor's prisoner. As such he had not been legally bound, she argued. This time would be different. She herself would see to it that Francis held to whatever agreement was made, as he would enter into it of his own volition.

"If he sticks to any agreement, it will be because his mother forced him to," Margaret griped to Gattinara.

"He will not see his two sons again if he does not abide by whatever terms you and Madame Louise agree upon," her counselor pointed out.

Margaret's tone was dry. "He does not seem to have been unduly concerned with their welfare these past few years while they have been held in Spain."

"I would imagine their grandmother is desperate to get them back," Gattinara speculated.

"I am desperate to see them freed, too. It is not right for children to be held hostage for so long," Margaret worried.

"Then tell the French king's mother that you are willing to sit down with her." Gattinara advised. "Who knows, Madame? This may be your finest hour."

Margaret wrote back to say she was willing to meet, but talks must take place on neutral ground. She suggested Cambrai, where she had won her greatest diplomatic triumph in 1508. Such a setting might prove auspicious again.

While exchanging letters with Louise, word came from Spain. The emperor had sent a proposal to the Duke of Guelders on terms Margaret had suggested. Charles V would recognize Charles of Egmond, Duke of Guelders, as Lord of Guelders, Groningen, and Drente, in exchange for his feudal allegiance. Upon the duke's death, should he die without issue, his lands would revert to the empire, passing to Charles V.

To her great satisfaction, Egmond agreed. On October 20, 1528, the treaty was signed, putting an end to the decades-long war with Gelderland.

"He has gone for the suggestion you put in the emperor's head to make," Gattinara exulted.

"Which you helped me to craft," Margaret said.

"It is what I am here for, Madame."

"And may you be here forever."

Gattinara dipped his head. "For as long as I walk the earth, my lady."

Margaret's heart swelled. She had chosen wisely when she had given Mercurino di Gattinara a position at her court decades earlier. She could not imagine life without him, with his wry humor and unwavering devotion.

With the worst of the Netherlands' interior problems resolved, Margaret threw her energies toward brokering peace between Europe's two most powerful realms. Although the French king had less ground to stand on than the emperor, Margaret's long experience in statesmanship told her not to whip a wounded dog. If Charles V treated Francis too harshly all of Europe would rally to the French king's side, as had happened with the Treaty of Cognac.

And it did not do to look too powerful. Recalling Louis XII's Italian problems in 1509, she thought of his great victory at Agnadello. Provoking the envy of every other prince in Europe, they had banded against the French king to curb France's dominance in Italy.

The same finesse must now be applied so that her nephew did not become Europe's most hated figure. Too strong a display of power was never a good thing, as Charles the Rash had learned, ending up in a frozen bog, hacked to death beyond recognition.

Margaret weighed her strengths. Bringing flexibility and a willingness to compromise to the table, who better than a woman to represent each of Europe's two most powerful rulers to achieve a peaceful outcome between their realms?

Over the winter Margaret prepared for that summer's meeting with Louise of Savoy. Both had been shaped under the cold, clear eye of Europe's most powerful regent of the century before. They would rely on Anne de Beaujeu's dispassionate schooling in their negotiations ahead.

But one sticking point remained—England. No peace for Europe could be concluded without the English agreeing to abide by it. Henry VIII was in treaty agreement with Francis I with the 1526 Treaty of Cognac. But he had been in close relation with Margaret for far longer, due to England and the Low Countries' extensive trade history.

Margaret needed to include the English king and Wolsey in whatever outcome she and Louise of Savoy achieved. But with each envoy she sent to warm the English to the upcoming talks, she only received back news concerning the king's desired annulment. Her contact said the English court referred to it as the king's 'great matter,' eclipsing all other affairs.

She was incensed to hear that the king had installed his favorite in a nearby palace with her own court. It was said that many visited her to curry favor. Increasingly, Queen Catherine was being isolated, her influence diminished daily.

In addition, her contact reported that Anne Boleyn had gifted Henry VIII with a copy of a new book by William Tyndale, the English Lutheran who had translated the Bible into English.

"What is this new work called?" Margaret asked.

"*The Obedience of a Christian Man and How Christian Rulers Ought to Govern*," the man related.

"And what does this Tyndale say about such matters that Mistress Boleyn thinks to plant in the king's head?" Margaret asked.

"It is said, Madame, that his book proposes that it is the king of a country who should head up its church, and not the pope."

"But Christendom would break into small pieces if such a heresy came to pass," Margaret protested, alarmed to hear Henry VIII was entertaining reformist ideas.

"It is an idea that might hearten the king, should the pope refuse to grant his annulment," her contact said dryly.

"I wonder that the English king is so set on his course that he does not see the danger in it to all of Christendom," Margaret exclaimed.

"If I may say so, Madame, the English king is a man who wants what he wants. And it is beginning to look like he will do whatever is necessary to obtain it."

"Let us hope he will come to his senses once this infatuation has passed," she fretted.

"It does not look to pass anytime soon, but even if it does she will have convinced him that he has the authority to change the law to suit his will," the man noted.

Shocked to think that her bright young maid of honor was swaying England's king to overturn the most basic tenets of Christendom, Margaret pondered her path forward. It was galling to think she must win Henry VIII over to whatever agreement they came up with, when she was finding him less palatable with every report from London.

In June 1529, two events occurred that strengthened her position in the summit meeting to come.

On June 21 the French Army in Landriano near Pavia in Northern Italy was defeated by Charles V's Spanish-Imperial forces. Finally, the French presence in Italy was finished, both in the south and in the north.

Eight days later Charles V signed a treaty with Pope Clement VII, restoring their relationship after two fractious years following the sack of Rome.

With the French booted from Italy, the emperor and the pope agreed to pursue peace in Italy and join forces to repel the Turks. Charles V promised to restore Medici rule in Florence, with the pope's nineteen-year-old nephew, Alessandro de Medici, at its head.

In return, Clement VII agreed to crown Charles V, raising him from emperor-elect to Holy Roman Emperor and Protector of the Church. In true Habsburg fashion, the agreement was sealed by the promise of this same nephew of the pope to Charles V's natural daughter, Margaret, age six.

Margaret rejoiced. Her journey to Cambrai only days away, she had two more arrows in her quiver with which to do battle with her summit adversary. Especially satisfying was that her nephew had provided for her namesake, his only child born and raised in the Low Countries.

"Let Margaret's mother know that her father has arranged a marriage for her with a young prince of the House of Medici," she instructed Lady Elisabeth.

"'Tis a high honor for a natural-born child to marry a Medici prince," her lady-in-waiting remarked.

Margaret looked at her sharply. "Why should not the daughter of an emperor marry the son of a Medici prince?"

"Which one, Madame?"

"Alessandro, the son of Lorenzo de Medici."

Lady Elisabeth raised a brow. "Is he?"

"I have just told you so," Margaret retorted.

Margaret's lady-in-waiting cast a knowing glance. "As the pope tells all the world."

Margaret returned the look. "You think he is the pope's son?"

"Giulio de Medici was a man before he became pope," Lady Elisabeth noted.

"Sworn to the cloth," Margaret pointed out.

"Yes, and we both know that the cloth is often underneath the couple who bed upon it," her lady-in-waiting quipped.

Margaret stifled a chortle. "Lady Elisabeth, you shock me."

"Lady Margaret, you have seen too much of the world to be shocked by any such thing."

"Well then, will it not be a marriage of equals in more ways than one?" Margaret asked, thinking it might prove a practical match.

Neither bride nor groom could lord it over the other that one was legitimate and the other natural-born.

"It will prove a fine match should it come to pass," Lady Elisabeth agreed.

"'Tis a good way to plant a foothold in Florence for the empire," Margaret observed.

"It appears your nephew continues your father's tradition of using marriage to expand his house across Europe."

A smile played on Margaret's lips, her father's seamed and loving face coming to her. "'Tis a tried and true method."

"Even if he is marrying his daughter to the son of a pope."

"Perhaps popes should be allowed to marry," Margaret suggested.

Her lady-in-waiting raised merry eyes. "My lady, it is now you who shock me."

Margaret held up a hand in protest. "I will never be a reformist. But legitimizing the children of priests and popes would be a good idea for all concerned." She had thought as much for years, but her foremost preoccupations were governance and diplomacy, not so much the Church or what men of it chose to do with their bodies.

"You know that Martin Luther married a former nun," Lady Elisabeth divulged.

Margaret had heard something to that effect. "May he do what he likes, but I will not have his teachings spread in my domain."

Her lady-in-waiting tutted. "No, of course not."

"I have noted already that times are changing, and I am going to Cambrai to see that they don't change too far. Now take my message to Margaret's mother so you can get back here to help me pack."

"On my way, Madame."

After her lady-in-waiting left, Margaret peered into the Venetian looking glass on the wall. Good news had invigorated her for the battle ahead with Louise.

In the mirror the years fell away, and a younger woman appeared. A shadow of the fresh-faced princess at Amboise gazed back, the girl Louise had once called "blonde like the wheat from neighboring Beauce, and with cheeks the color of roses of Provence."

Margaret had laughed at such a description from the companion she had played with as she awaited the day she would wed the King of France. Who could have foreseen that it would be her friend's brother that she would marry instead, falling so deeply in love that she never looked for another to take his place?

Buttoning up her heart, she wondered what remained of the Louise she had once known. If not as firm a jawline or as slender a waist, Margaret guessed she might expect the same sharp wit and strong spirit she had shown as a girl.

With a tug Margaret straightened the points of her collar, reminding herself that they would not negotiate as friends—but not as enemies, either. Her former sister-in-law had written that they must necessarily tussle, but she hoped it would be without anger or ill-will.

Margaret gave herself a confident nod. Of course it would be. Provided that she won.

Portrait of Louise of Savoy (1476-1531), mother of Francis I
By the School of Jean Clouet, c. 1528
Fondation Bemberg
Toulouse, France
Photo by Didier Descouens

Portrait of Margaret of Austria, Duchess of Savoy
By Bernard van Orley, c. 1515-1520
Royal Museums of Fine Arts of Belgium, Brussels
Photo unattributed, courtesy of museum

23

THE LADIES' PEACE

1529

"Women 'have often corrected
many of men's errors.'"
— Baldassare Castiglione, *The Book of the Courtier*
Sarah Gristwood, *Game of Queens*[1]

At three in the afternoon on July 5, 1529, Margaret arrived in Cambrai. She had timed her journey to arrive first, before her sister-in-law turned up. With her leg giving her trouble, she intended

---

1. Sarah Gristwood, Game of Queens (New York: Basic Books, 2016), p. 145.

to be fully installed at the Abbey of St. Aubert so that she could gain the advantage before negotiations began.

Sending word to Louise of Savoy en route, she let her know she would be pleased to receive her upon her arrival. Marguerite of Navarre, sister of the French king, was accompanying her mother. She would serve as a hostage should any French aggression against Margaret and her entourage occur.

"You will entertain the Lady Marguerite while I treat with her mother," Margaret instructed Neuteken.

Her fool made a gruesome grimace. "Margaret, Marguerite—why am I forever fated to manage Margarets?"

"Just as I have been assigned the Charleses to attend to," Margaret quipped.

"At least you had a few Handsomes in your life, too," Neuteken pouted.

Margaret smiled wistfully. "That I did. And the great lady soon to arrive is the sister of the one I loved most."

Neuteken clapped her hands. "That decides it, Madame. Your favorite prince will call out to his sister from the grave and encourage her to make peace with you."

"Whether he does or not, I will be the one who will have to sell whatever we agree on to Charles," Margaret noted.

"These Charleses seem to cause a lot of trouble," Neuteken observed.

"Their troublemaking is nothing compared to the Francises of the world," Margaret retorted.

"Will you say so to your Handsome's sister?" Neuteken's tone was impudent.

"Most likely I will, Little Fool."

"Then I am less a fool than you, for you will stir the indignation of that overprotective hen."

Margaret wagged a warning finger. "So now you insult my opposition as well as me."

"You pay me well, Madame, so I deliver above and beyond." Neuteken tossed a sugared almond into the air and caught it in her mouth.

"See that you say nothing to Madame Louise and concentrate on Madame Marguerite."

Neuteken bounced in excitement. "I will dance and twirl for her in my new gown."

Margaret brushed her lively companion's cheek with her finger. "You are my good Neuteken, although you are very naughty."

"Someone must be naughty around here, since you are not allowed to be."

"Sadly true," Margaret agreed. "Now dance for me before they arrive so I may see what tricks you will get up to."

"I will trick them into conceding every one of your points, Madame."

Margaret snorted. "How I wish it might be."

"You will do the job yourself, my lady. I only serve as your mirror," Neuteken reminded her.

"Then you are a fine-looking one in your flashing colors." She had had a new gown made for her in a multi-hued silk brocade.

Neuteken preened and twirled, laughing aloud as the July sunlight caught the shimmering scarlets and blues of her gown and changed colors as she spun. "I am a rainbow, am I not?" she cried.

"Stop prattling and massage my leg." Margaret groaned as she shifted in her armchair. The indignities of age were creeping upon her at forty-nine. What shape would Louise be in, she wondered. Aging was unkind to all. But Louise had always been clever. Perhaps she had found a way to outwit the march of time, at least until her job of containing her son was done.

"Shall I give it a few thumps?" Neuteken lifted the hem of Margaret's gown and flung back her arm as if to thwack her left calf.

"Thump away. Just wake it up before they arrive so I may stand to greet them."

"Your wish is my command." Neuteken set to work smacking and kneading her mistress' leg, until Margaret began to laugh and begged her to desist. To no avail, she kicked at her to stop, then held out her arm for Neuteken to help her up from her chair.

At least she could stand. Going to the Venetian mirror, she frowned into it.

"That will not do, Madame. You must smile and put your best face forward," Neuteken objected.

"I am getting rid of my grimaces so they are gone when they get here." Margaret pinched her cheeks for color. How fast the years had flown, and with them her fresh, Flemish complexion. Now all that stared back was a careworn older woman, stately and well-maintained, but with youth's rosy glow replaced by hard-won lines.

"Why does my lady frown, when she is about to win peace for all of Europe?" Neuteken asked.

"You have not yet met my sister-in-law," Margaret told her.

The impish woman rolled her eyes. "She could not be as formidable as you."

"She has ruled France for the past fourteen years, while her son has cavorted and behaved like an arrogant ass."

Neuteken cocked her head, interest flashing across her face. "I hear he is very charming."

"He is as deceitful as he is charming, and my nephew is no longer amused," Margaret declared, puffing up the tops of her sleeves to ensure they would be as high as Louise's were bound to be.

"I don't think your nephew was ever amused," her companion retorted.

"You will keep my nephew off your list of targets." Insulting the emperor was going too far. But Neuteken had a point. A taste for amusement and frivolity was not one of Charles V's attributes.

"Forgive me, Madame. I am only a fool."

"You do not fool me, but you will steer clear of my lord and nephew."

"Another one of those Charleses."

Margaret reached out and cuffed Neuteken's chin. "That is enough."

The blare of clarions sounded outside, announcing the arrival of France's regent and her daughter.

With a final warning to her cheeky companion to keep her mouth shut while Louise was present, Margaret told herself she would keep her own mouth shut, too. At least until she discovered what hand Louise would play, so she could trump it.

MARGARET BOWED TO HER sister-in-law the moment Louise tipped her head toward her. There must be no slights of rank at their meeting. The fate of Europe hung in their hands, and neither woman wished to allow the rulers they represented to continue to war with each other.

Louise of Savoy lifted her head and smiled as Margaret held out her arms. Instantly, the years fell away and they were two girls greeting each other on the great lawn at Amboise. Enfolding her old friend into an embrace Margaret kissed her on both cheeks, inhaling the faint scent of patchouli.

Louise returned the kisses then stepped aside for Marie of Luxembourg, Duchess of Vendôme, who had offered her home to the regent and her daughter during their time in Cambrai. The great lady was senior in age to all of them, the daughter of the Count of Saint-Pol of Burgundy and mother-in-law of Henry of Nassau, who had served in both Charles' and Margaret's privy councils.

"My dear Lady Margaret, what a pleasure to be part of bringing you and Madame Louise together," the duchess greeted. She looked both dignified and frail as she took Margaret's hands in hers.

Margaret warmed toward Louise for having the foresight to bring the duchess along. Knowing how close the noblewoman's family ties were to the emperor, with her son-in-law a firm Habsburg ally, Louise was signaling that she was there to reach accord.

The Duchess of Vendôme stepped back and Margaret turned to greet Louise's daughter. France's princess royal was now Queen of Navarre since her 1526 marriage to Henry of Navarre. She had worked tirelessly to secure her brother's release from his imprisonment in Spain. Yet she had not been able to control Francis once he was sprung and went back on the terms of the treaty he signed to gain his freedom.

But Margaret would not hold Francis' duplicity against his sister. Well she knew the travails of women working in the best interests of men they loved who thwarted their efforts.

"Madame Margaret, it is my great joy to see you again," the Queen of Navarre exclaimed. At thirty-seven Marguerite was tall and elegant, with the aquiline nose and almond eyes of her father, but a mouth shaped like her mother's.

"You were a young girl the last time I saw you." A sweet stab knifed Margaret to think of when it was.

"At your wedding celebration with my mother and brother," Marguerite recalled.

"And now you are a mother yourself." Eager to move on from references to Philibert, Margaret would not let sentiment sway her from the task ahead. If she failed to win enough concessions for her nephew, Charles would not agree to whatever they came up with and peace would not be made.

"My daughter Jeanne was born last November," Marguerite related, a smile breaking out on her face.

"How happy I am for you," Margaret enthused.

"It took long enough," Louise put in, giving her daughter a caustic glance.

"Happiness flows to each of us in its own time," Margaret smoothed over as she took in the details of Louise's face. A keen intelligence shone there, along with pride and a shopkeeper's shrewdness. France's regent was still handsome, yet pain lines ran down each side of her mouth. Margaret wondered what troubles had put them there. Was it her son's imprisonment, or did she struggle with her own health?

"I would like it to flow back to me once more," Louise retorted.

"Let us take a moment to recall happy times we spent together," Margaret said, signaling to the attendants to bring refreshment.

Sitting, she motioned to the ladies to join her. Tapestries she had brought from Malines draped the walls of the well-appointed receiving room. The July day was fine, and the tall windows had been flung open to allow in the late-afternoon sunlight. Margaret hoped the golden warmth that streamed over them would put them all in a conciliatory mood.

"Let me see... you were the future Queen of France and I the poor relation of Madame la Grande," Louise began, an ironic smile on her face.

"Until I lost my position before gaining it and was sent away to marry another future king," Margaret finished for her. She remembered the same acerbic tone in Louise's voice when she had introduced her brother to her, a boy so blessed with high spirits that irony had found no foothold in his sunny nature. How different the two siblings had been.

"You certainly made the rounds of Europe," Louise remarked.

"Which is why I can help you now," Margaret responded, hoping she didn't sound patronizing. She must seize the upper hand, but not make Louise feel as if she did not hold it herself. "Although I did not have the good fortune to mother a king," she added.

"Raising an emperor has caused you similar worries, I should think." Louise popped a piece of candied ginger into her mouth.

"We both know what it is to manage men who do not always listen to us," Margaret said.

"Let us hope that they will listen now, as all of Europe is outside our door, eager to eavesdrop on what we discuss here."

"Did you see the passageway I had built to hide us from prying eyes?" Margaret asked.

Louise's face brightened. "Brava, sister-in-law. I could not have thought of a better idea myself."

"I shall visit you in my dressing gown if inspiration hits at an odd hour," Margaret jested.

"And I will not have to put on a good face when my gout acts up," Louise said.

So France's regent suffered ailments too, Margaret thought. "I will have my cook send over dishes to ease you on those days," she offered. She would not mention her leg problems. Louise would see for herself the moment they strolled together.

Sipping cool Burgundian elderflower wine and nibbling sugared comfits, the four women basked in the long rays of the sun as they talked. Youth had fled, yet the even more potent elixir of power had taken its place.

THE NEXT DAY MARGARET and Louise faced each other across the polished oak conference table in the upstairs quarters of Cambrai's Hôtel de Ville. Papers, quills and ink sat at each woman's elbow, their secretaries tucked into far corners of the magisterial room. The Queen of Navarre and the Duchess of Vendôme had been sent on a tour of the town, attended by the Mayor of Cambrai and a party of officials.

Much was on the table to discuss. Disputed claims to Burgundy, Artois, Flanders, Milan, and other Italian holdings all must be addressed. Then the amount of ransom required for the return of

Francis' two sons from Spain, where they had been held hostage since 1526. The League of Cognac that Francis had formed against Charles must disband. And finally, the Treaty of Madrid's clause stating Francis was to marry Charles' sister, Eleanor, needed to be concluded as a way to maintain peace between France and the empire.

"Where do we start?" Louise asked.

"To begin, dear sister-in-law, did you sleep well?"

"As well as I do these days. My gout comes and goes. It visited last night, but today I am better. And you?"

"My leg acted up, but by God's grace and the passage I had built I got here without too much pain."

"I see we both rely on our own solutions to aid the good Lord in doing His job," Louise remarked.

"Does He not help those who help themselves?" Margaret quipped, thinking her sister-in-law operated along similar lines as she.

"We are both practical thinkers, God be praised."

"If we are going to get anywhere, let us leave God aside for the moment so we can argue our fill until we have reached agreement," Margaret suggested.

"Then let us begin with something we don't hold too dear," Louise said.

"A good idea. You first." Margaret sat back and waited. She had learned from Jakob Fugger how to gain the advantage by hearing out others before committing oneself.

Louise glanced over her talking points then looked up at Margaret. "It is your nephew, dear sister-in-law, who claims Burgundian lands France has held since your mother's father died."

Blood rushed to Margaret's head. "And it is your son who still claims Milan for France, when he knows it has done him no good and will divert the resources of his realm if he doesn't let it go," she countered. How accurately Louise had put her finger on the least valuable concession her nephew required from France.

Charles couldn't care less about French-held Burgundian lands. He had an empire to run, and if France wished to hang onto the largely agricultural backwaters of Burgundy it had seized in the wake of Charles the Rash's death in 1477 Margaret knew he would gladly relinquish them. She had not intended for Louise to divine this so early on, but apparently she had already guessed.

"Francis will never withdraw his claim to Milan," Louise stated flatly.

"Then you will never see your grandsons again, for he has already promised to drop Milan and gone back on that promise," Margaret rebutted, wondering how the conversation had hurtled into sensitive areas so quickly.

"A promise made under duress cannot be expected to be kept," Louise argued, her face falling at mention of her grandsons.

"But now that Francis is freed, any promises made as a result of whatever accord we reach must be honored." Margaret sensed that the issue of Louise's imprisoned grandsons would be her opponent's weak point. God forbid that it would spiral downward into a tragedy similar to England's princes in the tower. The mystery of their disappearance had played out in their childhood, leaving all of Europe guessing at what horrors might have befallen the two doomed sons of Edward IV. Such a stain on England's history could not be allowed to happen to France, with the Holy Roman Emperor to blame.

"So long as we reach an accord that we can reasonably fulfill, I will see to it that Francis keeps to it," Louise promised.

"You were not so effective at seeing he kept to the last one," Margaret pointed out.

Louise looked sour. "I was not there to argue its terms, but I can imagine my son would have agreed to anything to save his life and return to his realm. Would not your nephew have done the same in similar circumstances?"

"He would not find himself in similar circumstances." Margaret gave Louise a thin smile, hoping it would not be construed as a smirk.

"Fine words, fair sister-in-law. I pray fate does not deal a bad hand to your nephew."

"Sooner or later we all get bad hands—but my nephew plays fairly, as your son does not," Margaret jabbed, then bit her tongue. She had meant to refrain from direct attacks. But how quickly talks were taking a piercing turn.

Louise's face hardened. "Does imprisoning two young boys for years count as fair? Or as harsh and inhumane treatment of princes of Europe?"

Margaret couldn't agree more that Charles had acted excessively in keeping the French princes imprisoned year after year. She, as much as Louise, wished to set them free. But Charles would not agree to it unless concessions were made. "It is your son who agreed to hand over his two sons to gain his freedom," she told her. "I cannot imagine too many fathers who would do so, outside of a Greek myth."

Louise turned red. "He had a country to rule, and never expected your nephew to hold onto his children for as long as he has."

"Only because your son went back on every promise he made in the treaty he signed," Margaret countered.

"It is a disgrace to keep such young boys imprisoned, and you know it."

Margaret blanched. Indeed, she did know it. Her nephew could be strangely unfathomable at times. So unlike Louise's son, whose capriciousness and nimble abandonment of promises were far more human traits; flawed but forgivable. "I will not argue such a point, Louise. I want to see them released as much as you, which is why we are here."

Louise's eyes flashed. "At the very least you could see to them being treated according to their royal dignity, with tutors and exercise, and decent food to eat."

"Are they not receiving all this already?" Margaret asked.

"It is said that they are left in a locked room for hours each day, with no tutor, no companions, and no exercise of body or mind."

Surprised, Margaret hoped Louise was exaggerating. "If it is so I will see that amends are made until we reach terms to gain their release," she promised.

Louise looked mollified. "It is something, sister-in-law. Improve their condition as soon as possible and you will soften my heart."

Margaret clapped her hands twice and her page appeared. Pointing him to her secretary, she bid Marnix to give him a message to get to Charles in Spain immediately. He would respond favorably, she knew. But he would draw the line at their release.

"It is done, sister-in-law. Now let us move on to a point we can more easily agree on," she urged.

BUT FRANCE'S MOST POWERFUL woman was proving to be a tough opponent. Over the next three weeks Margaret discovered there were few points they could quickly come together on. Not as susceptible to the seduction of creature comforts as Amboise or Wolsey had been, Louise of Savoy displayed a singlemindedness of passion to protect her son's interests that alarmed Margaret.

The weeks flew by, fiercely confrontational by day, but assuaged by evenings filled with childhood reminiscences. Over lingering dinners they talked and laughed, satisfying both hearts and palates.

Margaret's leg gave her increasing discomfort but she was determined to work through the pain. Summoning her physician from Brussels she brushed off the draughts he prescribed to dull the ache. Above all, her mind must stay clear to negotiate the outcome she sought—peace between Charles V and Francis I, with conditions acceptable enough on both sides to maintain it.

By July 26 the two women had pieced together a draft of an agreement, with only a few territories left to be decided upon.

"The county of Burgundy goes to France." Louise pointed to the map spread out on the table before them.

"As long as Charolais remains mine," Margaret qualified, pointing to an area in French-held territory, just to the west of Bourg-en-Bresse, where Brou was located.

"You know your nephew doesn't want it," Louise protested, shooting her an annoyed look.

"My grandfather was the last Duke of Charolais. It was given to me through my mother's estate," Margaret argued.

"The King of France will not agree to this treaty if Charolais alone is carved out of the county of Burgundy you have ceded to France."

Margaret dug in her heels. "I cannot let it go," she pushed back. Her yearly revenues from Charolais helped to pay for the church she was building. If she was to see her masterpiece completed and be buried there one day, she must retain her rights to the region.

"Then there is nothing more to be done. I have conceded much, sister-in-law, but I cannot cede you more." With a swish of her skirts, Louise of Savoy rose and swept from the room.

Margaret sat back, stunned. It wasn't her nephew she was fighting for. It was her own honor as a Burgundian princess. There was no way she could hand over the territory she herself held a claim to so deep in the heart of her mother's ancestral lands.

"Where is she going?" she exclaimed.

Marnix shrugged his shoulders. "Back to her quarters, and then we shall see," he replied.

Margaret set both elbows on the table and put her hands to her temples. "She cannot leave now after all this hard work we've put in," she moaned.

"You must concede something, Madame, if you wish to stop her," Marnix advised.

"Why should I concede anything more, when it is her son who has broken his promises to my nephew!" Margaret cried.

"Madame, you are within your rights. But if you humiliate too harshly those you have vanquished, the consequence is not peace but further war."

"I will not hand over Charolais!"

"If I may say so, Madame, it is of no strategic importance to the empire."

Margaret slapped the table with her hand. "It is of importance to me!"

"Then insist on your claim to it for the duration of your life, but no longer," Marnix suggested.

"One day when my nephew realizes the splendor that was Burgundy, he may want it, too," she argued. But it was no use. She was hanging on to a past that was no more. The point of their meeting was to secure the future.

"Madame, you might sue for rights for your lifetime to be passed to the emperor upon your death, but when he dies it goes to France."

"I do not wish it to go to France!" Margaret railed. Charolais had lain deep in the heart of Burgundy at the height of its glory. How painful it was to admit to herself that that glory was past.

An attendant appeared at the door. "Excuse me, Lady Margaret, but the steward is here."

"I am busy."

"He says it is urgent, my lady."

"What is it then?" Margaret snapped.

Her head steward from Malines entered the conference room, followed by the steward of the Abbey of St. Aubert. Both wore pained expressions.

"Madame, the Lady Louise has ordered her carriages to be readied for departure," her steward announced.

"That's impossible. She just left!" Margaret exclaimed.

"As she was going down the passageway, my men overheard her give orders to prepare for departure in one hour. She was in quite a huff."

"Good God, we must stop her!" Margaret cried.

"Madame, only you can stop her. There is no other of sufficient rank who can reason with her," Marnix pointed out.

As Margaret half-rose a searing pain shot down her leg. She fell back with a thump. "Someone get a message to her not to leave before I see her," she got out through gritted teeth.

"As I passed the Lady Louise, she said 'I am done speaking with her. I have done all I can,'" Margaret's steward related.

Racking her brain, she scrambled for a way to stop her. "Run quick and offer her something," she ordered.

"What shall it be, Madame?"

What could she offer? Casting her eyes over the room, she wished she was back in Malines. There she could have offered any one of the exquisite artistic pieces that filled her palace. But here?

"Help me to my quarters," she ordered her men. Perhaps she could find something in her trunks to give to Louise as a peace offering.

Within minutes she was back in her rooms, rifling through her jewel case. As she looked for a bauble to offer, Neuteken slipped in.

"Is my lady in need of something?"

"I need a miracle!" Margaret shouted. She hadn't brought any significant jewels; she rarely wore them. Louise didn't care about jewels either; she cared about the return of her grandsons. A way must be found at once to leverage that point into getting her to stay.

"Miracles are hard to come by, but what can I do?" her fool asked.

"I am sunk! The Lady Louise is leaving and we have not yet reached an accord."

"Were you too harsh with her, my lady?"

Margaret glared at her. "I have every right to be harsh. Her son was the emperor's prisoner until he lied to gain his release."

"All that is past, and now is the present. How can I be of help?"

"I need to stop her from leaving! Think of something for me to give her so she won't rush off before I speak to her."

"You must offer something that charms her so her anger abates," Neuteken advised.

"Louise is not easily charmed. And I am not at home, so I have nothing of value to offer."

"Then let me try charming Madame Marguerite."

"How so?"

Neuteken thought for a moment. "What about that crimson hood you had made for me?"

"It was for you to wear at the celebration dinner once a peace treaty is signed!" Margaret cried. Good God, she could not allow all their hard work to go up in flames.

"I can give it to Lady Marguerite to give to her fool," Neuteken suggested.

"What good will that do?"

"It will gain time and soften them while you make your way to the courtyard to stop them."

"Then get the hood and run! I will have my men help me down there."

"And be sure to come up with a solution to whatever you quarreled over," Neuteken tossed out as she rummaged for the hood in Margaret's trunk.

Margaret snapped shut her jewel box. "There is no solution save the one I want."

"You want peace as much as Lady Louise does, so sweeten your plan to one you both can live with."

"Get along with you." Margaret barked as Neuteken scurried from the room. She had offered to give up something dear for the sake of a greater good. Was her fool going to shame her for not being able to do the same?

DOWN IN THE COURTYARD, Margaret caught her breath. Collapsing onto a stone bench, she gasped.

Louise of Savoy had emerged from the Hotel Saint-Pol and was walking briskly toward the carriages. The Queen of Navarre trailed behind with their attendants bustling about. All were dressed for travel.

"Help me up," Margaret ordered the two men who had escorted her from her rooms.

Rising with difficulty, she dragged herself across the courtyard to bar Louise from stepping into her carriage.

"Take my arms," she hissed to her men, cursing her bum leg acting up just when she needed it most. Yet the pain she felt was nothing compared to her mental anguish.

As Louise of Savoy waited for her equerry to bring the mounting block, she ignored Margaret's approach.

Swallowing her pride, Margaret thought of the hood Neuteken had offered to Marguerite's fool. She herself must offer something before it was too late.

"Sister-in-law, wait. I have something for you," Margaret called out.

"I do not need anything more from you, Lady Margaret. We will be on our way." With head held high, Louise avoided her gaze.

"But you do, Lady Louise. You need this from me."

"What is it, then?"

Margaret lowered her voice as she reached her. "A proposal."

Louise's face looked carved out of granite. "I believe we have exhausted all our proposals."

"We have not, sister. We ourselves may be exhausted, but we are almost at our goal."

"My goal is to get into this carriage and bring the news to my son that we were unable to come to terms. Allow me, Madame."

"I will not!" Margaret hissed, heaving herself between Louise and the carriage. A streak of pain ran down Margaret's leg. She braced herself against the side of the carriage, willing the ache to disappear. Now was not the time.

"You will not allow me to leave? You are beginning to sound like your nephew with my son," Louise said sharply.

"Hear me out, sister."

"Sister-in-law, I have heard you out and I cannot concede anything more."

Margaret swallowed the lump in her throat. "Then allow me to take my turn."

Louise's eyes flickered as she motioned her attendants away. "Something new?"

Margaret nodded, pushing down her pride and thinking of all she cared about: the well-being of the Netherlanders she governed, the Habsburg dynasty, the future of Europe. "About Charolais," she said.

Louise tapped her foot, looking impatient to be off. "What about it?"

"I wish to retain it for the duration of my life, then pass it to my nephew to hold until he dies."

"We have been over this, and it is now time for me to go."

Margaret's eyes bored into Louise's. "... after which time it passes to France."

Louise cocked her head, studying her. "Why does your nephew need it once you are gone?"

"Because I may be gone soon, and he will wish to be the one to cede it to France."

"Sister-in-law, I will be gone soon, too, if this gout keeps up. Do not speak of death and the glory beyond, when we were unable to achieve glory here."

"Then let us achieve it, sister. You and me. Here and now. No one knows what waits on the other side, but this is our moment to win something real," Margaret pleaded. She was not accustomed to begging. But this was too important to let go.

"So Charolais goes to France," Louise spelled out.

"Once I, then the emperor, dies."

"Do not talk of death, Margaret. You are too full of life for that."

"And you are too wise to walk away from the glory we are about to achieve here on Earth," Margaret countered.

"If I agree to Charolais for France only after the emperor is gone, I want something in return," Louise bargained.

"I will see to it personally that your two grandsons are returned to France within the year."

Louise blinked. "What if I cannot raise the full ransom?"

Margaret leaned closer and put her mouth to Louise's ear. "Then I will lend you the difference. Just don't tell anyone," she whispered.

"I cannot bear to think of them imprisoned a moment longer." Louise's voice quavered.

"Don't get into that carriage, sister. Take my hand instead, and the concession I offer."

Louise paused, searching Margaret's eyes as if seeking the bonds of childhood they once had shared.

"Please," Margaret added, willing her to remember the friendship that had sustained them under Anne de Beaujeu's loveless care.

For a long moment the two women held Europe's fate in each other's gaze. Then France's most powerful woman put her hand atop Margaret's.

"So let's get on with it," Louise said. Turning to her equerry, she barked orders. "A change of plans. Return the carriages to the stables."

Margaret's heart leapt to see her proud sister-in-law recognize the same thing she did. Peace at hand was too important to lose. Pride was at play, too, but both she and Louise knew that pride in achieving peace for Europe was something God was likely to forgive them for.

THREE DAYS LATER THE treaty was finalized. Francis I's two sons were to be returned to France for a payment of two million crowns, 1,200,000 of which was to be paid before handoff. If they were not returned to France after payment was made, Margaret and the

Netherlands' senior lords would be responsible for paying one million crowns to Francis I.

The proposed marriage between Charles V's sister, Eleanor, and Francis I was to be concluded.

The French king was to renounce all claims to Flanders, Artois, and all lands in Italy. He would withdraw from the Cognac League he had formed against the emperor, and would cease all aid to the Duke of Guelders, once and for all.

Charles V would give up the Free County of Burgundy to France; although in the case of Charolais, not until his demise. He would hand over to Francis all possessions of the Duke of Bourbon, whose death had ignited the 1527 sack of Rome.

The treaty was ratified the following day. On the evening of August 1, 1529, Margaret, Louise, and Marguerite attended vespers at the Abbey of St. Aubert. Taking each other's hands, they prayed that the princes they represented would abide by the treaty they had fought so hard to conclude.

Four days later a Mass at Cambrai's cathedral was celebrated, with Margaret and Louise both swearing to uphold every clause of the treaty they had made. The Mass concluded with a Te Deum sung. As attendees poured out of the church clarions sounded, followed by heralds announcing to the crowds that peace had been made.

By the end of that day, the Treaty of Cambrai was referred to as "the ladies' peace" by all. Messengers were sent off to every corner of Europe with the triumphant news.

That same afternoon, Margaret met with Thomas More and two other English ambassadors. Once more she dipped her quill to sign a treaty of cooperation to enhance commercial relations between the Netherlands and England.

Cambrai erupted into jubilation with music and dancing. Wine flowed from its public fountains and coins were tossed to the joyful crowds. Celebrations culminated in the King of France's arrival on August 9.

As Margaret watched Louise's son ride in on a white horse, she secretly agreed with Neuteken. Francis I of France exhibited every gift that Heaven could bestow on a prince. Debonair and graceful, he turned to right and left in his saddle, greeting the crowds as he dazzled every woman whose eyes he met.

At the reception for the townspeople his mother hosted at the Hotel Saint-Pol, the French king bowed low over Margaret's hand, kissing it with feather-light lips that caressed her skin, making her insides tingle. Louise's son was unbearably dashing, blending urbane sophistication with a joyful vivacity that lightened the hearts of all.

Drinking in his effortless style, Margaret's thoughts flew to Philibert. Although Francis was dark and suave unlike her lighter-haired and sunny husband, the similarities in the two members of the House of Savoy were apparent.

Which of Philibert's and Louise's parents had passed on such gifts? Had it been Margaret of Bourbon or Philibert's father, Philip II of Savoy?

With a name like Philip, Margaret decided it must have been their father. Sighing, her long-dead brother's handsome face came to her. As perfect as an Adonis, as cruel as Narcissus.

"Has your brother always been like this?" she asked the Queen of Navarre at that evening's banquet. Seated next to her, they both watched as Francis presided over a gaggle of demoiselles, each vying for his attention.

Marguerite de Navarre fluttered the same long lashes her brother possessed. "From the moment he first laughed in his cradle."

"What was he laughing at?" Margaret asked.

"The sunbeams that danced above his head. He reached out and wanted to dance with them, and he has been like that ever since," the Queen of Navarre described.

"You and your mother must have enjoyed many gay moments with him as he grew up."

"We did, Lady Margaret, as I'm sure you enjoyed your moments with the emperor and his sisters."

"Of course," Margaret agreed, although memories of her taciturn nephew did not make her heart leap as it did now, watching Francis pay court to the ladies, complimenting them in turn and making each feel special. What a gift some men had, one that gave them tremendous power that could be used both for good and for bad.

Her mind wandered to her once-favored master of the horse. Did Mary Tudor rue her marriage to him? She had heard she been put out to pasture in the English countryside while her husband kept company with Henry VIII at court.

Grateful that both Charles and Eleanor were still in Spain and not at Cambrai, to be shown up by Francis, Margaret thanked God for her nephew and niece. They were all that a parent or guardian aunt could ask for, as much as neither would ever be scintillating.

Turning her eyes back to the effervescent King of France, she recalled one of her own sex who had exhibited similar gifts.

Anne Boleyn had possessed that same sparkling quality, a sort of quicksilver grace that poured over a chosen target, beguiling them instantly. Her former maid of honor had captured the King of England in her gossamer web. Was Charles Brandon now fanning the flame of the king's obsession with his favored lady?

She imagined Mary Tudor and her husband arguing over Anne Boleyn. Margaret guessed he would back the king, as she would back Queen Catherine, at whose court she had served. Should Henry VIII wish for the daughter of a minor diplomat from the merchant class to replace the daughter of the Catholic monarchs as his queen, Brandon would support him in that desire. A man like him would turn like a weathervane in the direction of opportunity, no matter from whence it blew.

"Of what do you think, Lady Margaret?" the Queen of Navarre queried, breaking into her thoughts.

"I think of Queen Catherine of England, who is as much a sister-in-law to me as your mother," Margaret replied.

Marguerite de Navarre sucked in her breath. "'Tis a heartbreak to see that great lady dishonored."

"By a courtier we both know."

The Queen of Navarre's almond eyes darkened. "She was briefly at my court and she learned her lessons all too well," she related.

"I am to blame, too," Margaret bemoaned, "for she began her career with me in 1513 after her father had been posted to my court."

The Queen of Navarre shook her head. "Neither of us is to blame for what a man or woman of abundant gifts chooses to make of them."

"I should think the king has some agency in the matter," Margaret noted, reasoning that blame should be laid on the offending party, not the one who had turned his head.

"He has spent years trying to get the pope to agree to end his marriage."

Margaret raised a brow. Always ready to deepen ties with the English, in this case she could not support the English king. His cruelty to Isabella of Spain's youngest daughter was too harsh, his attention to duty sorely lacking. "His argument that he is unlawfully wed to my sister-in-law for full twenty years is absurd," she declared.

"It is all he has to hang his case on to gain a divorce, and the pope will not grant one."

"What next, I wonder?" Margaret asked.

Louise's daughter lowered her voice. "With a woman like that at his ear, he may break with Rome to get what he wants," she speculated.

"'Tis unthinkable," Margaret whispered back.

The Queen of Navarre cast her a meaningful glance. "Much that has been unthinkable has recently passed with Rome, Lady Margaret."

"My nephew was horrified by the actions of his army," Margaret shot back, still mortified by the sack of Rome.

"It was that traitor, Bourbon, who led the attack. I do not blame your nephew the emperor."

"I thank you, Lady Marguerite, but we take the blame upon ourselves and hope never again to see such actions by any who serve the House of Habsburg."

"The times are changing, Lady Margaret. I pray we will be able to change with them."

Margaret rapped the table with her hand. "I will never change. I am too old for that sort of thing."

Marguerite giggled. "You sound like my mother's past rival, Queen Anne. Her motto was '*non mudera*—I will never change.' And well did her husband know it."

"Yet Louis was devoted to her," Margaret recalled, thinking of Philibert.

"She was his anchor," Marguerite agreed.

"As I am my nephew's."

"As my mother is my brother's," Marguerite added.

Margaret cocked her head. "Perhaps it is not so bad to be unchanging."

"It is not, Lady Margaret, but we must open our eyes to the world changing around us."

"Do you think some changes are going too far?" Margaret asked.

"I do not know. But what has already begun cannot be reversed," the Queen of Navarre observed.

"Then I am happy to be old, for I cannot move into a new age," Margaret declared. "It is all I can do to uphold the one I was born into."

Marguerite laughed with the same easy grace of her brother. "That is what my mother says, too," she exclaimed, casting a fond glance in her direction. Louise of Savoy was conferring with one of the servers, as tightly wound as ever, a commanding look on her face.

"Then I toast your good mother, for she and I are fated to be remembered to history together," Margaret proclaimed, thinking back to their ties of childhood days. How far they both had come.

The Queen of Navarre raised her goblet and clinked it with Margaret's. "To the two great ladies of the Ladies' Peace. May it last long, as may you both."

Margaret drank deeply and set down her goblet. Instinct told her the peace they had made would endure longer than she. But so be it. She had accomplished her most important goals. Satisfied with what she had brought about, she did not wish to last long enough to see it all come crashing down.

Treaty of Cambrai

By Francisco Jover y Casanova, 1871

Museo de Prado

Madrid, Spain

From Fine Art America

24

THOUGHTS OF RETIREMENT

1529-1530

IN THE AFTERMATH OF the Treaty of Cambrai, Margaret began to long for a quieter life. The Queen of Navarre's words on how the world was changing had struck a nerve. But no answering chord within Margaret sounded in response.

As with many who were fortunate enough to grow old, she was beginning to tire of all the wrangling—the bad behavior of perfidious princes, most notably the King of England in whom she had rested so much hope. Her heart raged to think of him destroying his queen's happiness by demanding a divorce, although all of Europe decried his actions.

It was one thing to have a favorite. God knew Henry VIII had had a few, and Queen Catherine had looked the other way in noble dignity befitting her station. But the woman who currently had hold of the king's heart did not know her place. It appeared that instead of serving the Queen of England, Anne Boleyn wished to replace her. It was an outrage.

"Sire Erasmus, what do you think of the English king's call for a divorce?" Margaret asked while passing through his hometown in Brabant on her way to check on Gelderland's borders.

The esteemed theologian was blunt. "I think it despicable, Madame."

"Do you think the pope will grant his request?"

"I do not, Madame. The pope will stall for time, in hopes that the King of England's reason returns to him once passion's comet has arced."

"I worry that my sister-in-law is isolated," Margaret said. "My contacts tell me she has been abandoned by those who flock to the king's side. They fear to lose his favor if they support her."

Erasmus looked pained. "The Queen of England has not led an easy life as a foreign princess far from her land."

"It is the fate of princesses, and was my own tale," Margaret mused. "Not just once, but three times."

"It is a practice that should stop," the theologian opined. "Why should princesses be sent to foreign lands at tender ages, to be used as hostages in their fathers' fights over lands and dowry?"

"I spent two years in France before terms could be reached so I could return home," Margaret recalled. "Then another two years in Spain while my father-in-law tried to find a way out of returning my dowry. But I was cared for and treated well, as I fear Catherine no longer is."

"I have heard that Queen Catherine is beloved by the common people. But power is in the hands of her husband and he is desirous of heading the Church in England himself instead of the pope," Erasmus noted.

"Is this due to religious conviction, or in order to get what he wants?" Margaret asked.

The theologian's brow darkened. "We see many now, Madame, who hide behind the name of reform in order to abandon the Church in search of their own aims."

Margaret's heart was heavy, not just for the Queen of England. "We are entering a time of upheaval, are we not, Monsieur?"

"A time of great upheaval," he agreed. "And not always for the sake of seeking God's righteousness."

"Please tell me you will not leave the Church." Margaret set great store by the famed theologian's opinions. He had written a guide for her nephew in 1516 which had helped shape Charles into the sober prince he had become. *Unlike the self-seeking Henry VIII and Francis I,* she thought darkly.

"I have no desire to abandon the Church, Madame. Only to clean house from within, as our Lord swept the moneylenders from the temple," he replied.

"It is reassuring to hear, Monsieur. I beg you to use your influence with the pope to prevent the English king from divorcing his queen," she requested.

"I have already written to him of the matter, and will write to him again. But it may soon move out of the pope's hands and into the English king's own to decide."

"Such disobedience goes against all rules of Christendom," Margaret exclaimed.

Erasmus looked grave. "Madame, those rules are being rewritten as we speak."

"I pray you, Sire Erasmus, uphold the Church and do not let the rules be rewritten to the point they are swept away."

"My lady, if only I had it in my power to withstand the winds of change. But I cannot, as none of us can." The elderly scholar shook his head slowly, his craggy features a stark landscape of valleys and bluffs.

"Then do your part to see we are not all swept away in its forces," she pressed.

"I will do so, Madame. And I will pray for your sister-in-law that she stands firm."

"My sister-in-law is the daughter of Isabella of Spain, God rest her soul. I am sure she will." Margaret bid the venerable scholar goodbye, hiding the worry she felt at his final words. Catherine would stand firm, if she knew her at all. But at what cost?

ON HER RETURN TO Malines, Margaret stopped in Bruges to visit her mother's tomb. Maximilian's heart was there, too, enclosed in an urn placed beside Mary of Burgundy's resting place. He had lost his one great love at age twenty-three, so similar to Margaret's own loss. Closing her hands around the marble urn, she took comfort in knowing that she, too, would rest beside her greatest love one day.

After paying her respects, she continued on to the convent of the Annunciades outside Bruges. She had founded the convent in 1516 between appointments as governor, when she had finally had time to pursue projects close to her heart.

Greeting the Mother Superior, Margaret came straight to the point. "Mother Ancelle, I would like to end my days here, near to my mother's resting place and in quiet contemplation of the world beyond."

An amused expression flickered across the Mother Superior's face. "Lady Margaret, as Governor of the Netherlands, I do not imagine you to be spending time in quiet contemplation here or anywhere else," she replied.

"The time approaches when the emperor will return from Spain, and I will give him a full accounting of my government. Then I should like to hand it over to him and retire here until my days are done," Margaret said.

Mother Ancelle's gaze was piercing. "We should be pleased to have you among us, but you do not seem ready to renounce all that you manage so ably." She paused, scanning Margaret up and down. "Is it God who calls you, or is it you who have decided you've had enough?"

"That is the question I struggle with," Margaret confessed. "But my mind and body are weary of this world's affairs. I have less taste for managing them with each passing day."

"When you are ready, Lady Margaret, God will let you know. At that time we will welcome you with open arms."

Margaret wanted to dance for joy. Except that her aching leg precluded her from dancing at all. She would start at once on crossing off the remaining items on her list of needs, grievances, and meetings. Once all was in order and her nephew back in the Netherlands, she planned to pack a small case and enter the Annunciades' cloistered halls, where worldly cares were discarded at the door.

"I am grateful, Good Mother. You will see me here again soon." Margaret took a small velvet pouch from the folds of her gown and handed it to Mother Ancelle. "For upkeep, in the meantime."

THROUGHOUT THE WINTER A flurry of follow-ups ensued to ensure the terms of the Treaty of Cambrai were met. Margaret and Louise of Savoy kept in close contact, with an exchange of ambassadors between their courts. To resolve outstanding issues over border disputes since new lines had been drawn up by terms of the treaty, the two ladies set up committees to decide each claim as it arose.

Louise's task of raising the 1,200,000 crowns necessary for the release of her two grandsons in Spain was as daunting as Margaret's 1519 fundraising campaign had been to see her nephew elected King of the Romans. Mindful of the promise she had made to help Louise if she couldn't raise the ransom within a year, Margaret hoped she would find a way to collect the full amount. Otherwise, she must channel funds to her sister-in-law that she needed to pay back the Fuggers.

There was only one further goal Margaret longed to see attained by her nephew. Although emperor-elect, he had not yet been crowned by the pope.

With the Ladies' Peace restoring relations between Charles V and Clement VII, the time had finally come. In 1520 Margaret had gladly traveled to Aachen to see Charles crowned by the prince-electors.

But now she was ten years older. Her leg was giving her too much trouble for the journey to Italy to see the pope place the imperial crown on her nephew's head.

No matter. On her nephew's thirtieth birthday—February 24, 1530—Pope Clement VII crowned Charles V as Holy Roman Emperor in the Basilica of San Petronio in Bologna. Margaret was overjoyed to hear this great honor had finally been achieved. Soon, she hoped Charles would return to the land of his birth so she could hand over her government and be done with worldly affairs.

Yet Charles had his own list of affairs to attend to before he could return to the Low Countries. At the top of it was what to do about Martin Luther's protests against the Church, now spreading like wildfire through German lands and beyond.

From Bologna, Charles V traveled to Austria. He had taken Gattinara with him and Margaret found herself missing her closest counselor. Anticipating his return, she was shocked when news arrived in mid-June that her faithful Piedmontese advisor had died in Innsbruck on June 5th.

Grieving his loss, Margaret learned that Charles had journeyed on to Germany to host the Diet of Augsburg. There he would grapple with what to make of the doctrinal differences between the new Lutheran reformers and the Church. Meanwhile, Margaret grappled at home with the loss of the man who had been at her side longer than any other in her life.

In mid-July she was not surprised to hear from Augsburg that nothing had been resolved. It was an outcome she was familiar with after presiding over council meetings year after year. Change was knocking at Europe's door, but her nephew, as Holy Roman Emperor, was duty-bound to uphold and protect the Church.

As she awaited his return, Margaret managed the usual stew of troubles in the Netherlands, with each province clamoring for its own privileges. None of the factors binding together subjects of other realms mattered much to the inhabitants of the Low Countries: neither a common tongue, nor a sense of fealty to a powerful monarch.

Margaret had learned from her father's tribulations that her people were not as receptive to the idea of a strong ruling authority as the French, Spanish, and English were. Long experience had shown her what they wanted: their practical, flexible Lady Margaret, adorned with her unthreatening white widow's coif, and promoting peace and stability to drive economic prosperity while keeping warlike princes at bay.

But that summer she was unable to go on her usual progress to the far corners of her domain. Gattinara was not just away; he was gone forever. And her leg was giving her trouble again.

Remaining in Malines she managed through a network of contacts, with a steady stream of supplicants visiting her at the Court of Savoy. Most sought favors for their own regions while grumbling against neighboring ones that received privileges not granted them. Margaret saw them all, using her usual combination of charm, hospitality, humor, and flexibility to convince each supplicant that they came away with a net gain.

But something had hanged within her. She was no longer as quick with a smile, a deft gesture, or a clever jest to put her constituents at ease to achieve a solution.

She was tired. And her leg hurt. The pain came and went, but its never-ending return had begun to wear on her nerves. She had always been a solid sleeper, having been spared the indignity of a snoring partner of which some of her married ladies-in-waiting complained.

But now there were nights when she tossed and turned, unable to find comfort in any position. The day after such nights, she was quicker to snap and less tolerant of complaints.

Her sharpness at cards and backgammon had not tailed off, but her chess game had. She no longer had the patience to consider the consequences of each play. Instead, she simply made her move to advance the game.

"Good aunt, you have put your queen at risk by taking my pawn. Do you really want to do that?" her grandnephew asked one sunny July afternoon as they sat in the gardens of the Court of Savoy.

Margaret studied her move, thinking she didn't care anymore if she lost. She had done enough maneuvering in her fifty years to last a lifetime. "Let's just get on with it," she answered, knowing her niece's son was about to take her down. But seeing the disappointment on her twelve-year-old opponent's face, she took back her move and played her queen in another direction.

"You've just left your king unprotected!" John of Denmark cried. Oldest son of Margaret's niece, Isabella, and Christian II of Denmark, Prince John was motherless and stateless, being raised under Margaret's care and funding.

"My king is perfectly capable of managing himself," Margaret retorted, thinking of her nephew.

"You know that's not so. The king will be checkmated if the queen doesn't protect him," John protested.

"My boy, I have protected him his entire life. He can do the job himself now while I take a rest," Margaret declared, forgetting about the chessboard before her.

"Do you really want to play this game?" John asked, a precocious understanding swimming in his bright blue eyes.

"No. Not anymore," Margaret answered frankly. "What about you?"

"Not really. It's no fun with you if you don't even try to win. Let's play something else."

Margaret threw her head back and laughed. It was a joy not to have to be good at everything anymore. She still needed to govern her realm until Charles showed up. But if she let her chess game go, so be it. What freedom it was not to care anymore.

"My darling, I have won all that I need to win, and now I've won my rest," she exulted.

"What's so exciting about that?" The young prince eyed her doubtfully.

Margaret gave him a sly smile, enjoying her age and experience for a rare moment. "You will know when you are my age," she told him.

"*Bonne tante*, with all due respect, when I am as old as you I shall still want to win at whatever I do."

"I didn't say I don't want to win. I said I have won all that I need to win. And you can be sure I cared about winning it," she specified, a surge of her old energy crisping her words.

John stared at her with the perfect charm of uncomprehending youth. "I don't understand anything you're saying, good aunt."

"That's just as well. Let's play cards, shall we?"

"But you always win at cards!" John objected.

"Even when I don't care if I do or not," Margaret retorted gaily. It was mostly true. Her skills at bluffing had not tailed off. She enjoyed it, with no effort at all. Having spent a lifetime dissembling, it was as natural to her as breathing.

"Well, all right, but you must let me win once in a while," John grumbled.

"I don't have to do anything anymore that I don't want to do," Margaret said. It wasn't entirely true, but it would be, once she handed over rule of her realm to someone else. She had begun to think of her niece as a successor to her position. Capable Mary now ruled Hungary as regent on behalf of her brother, Ferdinand, who was busy in Austria and Bohemia. As a Burgundian princess born in Brussels, Mary might be favorably received by the people of the Low Countries so long as she did her job well. "But I'll make sure you win a hand here and there," she offered.

"Do you promise?"

Margaret smiled wickedly. "Of course I do."

The boy's eyes narrowed as he picked up the card pack and cut the deck. "*Bonne tante*, do you bluff or speak true?"

"There's only one way to find out," she chortled, feeling young again for the first time in much too long.

AT THE END OF July, good news arrived. Eleven months after signing the Treaty of Cambrai, Louise of Savoy had scraped together the ransom money of 1,200,000 crowns.

Margaret breathed a sigh of relief. She was off the hook with making up the difference, as she had promised to do within the year.

Margaret's niece, Eleanor, had met the two sons of her new husband, Francis I, near Bayonne, where they had been rowed across the river that separated Spain from France. The French king had sent a highly-placed noblewoman from court, Diane de Poitiers, to accompany her.

Margaret could only guess at what toll four years in captivity had taken on the young boys. What must their feelings be toward their father, who had sent them to their imprisonment in exchange for his own freedom?

That would be Francis I's cross to bear, but she doubted that the French king bothered himself overmuch with concern for the feelings of others. She prayed that Eleanor would have the fortitude to carve out her own place at court as the new Queen of France.

In October 1530 Louise of Savoy wrote to Margaret to say that she was ailing, but that she was strengthened by thoughts of the peace they had forged for their countries.

As she read Louise's heartfelt words, Margaret sat by the fire, warming herself to stave off the ache in her leg. It had worsened with autumn's advance. She, too, was ailing in body, but buoyed to think that she and her sister-in-law had worked together to unite Europe. All that was left for her to accomplish was to see the church in Brou completed.

But now that Gattinara was gone, there was no one she cared to confer with on the project that had sprung from her once young and impassioned heart. All who served her saw her as what she had become: capable administrator of the Netherlands, elder statesman of Europe, foster mother to two generations of Burgundian-Habsburg princes and princesses left behind by dead or incompetent parents, and the one to whom all came with their problems, troubles, and requests.

Margaret let out a great sigh as Neuteken entered the room.

"My lady, something I can do?" her fool asked.

"There is always much to do, little one. And I am ever the one to see that it's done."

"Then you are doing the right thing now, for you are doing nothing, which you well-deserve for all that you do," Neuteken said.

"I am trying to do nothing, but I am thinking of plans, as usual," Margaret admitted.

"Madame, why not leave the planning to others and take a moment for yourself?" Neuteken pulled up a low stool to where Margaret sat. She lifted her mistress' leg as if taking a babe from its cradle.

Margaret's smile was wan. "It eases me to be planning. If I think of nothing, my leg acts up and I have nothing to distract me from the pain."

"Then tell me what you are thinking while I rub your leg, so we may both bat the pain away."

"Two is better than one, isn't it?" Margaret mused.

"I would hardly know, as I'm just one myself," Neuteken replied.

"And I have been just one for so long that all who know me think of me as such. But once I was part of two, and it is for him that I make my plans."

"I know of whom you speak; he is long-dead, so make your plans for yourself," Neuteken said flatly.

Margaret stared at her brash fool, thinking her impudent. But she would not punish one already punished by God. "How do you know of whom I speak?" she asked.

"I know, Madame, that your heart flies to Savoy where your prince lies."

"Nonsense. My heart is with my nephew and nieces, and their children," Margaret insisted, wishing to keep her deepest desires to herself.

Neuteken's eyes flickered. "Madame, I do not speak of the heart of a mother, but the heart of a wife."

"And you have said yourself, you know nothing of it."

A coy smile curled the corners of the little woman's mouth. "I said that I am just one, but I was not always so."

Margaret leaned forward, forgetting about her leg. "Dear imp, do you have a story to tell?"

Neuteken pulled back. "It is a secret so precious that I dare not share it, lest I tarnish its wonder," she said.

"You can be sure I would be careful with your secret, so tell me," Margaret coaxed. There was nothing she liked better than a good story. Especially over a card game, but a blazing fire would do.

"Madame, you know better than others that once a secret is told, no matter how carefully it is kept, the chances increase that it will be told again to someone less careful," Neuteken noted.

"You are discreet, little helper. But I know how you feel, for I feel the same when I think of my sleeping husband and all the joys we shared that coarse ears might receive lightly."

Neuteken nodded, her blue-green eyes luminous in the firelight. "It is better to keep our best secrets to ourselves, is it not, my lady?"

"That is exactly what I do, and you are wise to do so yourself."

"I am your mirror, my lady. One that you see or ignore, as you please."

Margaret gazed at her faithful companion, contemplating her with new eyes. "I see you more clearly now, little one."

"I am glad, my lady. For we have forgotten all about your leg, have we not?" Neuteken gave her mistress' foot a forceful tickle.

"Stop!" Margaret pushed her off as laughter burbled from them both.

"I will not stop until you tell me your plan," Neuteken resisted.

"I will not tell you, for it is mine alone to savor just as your secret is yours alone," Margaret countered.

"Then we are sisters in the order of the secrets, are we not?" Neuteken quipped.

"Finally, someone has offered me an order to join," Margaret sang out, her spirits as bright as a summer day. The shackles of her bitter thoughts against the order that had excluded her had burst open, powerless to hurt her anymore. What satisfaction it was to think she had brought peace to Europe without the help of any of them. "Let us call it the order of the golden secrets," she amended.

"They are golden indeed, are they not, Madame?"

Margaret felt her lips curl into the same coy smile Neuteken had worn a moment earlier. "They are, indeed."

As bounteous October passed into gray November, Margaret tried to tie up affairs so she could get to Savoy to see what work remained to be done on her church before winter set in.

Yet endless matters demanded her attention, including a visit to the Fuggers' banking office in Antwerp to discuss repayments for Charles' election of ten years earlier. She didn't doubt she would be repaying them for the rest of her life. But it was money well spent to see another Habsburg prince wear the crown of Charlemagne.

Groaning, Margaret cursed her bad leg. Antwerp was only a day's carriage ride north, yet already she was uncomfortable. Savoy was a long journey south into the foothills of the Alps, where the first snow fell as early as late November some years. She dreaded the trip, but she needed to go.

Sneaking a peek at Marnix, she considered him as they traveled back from Antwerp to Malines. He was not Gattinara, who had understood her vision for Brou more than any other. But perhaps she could send Marnix in her place.

As the carriage bumped and jolted along the road, Margaret weighed her options. Retiring to the convent of the Annunciades did not seem to be one of them anytime soon.

"Every time I try to slow down, something thwarts me," she grumbled, thinking Mother Ancelle had been right.

"Madame, I am reminded of the later years of that good lady, Eleanor of Aquitaine," Marnix replied.

"She was formidable, but I'm not so sure about good," Margaret quipped, then felt her conscience prick her. What would posterity say about her if she did not manage to discharge the debts incurred to see her nephew elected Holy Roman Emperor? And what would be said if it was discovered just how many she had bribed to ensure he won?

"Was she not close to eighty years of age when she traveled to Castile to pick out a bride amongst her grandchildren for the King of France?" her secretary asked.

"At least she didn't owe vast amounts of money," Margaret griped, thinking of the notes she was also paying off to the Welser and Gualterotti banking houses.

"Madame, she was taxed with cares all the same, and saw to every one of them before retiring to Fontevraud," he noted.

"Good God, if only I could get to the end of my own list," Margaret complained.

"There is never an end to the list of a conscientious ruler, Madame. There is only a final day. And a Heavenly accounting once that day arrives."

"Then I am sunk, for I need these debts paid off and I also need to see my church in Brou completed." Her plan to retire to the Annunciades was now a speck on the horizon, sailing in the wrong direction.

"I am sure Eleanor of Aquitaine was worrying along similar lines as she made the trip to Castile," Marnix conjectured.

"Did she not part from her granddaughter in Fontevraud on her way back from Spain?" She had heard that once Eleanor disappeared behind the gates of the great Loire Valley abbey, she had emerged no more, even as her legend spread across Europe.

"She did, my lady."

"What a moment that must have been." Margaret tried to envision herself shaking the dust from her travel garments and entering the cloistered gates of the Annunciades. But what would she do without any to-do lists to complete? Had Eleanor of Aquitaine become a contemplative creature overnight? She couldn't imagine that doughty queen sitting still any more than she could imagine herself doing so.

"There she rested from her labors until God called her home."

"I don't see how I am ever to rest from my labors until that time comes."

Marnix crossed himself. "Good Madame, let us pray you may enjoy a long chapter of rest before that day."

Margaret glanced out the window to the east, in the direction of the Rhine. "I cannot rest until my nephew comes. Yet he lingers in Germany."

"He has much to attend to there, with that monk stirring up Christendom," Marnix replied.

"I wish this Luther could go head to head with our Sire Erasmus and be done with their squabbles once and for all," Margaret groused.

Marnix shook his head, his tone doleful. "I'm afraid this is much more than a squabble."

Margaret studied her secretary. "Do you ascribe to any of his teachings?" She knew many did; among them members of her own house. Before her niece, Isabella, had died, she had been rumored to have been won over to the reformists' cause. She had also heard that her niece, Mary of Hungary, was sympathetic to those who protested against the established Church. She hoped Charles would talk his younger sister out of whatever leanings she might have so that she could drop the reins into Mary's lap when the time came. God knew he would never entrust his sister with governance of the Netherlands if she left the Church.

"Madame, I am a sentient being. I cannot help but hear from many places that not all of the reformists' points are without merit," Marnix said carefully.

"It is reasonable, Monsieur. But remember that the Houses of Burgundy and Habsburg stand with the Church, and my nephew is sworn to uphold both his lineage and the Church." She cast a sharp eye to remind him of his allegiance.

"I am at your service and at the emperor's forever, my lady. I simply see what all of Europe sees at this time, especially across the Rhine."

Margaret sighed. It was true. Fortunately, the burghers she met with daily were more concerned with commerce than they were with religious doctrine. But Luther's reforms would suit their agendas nicely, freeing them from the need to buy assurances of their salvation with costly indulgence purchases or contributions to pay for the pope's building projects in a far-off land.

It was only a matter of time before the wind blew westward and the Low Countries embraced new doctrines that would give them more autonomy. Should they shrug off the Church, she could imagine what next they might shrug off.

A groan escaped her as a sharp pain traveled down her left leg. God grant that she would be gone before that moment arrived.

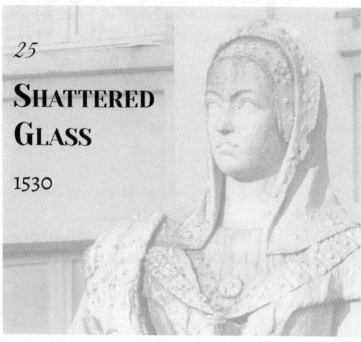

25

SHATTERED GLASS

1530

MARGARET AWOKE THE MORNING of November 15, 1530, still tired from her journey. She had reached Malines from Antwerp just as the sun set the previous afternoon. How she wished Gattinara was on his way to meet with her at nine, as they had done every morning for years.

It was a huge loss. Watching the sunbeam grow on the floor of her room she imagined Louis XII's grief after losing his own right-hand man, Georges d'Amboise. There was not a day that went by that Margaret did not miss her steady counselor who had been at her side since Savoyard years.

Her thoughts flew to that momentous November of 1501 when she had journeyed to Savoy to meet her new husband. She must travel there again before the Alpen snows set in. When she returned, winter's dull days would be upon them, cloaking the Low Countries' skies in gray for months. But she would be cheered by having moved one step closer to seeing her dream come true.

"A glass of water, Magdalen!" she called. Magdalen Rochester had remained in her household after Anne Brandon and Anne Boleyn had left years earlier. She had proven to be as faithful and loyal to Margaret as the man who had sent her had not.

She watched with affection as her lady-in-waiting went to the sideboard to fetch it.

Taking a sip from the glass goblet she held out, Margaret handed it back.

The glass slipped from Magdalen's hand, shattering on the floor.

"Ouf, Madame, I am sorry!" she exclaimed, stooping to pick up the pieces.

"An accident. Just clean it up, my dear."

As Magdalen picked up the shards, Margaret thought of the shards of broken hearts the young woman's sponsor had scattered in the wake of his climb to power. How fortunate she had been to move on from the man who had never returned her ring. If only she might escape occasional visits from him in her dreams.

Lingering in bed, she mulled over plans for the day. Everything must be in order before leaving for Savoy. For once, the to-do list was not so long. Perhaps when she returned she could be done with it once and for all.

A peaceful sigh escaped her. She had succeeded in her life's aim for her nephew—to see him crowned Holy Roman Emperor by the pope.

Now she was ready to accomplish her life's work for herself—the completion of her masterpiece in Brou. She would rest from her labors there one day, far from the bustle of politics and intrigue. It was a world she had enjoyed, truth be told. But she was ready to leave it behind.

Rising, she stepped into her slippers.

"Ahh!" she cried.

Falling back on the bed, she writhed in pain as Lady Elisabeth and Neuteken came running.

"My foot!" she moaned.

Pulling off the slipper, Lady Elisabeth gasped. Blood dripped from Margaret's foot where a shard of glass from the broken goblet had embedded itself.

"Forgive me for being so clumsy, Madame!" Magdalen wailed, handing a cloth to Lady Elisabeth to stanch the blood.

"Shh, my dear; you did not mean to be." Margaret winced as the cloth pressed against the wound. It was on the foot of her bad leg, too.

"Call for the doctor," Lady Elisabeth told Magdalen, who fled from the room.

Margaret's personal physician Philippe Savoien soon arrived. Immediately, he set to work extracting the glass shard.

The pain was excruciating. Margaret bit into the cloth that Neuteken placed between her teeth, squeezing her attendant's hand so tightly that Neuteken's wince mirrored her own.

In a moment the doctor was done and Margaret's foot bound. As the pain subsided, she felt her composure return.

Motioning to Neuteken, she held out her arm to be helped up. She had much to do to attend to state and household matters before leaving for Brou.

With Neuteken supporting her she hobbled to the center of the room, motioning to her ladies' maid to dress her. The day's cares were upon her and it was just as well. Busy at her desk, she would forget all about her injured foot.

But several days later the pain had not abated. Instead, it was worse. Unwrapping the bandaging, her doctor probed, making Margaret almost faint.

"The wound is infected," Philippe Savoien announced.

"What can you do?" Margaret asked, desperate to be relieved of the throbbing she felt in her foot. By day she could no longer walk on it. By night, its incessant drumbeat robbed her of sleep.

"I will call in my colleagues, Madame. Then we will decide," he answered, looking at her foot and not her eyes. She had sat at the negotiating table enough times to know that no eye contact was not a good sign.

"I cannot bear this much longer," Margaret said. Unable to think, make plans, or focus on anything but the pain, she wanted to scream for release. The journey to Brou would have to wait.

"We will give you a potion, my lady, so that you may rest," the doctor prescribed, gesturing to his attendant.

Margaret knew that a sleeping draught was not a solution. But she drank it down, desperate to escape into slumber.

THREE DAYS LATER, HER almoner came to her. His grave eyes told her the news was not good.

"Madame, may God give you the strength and grace to receive my tidings from your doctors," he intoned.

Margaret felt an uncanny peace settle over her. Antoine de Montécut was an old and faithful member of her household.[1] The doctors had sent him in their place for a reason.

"Why didn't they come themselves?" she asked, girding herself for the answer.

"They do not know your courage and strength as I do, Madame, and fear to speak with you."

"I gather it is bad, but nothing could be worse than this pain that grips me night and day," Margaret replied, thinking of Anne of Brittany. France's former queen had died in agony from kidney stones years earlier. Now she had an inkling of what she had gone through.

Antoine de Montécut sighed deeply, then held out both hands. She took them, gaining strength from his grip as he gazed into her eyes with sadness in his own.

He squeezed tightly. "With your consent, Madame, the foot will need to be amputated."

Margaret stared at him. Already she had guessed what he might say. The infection had spread, and only two possibilities could stop it: amputation or death. By facing the first, she also faced the second.

"Of course I consent. I cannot live another week like this last one," she answered matter-of-factly.

"I will let the doctors know."

"You will arrange for my confessor to give me the sacraments," Margaret told him.

---

1. Marian Andrews, *High & Puissant Princess Marguerite of Austria* (London: Harper Brothers, 1907), p. 330.

Her almoner's face fell. "Yes, Madame. But I have no doubt you will come through this with all the spirit with which you have already come through so many of life's blows."

Margaret gave him as serene a look as she could muster. She had confronted death by shipwreck on her way to Spain at age sixteen. She had held two dead husbands and one stillborn daughter in her arms. She could face what lay ahead.

"I will come through this and out the other end in the place God calls me to," she said. For once, she didn't feel she was being called anywhere by anyone on Earth. She had done her duty by both her father and her nephew. The only one calling to her now was Philibert, humming to her to stop running about and come join him.

Antoine de Montécut bowed deeply and backed from the room, his eyes remaining on hers as if to give her courage.

That afternoon Neuteken came to cheer her.

"You have heard the news?" Margaret asked.

"My lady, we have heard the news. And all in your household know you have the strength to get through this," her faithful companion assured her.

Margaret grimaced. "But do I want to get through this?"

"Of course you do. We need our Lady Margaret!" Neuteken cried. "And the government is on your shoulder," she added.

"Stop being so serious and cheer me. I am done with ruling for the moment, and perhaps forever." Margaret moved her foot, hoping to find a better position to dull its throb. But there was no better position.

"Do not say so, Madame!" Neuteken's face looked as if it was shattering into as many pieces as the goblet that had gouged Margaret's foot.

Margaret waved a commanding hand. "You bore me with that grim face. Do your job and take my mind off my pain."

Neuteken flung her body across Margaret's bed and pounded her head up and down on her good leg. "How's this, Madame?"

Margaret laughed weakly. "Not your best. But now that you've hurt my other leg, at least I've forgotten about the one I am to lose."

"Don't say so, Madame! It is only the foot you are to lose, not your whole leg!" Neuteken protested.

"Not a great solace, little one. I'm sure you can do better." Besides, she knew better. The infection had traveled up her leg from her foot. If she were to wake from the operation the doctors would perform, she would likely find her entire leg gone.

"What about this, Madame?" Neuteken executed a somersault off the bed and landed on her feet. Turning, she made a graceful bow then fell onto the bed, burying her face at Margaret's side.

"Better." Margaret stroked the fine blonde curls on her fool's head. Once her hair had been the same color and texture. Once she had been young. In a few days' time she would be saying 'Once, I had two legs.' She did not wish to face such a moment.

On November 27, 1530, Margaret received the sacraments of last rites. Her only regret was that her nephew had not yet arrived. But no matter. The pope had crowned him Holy Roman Emperor. The Netherlands were at peace. And she herself was at peace, knowing she had fulfilled every duty of the position God had put her in as a Princess of the Houses of Burgundy and Habsburg.

Only the church and monastery in Brou remained to be completed. But the funds had been set aside for the remaining work. And she knew her nephew.

Charles would get it done. The boy she had raised to rule over most of Europe lacked spontaneity and gaiety, but he understood commitment. She had been like a mother to him, and he would see that her final wishes were carried out in full. Of that, she had no doubt.

Downing a sleeping draught, Margaret slipped into slumber.

TWO DAYS LATER THE pain was worse.

"Get my notary," Margaret ordered.

Lady Elisabeth looked worried. "Do you not want me to call the doctor instead?"

Margaret waved a dismissive hand. "I am through with doctors. They have done all they can for me. Now I must do all I can for those in my household before what is to come."

"Madame, you will sail through this and be on the mend in no time," Lady Elisabeth assured her. Plumping a pillow, she placed it under Margaret's head.

"Do not waste your words," Margaret said. "Just get the notary. And tell your husband to come, too. I must put my government in his care before I face what lies ahead."

Lady Elisabeth nodded, then turned and hurried from the room.

As Margaret watched her leave, she marveled at sight of her swift steps. Within days she would no longer have two feet to carry her anywhere, swiftly or otherwise. How splendid was the gift of a fully intact body.

Like a vision, an image of the most beautiful body she had ever known wafted into her mind. Philibert had been as magnificent a physical specimen in death as he had been in life. To be worthy of him, she wished to lie next to him as fully intact as he had been. She abhorred the thought of her remains lying beside her beloved for all eternity, missing one leg. It was a thought that others would try to dissuade her of. She would keep it to herself.

The notary arrived and Margaret spent the day making bequests to members of her household. Lady Elisabeth, Magdalen Rochester, and her other ladies-in-waiting were remembered with generous monetary gifts. To Neuteken she bequeathed a pension that would sustain her for life and release her from service. To Jean de Marnix she left her writing desk, implements, and a substantial sum for his loyalty through the years. To her nephew, Charles V, she bequeathed the entirety of the remainder of her estate.

Once Margaret was done, she handed over the reins of her government to Antoine de Lalaing, Count of Hoogstraten and knight of honor of her household. As dedicated to Habsburg authority in the Netherlands as many of the other Burgundian nobles were not, she trusted him to conduct affairs of state while she was incapacitated or worse, in the absence of her nephew.

The document of temporary transfer of power was duly signed and stamped and Margaret fell back on her bed, satisfied that she had seen to all in her care.

November 30th dawned, gray and chill. The amputation was to take place the next day.

"Get Marnix in here," Margaret told Lady Elisabeth.

With her secretary at her bedside, she dictated a letter to her nephew.

'Monseigneur, the hour is come when I can no more write to you with mine own hand, for I find myself in such a disposition to believe my life will be brief. With a quiet conscience, and resolved to receive all that it may please God to send me, with no regret whatever save the privation of your presence, and that I am not able to see and speak to you once more before my death, which I would supply in part by this my letter, which I fear will be the last which you will receive from me.

I have instituted you my universal heir alone and for all, save the charges in my will, the accomplishment of which I recommend to you.

I leave to you your lands of "par deça,"[2] which during your absence I have not only kept as you gave them to me on our departure, but greatly augmented; and I return you the government of the same, of which I believe that I have loyally acquitted myself, so that I hope for divine reward, satisfaction from you, Monseigneur, and thanks from your subjects; recommending to you particularly peace, and especially with the kings of France and England.

And to end, I beg you, Monseigneur, for the love

which it has pleased you to bear to this poor body,
that you will keep in memory the salvation of the
soul, and my recommendation of my poor servants,
for the love of God, to whom I pray, Monseigneur,
that He will give you prosperity and long life.

From Malines, the last day of November, 1530.
Your very humble aunt,[3]
Margaret'

Jean de Marnix looked grave as he handed Margaret the letter to sign. "Madame, I hope there will be no need to send this."

"One may hope, Monsieur, but it is best to be prepared."

"Madame, you have always been prepared."

"And so I will continue to be until my last breath," Margaret declared, wondering how soon that might be. But the peaceful sensation that had appeared since her almoner had brought the doctors' news was still with her, calming her senses and quelling her fears. Whatever was to come, she had done her duty in this world. All cares were behind her; she had earned her rest.

THAT EVENING, NEUTEKEN CURLED up at the bottom of Margaret's bed. Lady Elisabeth had gone to fetch the draught the doctors had prepared. It would send her into a sleep so deep that she would not awaken until after the operation was over the next morning.

"Do you not wish to go to your own couch, little one?" Margaret asked.

Neuteken's blue-green eyes beamed large and bright. "My place is here with you tonight," she said.

"Then stay, for you have blessed me from the day you first arrived."

"Tormented is more like it, but at least entertained," Neuteken amended.

Margaret's chuckle was soft. "May you entertain others in your future, but for your own pleasure."

Neuteken frowned, shaking her head. "My future is with you, Madame. I will never leave you, as I told you long ago."

"Ah, my dear one, but I may leave you. So I have seen to it that you no longer need to work for a living," Margaret informed her.

The little woman looked puzzled. "Then what will I do?" she asked.

"You will light candles in my memory and give alms I have left for you to give to others like you, whom God has blessed in a special way."

"May I take a tumble as I give them out?" Neuteken asked with an impish gleam.

"No tumbling with the candles, but when you give out alms take a tumble or two so I may laugh in Heaven."

Tears glittered in Neuteken's eyes. "Ah, Madame, I have loved being your mirror."

Margaret smiled at her. "And I have loved having you as one."

"I will be at your side tomorrow when you awake," Neuteken promised.

Without answering, Margaret smoothed her hand over her beloved dwarf's unruly curls. Nothing more needed to be said. All she had been called to do in this world had been done.

Reaching for the draught that Lady Elisabeth held out, Margaret drank it down.

That night, between the hours of midnight and one in the morning of December 1, 1530, Margaret of Austria passed into the world beyond. The opium draught the doctors had prepared to sedate her had been too strong. It was an unexpected result, but perhaps not an entirely unwanted one.

The Netherlands' redoubtable ruler met her well-deserved rest with her body intact and her mind at ease. She had fulfilled all she had been entrusted with on earth.

It had been a life well-lived.

Tomb of Margaret of Austria
By Conrad Meit (sculpture)
and Lodewijk van Boghem (architecture)
Royal Monastery of Brou, Bourg-en-Bresse, France
Photo by Christophe Finot

Brou at Bourge-en-Bresse, France

www.map-france.com, edited by R. Gaston

Tomb of Margaret of Austria
By Conrad Meit (sculpture)
and Lodewijk van Boghem (architecture)
Royal Monastery of Brou, Bourg-en-Bresse, France
Photo above courtesy of Sue Ross, photo below courtesy of Frantz

EPILOGUE

Margaret of Austria, Duchess of Savoy, is buried next to her husband, Philibert of Savoy, at the Royal Monastery of Brou[1] in Bourg-en-Bresse, France.

The church of the monastery, a masterpiece of flamboyant Gothic architecture, and tombs of Margaret, Philibert, and his mother, Margaret of Bourbon, were commissioned by Margaret and completed two years after her death, at which time her body was laid to rest there.

Tucked away in the southeast central Auvergne-Rhône-Alpes region of France, about 43 miles northeast of Lyon and 68 miles west of Geneva, the royal monastery escaped desecration in the 1789 French Revolution due to its obscure location.

---

1. http://www.monastere-de-brou.fr

The tombs of Margaret, Philibert, and his mother are perfectly preserved. It is to be noted that Margaret gave her husband's tomb place of honor in the center of the church, with the open eyes of his effigy gazing in the direction of her own effigy. This arrangement tells the tale of their love for each other.

— *Rozsa Gaston*
Bronxville, New York

Margaret of Austria and Philibert of Savoy's tombs
Royal Monastery of Brou Bourg-en-Bresse, France
Photo courtesy of Sue Ross

Eulogy for Margaret and Philibert

"So rest, for ever rest, O princely pair!
In your high church, 'mid the still mountain air,
Where horn, and hound, and vassals never come.
Only the blessed Saints are smiling dumb,
From the rich, painted windows of the nave,
On aisle, and transept, and your marble grave;
The moon through the clere-story windows shines,
And the wind washes through the mountain-pines.
And, in the sweeping of the wind, your ear
The passage of the angels' wings will hear,
And in the lichen-crusted leads above
The rustle of the eternal rain of love."

— Matthew Arnold's eulogy for Margaret of Austria and Philibert of Savoy in their final resting place of the Church of Brou

From Eleanor Tremayne, *The First Governess of the Netherlands* (New York: G.P. Putnam's Sons, 1908), p. 303.

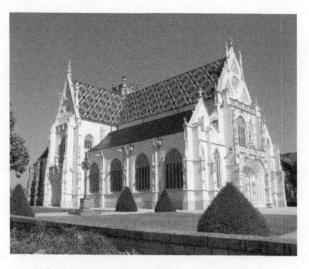

Church of the Royal Monastery of Brou
Bourg-en-Bresse, France
Photo from www.camping-mepillat.fr

Church and monastery of the Royal Monastery of Brou
Bourg-en-Bresse, France
Photo by Herwsy, from Auvergne-Rhone-Alpes Tourisme

BIBLIOGRAPHY

Abernethy, Susan. *Margaret of Austria, Duchess of Savoy and Regent of the Netherlands.* The Freelance History Writer, 2014.

Andrews, Marian (Christopher Hare). *The High and Puissant Princess Marguerite of Austria.* London: Harper and Brothers, 1907.

Barker, Juliet, *Agincourt.* London: Little, Brown, 2005

Besson, André, *Marguerite d'Autriche.* Paris: Nouvelles Editions Latines, 1985.

Blockmans, Wim and Prevenier, Walter. *The Promised Lands: The Low Countries Under Burgundian Rule,* 1369-1530. Philadelphia: University of Pennsylvania Press, 1999.

Bonner, Shirley Harrold. *Fortune, Misfortune, Fortifies One.* Shirley Harrold Bonner, 1981.

Boom Ghislaine de. *Marguerite d'Autriche–Savoie et la Pré-Renaissance.* Brussels: Librairie Falk Fils, 1935.

Brantome, Pierre de Bourdeille de. *Lives of Fair and Gallant Ladies, Vol. I*. London and New York: The Alexandrian Society, Inc., 1922.

Carlino, Linda. *That Other Juana*. Durham, UK: Veritas Publishing, 2007.

Castiglione, Baldassare. *The Book of the Courtier*. New York: W.W. Norton & Company, 2002.

Dapelo, Nichole Christakes. *Making of Margaret of Austria: Queen. Duchess, Regent*. 2022.

Davis, William Stearns. *Life on a Mediaeval Barony*. New York: Harper & Brothers, 1923.

Downey, Kirstin. *Isabella: The Warrior Queen*. New York: Anchor Books, 2015.

Eichberger, Dagmar, "A Noble Residence for a Female Regent: Margaret of Austria and the Construction of the Palais de Savoy in Mechelen," 25-46 plus illustrations, in *Architecture and the Politics of Gender in Early Modern Europe*, hrsg. von Helen Hills, Aldershot and Burlington: Ashgate, 2003.

Eichberger, Dagmar, "Margaret of Austria's Treasures: An early Habsburg Collection in the Burgundian Netherlands," 71-80, in: Fernando Checa Cremades (Hrsg.), *El museo imperial. El coleccionismo artístico de los Austrias en el siglo XVI*, Villaverde Editores:

Madrid, 2013.

Frieda, Leonie. *Margaret of Austria, Duchess of Savoy.* https://engelsbergideas.com/portraits/margaret-of-austria-duchess-of-savoy.

Gristwood, Sarah. *Game of Queens.* New York: Basic Books, 2016.

Habsburg, Otto von. *Charles V.* Westport: Praeger, 1970.

Henry-Bordeaux, Paule. *Louise de Savoie: Régente et "Roi" de France.* Paris: Plon, 1954.

Iongh, Jane de, Margaret of Austria. *Regent of the Netherlands.* New York: Norton, 1953.

Lemaire de Belges, Jean, *Oeuvres.* Geneva: Slatkine Reprints, 1969.

MacDonald, Deanna. *Acknowledging the "Lady of the House: "Memory, Authority and Self-Representation in the Patronage of Margaret of Austria.* Montreal: McGill University, 2002.

Mayer, Dorothy Moulton. *The Great Regent.* New York: Funk & Wagnalls, 1966.

Michelet, Jules. *History of France,* Vol. 7. Paris: A. Lacroix, 1876.

Nassiet Michel. *Anne de Bretagne: Correspondance et itinéraire.* Rennes: Presses universitaires de Rennes, 2022.

Putnam, Samuel. *Marguerite of Navarre*. New York: Grosset & Dunlap, 1935.

Richardson, Walter C. *Mary Tudor: The White Queen*. London: Peter Owen, 1970.

Shaw, Christine, and Mallett, Michael. *The Italian Wars: 1494-1559*. New York: Routledge, 2019.

Stecher, Jean. *Jean Lemaire de Belges*. Louvain: Lefever Frères et Soeur, 1891.

Steinmetz, Greg. *The Richest Man Who Ever Lived: The Life and Times of Jacob Fugger*. New York: Simon & Schuster, 2015.

Tremayne, Eleanor E. *The First Governess of the Netherlands*. New York: G.P. Putnam's Sons, 1908.

Wellman, Kathleen. *Queens and Mistresses of Renaissance France*. New Haven: Yale University Press, 2014.

Willard, Charity Cannon. *Christine de Pizan: Her Life and Works*. New York, Persea Books, 1984.

Williams, H. Noel. *The Pearl of Princesses*: London: Eveleigh Nash Company, 1916.

ABOUT THE AUTHOR

ROZSA GASTON is a historical fiction author who writes books on women who reach for what they want out of life. Her focus is on 16th-century European female rulers. She studied European history at Yale, and received her Master's degree in international affairs from Columbia University, including one year at Institut d'études politiques de Paris (Sciences Po). She worked at *Institutional Investor*, then as a columnist for *The Westchester Guardian*.

Her other works include the award-winning Anne of Brittany Series: *Anne and Charles, Anne and Louis,* winner of the Publishers Weekly 2018 BookLife Prize for general fiction, *Anne and Louis: Rulers and Lovers, Anne and Louis Forever Bound*, first place category winner of the 2022 CHAUCER Book Awards for pre-1750s historical fiction, *Marguerite and Gaston, The Least Foolish Woman in France,* and *Sense of Touch.*

If you enjoyed *Margaret of Austria*, please post a review to help others find this book: bit.ly/margaretofaustria. One sentence is enough to let readers know what you thought. Drop Rozsa Gaston a line on Facebook to let her know you posted a review and receive as thanks an eBook edition of any volume of the Anne of Brittany Series.

Gaston lives in Bronxville, New York, with her family and is currently working on a book on Anne Boleyn at Margaret of Austria's court.

bit.ly/RozsaGastonbooks
www.facebook.com/rozsagastonauthor
Instagram: rozsagastonauthor
TikTok: @rozsagastonbooks
Twitter: @RozsaGaston
www.rozsagaston.com

OTHER BOOKS BY
ROZSA GASTON

The Anne of Brittany Series
Sense of Touch: Prequel
Anne and Charles: Book One
Anne and Louis: Book Two
Anne and Louis: Rulers and Lovers: Book Three
Anne and Louis Forever Bound: Book Four

The Ava Series
Paris Adieu: Book One
Black is Not a Color: Book Two

Novellas
Marguerite and Gaston
The Least Foolish Woman in France

THE ANNE OF
BRITTANY SERIES

The gripping tale of a larger-than-life queen

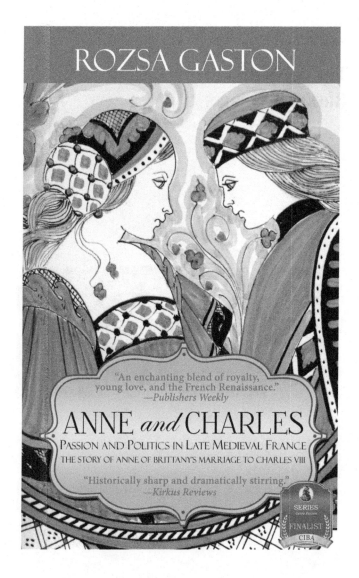

"An engrossing depiction of the meeting and marriage between Anne of Brittany and Charles VIII of France. This book excels in humanizing one of the most misunderstood of French kings."
—*RT Review Source*

*I*t's 1488, and eleven-year-old Anne of Brittany is thrust into a desperate situation when she becomes ruler of her duchy. Besieged on all sides, she eventually agrees to marry Charles VIII, King of France, to save Brittany from plunder.

A passionate relationship ensues as they unexpectedly fall in love. Yet Charles cannot shake the bad habits he brings to their marriage, and Anne cannot pull him out of his darkest depths of struggle.

Together, they usher the Italian Renaissance into France, building a glorious court at their royal residence in Amboise. But year after year, they fail to accomplish their most important aim: to secure the future of their kingdom.

As they pursue their shared dream, will an unexpected twist of fate change the fortunes of Anne and Charles, two of fifteenth-century Europe's most star-crossed rulers?

Book One of the Anne of Brittany Series

"Masterfully conveys the passion, heartbreak, and determination of this royal couple."
—*InD'tale Magazine*

RENAISSANCE EDITIONS
WWW.RENAISSANCEEDITIONS.COM

Fiction/Historical $14.95

ISBN 978-0-9847906-5-4

9 780984 790654

90000

Cover image by Adriano Rubino, courtesy of 123RF.com
Back cover photo of the Royal Chateau of Amboise, courtesy of Wikimedia Commons
Cover design by Cathy Helms/Avalon Graphics

"Sharp and engaging." —*Publishers Weekly 2018 BookLife Prize*, Winner, General Fiction

ROZSA GASTON

"Dramatically engrossing and
historically searching."
—*Kirkus Reviews*

ANNE *and* LOUIS

PASSION AND POLITICS IN EARLY RENAISSANCE FRANCE

THE FIRST YEARS OF ANNE OF BRITTANY'S MARRIAGE TO LOUIS XII

"A masterpiece . . . satisfying, educational,
and hard to put down."
—*Midwest Book Review*

France admired her but Brittany loved her. Just as Louis did.

Anne, Duchess of Brittany, is the love of King Louis XII of France's life. Too bad he's already married. While his annulment proceedings create Europe's most sensational scandal of 1498, Anne returns to Brittany to take back control of her duchy that her late husband, Charles VIII, King of France, had wrested from her.

At age twenty-one, Anne is sovereign ruler of Brittany as well as Europe's most wealthy widow. But can she maintain Brittany's independence from France if she accepts Louis' offer to make her Queen of France once more?

With Italian arrivals to the French court from Cesare Borgia to Niccolò Machiavelli, Anne and Louis' story unfolds as the feudal era gives way to the dawn of the Renaissance. Their love for each other tested by conflicting duties to their separate countries, they struggle to navigate a collision course that will reshape the map of sixteenth-century Europe.

Book Two of the Anne of Brittany Series

RENAISSANCE EDITIONS
WWW.RENAISSANCEEDITIONS.COM

Fiction/Historical $14.95

ISBN 978-0-9847906-8-5

90000

9 780984 790685

Cover image by Massimo Santi,
courtesy of shutterstock.com
Front and back cover illustrations
courtesy of Wikimedia Commons
Cover design by Cathy Helms/Avalon Graphics

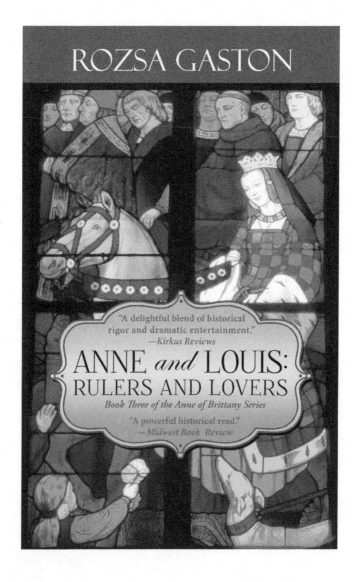

"As Petrarch has been called the first modern man, so Anne
might be called the first modern woman."
—Helen J. Sanborn, *Anne of Brittany*

In 1501, Anne of Brittany devises the perfect match for her only
child by Louis XII, King of France. Their daughter will become the most
powerful woman in Europe if she marries the future Holy Roman
Emperor. But Louis balks. Instead, he wishes her to marry his successor. How
else to keep his own bloodline on the throne?

Anne is incensed. Why should her daughter not rule Brittany one day as her
successor? Better to be a decision maker as ruler of Brittany, where women are
not forbidden to rule, than only to sit next to France's future king as queen-
consort, bereft of political power.

Anne wants Louis to stay out of Italy, but Louis is determined to gain
a foothold there for France. Joining Ferdinand of Spain in a secret
pact to partition southern Italy, Louis soon discovers, with devastating
results, the age of chivalry is over.

As lovers, Anne and Louis are in accord. As rulers, their aims differ.
Who will prevail?

Book Three of the Anne of Brittany Series

RENAISSANCE EDITIONS
WWW.RENAISSANCEEDITIONS.COM

Cover image from Church of St.-Malo
of Dinan, Brittany, France
Back cover illustrations courtesy of
Wikimedia Commons and Pixabay
Cover design by Cathy Helms/Avalon Graphics

Fiction/Historical $15.95

ISBN 978-1-7325899-4-0

90000

9 781732 589940

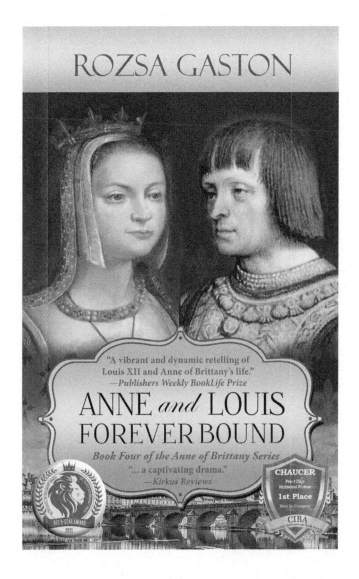

"It is difficult to quench a great fire when once it has seized the soul."
—Pierre Brantôme on Louis XII's love for Anne of Brittany

The year is 1508. Louis XII, King of France, wants to stamp France's footprint upon Italy.

Anne of Brittany, Queen of France, and ruler of neighboring realm Brittany, wants to produce a son and heir for Louis and to save the independence of Brittany from France.

Louise of Savoy, the mother of the king's intended successor, the future Francis I, wants to see her son on the throne of France.

All three have suffered the twisting of their fates by Anne de Beaujeu, the spider king's daughter, who ruled France from 1483-1491. Two shake off her shadow; one does not.

One sees their dreams come true; two do not. But in this game of thrones, winners lose and losers win the greatest prize of all.

Book Four of the Anne of Brittany Series

RENAISSANCE EDITIONS
WWW.RENAISSANCEEDITIONS.COM

Fiction/Historical $15.95
ISBN 978-1-7325899-7-1

Cover image of Anne of Brittany from Chateau de Chaumont, courtesy of C.S. Carley
Cover image of Louis XII, back cover images of Louis XII, Anne of Brittany, Anne de Beaujeu (lower right) and Louise de Savoy (lower left) courtesy of Wikimedia Commons
Cover design by Cathy Helms/Avalon Graphics

9 781732 589971

ACKNOWLEDGMENTS

THANK YOU TO DAGMAR Eichberger, art historian and leading expert on Margaret of Austria, eagle-eyed manuscript readers Angela Loud Morris and Sasha Pinto-Jayawardena, the meticulous Kim Huther of Wordsmith Proofreading, Susan Schulman of the Susan Schulman Agency, Cathy Helms of Avalon Graphics, Anne McClellan, Keira Morgan, Cynthia Louise Moore, Laura Finger, Susan Abernethy, Sue Ross, Jessica Russell, Michael Dandry, Christine Axen and Sara Georgini, who encouraged me to include Neuteken in this story. With you, and readers like you, may Margaret of Austria's story reach across the centuries to inform women in the art of political leadership.

I am indebted to Jane de Iongh, author of *Margaret of Austria, Regent of the Netherlands* (W.W. Norton & Co.: 1953), whose book colors in Margaret of Austria herself, rather than the times she lived in, the historically significant people she knew or the important deeds she carried out. Until I read de Iongh's work, I was unable to grasp the essence of Margaret herself. But in de Iongh's historically sound and evocative work, Margaret of Austria springs alive.

It is in de Iongh's book that Margaret's dwarf Neuteken is mentioned, filling in a missing piece of the puzzle Margaret became to me as I researched her. The more I read her story, the less I understood how her emotional needs were met in the years after losing her husbands and without her own children. Members of Margaret's household such as Mercurino di Gattinara and Jean de Marnix played important roles in supporting Margaret, but I wondered who comforted her once the bustle of the day was through.

Once I discovered Neuteken in de Iongh's work, I sensed I had found her. The role of court dwarves in the lives of royals is little-documented but worthy of deeper historical examination. The court dwarf was engaged to add stature to his or her patron's appearance in portraits by virtue of size difference. But a more important function was to comfort his or her royal patron as well as tell the truth about them to their face when no one else dared to. The court dwarf was exempt from punishment, due to his or her status as one of God's special children.

The role Neuteken played in Margaret's life is not recorded, other than her name and that Margaret treated her well. Thus, Neuteken's details in this tale are fictitious. But the important role court dwarves played in serving royal historical figures of the past is fact.

May this work serve to gain Neuteken and others like her their historical due. And may Margaret of Austria receive hers as one of the most important female rulers of the Renaissance.

Made in the USA
Las Vegas, NV
09 January 2025

16061634R00249